HELIX GENESIS

HELIX GENESIS

A vengeful war hero. A politician's wife.
A lethal pathogen. Scores to settle.

Chris Lofts

2020

HELIX GENESIS
By Chris Lofts

Produced and published in 2020

ISBN 9798653369230

Typeset in Libre Caslon 11pt by Blot Publishing
www.blot.co.uk

For my brothers Dave and Phil.
For brothers and sisters everywhere.

1

Helix knew a lot about pain, dishing it out and getting it back. The balance was probably in favour of the former, but he didn't trouble himself with records. Records were for those who gave a shit. Pain, at the excruciating end of the spectrum, was what the man opposite him would be enduring as he reeled away from the hammock. The room was awash with blinding pulses of staccato white light. The luminosity of the strobes would be nothing compared to the ringing in his ears or the grating he'd be feeling on the back of his eye sockets, like someone scratching your eyeball with a fingernail. Helix side-stepped, jabbed and connected, his titanium and carbon-fibre fist pummelling the trespasser's nose.

Helix killed the strobes with a wink of his right eye as the man crumpled to the floor, rolling in the gloom. His fingertips tried to staunch the flow as crimson-streaked bubbles bloomed from his nostrils.

Helix hauled him to his feet by his shoulder flashes. 'Get up, Inspector.' He aimed another jab over the inspector's shoulder at the light switch. A naked bulb in a decrepit wall fitting complained into life, casting a weak patch of yellow light onto the floor below.

The inspector blinked. 'Who the hell are you?' he said, swaying on the balls of his feet. 'Give me your name!'

Helix stepped forward, his hands on his wide hips. 'Major Nathan Helix, investigating officer in charge.'

'Helix?' the inspector wheezed. 'OK, Major Helix, I'm arresting you for the assault of a police officer. You do not—'

Helix ignored the muffled howl, as he snapped his right hand over the inspector's mouth, squeezing the hollows of his cheeks, forcing his jaw open.

'Assault? I don't think so.' He grimaced. 'Christ. Halitosis, fags and shit for breakfast. Don't they have toothpaste out here?' He extended his arm. 'You're lucky I haven't thrown your scrawny arse off the balcony.' He shook him loose and wiped his hand on the inspector's jacket. 'As we're doing names, who the fuck are you?'

The inspector swallowed a nauseous retch. 'Neville Lafarge, Inspector, 593421.'

'Shit to meet you.' He turned away. 'What's with the bloody lights in this dump?'

He poked another switch next to the patio doors. The blinds crept upwards, casting a mountainous shadow as daylight squeezed in around him. He scanned the bedroom, the silhouette of the lifeless woman cocooned in the hammock emerged from the twilight. A simple vase of wilted blooms kept vigil alongside the hollow burned out candles, their scent still lingering. Another body, but it was far from the

Ebola death pits where bodies were part of the endless monotony and fatigue that putrefied into a kind of tedium that ate away at your soul. At least she would be laid to rest with dignity. It was almost twenty years since the outbreak of Ebola. The coming days would be filled with anniversaries of one sort or another, most of which he'd rather forget.

'What were you doing in the bathroom, Lafarge?'

Lafarge wrung his hands. 'Securing the scene, waiting for forensics.'

A blue nylon bag lay on the floor by the bathroom door, the outlines of boxes and bottles distorting the thin material. Helix frowned, pursing his lips. 'I'm not sure what they teach you people after they've flushed you out of the drains, but I'm sure securing the crime scene doesn't involve moving or touching items that might be related, or did I miss something?' He nudged the bag with his boot.

Lafarge nodded. 'I was collecting the medication.'

'Collecting the medication? What's that, some kind of hobby, like collecting teaspoons? This is a crime scene, Lafarge. So, what were you doing tampering with potential evidence?'

Lafarge flinched. 'It's for a friend. She's not well.'

Helix swung at him and grabbed a thick handful of his greasy hair.

'OK, OK. I was going to sell it, I'm sorry – please.' Free of Helix's grip, he crumpled to his knees onto the threadbare carpet, his hands clamped to his scalp.

'And what about her?' Helix said, nodding towards the hammock.

Lafarge wiped his nose across the back of his hand. ‘What do you mean, what about her?’

The Sig Sauer P226 swayed in its shoulder holster as Helix unzipped his jacket. ‘What were you doing drooling over her left breast with your fingers between her legs? Searching for a pulse?’ The catch on the patio door clicked as he thumbed it down.

Lafarge recoiled. ‘What are you doing?’

Helix shrugged. ‘I thought a bit of fresh air might clear your head.’ He heaved the door aside and sniffed over his shoulder. ‘If you can call it fresh air.’

‘I knew her from the surgery.’ His eyes darted at the hammock. ‘I was a patient.’

‘Treatment for your sexual attraction to corpses, was it?’

‘I’ve got an infection. Antibiotics are difficult to get around here. She ran a daily surgery. You have to queue for a couple of hours, but it’s worth it.’

‘An infection? That’s one word for it. When was the last time you saw her alive?’

Lafarge swallowed. ‘What? It was... er, yesterday. Yes. It was yesterday.’

‘At the surgery?’ Helix stepped towards him and folded his arms. ‘Who else would have seen you?’

Lafarge shuffled across the carpet on his backside. ‘Other patients and the nurse. Sometimes there was another doctor, but I never saw her.’ His back pressed against the wall, halting his retreat. ‘I always waited for Miri... Professor, Doctor Polozkova.’ He pressed a hand against the peeling wallpaper and clambered to his feet. ‘Anyway, what’s so important about her?’

Helix twisted the front of Lafarge's jacket in his fist. 'She was a member of the Scientific Elite, you maggot. Do you have any idea what she did before she lost her marbles and came to this cesspit, so she could treat the likes of you?'

Lafarge squirmed, looking towards the apartment door.

Helix shook his gaze back to his and gritted his teeth. 'Now you listen to me. If I ever see your ugly mug again, or hear another word from that arsehole you call a mouth, my video of you sticking your nose and fingers where they don't belong will go viral amongst the militia, just like Ebola back in the day. Do you understand?' He shoved him towards the kitchen. 'Now get out!' He locked his eyes on Lafarge and watched him back away through the police tape into the unlit stairwell.

He turned and stepped onto the balcony. At one time the view from the fifteenth floor might have been worth looking at. The only things that dominated it now were broken windows, weed-knotted streets, overgrown gardens, trees festooned with shredded paper and plastic and the discarded remnants of life. He arched his eyebrows, dropping his sunglasses back onto his nose. The sun glinted off the river Medway in shards of oily silver between the islands of detritus and fatbergs that jostled for space.

He spun back towards the sound of footsteps in the bedroom. Maybe Lafarge had returned with reinforcements. He slipped back into the room, disappointed that it was the forensics team preparing their equipment. He dodged a busy scan-orb, with its fans of green laser light, gathering data for a 3D holographic rendering of the crime scene. Two other orbs went about their business in the bathroom and kitchen. A technician flicked the catches on an aluminium carry case, releasing two CSA bots that sniffed, probed and sampled the surfaces, seeking wet and dry matter for analysis. Helix recognised the team leader but didn't know him by name. Nodded greetings were exchanged.

A faint beep in his ear caught his attention. He peeled back the flap of material in his jacket sleeve reading the short message on the graphene display. "There's something you need to see."

2

The lift door opened with a laboured squeak, casting a puddle of piss-coloured light out into the murky underground car park. Helix strolled past the skeletons of what were vehicles, picked over and stripped of anything useful before being set alight. Cars were rendered useless and illegal with the passing of the Autonomous Vehicle (AV) Act 2025 that prohibited the use of any driver-controlled vehicles on the roads. The effect outside London and the regional centres had been minimal. Those who could find and afford fuel didn't care and the underpaid militia were too depleted to bother enforcing the law. The shadows echoed to metallic clatter and a cat's scream accompanied by shouts of hungry excitement. There would be meat on the menu for someone that night.

The matt black door of his AV sighed open. Two large holographic displays glowed into life as he slid into the black faux-leather seat. Taking a bottle of water from the centre arm rest, he took a large slug and wiped his mouth on the back of his hand. The vehicle's systems established secure comms and data links. The compartment lights adjusted as the ghostly image of his younger brother, Ethan, appeared on-screen, wisps of smoke swirling from a fat joint held between his lips. The vehicle filled with the familiar sound of small arms fire and dull explosions.

'Nate. How's it going?' Ethan said, in between volleys of gunfire.

Helix grimaced. 'Hi Bruv. Not too bad. What the hell is that noise?'

'Watching a film, *Blade Runner 2049*, it's a classic.'

'Ethan, it's 2039, they got the previous film wrong. 2019 wasn't great, but nowhere near the grim dystopia they predicted, and I doubt 2049 will be either. No need to leave the planet just yet.' He drained the bottle, before crushing it flat and screwing the cap back on.

Ethan coughed, phlegm ratting in his throat. 'Maybe not, but we came close.'

'And those things will kill you,' he sighed. 'I take it you saw what happened upstairs?' He fished a small green box from his jacket pocket and shook a breath-mint into his palm. 'Or were you too busy watching Officer K wasting skin-jobs?'

'No. I was with you all the way; the stream was perfect. That new UHD sensor in your eye is better than I expected, even with the strobes. You should have chucked him out of the window.'

'It was tempting, but I can do without the desk work. Anyway, there's something I need to see?'

Ethan paused the film and drew hard on his joint. 'CCTV coverage. I'm surprised we have any at all. It's patchy, but at least we have something to work with.' He flicked his blond hair from his eyes. 'I'm just stitching together an accelerated time frame. It'll be done soon.'

Helix studied the flat bottle. 'OK, good work. Have you got a full run down on Prof. Polozkova?'

'Yep. Here we go: Miriam Polozkova, born 1991, parents Aneta and Anatoly Polozkova, Polish immigrants, both died back in the late unpleasantness, August 2020. Professor Miriam was a member of the Scientific Elite. She established ground-breaking methods of mass inoculation for Ebola, saving thousands of lives that would otherwise have been lost. Media-shy, bordering on reclusive, which might explain why she was down there. Emeritus Professor of Tropical Medicine 2022 to 2025. Re-trained for gynaecology, obstetrics and general practice 2025 to 2029, gave up her grace and favour house in the Meridian 2032.' He picked a small strand of tobacco from the tip of his tongue and flicked it over his shoulder.

'What was she doing in this dump?'

'As your new friend said, she established the charity medical centre in the old dockyard. Doctors are as rare as honest politicians in these parts, so the locals show restraint and respect.'

'My friend? I know things are tough outside, but the militia must be desperate if Lafarge is the best they can find.'

'Hmm, agreed. I'll do a bit of digging into him when I get a moment. Oh yes, Miriam had a housekeeper.'

'What's her story?'

Ethan ground the remains of his joint into an ashtray. 'Nothing special, her statement is included with the file the locals sent you. Turned up for work as usual at 07:00, let herself in, started tidying the kitchen, wandered into the bedroom and there she was, in the buff, fast asleep. Well, not asleep as it turned out. Militia were called and there you are.'

'List of Polozkova's associates and patients? I'd be interested to know if Lafarge is on it and to see if his infection story checks out.'

'I'm working on it.'

Helix pressed a button on the door panel, the opaque glass cleared. The militia were wielding their batons, discouraging a group of curious locals who'd got too close to the forensic vehicles. 'Looks like they're bringing her down. Once they've loaded her up, I'll get weaving.'

'OK. Best route for your return is via the old A2 up to Ebbsfleet and onto the loop. I'll nick a pod out of the international schedule for you. Your AV can find its way back home.'

'Thanks, Ethan.'

The AV picked its way out of the underground garage and back into the sunlight. Ethan had recovered well. Risk of injury in the military came with the turf, everyone knew that. What you don't expect is to lose your legs while driving a desk. He'd refused to be diminished by his injuries. To him, they were just another server to be hacked or encryption key to be broken. He wasn't interested in pity, however well-meant. He'd met the challenge head on, bear-crawling and clambering out of the pit he'd found himself in and God help anyone who'd got in the way. He enjoyed his new life of isolation, his view of the world augmented via Helix's eyes and ears whenever he needed it. Ethan had always said it could have been worse, like Jon and the others.

Helix worked the fingers of his right hand. The AV accelerated, chalky dust billowing around the windows. It was the same colour dust that had scratched his eyes and clogged his lungs as he'd lain in the wreckage of that flattened school building, in a place the Government denied even existed. The medic's shouts on the radio: "Three dead, one double amp, lucky bastard, immediate medivac required." Lucky? In the months following, he'd discovered there were worse things than dying.

'Got that time frame. I'll put it on screen two,' Ethan said. 'I've kept the best of what we have from around the approaches to Professor Miriam's apartment.'

A mosaic of high-definition images and grainy black and white footage organised itself across the screen.

'Dogs, cats, pigeons and old ladies with shopping trollies, Ethan. Come on.'

'I know, I know. Give it a moment. Here we go.'

Basic AVs were seen swarming around London like ants. The same photo-voltaic skins, the same pregnant skateboard shape, available in all shades of black. Swarming outside of London was rare, and the sight of one manoeuvring down the slope of the underground garage that Helix had just left grabbed his attention. 'What time is this?'

'Just before 23:00 last night.'

'Do we have a tag? Who owns it and what are they doing outside London?'

'All good questions but I don't know yet. Once I can access the licencing authority systems, I should be able to see how many trips outside correlate with the information we have.'

'We might get a facial ID before then.' He rattled his mint box. 'Can you fast forward it?'

'Patience, my friend, patience.'

Helix tossed his sunglasses onto the seat and leaned in closer. 'We won't see their face if they walk directly into the lift.'

'Her face. Around five-foot seven inches tall I would say, full length black coat, hood up, flat shoes, straight into the lift, no face to see. Bugger.'

'OK. Move it on, Ethan.'

'It'll move on. That's what it's been doing, removing all the bits without vehicles and warm bodies.'

Helix drummed his fingers on the arm rest. 'We don't have anything from inside the apartment, do we?'

'No, but if you look, she's coming out on the fifteenth floor.'

'It's her back again. Is that Polozkova's door she's standing outside of? It doesn't look like she's trying to hide herself. The angles of the cameras are just wrong.'

'It's the Prof's door. We'll be fine, she's made her way in, she needs to come back out. Let it play.'

The image stuttered again. The timestamp advanced.

'Here she comes. Two hours fifty-eight minutes total time elapsed.' Ethan sniffed. 'Let's slow things down, frame by frame. Come on, milady.'

Helix tapped the water bottle on his knee as he watched the lift door stagger open, the same pool of yellow light rendered white-grey on the screen as she stepped out. She paused and looked around before stepping towards her AV.

'Stop there, Ethan. Zoom in and enhance it. She's almost looking up at the camera.'

'Hold on.'

The image froze. The woman's head was shrouded in the deep hood of the coat. She advanced, frame by frame. Her hand rose to the hood, sweeping it off her head, revealing dark shoulder-length brown hair. Ethan zoomed in, the image pixilating and then re-rendering into sharper focus.

The empty water bottle slipped from Helix's hand as the gentle oval face came into focus. 'Well, well, well. You know who that is, don't you, Ethan?'

3

Helix's eyes lingered on the frozen image of Doctor Gabrielle Stepper, Dame of the realm and hero of the nation. 'Ethan, I'll stick with the AV. I miss the gridlock days. At least you had time to think.'

Ethan laughed his mouth empty of smoke. 'Roger that. Time to think about what might have been if only she had chosen you and not Justin Wheeler?'

Helix grinned. 'Fuck off. She doesn't even know me.'

'Not yet,' Ethan mumbled. 'OK. Where you gonna go?'

Helix tilted his head, his fingers rasping the emergent stubble on his chin. 'Navigation. The Meridian.'

The dashboard display confirmed the order. A rush of acceleration pressed him back in his seat. 'For fucks sake! Navigation. Max speed fifty.'

Ethan laughed. 'You finished fighting with the technology now?'

Helix reclined his seat and closed his eyes. 'Where were we?' He stretched his legs, crossing his feet at the ankles.

'Dame Gabrielle Stepper, born 4th June 1992, Cambridge. Making her—'

'Forty-seven?'

'Are you sure? She looks more like twenty-seven.'

'Maybe she discovered the secret of eternal youth. And why Dame, not Doctor?'

'They don't use their medical qualification if they have been elevated to the nobility.'

'Right. I thought she turned it down?'

'That was the Nobel Prize. Don't you know nuffink?'

'Get on with it.'

'Sorry. Mum was a teacher, dad a barrister, twin sister Sarah-Jane.'

Helix's eyes sprang open. 'I'd forgotten about Sarah-Jane. Anything else on her?'

'Hmm. Twin sisters. Imagine that. Dunno. I'll have a look in a minute. Dr Gabrielle has degrees in microbiology, tropical diseases, botany and genetics. Sounds like a right swot.'

Helix scratched his chin. 'Is that it?'

'No. She had a daughter, Eve. Born in 2025, died 2031. That's grim.'

'Yeah. I read about that. Grim is one word for it.'

'And finally, as you know, she's married to none other than Just Wheeler, the Chancellor of the Exchequer and turd of the first order. I added that last bit.'

Helix snorted. Turd was one of the politer names. He couldn't believe she'd married him. She was all over the media. He was a rising star in the discredited Government, trying to claim all the credit for her work in ending the pandemic.

He leaned forward and rubbed his right ankle. 'I remember the media frenzy around their wedding. Some sort of spirit of hope thing, the two of them standing on each side of the prime meridian. The future and the past.'

'And he approved the funding for the remembrance garden.'

Helix shook his head. 'Paving over the entire length of the bloody Thames, from Hammersmith to Greenwich, to plant fucking trees and bushes so the scientific elite and the green party could tiptoe through the tulips together.' He looked up at Ethan's smiling face on the screen. 'What are you smirking at?'

Ethan rested back in his seat. 'You don't like him much, do you?'

'Can you tell? I still can't believe she married him.'

'Oh yes. I almost forgot SJ. Now, let me see.'

Helix knew what a shit storm looked like and this had all the hallmarks. What was she doing outside London? It wasn't illegal, but in the middle of the night visiting someone who turned up dead the next morning? That would take some explaining. A national treasure and very vocal, high-ranking politician? It was time to check in with the old man. He snapped the voice command. 'Call Yawlander.'

'Wasting your time, buddy,' Ethan mumbled. 'He's out and about.'

'Cancel.' He frowned at the monitor containing his brother. 'How do you know?'

'Cos I got all the gear and all the ideas, unlike some people, and—'

'And two wheels. Unlike some people.'

Ethan gasped. 'Now that's harsh. I think you need to attend an embracing diversity course, Major Helix.'

'Sign me up. Anything on the sister?'

'Yep. Here we go. Same birthday—'

'Amazing work, Poirot. She's her twin sister.'

'How rude. If I may continue. Interesting. Twin sister maybe, but polar opposites. Dropped out of uni' after six months, odd jobs, dossing about, claiming benefits, left the country 2019, aged twenty-seven.'

'Just before the outbreak. Where'd she go?'

'Canada. Active on social media for a while, Instagram account, Facebook, hellooo baby. Some sort of extreme sports junky. Seems to be having a good time. Here you go.'

Helix glanced up at the screen. The likeness was unmistakeable. 'Where's that cliff she's jumping off?'

'Canada, British Columbia, the Stawamus Chief. It's a granite dome over seven-hundred metres in height. Irresistible to base jumpers. There was a guy killed the week before when his chute didn't open.'

'Ouch. What else?'

Ethan scrolled through the photos of the athletic, often half-dressed, Sarah-Jane, also known as SJ to her friends. 'Not much. Things go quiet after the outbreak.'

'Canada managed better than most. Maybe she headed for the wilderness. No connections to anything out there. Do we even know if she's alive? You can answer that when you've finished drooling over her photographs.'

'Hmm. I can have a look around.'

At the side of the road, a weed-draped sign announced his approach to Blackheath. One urban myth replaced with an urban truth. The stories about the name telling how it was associated with the 1665 Black Death and used as a burial pit became an eerie truth three-hundred and fifty years later. There must have been thousands under there. Row after grim fucking row. He'd spent hours cooped up in an excavator in a sweaty bio-suit gouging out new pits or back-filling them. Nature had done its job. If there were any lingering reminders, they were shrouded by the undergrowth.

Estimated time of arrival was four minutes according to the scrolling map on the dash display.

'Maritime Museum,' he said.

The new destination registered, ETA unchanged.

'I'm going to park up for a bit, take some air and clear my head. Anything from the forensic team yet?'

A gap in the trees provided a fleeting glimpse of the onion-shaped dome of the Royal Observatory. 'Ethan. Anything from the forensics team?'

'Yep. There's some chatter going on.'

Ethan manoeuvred the hacked communication onto the shared screen. 'Here's the first one,' he said, his earlier levity absent.

```
High probability that subject died from
cardiac arrest caused by toxic substance
of unknown origin. Samples inbound by
drone. Request detailed analysis
prioritisation.
```

Ethan cleared his throat. 'There's more.'

```
DNA evidence suggests possible matches
with three female subjects. Searching
national DNA database.
```

Helix's stomach groaned. 'That won't take them long. No prizes for guessing who two of them are. Where's your money?'

'Same as you, I guess. The housekeeper and Doc Gabrielle.'

'Hang on. Is that it? Three females. Have they ruled me and Lafarge out? With the amount of claret leaking from him, I'm surprised they didn't pick up on it.'

'Dunno, Nate. Unless they have and they've only mentioned the unknowns. I'm guessing he's on the database. Same as you. I'll check.'

'OK. Stay on it. Let's see what else comes up.'

* * *

Earlier thoughts of death trenches crept back upon Helix as he walked up the empty gravel path to the Queen's House. Designed by Inigo Jones for Anne, the Queen of Denmark and Queen to King James I, it had been repurposed as the administration and facilities office for the Meridian, the home of the Scientific Elite. Six autonomous lawn mowers performed their choreographed manoeuvres, sculpting faultless geometric patterns in the lush grass. He paused under the covered walkway connecting the maritime museum and looked out over the expansive lawns.

The former world heritage site was a gift from a grateful nation. Its proximity to the city was convenient for the increased role played by science in Government. Rising behind the Queen's house, the undulating parkland was empty apart from a few walkers and joggers. The historic Royal Observatory, home to Doctor Gabrielle Stepper and her husband, dominated the horizon. It was another one of Wheeler's "statements". It always reminded Helix of fussy wedding cake balanced on top of a monstrous glass and polished steel shoe box.

Helix activated the microphone incorporated into the collar of his jacket. 'What access do we have to the residence, Ethan?'

'Not a lot at the moment. Never felt the need,' Ethan replied via the cochlea implant in Helix's right ear. 'I should be able to get the data links without too much hassle. If they've got CCTV around the place and cameras inside, I'll get those too. Why's that?'

'Don't know. Just a little tingle down below. I think we'll be getting to know Mr and Mrs Wheeler a lot better.'

Anything else from the forensics? And is Yawlander back in yet?'

'Who am I, your bloody secretary? Ethan rapped out a command on his keyboard. 'Yes, and yes. Which do you want first?'

'Forensics please, ducky.' The link went silent. 'Whassup, Bruv?'

Ethan sighed. 'No prizes, cos there's no surprises. This just came in. Listen up.'

```
Three female subjects, DNA confirmation.
Professor Miriam Polozkova, Doctor
Gabrielle Stepper and Monica Estevez.
```

Helix nipped the inside of his mouth as he listened. 'No shit. Anything else?'

'Shit is probably the best word. Hold on to your hat, here it comes.'

```
Initial analysis confirms cause of death
– cardiac arrest. Agent used is not
military or commercially available and
likely hand-crafted by person(s) with
significant expertise in genetics and
biochemistry. Full results and report
expected in less than 24 hours.
```

4

Gabrielle's eyes lingered, her finger stroking the edge of the gilt-framed photograph. Eve would have been fourteen next month. The years had fallen away, into an abyss, six-years deep. She focused her thoughts back on the screen, prompting a steady flow of text, completing her notes. She paused, the cursor blinking in anticipation of the next sentence or paragraph. Her finger rose to the bridge of her glasses that doubled as the human-machine interface, or HMI, capturing her thoughts and processing them. Her eyes followed as the commands played out. File > Save As > Miriam Polozkova Clinical Trial Update D16.5.

She had been diligent with her notes and record keeping as usual. Because she was treating a dear friend didn't mean there might not be the possibility that the science could be of benefit to others. But it was hard not to allow her feelings to colour her thoughts. Was there anything she could have done to prevent this? Miriam had known the risks, she'd always been open about her lifestyle and her choices, the thrill of the chase. "Better to burn out than fade away" she used to say. Her discovery of a shadier side of Chatham had played a part in Miriam's move there. She'd begged Gabrielle to explore with her. Gabrielle snatched another glance at the photo. Her cheeks flushed. Dark times in her own life had led her to some poor choices, too. Miriam had done nothing to discourage her. Following another drug and alcohol fuelled orgy in a grimy basement squat, they'd returned to Miriam's apartment and discovered each other. Gabrielle suspected it was the cocktail of chemicals and booze, but the morning after had disproved the theory. It had been unexpected, and she'd surprised herself by feeling happy and excited. Miriam had insisted they keep it an open relationship, no rules and no shackles. Gabrielle always felt loved when they were together, but she also knew that Miriam hadn't stopped exploring when they weren't.

She turned and smiled in response to the hand on her shoulder. 'All done, Rachel?'

'You were miles away.'

'Hmm, just thinking over my notes, making sure I hadn't forgotten anything.'

Her lab assistant peeled off her white nitrile gloves with practiced efficiency. 'Anyway, I'm done. If there's nothing else, I'll head off.'

Gabrielle tilted her head towards her friend. Something was up. 'Are you OK, Rachel? You've been quiet this morning,' she said, resting her hand on Rachel's arm.

Rachel patted the back of her hand. 'Sure. I'm fine. Late to bed last night. Studying.' She rolled the gloves into a ball and tossed them into the bin. 'I have a paper that I need to complete before the end of the week and I'm a bit bogged down. That's all.'

'Not enough hours in the day?'

'You could say that. Full-time job, eight-year old plus studying. But needs must. I didn't have the same immersive education you did, so I have to do things the hard way.'

'Hmm. Careful what you wish for,' Gabrielle shrugged. 'Want me to take a look at the paper?'

'No thanks. It's fine. I know what I need to do.'

'Alright, but if you change your mind just send it over. The last time I felt like I'd cheated you, because it was a superb piece of work.' She glanced at her empty screen. 'I'm not going down to Miriam's for a couple of days. I've got time.'

Rachel nipped at her lip. 'Hmm. Thanks for the offer.'

Gabrielle trapped the sigh. She rested her glasses on top of her head and tucked her hair behind her ears. 'Miriam was better last night. Still questioning everything we're doing, but that's a good sign.' It *was* a good sign and it was what they needed. 'There are some positives. The treatment is helping, so we might have this thing on the run...'

She glanced up at Rachel's brown eyes, forced a smile and slipped off the lab stool into the gap between them. She needed a hug. As she held her friend, her eyes returned to the photo of Eve. She couldn't fail again. 'Sorry, Rachel.'

'It's OK. You're doing your best.'

Gabrielle pulled a tight-lipped smile and turned towards the door. 'I'll come up with you.'

* * *

It was Gabrielle's turn to be quiet. She leaned into the corner of the small lift as it made its way back up to the extensive two-level apartment beneath the Royal Observatory. She ached for Miriam, ached for conversation, comfort and physical warmth. She hesitated, watching Rachel looking at her shoes while they waited for the doors to open. 'Listen, Rachel. I was going to jump in the shower and then maybe we could have a drink after.' She took Rachel's hand giving it a squeeze of encouragement.

Rachel flushed as she smiled. 'I can't. Not now, Gabrielle.' Her eyes widened as she glanced at her watch. 'I need to pick Lauren up from school.'

Gabrielle stepped back, wringing her hands. 'Sorry. I didn't realise the time.'

Rachel leaned in to kiss her cheek. 'Take care, Gabrielle.'

Gabrielle turned her head, their lips coming together. She snatched another quick hug before Rachel smiled and drifted away.

The door closed on the yawning emptiness of the apartment. That, together with the equally empty gardens and surrounding parkland, echoed her life.

* * *

The bookshelves of Gabrielle's study overflowed with academic journals and books. Somehow the paperless office still hadn't arrived in her world. Almost tripping over an archive box, she pulled back the large leather chair and slumped in front of her computer. The scent of stale potpourri rose from a fluted porcelain dish on her desk to meet her as she slipped her glasses from her head. The screen bloomed into life. An email icon blinked in the corner of the screen. She reached for the lime-green stress ball on her desk.

Squeezing the ball in her right hand, she hesitated as she noted the email sender's address – Meridian Campus Admin.

She slid her glasses up onto the bridge of her nose. A single blink of her eye opened the two-word message.

`See invitation`

She gasped. The wheels of the chair squeaked as she distanced herself from the words. Thirteen characters. Always the same. Her heart rate soared. A further blink opened the path to a shared folder – one new document. She bit at her bottom lip and forced her eyes open, daring not to blink. She allowed the faintest twitch in her left eye. It was enough. The message opened.

```
I warned you. Remember the past, think
about the present and consider the
future. Time's up. Time to share. Don't
squander this opportunity. Join me or
regret it.
         Cerberus.
```

5

The leering cameras blinked their menacing red eyes as Dr Vincent Berdiot perched on his lab stool. The conference call had ended abruptly but he had no idea if he was still being watched. The voice, which had been impatient, had seemed calmer, more resigned and knowing that in science, it was necessary to take a few steps back to move forward.

An intense hiss, like air escaping a slashed tyre, came from over his shoulder. He spun around on his stool. The black emergency hermetic seal bulged into the gaps around the laboratory door. Something must have triggered the contamination alarm. He pushed back, toppling his stool. Something brushed the bottom of his trouser leg and rolled across his foot. A white lab rat lay on the tiled floor beneath the bench. He reached down and picked up the creature, cupping it between his hands. Its pink snout twitched in time with its irregular and laboured respiration. The stricken animal convulsed, emitting a strained wheeze. Something Berdiot had witnessed before. He dropped it. Contact with the hard floor was the catalyst for its demise as it exploded, spattering his blue lab trousers and left hand with blood and gore. His first convulsion followed immediately. He clutched his hands to his stomach. The overwhelming nausea and cramps weakened his knees. He pitched forward and flailed against the edge of his workbench, dislodging his glasses as he fell to the floor. He looked up at the blinking eye of the camera, felt the cold of the tiled floor against his face and then the final devastating convulsion and darkness.

* * *

The Chairman poured mineral water into a shimmering crystal tumbler. He studied the ashen faces of the two men before him. Berdiot's lab coat, in its 3D holographic rendition, hung on his stool, shredded and bloodstained at the centre of the conference table. Part of his exploded liver slid off the bench onto the floor with a slop. The General flinched, as if it was actually steaming on the conference table in front of him.

The chairman shaped his words, the way his speech therapist had taught him. 'Berdiot was an id-idiot. He squandered the remaining active pathogen on his t-trivial animal experiments instead of advancing to where I needed him to be. But gentlemen, what we have just w-witnessed is, as I have always known, science with huge commercial potential. Something my late f-father could only have dreamed of.' He sipped his water as his eyes darted between the two impassive faces that stared back at him.

He tapped the glass table-top. The live stream from the lab morphed into a document in front of each of the men. His chair spun as he got up and turned away, allowing them time to read and absorb the text. From the panoramic window, he looked out over the verdant, crystalline, polished steel city. His tailored suit trousers fluttered in the gentle breeze from the air conditioning vents at his feet. For every ten degrees of travel, he could name at least one bridge, office, retail outlet or apartment block that his late father's company had built, or rebuilt, thus dragging London back from the cusp of oblivion. Artificial Intelligence, automation, autonomy and the harnessing of renewable energy sources were the pillars upon which his father's empire had been built.

He turned, his hand on the back of his tall green leather chair. 'What you see before you, gentlemen, is a personalised grant of shares in LR e-enterprises. An appropriate n-number, given your relative seniority. At their current price, even yours, Colonel, are worth several m-millions.

He retook his seat, his elbows on the table. 'Berdiot only ever seemed to bring me problems. I prefer solutions.' He interlaced his fingers. 'This is where you come in.'

He'd chosen well. He saw his own steely determination reflected in their faces. Time would tell. 'Bring her to me, gentlemen, that is all I ask.' He waved his hand across the glass table-top, restoring the live stream from the lab. 'Bring me more problems and it will be you picking up the p-pieces. Now g-go.'

He pressed his foot at the leg of the table, rotating his chair. He watched the reflections of the departing men in the window as he held his glass up to the light. His eyes drifted across the skyline to the east. To say his late father had exploited the post-Ebola years would have been considered impolite. His father found the word *capitalise* more appropriate. The legacy spread out before him was a living testament to his zeal.

In the corner of the office stood an imposing leather chair behind an antique desk, with marquetery panels and an inlaid leather writing surface. The two items were incongruous beside the brushed metal and glass office furnishings, but it was how he preferred to keep the memory of his father alive. It was from that same seat that his father had given his account of the tensions in Ukraine that had hastened the family's departure from their adoptive homeland. His father had shouldered the burden of responsibility for what had happened, unable to forgive himself for the events that unfolded as they fought to escape the purges orchestrated by the ruling party. Once settled in London, he had made it his remaining life's work to track down and punish those responsible for his daughter's disappearance and the murder of his wife.

He approached the desk, running his finger along the carved edge. Rare were the days when he was not reminded of what had happened and how it was *his* duty, should his father fail, to complete the task. The demand was always reinforced with a hefty slap of the leather surface.

He reclined in the chair, his hands on the fraying leather arms, glancing at the rare family photograph. It was the only one salvaged during their escape. A faint whiff of Cuban tobacco reached his nose from the humidor, next to the glasses and decanters on the drinks cabinet. The luxury of fine whisky and brandy, enjoyed with a cigar, was something his father would never have approved of.

His father may have gone to his grave tormented by guilt and failure, but *he* had kept his promise. Two years later, he had succeeded where his father had not. The architects of the purges had themselves fallen victim to political infighting and assassination. Some had found sanctuary in Moscow, Baghdad or Damascus. Wherever they'd tried to hide, he'd tracked them down and now had them where he wanted them.

6

Mounds of soft white bubbles bloomed across the surface of the steaming water as the bath filled. The flames of the scented candles danced in the clouds of steam rising beneath them. A half-filled glass stood next to an emerald-green bottle on the wide edge of the bath, swathed in condensation that coalesced into crystal beads that hung briefly, before tumbling down the stem.

The steam billowed away from the frosted glass door as it pushed inwards. Gabrielle entered, a silk kimono draped around her. Pulling up her sleeve, she ran her fingers through the water and found the temperature to her liking. The kimono whispered to the floor around her ankles as she shook it off. Perched on the edge of the bath, she took up the glass and breathed in the wine's aroma. Closing her eyes, she took a generous sip and rolled it around her mouth. The subtle crisp fruit with hints of oak, and the aroma of the candles combined to remind her of the last time she'd shared a bottle with Miriam.

She spun around on the edge of the bath and slid her feet into the deep water. She topped up her glass before slipping below the surface, the clouds of bubbles closing in over her. Images of the previous night with Miriam flickered inside her head. The simple but comfortable apartment was free of modern accoutrements, but full of tenderness and alive with laughter. She relived the warmth of the bath they'd taken together, Miriam in her arms and the giggling in that crazy hammock where she slept when alone.

Her lips trembled apart, sending her back to the surface. She smeared away the foamy suds from her face and smoothed her hair back. Resting her head back against the bath cushion, she closed her eyes again. Small ripples shivered across the water with each choking sob. Why the saviour of humanity but not those closest to you? Why Gabrielle?

* * *

She opened her eyes. One of the candles had burnt out, a thin finger of dark smoke snaked towards the ceiling and the water had cooled. "Join me or regret it." She pushed the words to the back of her mind as she had before. She'd been over it before, again and again. But this one was different, more direct, more menacing. Any normal politician's wife wouldn't hesitate to ask her husband for help. Fat chance of that. Unless it benefitted him.

She allowed herself to float free in the water, determined to relax. Brushing her finger over a touch-sensitive screen next to the bath, a warm current of hot water enveloped her as the thermostatic control adjusted the temperature. With a second touch, a small panel hinged open beside the wine bottle allowing eight cypribots to escape and tumble into the water at her shoulder. The small fish-like devices swam between her feet and kissed their way over her skin. A final touch on the panel increased their intensity before she took up her glass again and laid back, focusing on the tiny bots as they began to massage their way across her feet and calves. Her ankles drifted away from each other, a warm sense of anticipation growing between her thighs. She bit her lip lightly following her breathing but found herself drawn back to thoughts of those bloody emails. She resisted, urging the cypribots on in spite of the tightening of her muscles.

What's that? She stiffened, knocking her glass against the bottle, trapping a bot under her leg. She tilted her head, the silence punctuated by a single drop of water from the tap. You're hearing things, he wouldn't be home this early. A second drip from the tap convinced her it was nothing. She drained her glass before refilling it and relaxing back into the water. The trapped bot wriggled free and resumed its task.

She tensed and released her muscles in groups from her toes up to her neck and face, the alcohol playing its part, as she returned her focus to the tiny shoal sharing her bath. She floated serenely in the water, her face barely clear of the surface. Her jaw relaxed; her tongue played across her lips as the eight tiny soft mandibles of the cypribots converged between her legs. She listened to the beat of her heart through the water and as the bots pressed closer, the tips of her fingers played across her breasts. She gasped, arching her back, slipping below the surface, her fingers working in concert with the bots. Her deep groan echoed through the water. Her eyes opened as a second rush engulfed her. She held her breath and closed her eyes anticipating the next. With the quivering onset, her eyes flickered again. But something was different. A shadow above.

She blinked in terrified confusion at the silhouette of someone peering down between islands of foam. Flailing, she erupted back to the surface, scrabbling for grip on the edge of the bath as her eyes focussed. 'Justin. What the hell are you doing?'

'Watching you.' He scratched at the front of his trousers. 'Thought I might slip in there with you.'

'I'm not that desperate.' She glanced over her shoulder, looking for her glass. 'Bugger off and leave me alone.'

'Not desperate? Unless it suits you.' Wheeler shrugged, nodding at the bottle. 'Perhaps another time then. First or second one today?'

'Second – thank you.' She tilted the almost empty bottle as if checking her facts. 'Keeping count now, are we?'

'Bottle?'

'Glass, you idiot.' She emptied the remaining wine into her glass. 'What do you want, Justin? Parliament on fire? Must be to get you out this early.' She wiped the remaining water and bubbles from her face and took a defiant sip of wine. 'Well?'

Wheeler shoved his hands in his pockets. 'Get dressed.'

'Why? No. I haven't washed my hair yet or done my nails.'

'Just hurry up and get out. There's something I need to tell you and it would be better if you weren't inebriated.'

She took a long look at the glass before putting it back next to the empty bottle. What could be so important? He's been in the house for hours before now and hasn't even bothered to tell me he's back. Perhaps it was him earlier. 'Justin, I'm tired. Whatever it is you want to say just spit it out and leave me alone, or wait until I've finished my bath.' She pulled her knees up and wrapped her arms around them. One of the cypribots clung to her knee. She flicked it back into the water.

'Not finished playing with your toys?'

She pressed her palm to her forehead. 'You have no idea,' she said, floating the empty bottle in the water and watching it bob around.

'At least that doesn't need batt—'

She brandished the bottle by the neck. 'Just say what you've got to say and—' A slick of bubbles ran down the bottle and across the back of her hand as she held it above her head.

Wheeler held his hand up. 'It's about Miriam.'

'Miriam? What is it?' The bottle slipped from her hand, splashing into the water. Why would he be interested in Miriam, let alone know something, anything, about her? She held her hands out. 'What is it?'

Wheeler cleared his throat. 'I heard a rumour in Parliament that—'

Gabrielle arched an eyebrow. 'Wow, call the police, there's a rumour in Parliament.'

'Yes, very amusing, Gabrielle.' He folded his arms. 'It was about Miriam.'

'Why would there be rumours about Miriam? Is she OK, Justin? Is that why you're here? What's wrong?'

'Well, in spite of Miriam's behaviour, she is a member of the Scientific Elite and wherever she is, she is afforded the protection of—' Wheeler stepped towards her, his hand extended.

Gabrielle fought to swallow. With one hand to her chest she scrabbled for grip as she tried to get to her feet. 'Go on.'

'Gabrielle. Miriam is dead.'

Barely on her knees, Wheeler's face diminished to a blur, a scream filled her head. Miriam's dead? Her stomach knotted, she clamped her hand to her mouth, but the alcohol laced vomit found a way through the gaps in her fingers as she retched, throwing her against the edge of bath. The force of the blow to her ribs didn't register as pain, the bruise to come would tell the story. Another heave, another yellow tinged spray over the edge of the bath. He's lying. The stench of vomit clung to the back of her nose. This is just another sick way of taking out his jealousy of Miriam. She toppled back, eyes closed, water against her face. She summoned all her energy, but no scream came, just a painful, hoarse moan from somewhere inside her chest.

Water filled her mouth and nose, the bottom of the bath smooth against her cheek, a cascade of tiny bubbles filling her vision. She closed her eyes – No Miriam. You were getting better. The test res— She fought against the sharp pain pinching at the top of her right arm. He's going to drown me. Justin. No. Get off me. Get— She scraped and pushed to her knees. Her hand fell on the bottle as it knocked against the side of the bath, she groped at it, catching it by the neck. Above water, she heaved it towards her attacker, hearing him curse as it connected with the side of his head.

'For Christ's sake, Gabrielle, get a grip. I'm trying to bloody-well help you.'

She coughed up another mouthful of watery phlegm. 'Stay away from me, Justin. Stay away.'

Wheeler rolled out of range on the marble floor, his shirt soaked transparent. He dabbed at his ear and checked his fingers for blood. 'I was trying to help you. It looked like you'd fainted. Jesus.'

The bath felt like ice, she shivered, her arms wrapped around herself. 'Miriam's dead? How? Justin. Tell me!'

Wheeler rolled onto his knees. He checked his ear again before getting to his feet. 'I don't have any more details at the moment.' He unbuttoned his shirt. 'The report was made by her housekeeper. The local militia called it in when they realised who it was. We've sent someone.'

'Why? We've sent... Why did they do that?'

Wheeler peeled off his shirt dropping it to the floor. He took a towel from the heated rail. 'You know why. Any member of the SE who dies under susp— I mean unexplained circumstances, they send someone. The bloody digger militia can't be trusted.'

Gabrielle's fingers groped for the temperature control. The warm rush around her back barely registered. 'Suspicious? Why suspicious? What aren't you telling me, Justin?'

'I said unexplained.'

'Don't bloody lie, Justin. What do you know? Tell me.'

'We'll know soon enough, once the initial results are in. They're sending samples back by drone for analysis.'

Gabrielle got to her feet, the mixture of shock and alcohol causing her to reel. 'Don't come near me.'

Wheeler backed off, rubbing his arms and chest with the towel. He sighed. 'I've told you what I know. Get dressed. I'll pour you another drink. Come on.'

'Miriam's dead?' She shook her head as if it would make it untrue. 'No. Just leave me alone, Justin. Get out. I want to be alone.'

'Gabrielle—'

'I said. Get out!'

The door sucked closed behind him. She sat on the edge of the bath, flanked by the candles. Reaching out, she ignored the small sting between her fingertips as she snuffed each one out, leaving her alone in the dark. The only light left in her life had gone out.

7

Closing his left eye, Helix zoomed in on one of the panoramic windows of the Royal Observatory residence. The overlaid range finder display confirmed the distance as three-hundred and ninety-nine yards. His own brain confirmed the tall brown-haired man standing in the window holding a glass of red wine as Chancellor Justin Wheeler.

Ethan sneezed. 'Excuse me. Look what the cat dragged in.'

'That's all I need,' Helix said, jogging down the steps back towards the road.

Perched on the door sill of his AV, he tore open a bar of ration-pack chocolate with his teeth. 'Phone Yawlander.' He took a generous bite of chocolate and settled in for the wait.

'Helix. I've seen the reports from forensics and the locals,' Yawlander said. 'More questions than answers it would seem. You didn't waste any time getting down there.'

Helix almost choked on the chocolate. Yawlander rarely answered his own phone. It was usually a game of being passed from pillar to post while they tried to track him down. He swallowed. 'I thought it best to make my way here while we waited for the forensics confirmation. Chancellor Wheeler has also just returned.' He put his hand over his mouth, stifling a cough.

'Right, next steps. Another forensics team is on its way. They'll be a while. It's one of the new mobile labs. Coming down from Potters Bar. I need you to contain Doctor Stepper in the residence. It would have been easier if the Chancellor wasn't there, but I know you'll be diplomatic. The locals still have the housekeeper in custody, so Doctor Stepper is unaware of Professor Polozkova's death. You'll need to inform her. Once the team arrives, they will look for a link. They have the DNA so they know she was there. You have the CCTV. Once the team have done a sweep of the place, they can do the analysis in the mobile lab and we'll take it from there. Understood?'

'Understood, sir. I'll keep you posted.'

'Good. I take it you'll be coming to the remembrance service at the Cenotaph tomorrow?'

Helix hesitated. It sounded like an order, not a question. The long tradition of remembering the fallen in November had been supplemented with an additional day of remembrance, but with less focus on the military. Helix knew which one he'd sooner attend. 'And Doctor Stepper, sir?'

'If she goes, you go. I don't want Wheeler in my ear about it. Yawlander out.'

'He sounded happy,' Ethan chirped, interrupting his chain of thought. 'Anyway, I've got access to the services going into and out of the house. There's no CCTV inside from what I can see, but we'll have you. The next best thing.'

Helix climbed inside the AV. 'Good to know I have my uses. Did I mention that this has the makings of a right dog's breakfast?' He leaned on the armrest as he teased the last of his snack out from between his teeth.

'Dunno, but you're probably right.'

'OK, let's get on with it. I need you on silent mode, I don't want you babbling in my ear. If I need anything, I'll do it via thought control.'

'Just think my name and share your inner-you with me.'

'Hmm, I'm not sure sharing my inner thoughts with you is all it's cracked up to be.'

'No, but you have to admit you've got a better grip on the technology now. It's improved since we installed the micro-switch on the inside your mush. At least with that you can activate it whenever you need to and I don't have to listen to your thoughts about morning glory when you wake up.'

'Er, yes alright. Thank you.'

'You started it.'

'Alright. I'll concede that along with the cochlea and optic nerve implants things have improved. Having you in my ear and behind my eyeball has had its uses. Radio silence has its uses, too.'

'Point taken. You be careful. I think there was almost a compliment in there somewhere.'

Helix grinned. 'Navigate – Royal Observatory.'

The AV moved off, heading towards the north-west corner of the Meridian and the private tree-lined drive leading to the observatory. Framed inside the holographic monitor, Ethan had his head down, working silently as requested. Helix appreciated his knack of knowing when a sense of humour was welcome and when it wasn't. They were always close. They'd each fought their own battles through recovery and he was glad to have him around.

* * *

Helix straightened his jacket and sunglasses as he stepped onto the pale green painted floor of the underground garage. A faint hum from the plant powering the expansive apartment came from behind an anonymous grey door. Wheeler's limousine leached the whiff of baked electrics as it ticked alongside its smaller cousin. Apart from the vehicles, the space was empty, devoid of any of the normal clues about family life, hobbies or interests. He glanced at the smaller AV.

'Same type of AV as we saw on the CCTV,' Ethan whispered.

'Ethan!'

'Sorry. But it is the same one.'

Helix sighed. He was probably right and it wouldn't take long to confirm. Four metallic marble-sized spheres rolled across the leather of his right boot and dropped to the floor. There was a momentary pause before they deployed into the ducting and cable trays around the perimeter of the garage ceiling. He pulled back the flap over the graphene screen to confirm the tiny HD cameras were online.

The voice of Justin Wheeler echoed around the garage. 'Major Helix. Do join us upstairs.'

* * *

The lift door opened to reveal Justin Wheeler tying a silk bathrobe around his waist. The hairs on the back of Helix's neck bristled, Yawlander's suggestion of diplomacy echoed in his ear.

Wheeler stepped forward with his hand extended. 'Major Nathan Helix, VC DSO. You *and* my wife, two of our nation's heroes, here together. I'm honoured.'

Helix was distracted by the involuntary tic around Wheeler's left eye that appeared as a wink. He accepted the offered hand, tempted to crush every bone in it before reminding himself to play nicely. He gripped the Chancellor's hand and looked into his steely blue eyes. 'Chancellor Wheeler, sir. Thank you for allowing me to meet with you. Is your wi—' He followed Wheeler's eyes down to their joined hands.

'Call me old-fashioned, Major,' Wheeler sneered. 'But isn't it polite to remove your glove before shaking someone's hand?'

'I'm sorry, sir. Yes, of course.' Helix tugged at the tips of his fingers, stripping off the black leather glove, revealing the inner workings of his prosthetic hand. Wheeler shrunk away.

'The skin made my hand itch sir, so I cut it off. Silly, as there are no pain or touch receptors in the budget skin provided to veterans. Unless it was my imagination.' He smiled and extended his hand again, working his fingers to a chorus of clicks as the joints flexed.

Wheeler grimaced, three winks escaping his eye. 'Blepharospasm, Major. In case you were wondering. Spasm of the orbicular muscle of the eyelids.'

'Excuse me, Chancellor?'

'Blepharospasm. I'm not in the habit of winking at people. Not chaps anyway. It's involuntary.' He waved Helix's hand away. 'Anyway. Itchy right hand you say. Must be coming into money soon. So goes the myth.'

'I doubt that, sir. But I eke out a living on the veteran's pension and the officer's salary you so generously—'

A movement at the top of the stairs behind Wheeler distracted him. Gabrielle Stepper ambled onto the mezzanine, tying a white silk kimono around her waist. She paused and glanced at her husband.

'Major Helix is here, darling.'

She nodded and pulled a white handkerchief from her pocket. She dabbed at the corner of her eye before turning back through the door.

Wheeler cleared his throat. 'Coffee, tea or something else to drink, Major?'

Helix raised his eyebrows. Did she already know?

'Still with us, Major?'

'Sorry, Chancellor. Coffee please. Thank you.'

The apartment was comfortably furnished. The ground floor comprised single open space with four doors, one of which was open. Helix tilted his head looking through at the unmade bed. The door to the ensuite bathroom was open, liberating a faint whiff of steam and shower gel, or shampoo. The large open plan kitchen and dining area filled one side of the space; a generous sitting area, with the biggest TV screen Helix had ever seen and with wide, brown leather sofas filled the other. An imposing oak bookcase formed the angle of two of the walls. It was crammed with a range of titles that would have graced an old-style library in the days before everything was digitised. Helix focussed on one of the shelves, discovering one of the nanocams had installed itself on top of a battered copy of Debrett's Peerage and Baronetage. There were no prizes for guessing who that belonged to.

Wheeler shoved the steaming cup across the kitchen counter, the dark brown contents almost breaching the lip. 'Milk and sugar?'

'No. Black is fine. Thanks.'

Gabrielle sauntered down from the stainless-steel and glass mezzanine, tucking her damp hair behind her ears. Her eyes were downcast, as she appeared to be applying an unusual amount of concentration to her descent. Her simple floral-print strappy dress, open at the back revealing her slim, freckled shoulders, swayed with each step. Her bare feet left fleeting condensation prints on the stair treads. Helix had often wondered what it would be like to meet her, albeit under different circumstances.

He settled onto a stool at the breakfast bar next to his coffee.

Wheeler leaned back against the kitchen counter studying his wife's progress towards them. 'Something to drink, darling?'

'Red. Thank you.' She slid up on to the stool next to Helix, crossing her ankles. She fixed her eyes on his and extended her hand. 'Gabrielle Stepper, how do you do, Major?'

Helix squeezed her perfumed hand gently. 'Doctor Step—'

'I know why you're here, Major. Miriam Polozkova is dead.'

8

Wheeler's constant fidgeting and interjections were grating on Helix. Gabrielle seemed far more practiced at ignoring it, focusing her attention as she listened to his summary of what had been discovered.

'I'd like to ask you a few questions, Doctor. To help me build a more complete picture.'

Gabrielle flicked her eyes up. 'Please, Major Helix, enough with the Doctor. Just call me Gabrielle.' She took a generous sip of her wine.

Helix allowed himself a small grin of satisfaction. He knew her informality wouldn't be echoed by her husband. 'Alright. Thank you. How well—'

Wheeler scoffed. 'And what do we call you, Major? Nathan isn't it? As we seem to be on first name terms.'

Helix did nothing to supress the heavy sigh before he took another sip of his coffee. This would take twice as long with a bloody audience. 'No. Helix will be fine. Thank you.' He pushed his sunglasses up on his head and fixed his eyes on the Chancellor. 'Now we've got the second round of introductions out of the way, I would like to speak with your wife. *If* I may, Chancellor.'

Wheeler smirked, giving up the staring competition with a wink. 'I thought that's why you were here, not just to drink coffee.'

Gabrielle slapped her hand onto the kitchen counter. 'Oh, for Christ's sake, Justin! Will you shut up and let the Major do his job?' She pressed her hand to her sternum and turned back to Helix. 'Please, Helix. Carry on.'

Wheeler shoved his hands in the pockets of his robe and stalked off to the bedroom, propping the door open.

'How did you know Miriam?' Helix asked, his elbow on the counter.

Gabrielle's eyes fell to her lap. 'We worked together during the pandemic.'

'What took her to Chatham? Why would she want to live outside London?'

'Why shouldn't she live outside London? It's not against the law is it?'

'No, but given her status I found it a little—'

'A little what?' She straightened her back. 'Miriam was a doctor. She wanted to help people get better and stay healthy.'

'I was going to say curious. Exchanging a comfortable life for—'

'Hah. Oh God. Is that what you think - comfortable?' Gabrielle cupped her glass in both hands, her hands trembling. 'She was sick of the life here, hated all the attention. I hate it too, but some of us don't have the freedom to choose.' She glanced towards the bedroom door.

Helix nodded, finishing his coffee. 'How often did you visit?'

'Not as often as I would have liked.' She tucked a stray strand of hair behind her ear. 'Twice a week maybe. Sometimes Rachel would come too...'

'Rachel Neilson. Your lab assistant?'

'Correct. We'd spend the day helping out.'

'Helping out with?'

'I'm sure you already know that Miriam had a walk-in surgery in the old dockyard. In the Admiral's house. Just inside the main gate.'

'And you used to help out with the patients?'

Gabrielle nodded. 'Then we'd go back to her place, change and go out for the evening.'

Helix pinched his chin. 'Was there anything particular about any of the patients?'

Gabrielle examined her empty glass, tilting it in the light. 'Nothing more than usual for the area. Children with colds, cuts and bruises, aches and pains, mild infections. That's what we liked about it.'

Helix raised his eyebrows. 'What you liked?'

'Sorry, poor choice of words. I shall have to be more careful. Don't want to give you the wrong impression. It was proper general practice. Real people with real maladies. None of the attention seeking and complaining you get here.' She waved her hand at the window. 'My breasts are too small or too big, my wife's not satisfied, can I have a penis enlargement, my bottom's sagging. I think you get the picture, Major.'

Helix tilted his head. 'Yes, I think so. You said you went out. Where did you go?'

Gabrielle slid off the stool to collect the wine bottle that her husband had left out of reach. 'We would go to one of the meeting places, have—'

Helix looked up from his empty cup, studying her back as she peered from the window. Her hair swayed across her nape as she shook her head. 'Gabrielle?'

She cleared her throat. 'Sorry... we'd have a few drinks. Try to relax a little.' She plucked the cork from the bottle as she turned. 'Would you like a glass?'

Helix held up his hand. 'No. I'm fine, thanks.'

She poured the remaining wine into her glass, brushing his knee as she climbed back up onto the stool. 'Since my, *our* daughter died, it's been difficult.' She pulled her wedding ring down her finger towards its tip. 'He has his politics. I have my research. We put on a show when required. We smile for the cameras and attend the functions etcetera, etcetera. But our marriage is a sham and I have nowhere else to go.' She turned to her glass.

Helix drew back on his seat and cleared his throat. 'I was sorry to learn about your daughter. You mentioned the meeting places in town when you were visiting Miriam. I wasn't aware that Chatham or the Medway area had much in the way of night-life.'

Gabrielle pulled the thin strap of her dress back over her shoulder. Helix glanced away, distracting himself from the fact that she wasn't wearing a bra.

'Well, not in the conventional sense no. Things aren't always what they seem.'

'In what way?'

She stared at her glass, rotating its stem. 'To an outsider it looks run down, but people are doing well. They make their way and you'd be surprised what you can find if you look hard enough.'

'And what did you find? What did Miriam find?'

She raised her eyebrows. 'Men, sometimes women, sometimes both... Then each other.'

Helix smiled. Maybe it was the wine talking. He wondered how much had she had before he'd arrived? He leaned forward. 'Were you and Miriam—'

He sat back, surprised at the volume of her laugh, expecting Wheeler to reappear from the bedroom.

'In a relationship?' she whispered. 'We were lovers. No point in beating around the bush.' She reached across the counter for a tissue, her giggles fracturing into short sobs.

He hadn't seen that one coming. He looked at the empty bottle. Maybe he should wait. She was upset and the bloody wine wasn't helping. 'Gabrielle, do you want to take a break?'

'No.' She blew her nose. 'I want to talk about her. She gave me the things missing from my life. Love, comfort, someone to hold, someone who cared.' She screwed the tissue into a tight ball in her palm and managed a weak smile. 'Not quite what you would expect from the nobility is it?'

He returned her smile. 'It's not for me to judge, Gabrielle. I'm just trying to learn more about what happened.'

She was the total opposite to what he was expecting. A pale, fragile imitation of her confident public persona.

'Was Miriam unwell, Gabrielle?'

She tossed the tissue on the counter. 'What makes you say that?

'She seemed to have a lot of medication in her bathroom?'

She raised her blood-shot eyes, looking into his as she wrung her hands in her lap. 'Yes.'

Helix tilted his head towards her. 'Sorry, Gabrielle. Did you say yes? She was unwell?'

She took a deep breath. 'Given our sexual proclivities and a mixture of partners, we may have been a little reckless. We both had needs.' She ran her thumb across her fingernails. 'For me it was a way of dealing with the depression, getting control, getting close to someone, anyone. For Miriam it was the risk, the thrill, the danger...'

'What was wrong with her?'

Her eyes snapped on him. 'There was nothing wrong with her.'

'I'm sorry, I meant—'

'HIV. She had a form of HIV. Not one we'd seen before.'

'And what was the prognosis, was she—'

'She was getting better.' She rotated her shoulders. 'The medication you saw was for the symptoms.'

'That's a lot of symptoms.'

She raised her eyebrows. 'Sarcasm, Major? And we were getting along so well. I would have expected better from you.'

He fixed his eyes on hers. Did he just get a bollocking? 'Sorry. I didn't mean to question your—'

'I'd been working on a treatment. It had shown promise. It had begun to slow the progress and there were early signs of reversal. We were feeling more optimistic.'

Helix nodded. Was it her that had hand-crafted the "agent" as it was referred to in the report Ethan had found? He glanced at his watch, wondering where the forensics people had got to. 'Gabrielle, when was the last time you saw Miriam alive?'

She frowned. 'Last night. I went in my AV.' She snatched another tissue from the box. 'We had something to eat. Miriam was feeling tired, so we took a bath and after, I helped her into her hammock.' She leaned on the counter, the side of her head against her hand. 'I gave her an injection and she drifted off... I stayed for another half-hour and left her asleep. I know she was asleep, Helix. I felt her breath when I kissed her.'

He nodded back at her.

She tilted her glass back, studying the contents before finishing it in one mouthful. 'Where is she, Helix? Where have they taken her?'

'Miriam's been recovered to the capital for—'

'And their conclusion?'

'Their conclusion?'

'Yes. Please don't treat me like an idiot, Helix. I get enough of that already.' She nodded towards the bedroom. 'The initial post-mortem. The conclusion.'

Wheeler stood in the door, buttoning a white shirt over his jeans. He stepped barefoot from the door, trailing the whiff of aftershave or deodorant in his wake. He leaned into the fridge and pulled a bottle of white wine from the door. 'I think the question was, Major: what was their conclusion?'

Helix turned back to Gabrielle. 'The cause of death was cardiac arrest.'

Gabrielle scratched her head. 'Cardiac arrest?' Her eyes narrowed. She shook her head and slipped from the stool. Crossing to the patio doors, she folded her arms.

'So, what now, Major?' said Wheeler, folding the cuffs of his shirt back.

'There is a forensics team on their way here and—'

Wheeler frowned, looking across at his wife's back. 'A forensics team? Are you accusing my wife of murder, Major Helix?'

Gabrielle spun around from the window. 'Are they saying she was murdered, Helix?' She rushed back to the breakfast bar.

Helix stood, his hands held up. 'Hold on. The initial report is that Professor Polozkova died from cardiac arrest brought about by an unknown agent.'

The words seemed to float through the space between them as Gabrielle stared up at him. A shrill tone from the main gate intercom shattered the silence as it echoed around the apartment.

9

The evening sun reflected off the blue-black photovoltaic skin of the mobile forensics unit (MFU), stationed in front of the Royal Observatory. The main entrance door to the residence swept open, liberating the four scan-orbs and three CSCbots that had been queuing inside. A small panel in the skin of the MFU slid open, allowing the devices to return to their cradles and begin downloading their data and samples. Helix and Gabrielle stood by while Wheeler berated the Lieutenant for parking such a conspicuous Crime Scene Investigation vehicle right outside the home of the Chancellor of the Exchequer.

Helix leaned at the side of the door, waiting for the signal from the technician performing the analysis. 'Shouldn't be much longer now.'

Gabrielle clamped her hands to the side of her head. 'Justin! Will you shut up? Look outside, there are no media drones, nobody cares. The Lieutenant is just doing what she was told to do. Give it a rest, for heaven's sake.'

Wheeler relented, dismissing the Lieutenant with a wave of his hand as if swatting away a persistent fly. The officer couldn't resist smirking at Helix as he passed on his way out. Helix returned the sentiment with a nod. He caught sight of the analysis technician at the door to the MFU.

'Alright. I think we're on,' he said, tapping her on the shoulder.

He followed as she climbed up the steps into the brightly lit interior. Wheeler pushed in behind, not used to being at the back of the queue. They surrounded the technician seated in front of a complex instrument that Helix suspected was used for some kind of chemical analysis.

Gabrielle folded her arms as she studied the screen. 'Show me, please.'

The technician's fingers darted over the virtual keyboard projected onto the surface of the desk. The display cleared before a new stream of data appeared, accompanied by a jagged graph. Gabrielle shook her head again. 'Have you re-calibrated your instrument, Sergeant?' She reached around him, manipulating the controls, rotating the 3D graph on its axis.

He turned to face her. 'Yes, ma'am. The instrument is brand new, but I have re-calibrated it and I have re-run the same analysis, and here we can see the same result.'

Wheeler pushed in at the side of his wife, his left eye twitch more evident. 'Well run it again, Sergeant. There's obviously an issue with the equipment, or perhaps it's the operator.'

'Sir. I've run the same test three times now and I have re-calibrated the instrument each time, it's—'

Helix put his hand on the sergeant's shoulder. 'One more time please, Sergeant.'

The sergeant shrugged and turned back to the screen. Fifteen seconds later he had the same result. He turned and looked up at Gabrielle. 'I'm sorry ma'am. The chemical composition is identical to that found in the samples taken from Professor Polozkova. This is the syringe taken from your bag and the same one you said you used to prepare the injection.'

Gabrielle clamped her hands to her ears. 'Don't bloody touch me, Justin.' She flicked his hand away. 'The contents of this syringe are ten times the strength, according to this analysis. Ten times the strength! Of course Miriam suffered a massive cardiac arrest. A quarter of that strength would have been enough.' She looked up at Helix.

Helix nodded. 'Alright. Thank you, Sergeant. I'll take it from here. Let's go back inside, Doctor.'

They traipsed back towards the house. Helix stood aside. 'I just need to make a call to headquarters.'

Gabrielle brushed Wheeler's hand of consolation aside again as they moved towards the door. The Chancellor snapped to a halt, his finger raised. 'Hold on. What if someone tampered with the medication in the lab?'

Gabrielle turned back from the door and shook her head. 'Who, exactly?'

Helix folded his arms. 'Who else has access to the lab?'

'Rachel Neilson, my wife's lab assistant. She has access. She comes and goes as she pleases.'

Gabrielle snatched her hair in her hands. 'Oh, for God's sake Justin! Rachel is a friend. She was a friend of Miriam's, too.'

'Anyone else, Gabrielle?'

'What? No.'

'Alright, Chancellor, I'll consider Miss Neilson as a potential witness and—'

'And what, Helix? Then what? Gabrielle threw her hands up. 'While you're at it, why don't you consider him as a witness too? He has access. He does bloody live here, when he can extract himself from between Julia Ormandy's thighs.'

'For Christ's sake, Gabrielle, show some bloody decorum,' Wheeler snapped.

'If we're assisting the Major with his enquiries, we have to consider everyone, surely. The lab is not BSL level 4. Anyone with access to the house has access to the lab and everything in it.'

'And when was the last time you accessed the lab, Chancellor?'

'Me? Don't be bloody preposterous.'

'Holding high political office does not put you above the law, Chancellor. Until my enquiries are concluded, your wife, Miss Neilson and you will be considered as witnesses or suspects. If there is nothing else, please excuse me. I need to update headquarters.'

Wheeler had no response. A brief standoff ensued before they went their separate ways. Gabrielle slumped down on one of the wide leather sofas, head in her hands. Wheeler went to his study and slammed the door behind him.

Helix stared over the lawns at the city beyond. The MFU moved off behind him, the gravel giving way beneath the wide tyres. 'You there, Ethan?'

'I'm here. That's a bit of a shit sandwich. What's your take? Some kind of mercy killing?'

Helix sighed, 'Something stinks. She's not bloody stupid. How could she make such a mistake? To take a concentrated form of whatever it is instead of a diluted one seems too much of schoolgirl error, if you ask me. Plus, the vials were marked the same. The one in her bag was thc same as the one in her lab. Surely, you'd label them differently, no?'

'The lab assistant is an avenue of enquiry though?'

'Or his holiness.'

'Yeah, I loved that part. You certainly pissed on his chips.'

'Miriam was getting better. You heard what she said.' He pushed his fingers through his hair. 'But then all the evidence seems to suggest she did it. She hasn't denied any of it. Anyway, I need to talk to Yawlander. She will have to be arrested. Wheeler will go ballistic.'

* * *

A narrow footpath ran part way down the lawn away from the observatory. It levelled out into a paved area bordered by raised flower beds and partly covered by a wooden pergola. Helix recognised it from the media coverage. It was where they'd got married. It wasn't every day you got to meet one of your heroes, found out she's bisexual, married to a wanker in a shit relationship and based on the evidence, possibly a murderer.

Wheeler glowered down from behind his study window, his hands on his hips.

Helix stared back. 'Phone Yawlander.' He parted his feet as he waited for the call to connect, placing his hands on his broad hips. It had the desired effect. Wheeler jerked his head and walked away.

'Helix. What news from the Meridian?'

'Positive match to everything. DNA, the agent that caused the death of Professor Polozkova, samples matching the syringe found at the apartment and the medication in Stepper's bag. All pretty strong I would say.'

'Motive?'

'That's not such an easy one, sir. She was in a relationship with Miriam, she was open about it. Things seem frosty here, in more ways than one. Miriam wasn't well but, on the mend. No option but to arrest her, sir. We can hold her while we build the case to charge her. Not sure we have a precedent of one member of the SE murdering another, do we?'

'Other theories?'

'A bit too good to be true if you ask me, sir.'

'What the bloody hell's that supposed to mean?'

'By my reckoning, if something is too good to be true, then it probably is.'

'But you don't have any other theories or lines of enquiry?'

Helix tracked a V-shaped skein of Canada geese as they flew overhead towards the Thames. 'Nothing at the moment, sir.'

'Alright. Arrest her and tag her. We'll keep her under house arrest for the moment with you as her chaperone. Yawlander out.'

Helix folded his arms. The city glimmered in the distance. 'Arrest her and tag her. That's what the man said. This'll go down like the proverbial lead balloon, Ethan.'

'Aye. Rather you than me, Bruv. Wheeler's been trying to call Yawlander while you were talking to him. I took the call and told him he wasn't to be disturbed. I offered to take a message though.'

'And what did he say?'

'Nothing. Just huffed and hung up.'

* * *

Gabrielle hadn't moved from the sofa. She had her face in her hands and was rocking back and forth. She stopped as Helix approached. 'So, what now?'

He still had his doubts. The evidence proved otherwise and Yawlander was unequivocal. He cleared his throat, preparing to deliver the well-practiced words as Wheeler emerged from his study, halting just behind him.

'So, Major. What's to be done?'

Helix flexed his shoulders, straightening himself. Here we go.

The speed with which he turned surprised the Chancellor. Helix stepped on his toes, pinning him to the spot and grabbed him by the shoulders. 'Sorry, Chancellor. Didn't see you there. Difficult to judge distances with only one eye.'

'Ow! You bloody oaf, take your hands off me.'

He lifted his boot and loosened his grip, throwing Wheeler off balance. 'Now, if you don't mind. Once again, I need to speak with your wife.'

Wheeler flexed his bruised metatarsals. 'I do bloody mind. I've just tried to call your commanding officer. I want to get a few things straight before this goes any further.'

Helix folded his arms. 'And?'

'Got through to some cocky pleb. Told him who I was but he still refused to put me through.'

Helix turned back to Gabrielle. 'Sorry.'

She looked up at him and nodded. 'I understand. Carry on.'

'Doctor Gabrielle Stepper, I am—'

Wheeler hopped on his good foot. 'No, no, no. Hold on, Major, what the hell are you—'

Helix closed his eyes, his hands balled into fists. For fuck's sake.

He spun his heel, his thick prosthetic finger outstretched. 'Chancellor Wheeler. If you interrupt me one more time, I will arrest you for obstruction, place you in restraints and dispatch you to the police station. Now, if you have to be present, remain silent until I tell you otherwise.' He lifted his sunglass to the top of his head. 'Do you understand, Chancellor?'

A wave of winking spasms radiated around Wheeler's left eye as he retreated, brushing his hand over his hair.

Gabrielle shuffled herself into a crossed leg position as he addressed her.

'Doctor Gabrielle Stepper. I am arresting you on suspicion of the murder of Professor Miriam Polozkova. You do not have to say anything. But it may harm your defence if you do not mention when questioned something which you later rely on in court. Anything you do say may be given in evidence. You will remain in my charge and under house arrest. You will also be required to wear a monitoring tag at all times. Do you understand?'

Gabrielle coughed and straightened her back. 'Yes, Helix. I understand.'

10

The sinking sun cast long shadows across the observatory gardens and open lawns of the Meridian. The first beads of evening dew clung to the grass, glinting in the pool of light cast from the broad panoramic windows. As soon as Wheeler departed for an engagement in Westminster, the tension in the residence had diminished. It was quiet inside. The silence broken by the clink of utensils, glass and cutlery as a meal was cooked and two places laid in the dining area.

Helix propped himself against the side of the patio doors with his hands in his pockets. He shifted his focus to the reflection of Gabrielle keeping herself busy in the kitchen behind him. Ethan was right, she looked more like twenty-seven, particularly in that dress. Time hadn't aged her. She looked almost the same as the first images he'd seen of her in the early years when she'd first became known. Her resilience was extraordinary, given what she'd been through. But everyone had been through a lot.

'I hate those things.'

Helix turned from the windows. 'Those things?'

She paused the chopping of the parsley, pointing west with the broad-bladed knife. 'Those receptions and dinner parties at Westminster that Justin insists on dragging me along to.' She resumed chopping, laughing to herself.

'Something funny?'

'Sorry. Gabrielle couldn't make it tonight, been arrested for murder. Bloody inconvenient, but these things happen, blah, blah, blah.'

'Why do you go then?' He pulled back a stool and half sat on it. 'Sorry, that's none of my business.'

'It's a good question and one I've been asking myself for years.' She tidied the chopped parsley into a rectangular pile on the board. 'That, and many other questions.' She took up her glass of water and took a sip. 'Are you going to carry that thing around all night? I thought that was my job.'

Helix looked down at the tracker tag he was running between his fingers. She wasn't a flight risk; he could always tell the ones that were. It was an early first-generation tag, but it did the job. The new ones were injected beneath the skin of the forearm, but he hadn't wanted to put her through that. 'Not while we're indoors. I trust you.'

He dropped the tag on the coffee table by the sofa and loitered in front of the book case. The smell of the books reminded him of the school library. Does anyone read books nowadays? A small collection of children's books occupied the bottom shelf, within easy reach of small hands. 'Have you read all of these?'

He looked over his shoulder as she approached, a large glass of white wine in her hand.

She held the wine out to him. 'I suppose you're not allowed to drink on duty.'

He smiled, accepting the glass, his fingers brushing hers. 'The boundaries between on duty and off duty get blurred sometimes and I've never been one for rules. I like to make my own. Not having one yourself?'

'Perhaps with supper.' Her hand brushed his arm. 'And yes, I have read most of those. A lot of them date back from my school and university days. Some belonged to my parents.'

He took a sip of wine. 'I noticed there were a few legal titles in amongst the medicine and botany. Your father was a barrister I understand?'

'You *have* done your homework.'

He raised his glass with a nod. She grinned and turned away. He needed to roll back the charm and remember where he was. Christ, that dress. She intrigued him. Only a few hours earlier he'd arrested her on suspicion of murder, but she still refused to believe the evidence. He wasn't expecting a confession. In fact, she had made it clear that she expected to be found innocent. Instead of saying nothing as her husband had suggested, she'd shown no fear of self-incrimination.

Sidling up to the breakfast bar, he watched as she finished the simple dish of seafood linguine. She served him a generous plateful and poured herself a glass of white wine. She topped up his glass and sat next to him. 'Bon appetite.' Their glasses met with a gentle crystal clink.

'Thank you.' He wound some pasta around the tines of his fork. 'This looks nice. Do you do a lot of your own cooking?'

She laughed. 'If you knew what they put into those pre-packs, you'd do your own cooking too.'

'True. But back in the day, those pre-packs got us through some difficult times.'

'Fair point. And yes, I like cooking. Although there's not much fun in cooking for one.'

He let the comment pass. He knew what she was getting at. It had been a while since he'd shared a meal with someone. Slowing down, he tried not to finish the food too far ahead of her. The problem was that if he wasn't eating, he was sipping his wine and he was now well ahead of her. He waved her offer of a refill away politely, which she rebuked with a pout and another full glass for herself.

She shooed him to the sofas while she cleared and prepared coffee. Slumping into an armchair, he poked his tongue out at the beady eye of the camera ensconced on the bookshelf, unsure if Ethan was monitoring things or not. He rasped his hand over the stubble on his chin. Motive or not, he kept coming back to the evidence. Given who she was, would they take her service into account?

She poured the coffee, adding milk and sugar to her own. She handed him his cup and curled her legs up underneath herself. 'So, what's your story, Major Nathan Helix VC DSO?'

He took a sip of his coffee. 'Ah well, that's an easy one, ma'am. The government doesn't comment on special forces operations.'

'Oh God. Sounds like something my husband would say. You weren't born into the special forces, were you? And I was asking you, not the government.'

'Not exactly, no. But it's a long, dull story and I'm sure we can think of something better to talk about.' He reached forward towards his cup, a faint vibration of an incoming message on his wrist.

'Sorry, I didn't mean to pry. You must have done something very special.'

Taking a biscuit, he leaned back in the chair. 'A lot of people did similar things to me and didn't get recognised for it. I'm not so special.'

'Alright, I'll change the subject. Where did you grow up?'

'Now that's an easier one. Kent. Not a million miles from here. My dad was an IT consultant, mum was an art teacher. Two brothers, Jonathan and Ethan. The latter is a right pain.'

Ethan coughed in his ear. 'I heard that, and you need to look at that message.'

'Yes. So, summers spent up the woods, making camps, bows and arrows and climbing trees, or down the beach mucking about in boats. That was until I almost drowned.'

'What happened?'

'In spite of growing up next to the sea, I was the

last one to learn to swim. So, Jon, Ethan and a couple of mates thought it would be hilarious to throw me off the pier. I had a choice: swim or drown.'

'And clearly you swam.'

'Only just. Actually, not at all. After a certain amount of floundering around they realised they would probably watch me drown and jumped in. Luckily, they dragged me up onto the beach. I laid there for a while pretending to be dead, to scare the life out of them, but it left me with a fear of water. After that, my summers on the beach were literally that. Spent watching them from the beach. It's a lot better now than it used to be.'

'Goodness, that's horrible.' She nursed her coffee in her palm. 'My mum was a teacher too, that's the reason I'm a bit of a swot. And with my father backing her up, I had no chance. What I would have given for the woodland escapades you had. Our fun, if you can call it that, consisted of looking up the latin names of the trees we'd spotted during our ramble. I can't believe that I can remember that horse chestnut is Aesculus hippocastanum, but not to be confused with Castanea sativa, its edible cousin the Sweet Chestnut. Thank you, mother, for stifling fun with education.'

She topped up the cups. 'So, two brothers? What are they up to?'

Helix shifted his weight. 'Ethan is still serving, like me, but not in a frontline role. He's a desk jockey. He was injured but he's made a good recovery. Instead of knocking him back, he seems to have even more energy than before. I don't know how he does it. I wish I had half of his tenacity.'

Ethan sniffed. 'Oh Nate, I never knew you cared. Read the fucking message!'

'You said you had two brothers. What's the other one called?'

Helix cleared his throat. 'His name was Jon, Jonathan. Do you see the whole t-h-a-n thing going on? Jonathan, Nathan, Ethan.'

She bit her lip. 'Was called Jon? Was it the Ebola? I'm sorry, Helix?'

'No. He was killed in a military accident at Sizewell. He was the eldest, we both looked up to him.'

She stared into her cup. 'I'm so sorry.'

'I understand you have a twin sister, Sarah-Jane, isn't it?'

'Do you want a brandy? I fancy a brandy. Justin's got something nice hidden away.'

Before he could answer, she was up and jogging toward Wheeler's study. Helix grabbed the opportunity to glance down at the arm of his jacket. What was so bloody important? He scanned the message and folded the flap back over the screen.

She slid back onto the sofa, a victorious grin on her face. In one hand, she held a smooth, elegant decanter and in the other, she pinched two stemless brandy balloons between her fingers. 'Now, SJ. She is interesting and yes, my twin. Seven minutes younger than me.' She juggled the heavy decanter in both hands as she splashed a large measure of the amber liquid into a glass, getting almost the same quantity on the table. 'Oops. Justin would go mad if he saw me. Still, he's not here, so who cares?'

He needed to stay focussed. The wine was OK but the brandy wouldn't help.

She licked a small splash of brandy from her fingers before sliding his across the glass table-top.

Helix rolled the brandy in the glass, breathing in its aroma. 'Hmm, that's nice. She went to Canada, didn't she? Just before the Ebola outbreak?'

She laughed. 'I should have guessed. It's not just my dirty laundry. I expect you know all her secrets too.'

'Not exactly. There are one or two gaps.'

'Not much to say. She went to Canada and missed the worst of it over there. Came back a few years ago. We keep in touch, about once a month, a card or a letter, hers scrawled on the back of a piece of recycled paper.'

Helix cupped the glass in his hand. 'She's back in the UK?'

Gabrielle took a sip of her brandy. 'Oh, so you don't know everything then?' she said, her finger tracing a line across her eyebrow.

'The trail goes cold after the outbreak. Like a lot of things, comms with the outside world were difficult for a while.'

'Yes. She's living out on the Welsh border. In a commune, but they seem to do pretty well. Like a lot of folks outside the administrative centres, there's been a big return to the old ways of doing things. Grow your own, small farms, markets, a bit of bartering going on. It's as if the clock's been turned back to mid-nineteenth century, with a similar population.'

'She's a digger.' Helix raised his glass as a toast.

Gabrielle laughed. 'Yes, she is. And proud of it. Dig for survival. It sounds nicer the way you say it. Justin makes it sound disgusting, or he refers to them as marginals. Says it's more PC. Idiot.'

He rested his glass on his knee. 'So, Dame Stepper, what was it like to be ennobled?'

She laughed. 'Urgh! Honestly, I'd rather not have it. For reasons I think are obvious. As you said, there were lots of people who went without their efforts being recognised. But I'd only just been stood down from the research centre. I was exhausted and didn't know what was going on.'

'There was talk of the Nobel Prize, too.'

She shook her head. 'What a complete and utter waste of time. With everything that had happened. No. I was wide awake when that idea was floated. That's why I turned it down.'

'And all of this? The Meridian, the life-style, the glamour?'

'Glamour? I thought I told you. It's not all it's cracked up to be. I wish I was more like Miriam...' She swirled her brandy in the glass, staring into it.

A sip from his own glass did nothing to mitigate his clumsiness. She'd lost a close friend, seemed to be living in a loveless relationship with an arse and he'd suggested that she was living the dream. 'You alright, Gabrielle?'

She took a long deep breath. 'Yes, I'm fine. I'd allowed myself to forget why you're here. Sorry. I didn't mean that to sound rude. It is nice to have a chat with someone different, albeit in strange circumstances.'

He glanced at his watch. 'I'll just grab my stuff from my AV. Would it be a cheek to ask if I could take a shower?'

Gabrielle finished her brandy and wriggled to the edge of the sofa. 'Of course. There's a guest suite next to mine, you can use that.'

'No, that's OK. I'll just use the shower and crash on the sofa.'

'Don't be daft. Use the room.' She gathered the half-empty cups and glasses onto the tray. 'Nobody ever visits. You can leave the door open in case I try to make a run for it in the middle of the night.'

'Who told you about Miriam?' he said, getting up from the armchair. 'Anything concerning members of the Scientific Elite is kept under wraps as with all political affiliates. Was it her housekeeper?'

'Monica? I don't think she's got access to a phone, apart from the one in Miriam's apartment. She would let her use it sometimes.' She pressed her hands to her knees and pulled a sarcastic grin. 'No, it was Justin. I think that's why he came home early.'

'And that doesn't happen often?'

'I imagine Justin has all sorts of habits, but coming home early isn't one of them, Helix. His parliamentary calendar is a smokescreen, so I never know where he is. I doubt he'll be back tonight. He spends more nights at his apartment in Westminster than he does here. Odd that he came home to witness my humiliation though. Don't you think?'

* * *

Gabrielle yawned and stretched in the kitchen, clearing away the glasses and tableware. Helix stepped outside and slid the patio door closed behind him. The temperature had dropped with the sun and the earthy smell of damp leaves and grass filled the air. He walked to the far edge of the patio, out of earshot, and sat on a low wall.

'Ethan, where the hell did that come from?' He peeled the flap away from the screen and read the message again.

'Same place as before. They said they'd have the full report within 24 hours.'

He shook his head. 'She was *smothered*? Is that what they are saying, Ethan? Because I'm struggling to decipher the language here.'

'Yes. All the physical signs are there. The initial report of cardiac arrest brought about by the injection could still be right. But it isn't unheard of for someone to go into cardiac arrest when asphyxiated.'

'So, she was murdered twice?'

11

Helix checked the time again. It was three minutes later than the last time he checked and seven minutes later than the time before that. He was in no hurry to get to the Cenotaph and it appeared that neither was Gabrielle. He grinned to himself, as he recalled the previous night. She'd shown him to the guest suite and fussed around, making sure he would be comfortable. He'd seen shabbier multiple-starred hotels. It was only when he took off his jacket and started undoing his shirt she seemed to get the hint and had said goodnight. The scent of her perfume had lingered long after she'd left, adding another dimension to the images he saw of her when he closed his eyes.

Hours staring at the ceiling had passed, punctuated with short passages of restless sleep. In spite of rewinding and replaying the conversations with Gabrielle, he had the same answers this morning that he'd gone to bed with. But there was something niggling him, the itch you get inside your body armour and can't get at. Could Gabrielle have smothered Miriam to make sure? But she said she was getting better. Plus, she wasn't likely to screw up with the medication if that was how she wanted to kill her. No. If she'd wanted her dead, death by lethal injection seemed like a more likely modus operandi, death by asphyxiation didn't fit the profile.

He'd been up early enough to witness the shortening of the shadows that he'd watched creeping over the landscape the evening before. He'd helped himself to coffee, as instructed, passing more than an hour on a stool next to the window, watching daybreak. As predicted, Wheeler hadn't returned, but he wasn't sorry about that. The last thing he wanted this morning was more of his bullshit.

He turned as he heard Gabrielle on the stairs, her shoes swinging from her hand. At least she knew how to dress for the occasion. She wore a discreet black sleeveless dress that shimmered in the light, just below the knee in length, and a small handbag on a black strap tucked under her arm. She'd pulled her hair back and secured it into a tight bun on the back of her head. He swallowed the compliment. Investigators don't compliment suspects on their appearance and wardrobe, regardless of how stunning they looked. She paused at the bottom of the stairs and slipped on her heels. He looked down at the fluorescent orange tracking band in his hand.

'Not sure where you're going to put that,' she said, raising her arms to shoulder height. 'Can I put it in my bag?'

He ran his eyes over her ankles, thighs, waist, chest and arms. He lingered behind her and repeated the inspection. 'Hmm. You should wear it really.' Unobtrusive wasn't part of the design specification. He didn't want to embarrass her by strapping it around her ankle.

'I've got an idea. We can hide it out of the way here,' she said, reaching under her arm and pulling down the zip.

Helix followed its descent. A narrow V-shape opened in the material, revealing her lacey black bra. He could see what she had in mind. He distracted himself by separating the two ends of the band.

'I hope you've got warm hands, Major Helix.' She smiled. 'Loop it round my bra and zip the dress over it. Should be discreet enough.'

The scent of her perfume filled his nose as he followed her directions. He tried to minimise the contact. The left-handed operation was awkward and in spite of taking care, he brushed her side with one of his prosthetic fingers, causing her to gasp and twist away. 'Sorry, not used to such a delicate operation, but I think we're all good. Do you want me to zip...?'

'Please.'

He pulled the zip up, flattening the band a little to close the material over it. As predicted, it was almost invisible.

'Thank you.' Gabrielle smoothed the side of the dress. 'We could walk down to the hyperloop. It's a nice morning.'

Helix nodded. 'Sure. Why not?'

* * *

As they ambled between the parallel rows of horse chestnut trees, Helix scanned the branches. The spikey pods were maturing, readying themselves for the annual conker ritual enjoyed by kids over the years, probably centuries. He counted the years since he'd been charging around the woods with Jon and Ethan to see who could find the biggest, the best conkers, stamping on the fallen pods or teasing the nuts out with pen-knives before threading them onto old shoelaces.

He stole a glance at Gabrielle. Compared to last night, she'd been practically mute that morning. Ethan had said she'd been up during the night, roaming around the house. She passed ten minutes watching him from the doorway as he slept. Maybe he was losing his touch. He should have slept on the sofa. But there wasn't much chance of her getting away, thanks to the Nano-HD cameras. If she had done a bunk, Ethan would have squealed in his ear. He wasn't so sure about chasing her across the manicured lawns of the Meridian in his boxers though.

He turned to face her as she halted. She looked knackered, chewing at her lip and wringing her hands. How much kip had she got last night?

Her eyes darted between his poppy and jacket buttons before gazing upwards at him. 'Helix. I did not kill Miriam.' She shook her head. 'I may have administered the injection that brought about her death, but I didn't intend to kill her.'

He'd heard the same yesterday. Could she be telling the truth? He left her words hanging in the breeze.

She hesitated, clutching her bag to her chest. 'Someone switched the medication. You don't seriously believe I would make such a stupid error, do you?'

He didn't. And the new evidence Ethan had dug up had sown more doubt, but now wasn't the time. 'No. I don't think you would have made an error like that, but who could have made the switch? Rachel or your husband are the only other people with access.'

She turned away, slinging her bag strap over her shoulder. 'I think my husband blames me for our daughter's death.'

Helix fell in alongside her as they set off again. 'What makes you say that?'

She folded her arms, her bag rocking on her hip. 'After Eve died, we were devastated, as you would expect. We each fell into our own worlds. The more I craved physical contact the less he seemed willing to give it. It felt like he was punishing me, refusing to hold me when I needed it. So, long story short. Miriam filled the gaping emptiness between us.'

'I don't understand. Yesterday, when I arrived, and forgive me for jumping to conclusions, but it looked like—'

'We'd had, what shall we call it? A siesta?'

Their amble faltered to a halt again. 'OK. It might be me, but in a sham marriage, as you called it, I would have thought making love was the last thing on the agenda.'

She grimaced. 'Making love – definitely off the agenda. But it wasn't what it appeared, like most things in my life. I'd been in the bath and he'd just got out of the shower. His shower.'

'Did he know about you and Miriam?'

'Yes. He'd started making sarcastic comments and lewd suggestions. In front of Rachel, too. It was childish and embarrassing. Anyway, we got into a drunken row one night and I blurted it out. I wanted to hurt and humiliate him, but he just laughed it off. But then yesterday he turns up in the middle of the afternoon – never been heard of. He comes immediately to the bathroom – normally disappears into his study without even telling me he's back. And then tells me he's heard a rumour about Miriam.'

'A rumour?'

'I know, but that's how he put it.'

'Julia Ormandy – the Home Secretary?'

She shrugged her shoulders. 'You're the investigator, Helix.'

Helix followed as she turned towards a bench at the side of the drive. He imagined the salacious sound bites across the media platforms: "Gabrielle Stepper – Wife of the Chancellor in Lesbian Relationship – A Nation in Shock." Wheeler could have killed Miriam, or colluded with Ormandy to orchestrate it, but it felt far-fetched.

'None of this makes any sense, Helix. I took the meds from the cold storage in the lab, put them in my bag, left here in my AV, went to Miriam's and gave them to her.'

As much as he wanted to put her mind at rest, he needed to get his facts straight. If he told her what Ethan had discovered now, she might challenge Yawlander when they got to the service, or worse, tell Wheeler. It was all or nothing, he couldn't hint that there might be something else. He wouldn't get away with that, she was too sharp. Bollocks. It would have to wait.

She picked up a twig from the ground and flicked it amongst the fallen leaves. He unhooked his elbow from the back of the bench and immediately dismissed the idea. He was certain that a reassuring arm around the shoulder of the prime suspect wasn't in any of the operations procedures. Not that he'd read them.

'Helix, there's something else,' she said, turning on the seat next to him. 'If I don't get this out, I'm going to go insane. I'll keep it brief. I can go into more detail later.' She laid her bag on the seat between them and slapped her hands flat on her knees. 'OK.'

Helix leaned forward, his elbows on his thighs, hands clasped together. 'Go ahead, take your time.'

'Alright. Prior to the Ebola outbreak, I discovered a way to breed crops that were resistant to certain diseases in sub-Saharan Africa. But to be fair, I can't take all the credit. I was working with another scientist, Valerian Lytkin. We'd spend hours in the lab after everyone else had gone home, reviewing, planning – we even hid a secret stash of booze in one of the store rooms. We became close. Anyway, our research delivered the usual blend of expected and unexpected results. One of my more promising failures kept coming up in conversation and Valerian thought we should continue with its development. He'd say that we should work in the evenings and over weekends, so it didn't impact our main projects, etcetera, etcetera.'

'What was it?'

'You've heard of the expression: prevention is better than cure. The research looked into ways to protect affected crops by eradicating the insects that spread the disease. Resistant crops equal prevention, destroying the insects is more of a cure.'

'And why was he so interested in this particular failure – as you put it?'

'He'd say it could be our pension plan. Better still, it could set us up for life. I wasn't comfortable. You didn't need a lot of imagination to realise its real potential.'

'And Lytkin had plenty of imagination?'

She sighed. 'He was always more of a drinker than me, and when he got drunk, his ideas went off on crazy tangents. He'd rant about security and he didn't mean food security, he meant direct military application.'

'A kind of agent orange 2.0, an upgrade to what the yanks used in Vietnam.'

'That was a herbicide, but yes it was used by the US military and like Valerian's ideas, it had nothing to do with saving life.'

'And this is all relevant in what way to Miriam?'

'Yes. Sorry.' She tapped him on the knee. 'I am waffling on, but stay with me. So, I was worried and I patented the discovery, which was unethical but I didn't like the direction he was leaning in. Any hint of military use didn't sit well with my principles.'

'And the discovery was advanced enough to get a patent on it?'

She nodded. 'Yes. Then the outbreak hit us. We went our separate ways and I pushed it to the back of my mind.'

Helix scratched his belly. 'OK. I don't want to sound like a corrupted music file here, but the link to Miriam is?'

Gabrielle turned to look over her shoulder and then back up the drive. 'Death threats.'

'Excuse me?'

'For the last few months, I've been receiving increasingly threatening messages from someone calling themselves Cerberus.'

12

Helix followed at Gabrielle's shoulder as she emerged from the station exit. The hyperloop transit between Greenwich and Westminster had taken a little under three minutes to cover the 5.35 miles. It was another green and efficient way to murder precious thinking time, something he was craving.

They filtered into the colourful confluence of humanity as it meandered northward from Parliament Square towards the Cenotaph. The advertising holograms that normally littered the pavements and road had been stood down out of respect. In the warmth of the sunlight, reflected from the Portland stone façades of the government buildings, the congregants nodded and smiled as they recognised Gabrielle. A ripple of polite hand clapping arose as a path was cleared allowing her and Helix to pass unimpeded towards the Foreign and Commonwealth Office. Helix smiled back at her as she glanced over her shoulder.

He was impressed with how she switched to press-the-flesh mode and felt more like her minder as opposed to her jailer. Progress slowed to a crawl as they entered the impressive nineteenth century building; everyone wanted to greet her. In spite of her earlier revelations and the events of the last twenty-four hours, she handled it professionally. She smiled, remembered people's names and asked after their children.

Helix's nose twitched in the fug of perfume that competed with wood polish, which was made worse by the number of very warm bodies cramming into the space. The contrast between this summer carnival and the solemn act of remembrance in November was stark, which was why he hated it. He saw it like a bloody garden party with everyone competing to see who could stretch the boundaries of the dress code.

He dodged a uni-wheeled serving droid as it weaved its way through the crowd, balancing a tray of tea, coffee, champagne, and fruit juice. There was no sign of Wheeler. He was no doubt sucking up to the Prime Minister, or anyone else who could further his career. He glanced over Gabrielle's shoulder at a uniformed officer at the top of the grand Gilbert-Scott staircase. Around five-feet ten-inches in height, short cropped blond hair, piercing blue eyes, the Colonel surveyed the crowd, his arrogance worn as proudly as the row of medals on his chest. Helix followed his gaze as it made its way down the stairs, coming to rest on Gabrielle. Helix zoomed in closer with his right eye. Their eyes met; the recognition confirmed by the tensing of the Colonel's neck muscles. Helix knew who he was looking at. He balled his fists. His pulse accelerated. He dabbed the micro-switch at the base of his left molar, with his tongue, activating the TC comms interface. *'Ethan. Top of the stairs. Look now. Short blond hair.'*

'Terry McGill, that fucker, what's he doing there?'

'No idea, but I'd like a word with him.'

'Me too. Leave it with me. Stay sharp.'

Helix ground his teeth as McGill dissolved into the crowd. It was the wrong time and the wrong place. On this occasion.

He shadowed Gabrielle up the wide burgundy carpeted stairs and into the cavernous reception room. The hairs on his neck bristled as Wheeler turned away from the glazed doors that led onto a balcony. Helix held back as Wheeler deployed his best politician's smile for his wife, his worshippers and underlings at his shoulder. General Yawlander stood to his right in full dress uniform, his build belying his age. An angry scar traced a line across his right cheek, the result of an injury sustained earlier in his career that had also cost him his right earlobe. Helix snapped to attention in front of the General. 'Good morning, sir.'

'Major.'

He knew the General well enough to know that the single word greeting conveyed a message. It wasn't as if he carried his dress uniform around in his AV. Maybe the boss wasn't enjoying Wheeler's company – who could blame him? He stepped back behind Gabrielle, declining the offered glass of champagne. Gabrielle accepted one of the crystal flutes and greeted Yawlander like an old friend, and her husband with a perfunctory air kiss. Helix substituted a handshake with a nod, which seemed to suit the Chancellor.

'Helix, I have a task for you,' Yawlander said. 'A shame you're not in uniform, but one of the wreath bearers has thrown a sicky, we need a sub, and you're just the man.'

This was the last thing he needed. Being at this circus was bad enough, being part of it was worse. He approached the General trying to get out of earshot. 'But sir, what about Doctor Stepper? There are plenty of other uniforms around who would jump at the chance.'

Wheeler interrupted with a double wink. 'Nonsense, Major. Where are your medals? Unusual for the VC not to be given posthumously. You should be proud.'

Helix gritted his teeth, turning to the Chancellor. 'I sold my medals, Chancellor, to raise funds for those veterans less fortunate than myself.'

Yawlander gripped the back of his arm. 'OK, Helix, that's enough. Get downstairs and present yourself with the other wreath bearers. I'm not asking you, I'm telling you.'

'Yes, sir. As you wish.'

Gabrielle caught his arm as he turned. 'Thanks for bringing me, Helix. See you later.'

Without Gabrielle parting the way, progress was slow. Pausing at the exit, Helix hesitated and looked back over his shoulder. Yawlander was speaking to Wheeler and Gabrielle, the earlier warmth of the greeting now absent. The General placed his hand on the small of Gabrielle's back and nodded towards a side door. Wheeler didn't look impressed, pointing at his watch. Yawlander stepped around him and they moved off in single file, Gabrielle sandwiched between the General and her husband who was apologising over his shoulder. An open doorway led to a smaller, less crowded room. Helix read "sorry Gabrielle" on the General's lips as he stepped aside for her. She passed through and paused, framed in the doorway. Her brow furrowed as she listened to whatever Yawlander was saying. Helix's eyes narrowed as Terry McGill stepped into view and shook Gabrielle's hand.

* * *

Helix accepted a wreath displaying the logo of a company he'd never heard of. Still mystified by why Yawlander would introduce Gabrielle to McGill, he took his place at the head of a long line of other bearers. He looked ahead, the memorials a few hundred yards in the distance, and gave a brief nod in memory of Jon. He fell in beside a double amputee, regretting his own impatience. 'How you doing, fella?' The veteran's determination reminded him of Ethan.

'All good. Thank you, sir.'

A ripple of solemn anticipation ran through the ranks as an auto-band struck up a sombre slow march in the distance.

Ethan came online with an update. 'Nate. I've got the latest on McGill. After retiring, he was appointed three months ago as Director of Security for Lamont Rhames.'

'Roger that.'

He focussed on the original Lutyens Cenotaph, erected in 1919 and now flanked by two modern black granite memorials. He'd been told to lay his wreath on the steps of the third. The parallel lines of wreath bearers shuffled forward in time with the solemn dirge, the hushed crowd looking on.

The dignitaries assembled on the balcony overlooking the memorials, their eyes turned down. Helix selected the 3D facial recognition overlay with two rapid winks of his eye. The software tagged Yawlander and Wheeler along with assorted others unknown to him. He scanned again. *'Ethan. Gabrielle's not on the balcony. She's wearing that first gen tracker. Where is she?'*

'I've got her. She's on the move. Still in the building. Heading downstairs.'

'Have you got the cameras in there?'

'Not inside. I can plot her location against the floor plan. Standby.'

Helix picked up the pace, redefining the definition of a slow march. He crouched and placed his wreath on the steps, its hologram of cascading poppies bursting to life.

'She's going to come out of a service door. Two-thirds of the way down King Charles Street. We've got eyes on. I can see an AV. Not one of ours. There's a driver at the controls. They're going to go manual.'

Helix looked up at Yawlander on the balcony. The General barked an order at someone over his shoulder. Something was wrong. Helix broke ranks and elbowed his way through the five-deep crowd on the pavement. He sprinted towards the triple arches that linked the Foreign Office with the Revenue and Customs buildings.

A sentrybot, as wide as Helix was tall, dominated the central arch. 'Citizen, stop. There is no access or egress along this thoroughfare. Please turn back,' it said.

'Protocol 452. Stand down.'

The sentrybot scanned him. 'Biometric data confirmed. Please proceed, Major Helix.'

Helix was past the sentrybot before it had uttered the "b" of "biometric". Two ranks of waiting cleaning droids scattered as he burst through the other side of the arch. He sprinted past the entrance to the circular courtyard at the centre of the Treasury buildings and slowed to a running crouch towards the rear of the AV. The side window shattered under the weight of his clenched fist. The driver's hand snapped upwards, grabbing his wrist, surprising Helix with the speed of the reflex. 'Fuck!'

Helix ducked the counter punch and twisted his arm free, jabbing his thumb into the corner of her eye. With both hands clamped to his wrist, she fought to lever his grip from her face. A twist of his hand took out her eye. The leather between his fingers split around the spring-loaded ceramic blade that plunged into the soft tissue below her right ear. Shaking the driver's dead hands away from his arm, he reached into her shoulder holster and pulled out her weapon. He checked it was armed before tucking it in the back of his trousers. '*Where are they, Ethan?*'

'It's the wood panelled doors behind you. I'm assuming she's got company.'

Helix could tell from the hinges that the heavy doors opened inwards. He grasped the handle with his left hand and waited, his ear pressed to the door. The handle twitched down. He tensed his grip preventing its travel. Voices on the other side. At least two men.

'This is meant to be open, what's going on?' one of them said.

'It is open. I unlocked it myself.'

Helix focussed, drawing a mental image of the scene inside: the two men close to the door, Gabrielle a few steps behind them. Another twitch of the handle.

'Get out of the fucking way. Let me try.'

Helix took a deep breath and waited for the pressure to return. The handle pressed into his palm, stronger this time. He let it slip. The door flew inwards. Helix shoulder-charged it on the rebound. The doorman's head was punched between one of the heavy oak panels and the marble wall. Gabrielle screamed as she was knocked backwards by the second minder. Helix side stepped an attempted kick from him, driving a crushing uppercut beneath his chin. He went down and stayed down. The doorman was scrambling for traction. Helix spun on his heel and delivered his boot into his groin, following up with a punch to the temple. With the two men down, he lunged towards Gabrielle and pulled her up from the floor. 'It's OK. Let's go.'

She pulled back. 'Helix, what's going on? Who are those people?' She stared through the shattered window of the AV at the bloodied face of the driver. 'Oh my God. Did you kill them?' She twisted free and clutched her hands to her face.

'I don't know who they are. That thing's not real. It looks like blood, but it's hydraulic fluid. The other two aren't dead, they'll just have a hangover later.

She wasn't responding or moving.

'Gabrielle. Come on. We have to move.' He snatched her hand again, pulling her towards the Clive Steps. Her mouth gaped; her eyes fixed on the corpse in the AV. She was going into shock.

He ducked under her arm and folded her over his shoulder. She mumbled behind his back as he charged down the ramp and into Horse Guards Road. He hailed a passing taxi and helped her inside. 'Down Street.' The taxi responded and merged into the flow of identical vehicles.

Gabrielle stared ahead as she mumbled to herself. Helix lifted her left arm and fumbled with the zip of her dress. His cold fingers glanced her ribs.

'What the hell are you doing, Helix?'

'Good to have you back. Are you going to be able to walk in a minute or two?' He separated the two ends of the tracker and pulled it free.

She pushed his hand away and pulled the zip up. 'Yes, I think so. Who were those—'

'I don't know, Gabrielle, but I have a hunch they weren't taking you to the park for a picnic.' He peered through the front screen. 'Taxi. Stop.' The taxi obeyed.

He pressed his thumb against the payment terminal and shoved the tracker down the back of the black vinyl seat. Taking her hand, he helped her onto the pavement at the side of The Mall. The empty taxi circumnavigated the Victoria Memorial and disappeared from view. They waited close to the former Buckingham Palace, now converted into a memorial museum; the surviving members of the Royal Family being ensconced in Balmoral.

Helix hailed a second taxi. On their way to the same destination, he checked back over his shoulder as they made their way down Constitution Hill.

Gabrielle leaned into him. He wrapped his arm around her shoulder. 'Ethan, can you throw them off my scent for a bit longer?'

'Yep, but we need to make other arrangements. It won't work forever.'

Gabrielle pulled away. Her brow furrowed. 'Why do you keep barking orders at Ethan?'

He lifted his arm away and tapped at the wrist of his left sleeve. 'Ethan. Say hi to Gabrielle.'

'Hi, Gabrielle.'

She blinked towards the voice emanating from Helix's sleeve.

'By the way, Nate, the emails make sense. Had to dig a bit, but I got there.'

Helix raised his eyebrows. He hoped his hunch was right, otherwise he would be in a shit load of trouble. 'What happened in there? Why were you leaving with those men?'

'Those men? What about that woman you killed?'

'It wasn't a woman, Gabrielle, it was a—'

'You could have fooled me.'

'We call them shrink-wraps, Gabrielle,' Ethan said. 'Almost human skin over a titanium frame. Autonomous with limited mission parameters or controlled remotely.'

'I thought it was real, too. That's why I tried to take it out. Temporarily.'

'Charming.'

He let it go. There was no place left for chivalry the moment the UN allowed women to be combatant. Those he'd met were capable enough, and he'd met plenty just as ruthless as any man he'd served with. 'The men back there. Where were they taking you?'

Gabrielle folded her arms and stared out of the window. 'General Yawlander told me they were police officers and that based on new evidence, I was being transferred to the police cells.' She shivered, rubbing her arms. 'Justin wasn't happy and made a right stink about it. It felt like he cared for a moment... Anyway, they ushered me out into a service corridor where the General insisted I go with them. He threatened Justin with obstruction of justice if he didn't calm down.'

'That sounds familiar.' Helix rubbed his chin. 'I think we can say they weren't police officers. Their vehicle wasn't registered to the police. I don't suppose they told you what this new evidence was?'

'No.'

Helix's sleeve spoke again. 'One other thing, were you expecting a visitor at the house this morning, Gabrielle?'

Gabrielle frowned at Helix as the taxi navigated its way around Hyde Park Corner. 'Not as far as I know, Ethan, why?'

'I recorded this earlier. It was just as things were kicking off at the Cenotaph.'

Helix tore back the flap of material over the screen. 'Someone you know?' he said, angling his arm towards her.

'That's Rachel. Hold on. Where is that video coming from? We don't have cameras inside the house.'

'You do now.' Helix nodded. 'Free standing Nano-HD cameras, I brought them with me.'

'So, does that mean you saw me last night, Ethan?' She leaned towards the screen. 'Wandering around, disrobed, in the privacy of my home.'

'Er, yep. Sorry about that.'

'Rachel's working on a paper for her degree. I expect she needed something from the lab or my library. I'm surprised she hasn't got Lauren with her.'

'Who's Lauren?' asked Helix.

'Her daughter. Why's she carrying that holdall?'

Helix looked up as the taxi turned in from Piccadilly. 'Go to the end. Turn right. Travel fifty yards and stop.'

Back on the screen, Rachel pressed the call button and waited for the lift. 'Can you fast forward it, Bruv?'

The video feed juddered, showing Rachel walking into the lift. 'She was only down there for six minutes,' Ethan said as he advanced the footage again.

Gabrielle pointed to the screen. 'She's got something in the bag now, something heavy. What's she...?' She turned to Helix. 'You didn't put one of your cameras in the lab I suppose?'

'No. Ethan would have let me know if he'd seen you go down there.'

Ethan increased the playback speed again. Rachel scuttled into Gabrielle's study returning four minutes later, the bag heavier.

'How much weight in the bag do you reckon, Ethan?' said Helix.

'Approx. fifteen pounds I would say. Based on my measurements.'

Gabrielle looked up from the screen and shrugged.

13

Down Street carved its way between buildings like a deep river gorge. The empty silence was punctuated only by the sing-song whine of passing battery-powered traffic on Piccadilly. An oxblood-red brick façade, with its three grand arches, squatted amidst its ivory-white neighbours. Helix paused beside an anonymous grey door set into the bricked up left arch. He heaved the door outwards in response to a loud metallic clunk. 'Mind your step.'

He followed Gabrielle over the two small steps and across the wide cement threshold. What little natural light there was, vanished as he pulled the door shut, plunging them into disorientating darkness. Two further concrete steps gave way to the top of a spiral staircase that groaned as they stepped onto it.

Gabrielle's whisper echoed in the gloom. 'What is this place?'

A thermal of warm stale air rose from below with the heavy rumble of passing trains. 'It's a disused underground station. Down Street, between Hyde Park Corner and Green Park, on the Piccadilly line.'

She brushed his arm. 'I can't see a thing.'

Helix activated his night vision and took her hand, feeling her hesitate as she found her footing on the metal stair treads. 'I've got you. There are lights further down.'

Seventy-eight spiral steps deeper, Gabrielle bumped into Helix's back as he paused again. He pulled open a second door. A chorus of clicks welcomed them as the darkness surrendered to the automatic LED strip lights. 'Welcome to the bat cave,' he said, slipping off his jacket.

The expansive workshop was filled with a chillier version of the same stale air found on the stairs. Gabrielle's feverish rubbing of her arms did nothing to dispel it. 'So, this is home?'

'When I get the chance. Are you cold?'

She looked down at her stockinged feet. 'Cold going on freezing. It's like a fridge in here.'

'I can fix that.' He pointed towards a cracked and peeling grey wall. 'Stand over there.'

He spun out a three-wheeled stool from beneath a bench and sat. Four screens bloomed into life in response to the command he bashed out on a museum-piece keyboard. He twisted around on the stool to face her. 'A bit more to the left please. Hands down at your sides.'

She smiled as six bright red lasers rushed across the contours of her body. Helix inspected a wire frame image of her body as it appeared on a screen. 'We have any colour you like as long as its black.' He tapped out a further set of commands, nodding his approval as he heard a machine come to life deep in an unseen recess towards the back of the workshop.

Gabrielle folded her arms as she stepped away from the wall. 'So, is that the party piece you do for all the girls?'

Helix laughed. 'No. You're the first person to come down here.' He draped his jacket over her shoulders, swamping her. 'Shouldn't be too long.'

'Thanks. Do you have a kettle amongst all of this wizardry?'

'Of course. Let me show you around. There's not a lot to see, but it's got all the basics. Don't get too comfortable. We won't be here for long.'

Helix gave her the penny tour. 'Kitchen, sleeping, dining area. Door at the back to shower and thunder box. That's about it.'

'I love what you've done with the place. Any colour you like, as long as it's grey.'

'Boom boom. I get by and I've known a lot worse. I'm old-fashioned when it comes to hot drinks so the kettle's there, fridge underneath, hopefully the milk hasn't gone off, tea and coffee in the cupboard above with the cups. I'll just check on your stuff.'

* * *

Made of the same military smart fabric as Helix's, the 3D printed clothing was lightweight and warm, waterproof and breathable in winter and cool in the summer. The material comprised a complex composition of moisture and dirt-repellent graphene, Kevlar, and carbon fibre. It included the bonus of being able to protect against blades and small arms fire if required. A pair of black all-purpose walking boots with Velcro-type fastenings waited on a tray next to a second machine. The smell of hot plastic rose to meet him as he checked them over. Being on good terms with the Regimental Quartermaster had its advantages. The first machine completed its work and fell silent. He folded the eight items and took them back to his workstation.

Gabrielle appeared at his shoulder with the coffee. 'Here you go, no milk, no sugar.'

'Thanks. You remembered.' He nodded his appreciation. 'Your clothes are here. I hope they're alright.'

Looking at her eyes as she checked the clothes, he wondered if there'd been a few tears in the kitchen. 'Hey.' He tapped her arm. 'I know there's a lot of stuff going on, but we'll work it out.'

She yawned. 'I'm exhausted, Helix and confused. I don't know what to do.' She rubbed her bare arms again. 'Is running the right solution?'

He wrapped his fingers around the hot cup. 'I trust a gut feeling more than anything else and there is too much that doesn't seem right. Miriam, the threats, what happened earlier at the Cenotaph. If those guys weren't ours, whose were they? I'm not one for toeing the line, but I also don't step over it unless I'm sure it's the right thing to do and this feels like the right thing.' He pulled his lips into a tight smile. 'Why don't you change? Feeling warmer might help. Then we'll have a chat with Ethan to see what our options are.'

* * *

The grey-painted minimalist living space fought back against the relentless artificial light that crept into every corner and consumed every shadow. There were no windows, no clocks and no sense of time and once inside, it was impossible to know if it was day or night, raining or sunny, windy or calm.

Gabrielle stood in the middle of the room, clutching the clothes to her chest. She wondered if the place was a facsimile of her future. She dropped the clothes onto the unmade bed and sat down beside them. He'd said they wouldn't be here for long, so she could leave – couldn't she? The stark accommodation and the plain functional clothes conjured an image in her imagination of what it would be like in prison.

She couldn't hear everything from where she was sitting, but Helix was talking to Ethan. The earlier humour had been replaced with earnest conversation. She caught the mention of options and something about timescales. She laid the individual items of clothing out on the bed as she thought back to what Yawlander had said at the Foreign Office. Just what was the new evidence he'd referred to? There wasn't any new evidence. I've done nothing wrong. But that doesn't change anything – Miriam's gone. She leaned forward, elbows on her knees, looking at one of her toes poking through her laddered stockings. I'll miss her funeral. The funeral she asked me to organise and to make sure it was done the way she wanted it. No pomp and ceremony. A joyous event she said. No weeping, she said, and her ashes scattered in a bluebell wood in the spring. There was still time. Time to sort out this mess and time to carry out her wishes.

She shrugged Helix's heavy jacket off her shoulders. A different weight bore down upon her; that of being alone again. She missed SJ. When was the last time she'd heard from her? It was just before their birthdays, back in June. SJ had made a card from pressed meadow flowers that she'd picked. She'd been vague as usual. She was fine. Nothing special happening. Still living with Bo in a Mongolian yurt in the woods. It was somewhere near a place called Tintern on the Welsh border.

Mention of the yurt brought a reflective smile to her face. That tent SJ had sent to Eve. She'd loved it. Patched together from recycled bits of canvas and rope, with poles and pegs whittled from hazel cut from the wood. Goodness knows how SJ had managed to send it, but it had arrived just before Eve's fifth birthday with very specific instructions. It was a special place for Eve and her mummy, somewhere to go on an adventure. Justin had hated it. He refused to imagine how anyone could enjoy spending the night outside like a tribe of diggers. But she'd ignored him and together with Eve, they'd pitched the tent on a hill away from the house, overlooking the park. They'd laid together, their heads poking out of the tent while Gabrielle read a story and Eve tried to count the stars. Eve had loved it and would have spent the rest of the summer sleeping out if Gabrielle had allowed her. Three months later came the initial diagnosis and what proved to be a protracted losing battle. She smudged away a tear.

She glanced at the bed, desperate for sleep, desperate to escape, but the questions remained. What was she going to do once this was all over? How long was it going to take? And what about Justin? She flopped onto Helix's pillow, the faint smell of soap or shower gel, maybe aftershave, clinging to it. She breathed him in. Justin was every inch the career politician, but his earlier outburst seemed heart-felt: he did look concerned. Did he do that for me, or was it the right thing to do in front of an audience? And the way he'd told me about Miriam? No. You've waited too long. Whatever happens, it's over and you need to find a way out. Bugger the negative publicity. You've given enough. You need to get your life back.

14

Gabrielle pulled out the chair next to Helix and sat down.

'The clothes seem to be a good fit. Feeling warmer?' he said.

She rubbed her arms, now sleeved in the high-tech material. 'Much better, thanks.' She yawned, raising her hand to her mouth. 'Excuse me. Sorry, I nodded off for a while.'

Helix smiled. 'I know.'

'How do you know? Were you spying on me?'

'Ha. You're a fine one to talk. No. It was the snoring.'

'I do not snore, you fibber.' She punched his shoulder. 'OK, what do we have?'

The levity was good. He wasn't surprised she was tired, stressful situations have a habit of sapping the strength when they hit you. He nodded at Ethan waiting on screen.

Ethan rested his spliff on the side of the ashtray. 'OK, strap in because this has gone ballistic over the last ninety minutes.'

A frozen image of General Yawlander giving a press conference appeared on the screen; Justin Wheeler, standing to his right, eyes closed. A single tap from Ethan freed the General from his temporary paralysis.

'Ladies and gentlemen, good afternoon. It is with a heavy heart that I have to inform the citizens of London – and indeed the country – that Doctor Gabrielle Stepper, one of our nations heroes, was yesterday arrested for the murder of Professor Miriam Polozkova, a prominent member of the Scientific Elite. Doctor Stepper was placed under house arrest and close supervision while investigations continued. She was allowed to attend today's service as it held a special place in her heart, and also ours as a grateful nation. The ongoing investigation has uncovered more evidence and other crimes. Because of this, I had no option but to decide that she should be placed in a more secure environment.' He paused looking down at his notes.

Gabrielle shook her head. 'Oh my God. I can't believe they've gone public with that ludicrous accusation. And what new evidence, what other crimes? What is he talking about, Helix?'

Helix nodded at the screen as Yawlander continued.

'It was during the transfer that the officers escorting Doctor Stepper to the Westminster Police Station were attacked and killed. Doctor Stepper was helped to abscond from custody by Major Nathan Helix, who had earlier placed her under arrest.'

An inset image of Helix in uniform appeared on the screen.

'We have no idea why Major Helix would have taken this action. As a result, he is now wanted for the murder of three Police officers. There will be no further operational updates, however, Chancellor Wheeler has asked to make a personal statement.'

Gabrielle got to her feet and folded her arms. 'Hang on Ethan, can you pause it there for a minute.' She moved to the edge of the bench next to Helix. 'I thought you said you didn't kill those men.'

'I didn't kill them, Gabrielle. Believe me, I know what I am doing. If I'd wanted them dead, they would be. They were out cold, nothing more. This is a fit up.'

'And what about this new evidence? Do you know what they're talking about, Ethan?'

Helix touched her arm, nodding towards the screen. 'Ethan's trying to work it out. He's monitoring the comms. We'll know soon enough.'

Gabrielle sat back on the chair and leaned her elbows on her knees. 'OK, carry on, Ethan. I can't wait to hear what *he's* got to say.'

Wheeler cleared his throat, the spasms around his left eye worse than usual. 'Ladies and gent— I'm sorry, Ladies and gentlemen, I would like to thank General Yawlander for the opportunity to make a short statement. I am convinced that my wife Gabrielle is innocent of all the charges levelled against her. I will work tirelessly to support the authorities in finding the answers that will provide incontrovertible evidence to prove that she had nothing to do with any of this. I would also like to appeal to my wife directly.' He fixed his gaze on the camera.

'My darling Gabrielle, if you are watching this, please come home. The authorities have promised that your contribution and leadership in finding an end to one of the darkest chapters in our nation's history, will be considered. Please come home. And finally, to you Major Helix, I say this. Please take care of my wife and return her to us, and you also will be treated fairly in recognition of your own efforts and sacrifices. Ladies and gentlemen, I would like to end this short statement by saying that I am personally offering a reward of £25,000 for information resulting in the return of my wife and Major Helix. Thank you.'

Wheeler and Yawlander stepped away as the swarming media corps buzzed upwards and around them, a barrage of questions issuing from their tiny speakers. The two human journalists tried to elbow their way forward, their microphones thrust toward the backs of the departing speakers.

Yawlander leaned into Wheeler, appearing to say something. Gabrielle gasped as Wheeler appeared to lash out at the General. A police officer stepped in-between them as Yawlander pushed Wheeler away. Separated, the Chancellor pressed against the officer as Yawlander was led away. Ethan paused the image again, Wheeler's face frozen in rage, his left eye half closed.

Helix looked at Gabrielle, her face in her hands. He looked at Ethan's image on the screen and shrugged. 'Are you OK Gabrielle?' he asked, his hand resting on her back.

Gabrielle sat up. '£25,000! Is that what I am worth

to you, Justin? That's about one week's salary to him. What a joke. And getting into a fight over me.' The chair scraped across the bare concrete floor and she stood up. 'That is a first.'

Helix toyed with a small screwdriver as she paced around, looking at her new boots. She clamped her hands on the back of the chair. 'If this is a big fit up as you called it, Helix, I can't wait to see what their imaginations have conjured up with this so-called new evidence.' She spun the chair around and sat in reverse, her elbows on its back.

'We'll have to see but for now, it's smoke and mirrors time. You and I need to disappear, milady. Ethan, let's go over it again for Doctor G.'

Ethan belched. 'Pardon me. OK. At the moment, they are trying to track six different Helix's. But as we know, only one of them is real. Once you two get moving, I'll keep the charade going for a bit longer, but they will eventually discover the "real" Major Helix somewhere just outside Edinburgh.'

Helix grimaced. 'Scotland?'

Ethan held a finger up. 'Play nicely, Nate. Next, we need to arrange carriages for your trip to the seaside.'

'The seaside?' Gabrielle got up. 'Not staying in London?'

'Nope. Too many cameras, too many eyes and too many gadgets. Plus, too many guns with large people dressed in black attached to them,' Ethan said. 'Now, you can't use public transport for all of the above reasons. To get around this, Nate will take you through the tunnels from there towards Green Park station.

In one of the deeper cross-rail tunnels there will be a freight train, on its way to Paris. It will have stopped having suffered a small technical fault.' He took a slug of water from a bottle. 'While the engineers, with a little bit of help from yours truly, try to work out what's happening, our two fugitives will climb on-board and stowaway. Then, by some miracle of technology, the fault will fix itself and the train will move on to a staging area at Hoo Junction in Kent.'

Helix looked at Gabrielle, now perched on the side of the workbench again, taking it all in.

'Never heard of it,' said Gabrielle. 'Is that where we're staying?'

Ethan leaned back into his seat, tapping his fingers on his desk. 'Not quite. As the crow flies, it's another twenty-three point five miles. Once you're in Hoo, I'll have a modified AV waiting. I say AV as in autonomous, but it won't be autonomous. If it can navigate, it can be tracked and traced, and we don't want that. So, your driver today, Doctor Stepper, will be Major Helix.'

Helix gave a shallow bow. 'At your service ma'am.'

Gabrielle smiled and nodded at the screen. 'He's got it all worked out.'

Helix put his finger to his lips. 'Shush. Don't. His head's big enough as it is.'

'Heard that. Anyway, once you're on the road, it's about another forty-one miles until it's time to change modes of transport once more.'

Gabrielle pointed to the screen. 'Hang on. You said we were only twenty-three odd miles once we got to that Hoo Junction place.'

Ethan coughed. 'Yes, but you're not crows and you don't fly. Any un-scheduled flying activity in that area will arouse suspicion and we don't need any more of that either.'

Helix yawned and looked at his watch. 'Time's ticking, Ethan. Come on.'

'I know. Question for Gabrielle. Do you have any wearable tech about your person, no implants, hidden communication devices etcetera, etcetera?'

Gabrielle's brow furrowed. 'I have nothing unnatural inside me, nor do I allow anything without a pulse to enter my person.'

Helix fought to contain the mouthful of coffee he'd just taken. He rocked forward on his chair and wiped away a dark brown dribble from his chin. 'Thank you.'

Ethan grinned and lit up a fresh joint. 'Love it. Great answer. OK, that's the lady dealt with. It's not going to be as simple with the big man sat to your right I'm afraid, Gabrielle.'

Helix raised his eyes to the ceiling. 'You know what we need to do Ethan. That's enough bloody showboating. Get on with it.' A schematic image of a prosthetic leg materialised on the screen in front of him. 'Right, you said about three inches down from the back of the knee, correct?' Helix brushed his hand through a detritus-strewn bench, retrieving a box-cutter knife from under a discarded circuit board.

Helix felt her face close to his as she leaned over his shoulder, studying the schematic on the screen.

'What are you talking about and what are you planning on doing with the knife?'

Helix bent down, grasping the material at the bottom of his trouser leg. 'Just a little bit of work to help me disappear.'

'I'll explain, Gabrielle,' Ethan said. 'He's got a CPU in his leg. It controls all of his gizmos and communications and owing to a design flaw, mea culpa, I crammed pretty much everything we needed into the one modified unit. In order for him to disappear, we need to take it out. The downside is that he'll still be able to speak, but he won't be able to see anything with his right eye, hear anything with his right ear and his right arm and right leg will become something of an encumbrance. Apart from that, he'll be completely normal. But don't be surprised if he starts hopping around in circles. The really big downside is that once the CPU is on its way to the land of Rabbie Burns, I won't be able to track him or communicate with him. You'll be on your own.'

Helix pulled up the material. The schematic enlarged on the screen offering a three-dimensional view of his leg from just above the knee. 'This'll be a right faff.' He twisted around, looking down at his calf.

Gabrielle stepped forward and picked up the grubby knife. 'You're going to cut it out with this? And end up with an infection. I'm not sure that's a good idea.'

Helix took the knife. 'If it was real skin, I'd agree, but its only purpose is to provide a way of keeping dirt out of the workings and make it look sort of real.'

'Here, give it to me. You'll make a right mess trying to do this yourself. Off with the trousers. I don't want the material getting in the way.'

Helix didn't argue, quickly stepping out of his trousers as she dropped to her knees behind his leg. He angled the monitor offering her a better view of the schematic. She leaned around him, checked the location of the device with her thumb on his leg and went to work.

* * *

Helix tore off a strip of silver gaffer tape and pressed it over the opening in his leg. He pulled his trousers back on. 'Thank you, Doctor.'

Gabrielle gave his arm a gentle squeeze. 'You're welcome.'

He took the silver CPU, about half the size of an old-fashioned cigarette packet. Turning it over in his hand, he wiped it clean with a grubby blue rag.

Ethan coughed from his screen. 'OK. You know what you need to do with that, Nate. Just because it's not in your leg doesn't mean it's not waving to the world. There'll be two trains waiting when you get down into the tunnels. Yours, and the one to Edinburgh.'

Helix nodded and stumbled towards Gabrielle, his right leg and arm heavy. The muscle impulses would no longer be boosted by the servos and micro-motors weaved into the synthetic nerves, carbon fibre and titanium framework. He steadied himself with his left arm. 'I've got this.' He winked his left eye shut. Darkness. Back in hospital. Months spent recovering from the injuries that almost killed him. He took a deep breath and lumbered – half hopping – about the workshop gathering items, shoving them into a black daysack hanging from his right arm.

He peered at Gabrielle through a gap in the storage racks. What was she thinking? Half the man he was maybe? He placed the last few items he needed in the bag and crossed back to where she was waiting. He lowered the bag to the floor next to her as she rested her hand on his good arm. 'I'm fine. It'll take me a few minutes to get used to it again. We'll be alright.'

'Thanks for doing this for me, Helix. I really—'

They turned together as Ethan called out. 'Better look at this.'

Their heads almost clashed as they both bent down for the daysack. Helix looked at her. 'I can manage, Gabrielle. Thanks all the same.' He snatched up the bag with his left hand and led the way back to the bench.

Ethan coughed, his eyes darting around, fingers tapping on keys. 'Things are picking up. Police are reporting a break in at Doctor Stepper's residence. The suspect is Rachel Neilson. Seen on the exterior CCTV leaving the address with a large bag and heading out across the park. The police have entered Ms Neilson's apartment but have found no trace of her or her eight-year-old daughter, Lauren.'

Helix turned to Gabrielle. 'Not exactly your classic smash and grab raid was it?'

Ethan mumbled something to himself and then. 'There's more. Oh shit. Police now seeking the location of Rachel Neilson. Believe that she may be working with Doctor Gabrielle Stepper and Major Nathan Helix. Evidence found at the apartment.'

Gabrielle flung her arms out. 'What evidence?'

'Have you got it, Ethan?' Helix leaned into the screen to see what he was doing. 'Ethan, come on.'

'On screen two, Nate.'

Helix pulled his seat closer to the bench and leaned across to the large touch screen monitor. He tapped the bottom edge restoring a postcard-sized window. Gabrielle peered over his shoulder.

Hi Rachel. I'm frightened. I'll be attending the Remembrance Day service on Sunday with Justin. In my safe you will find all my classified research materials and archives backed up onto a silver memory pod. The pod is password protected but you'll know what to do. In the secure store in the lab, you'll find the supporting samples and the experimental compounds. Please be careful with these. Use all the normal safe-handling protocols.

I need you to take all of this and move it to a place of safe keeping until I get in touch to make other arrangements.

Please, not a word to anyone.

Love Gabrielle. xxx

Helix adopted a neutral expression as he watched Gabrielle gawp at the screen. She shook her head as she read it again, her lips moving as she scanned the words. Helix pushed himself up as she staggered away. Thinking she was going to fall, he caught her in his arms as her knees gave way. 'I've got you. Come and sit down.' He held the back of the seat until he was sure she was stable. He backed away, keeping his eyes on her. He dragged his chair over and sat close. Leaning down, his elbows on his knees, he looked into her eyes. 'Do you want something to drink?'

She shook her head.

He could hear her breathing slow steady breaths. She cleared her throat and mumbled. 'Think I'm going to vom—'

He leaned closer. 'What was that. I didn't hear you.'

She reeled away from the seat, threw her head forward and vomited. Falling to her knees, she splayed her fingers on the rough concrete floor as she strained from the pit of her stomach.

Helix stepped around her and went to the kitchen. 'Experimental compounds? Safe handling protocols?' He rinsed a glass and filled it. 'Christ, this gets weirder by the minute.'

He found her leaning against the wall, her head clamped in her hands, face streaked with tears. She took three small sips of water from the glass, nodding her head.

Her explanation of the video they'd watched in the taxi had seemed reasonable. She was helping a friend by lending her materials for her university course. But the content of the email – and her reaction to it – didn't tally.

Gabrielle stretched her legs out flat on the floor, crossing them at the ankles. She sipped her water and tucked her hair behind her ears. She looked Helix in the eye. 'I did not send that email. And I know what Ethan is going to say. It was in my sent items.'

Helix held his hands out and shrugged. 'And the bit about classified research materials?'

She pulled her knees up, resting her forearms across them. 'Short version?'

'Please. We need to get moving.'

'Remember me mentioning the discovery I made, just before the Ebola pandemic?'

Helix nodded. 'The bug spray recipe?'

'That isn't funny, Helix.' She dabbed the corner of her mouth with her thumb. 'I took the research to a new level, several in fact, just like Valerian wanted. It took at least two years.' She drank the rest of the water, blinking at the empty glass. 'That's why it was classified. I cancelled the original patent and registered it under the Official Scientific Secrets Act. I could lose my licence, face a heavy fine and or receive a prison sentence. Trust me. You do not want that research in the public domain or anywhere near it.'

15

The decayed ruin of the twelfth century Tintern Abbey slumped on the Monmouthshire bank of the sedate River Wye, facing the tree-covered hinterland of Gloucestershire. A magnet to migrants from English and Welsh towns, the Wye valley had almost everything that the self-sufficient survivor could have needed. Plumes of white smoke snaked from woods bordered by small fields of tilled land and a patchwork of allotments bursting with seasonal crops.

A young woman swam towards the English bank, her hair stretching out behind her in the cool, slow flowing water of the river. She clambered over the rocks back to her sun-dried shorts and t-shirt. The warmth coupled with the light breeze had dried the garments faster than she'd expected. The sloping rock doubled as a sunbed. She relaxed, flicked out her hair behind her to dry and tilted her eyes up at the white clouds, billowing from the west. In the time it took for the clouds to crowd the sun, her skin and hair had dried, which she accepted as the cue to dress and get back.

She slipped into her shorts and t-shirt and smiled

at the chorus of giggles and sniggers from the three children who had spied on her from the bushes while she'd bathed. 'I know you're in there, you little buggers,' she called, rushing barefoot up the gravel path in their direction. Shrieks of laughter echoed through the woods as the two boys and their younger sister scampered from the undergrowth.

SJ caught up with the youngster on the path. 'Hello, Milly.'

Milly brushed her wild blonde hair from her grubby face and beamed up at SJ, whom she worshipped. 'They're always leaving me behind,' she said, pointing an accusing finger in the direction her brothers had taken.

'Don't worry poppet, it won't be long before you can keep up with them. In fact, I reckon you'll easily be able to run faster than them. Shall we run up to the camp together now?'

'Yes. Let's go,' she said, gripping SJ's hand and tugging.

SJ scooped her up onto her shoulders as she jogged up the path between the trees. She danced around the bushes and ducked under low branches towards the comforting smell of wood burning in the community kitchen.

Bo waved from the porch of the dining hall as they rounded the bend. The hall was the hub of the community, with a dozen yurts radiating out from it like the spokes of a wheel. Twelve years her senior, SJ had met Bo in Canada while hiking. They enjoyed many of the same extreme sports and had become inseparable. She stepped up onto the porch, summersaulting Milly off her shoulders onto the wooden deck. 'Hey, Bo. What's up, you look worried?'

The dining hall door creaked as Bo pulled it open. 'A boy from the neighbouring village saw something on the news and he thought you ought to see it. He's in here.'

SJ took Milly's hand as they stepped into the octagonal dining hall with its thatched roof and exposed wood beams, garlanded with corn dollies. Four long trestle tables and benches were arranged in a square and laid up for that evening's dinner. A teenager with a dilapidated laptop sat at a table. He turned as Bo put his hand on his shoulder. 'This is Marvin.'

Marvin returned SJ's smile with a nod. He tapped the keyboard, bringing the cracked screen back to life. A frozen frame of the news bulletin he'd recorded via the school's shaky internet connection appeared.

'Hey, Marvin. What have you got?'

She watched General Yawlander and Justin Wheeler's press conference with Milly wriggling on her hip.

Milly pointed to the screen. 'You're on the TV.'

'That's not me, Milly. That's my clever sister Gabrielle. She's *very* famous.' SJ frowned at the screen. 'What the hell...'

The recording fizzed out. Bo stood with his arms folded, his usual casual demeanour absent.

'So, was that this afternoon, Marvin?' SJ said as Milly tried to wriggle inside her t-shirt. She lowered her to the floor.

Marvin nodded and turned back to his machine. SJ

took Milly's outstretch hand and swung her between herself and Bo.

She scratched her ear. 'It looks serious.'

'I wouldn't worry. The privileged elite have a way of looking after their own.'

'Of course, I'm worried, Bo. She's my sister.'

'You're not thinking of going up there, are you?' Bo shook his head. 'What about that winking prick of a husband, Wheeler?'

'Don't use words like that in front of Milly, please. The bandwidth at the school is too slow and unreliable to make calls, the email doesn't work and it's miles to the nearest working phone. But he might be the only one who can explain what the hell's going on.'

16

Three months in post and it wasn't the impression Terry McGill had wanted to create. It was his ruthless reputation and the ability to get things done that had landed him the job. He'd grown tired of all the politically correct nonsense: the accountability, checks and balances that had leached into the military. The once great fighting force had been rendered impotent and no better than the toothless United Nations. With remuneration of at least five times his military salary, before bonuses, his employer demanded a lot and expected to get it. He wasn't about to let him down.

He stalked around the dimly lit control room with his arms folded. His eyes darted over shoulders at the holographic monitors as the team sifted through evidence and leads that might lead to the whereabouts of Helix and Gabrielle Stepper. He snorted. Nathan Helix VC DSO. Fucking war hero with *his* reputation. Apparently, a reputation much more in keeping with the modern military that Wheeler and those other idiots espoused. It wasn't the humiliation of the enquiry, where they had ripped his record to shreds before declaring the outcome "inconclusive". It wasn't the whispers in the corridors after he had been removed from his post. It wasn't being assigned to some dusty backwater office, shuffling paper from one side of the desk to the other. The worst part was having to stand to attention in that committee room in front of Helix and what was left of his younger brother Ethan, listening to the chairman's bullshit. And then, his lawyer's parting shot: "No point in appealing. You were lucky not to have been dishonourably discharged."

The military had been his life's passion, his chance to prove all the doubters wrong. One in particular: his father. According to him, the young McGill would amount to nothing, a wastrel just like his mother. She had fought like any mother to protect her son, soaking up the abuse and keeping the fragile peace. She'd practically dragged him to the recruiting office, hoping and believing the military would be a place of refuge for him. She had been right. Two days after he joined up, she'd found the courage to leave his father and start a new life for herself. He'd visited his dying father the day after the hearing had ended. He'd sat at the edge of the bed as his father pretended to sleep. The TV was on, the sound low but audible. McGill had glanced up as they ran another summary of the hearing, the words "shamed and humiliated" stamped across the screen. He'd glanced back at his father, his eyes now open, finger pointing at the screen, "See. I told you. You're nothing, a nobody, a failure, a coward *and* a liar." Those were the last words he ever heard his father say.

He turned back to Yawlander, standing in the door to his office. 'I told you Helix was a fucking liability. Easily turned by an intelligent pretty face.'

Yawlander shrugged, his finger glancing across his scar. 'And I told you it would have been better to have taken her at the Meridian. But you knew better and now you've got a shit storm. Well done, Terry.'

McGill spun around, overlooking the two curved rows of agents with their heads down over their keyboards, fingers flitting across touch screens, whispering into their jaw-bone headsets. He ground his teeth. 'Will somebody please tell me what the fuck is going on!' He slammed his hand down on a desk.

The agent in front of him flinched and cleared his throat. 'We have six traces, all of which seem to be Major Helix, sir. I've noticed that in the—'

'I knew that thirty minutes ago, Corporal. Please tell me something I don't know.'

'Yes, sir. In the last couple of minutes, one trace is separating from the others.' He pointed at the screen. 'They had been following a random pattern within a defined area.'

McGill leaned in, studying the map, the six red pings pulsing as they moved around central London. 'Heading north. Speed?'

'One hundred and eighty-seven miles per hour, sir. I think it's a freight train.'

'I doubt that Major Helix is capable of more than two miles per hour these days, Corporal. Find out where that train is going, get in touch with the control room and have it stopped and searched by a team.' He clamped his hand on the Corporal's shoulder. 'We find him. We find her.'

He climbed the three steps to the brushed aluminium rail surrounding the platform from which the senior leadership could monitor operations. 'I need an update on the status of Ethan Helix. I need to know where he is, what he is doing and I need it now.'

An agent stood, her hand raised.

'Speak up, Private,' McGill barked.

The young woman snapped to attention. 'Sir. All access to government surveillance systems has been revoked, as you requested. We're running traces across the networks to establish his location.' She dropped back to her seat.

Yawlander laughed. 'Ridiculous.'

'Something amusing, General?'

Yawlander pushed himself away from the door frame. 'You don't know who you're dealing with, Terry. Ethan Helix is one of the best. Probably *the* best covert surveillance and systems operative the military has.'

McGill put his hands on his hips. 'You mean had.'

'By cutting him off, you think you've blinded him. You're wrong. Ethan may be half the man he once was, but he'll be way ahead of you. He'll know what you're thinking before you've even thought it.'

'Way ahead of *you*? I thought we were a team, General. I get a sense that you're not even in the boat, let alone rowing in same direction. It might be an idea for you to remember where you are in all of this. Careers are at stake, maybe even lives.'

McGill held Yawlander's stare. He may have been a General, but he was also an arrogant prick. A shit storm, that's how he'd put it. Well, he'd show him what a shit storm looked like. 'I need an update on the location of the Neilson woman and the child. Now.'

The glass wall of Yawlander's office shuddered as he slammed the door behind him. A victorious grin broke across McGill's face.

'On schedule to the destination, sir,' said a voice from the other side of the control room. 'ETA seventeen minutes.'

McGill leaned back against the barrier. 'I want to know the moment they arrive.'

17

The wagon emitted a metallic groan as the train negotiated its way through an unseen junction. Helix checked the fluorescent dial of his watch in the stifling dark. 'Shouldn't be too long. Have you got enough room, Gabrielle?'

'I'm fine, thanks.'

He stretched out his hand towards the shadowy outline of the massive packing crate in front of him and steadied himself. The lack of electronic assistance in his leg and arm wasn't impossible to live with, but he was already missing it. He looked up, unable to make out the roof of the wagon. It was strange how you took what you had for granted. Nature was a wonderful thing and he was grateful he still had one of the eyes he was born with, but he missed the edge his ocular prosthesis gave him. Gabrielle fidgeted beside him. 'You not going to grab some shut-eye?' he said.

She sighed. 'I'd like to. But every time I close my eyes, my brain goes into hyperdrive. What about you?'

'I'm OK. Doing a bit of the same if I'm honest. Where were you when the outbreak started?' At least it was more interesting than talking about the weather.

She shifted on the rucksack and leaned against him. 'Benziger Ryser Gersbach, a pharmaceutical company based in Berkshire.'

'German company?'

'No, Swiss. Maidenhead Office Park also known as MOP. We had most of the campus. It was one of the main R&D sites.'

'MOP, really? I was there, too. Just after it all kicked off. My unit was tasked with securing power and data. It had a small airstrip on one side and the railway line on the other.'

'That's the place. I liked it there when I first started. But I must admit I wasn't sorry to leave. Two years and two months they kept us there.'

'You make it sound like you were a prisoner.'

'We were pretty much. They screened everyone. Anyone who'd been to London – or anywhere near the first reported cases – was moved to an isolation area on the other side of the airfield. If there were no symptoms after twenty-one days, they were allowed back. After that, it was a grim choice. You could leave and not be allowed back or stay and help to find a solution.'

'Was the cause ever established? I heard a few theories. More rumours, actually.'

'It was the Zaire species which had mutated. We knew that much. Investigations seemed to be pointing to West Africa. But competing priorities meant that we never knew for sure. There were more pressing things.'

'So, you stayed at MOP. What about others?'

'A few left. I think they believed they would be allowed back, but they were wrong. We never saw them again. It was a terrible time. We all knew people on the outside and kept in touch to start with.' She cleared her throat. 'When you heard about someone's family or a friend, you expressed your sorrow for their loss in the normal way. But after a while you stopped asking and people stopped saying.'

Helix remembered that the Paras didn't fuck about. Everyone knew about the checkpoints along the road leading to the park and the snipers on the bridge over the railway track. Re-supply took place by air. The options were shit if you left and wanted to come back: a bullet, Ebola or a slim chance of survival, take your pick. 'Was that where you met Lytkin?'

'We met at uni. I was head-hunted by BRG. He applied.'

Helix crossed his ankles. 'But you worked together?'

'Sometimes. More towards the time of the outbreak. When it all started, there were major concerns about the clustering of expertise in one place. The forecasts indicated that the emergency response and recovery procedures would be inadequate. Cross-functional research teams were established to work in isolation. That's when they started moving people out.'

'And he was one of them?'

'Correct. He thought I'd orchestrated it, because of the research. He was furious and that was before he found out I'd patented it.' She sat up and stretched her back muscles. 'Patents aren't secret, well not the standard ones. Several years after the all clear, someone he knew with the necessary clearance recognised my name. They knew about our time together and told him. A lot of companies keep track of what's being filed. They did it out of a need to make sure they weren't working on something similar, or to spot licencing opportunities.'

'Knew about your time together?'

'Me and him. Our relationship. The personal one.'

'Oh right. You said you became close. I didn't realise...' He peered at his watch again, pressing his toes against the pallet.

She gave him a nudge. 'So, what happened to you after MOP?'

'Oh, not a lot. Apart from digging holes, some of them in people's front gardens. That and looking after Thanet Earth.'

'Holes. I assume you mean graves.'

'Yep. Nasty old business. Shit times, but someone had to do it. I spent a year at the best military academy in the world so I could spend months in a sweaty bio-suit looking for sites, and then organising blokes to come in with the earth movers.' He smiled at the reassuring squeeze she gave his arm. She must have known what was going on outside the fence.

'And Thanet Earth, I've never heard of that.'

'You've heard of the Isle of Thanet or Planet Thanet as we used to call it.'

'Margate?'

'Close. It's a huge industrial agriculture facility, known as Thanet Earth. Two hundred and twenty acres of greenhouses, about the size of the old terminal five at Heathrow. The surviving locals had ransacked the place of anything edible, but the facilities were left in reasonable nick. Our task was to secure it and get it back into production. It was used as a model for a lot of the new facilities that came later.'

'Digging different holes.'

'Those kinds of holes I didn't mind. It was the others, or more to the point, what we were planting in them that kept me awake at night.'

'It must have been strange to have been so close to home with everything that was going on.'

'Hmm. My parents were lucky, kind of. They'd taken a converted bothy in the Shetlands for a month. They were avid twitchers and spent their days watching bloody seagulls. Still, they ended up getting stranded. Probably saved their lives.' He scrambled to his feet as the train slowed. 'This should be us. You ready to move? We need to roll out of the wagon and get underneath until we know where the loadbots are. They won't be expecting passengers and they don't understand the concept of ladies first.'

They swayed into each other, as the train thumped over the jointed track. The brakes hissed as they came to a halt with a loud clunk, indicating that the doors had unlocked.

Helix reached forward in the dark, his hand resting on her back. 'Here we go. Standby.'

Thirty seconds passed. There was no movement, no sound. He leaned forward over her shoulder, his ear turned towards the door. If they didn't get out fast, they could find themselves somewhere on the wrong side of the English Channel.

'Are the doors meant to open on their own?'

'Maybe it's just a stopover to load something else. Let me squeeze past you.'

Gabrielle shuffled around him as he reached up to the edge of the door. He hooked his fingers into a gap and heaved it open. A welcome rush of evening air and the smell of damp grass mixed with brake dust filled the compartment. 'No welcoming committee. Come on. Let's go.'

Sliding out, he hopped around on his good leg, catching the rucksack as she swung it out. He glanced to his right at a dormant gun-metal grey loading bot, standing opposite the door of the neighbouring wagon. 'That was close,' he muttered to himself.

Gabrielle's fingers slipped from his hand as the door hissed and slid shut, trapping her inside. 'Fuck.' He hammered at the door, hearing the urgent whine of the bot's electric motors as it propelled itself along the guideway towards him. They could have done without this. The bot's orientation lasers stroked the side of the wagon as it elbowed him away from the door. He stumbled, executing a parachute landing fall under the wagon, narrowly avoiding headbutting the polished metal of the track.

He lay still for a moment. The smell of grease filled his nose as he spat out the gravelly dust from the side of his mouth. The bot was stationary. Gabrielle's muffled shouts leaked down from above his head. He needed to shift his arse. If she wasn't quick enough, she'd be crushed as it reached inside.

He rolled out from under the wagon and paused, looking up and the motionless bot. Precious seconds. What was it waiting for? 'Gabrielle, can you hear me?' He leaned into the door, his one good eye on the bot.

'Helix. What's going on?'

'There's a bot outside. Get ready. When the do—' He recoiled as the bot came back to life, scanning the barcodes attached to the wagon door.

The heavy machine stiffened. Its articulated legs thrusted upwards positioning itself across the door as it slid open. Helix rushed behind the machine. He struggled to see inside the wagon as it filled with strobing lasers. Gabrielle stood in the doorway, bathed in fluorescent green, frozen like a prisoner in a halo-cuff. 'Helix. What do I do? Help me.'

He braced himself as it lurched forward and froze. 'Don't move, Gabrielle.'

The machine creaked as it rocked back and forth. Its lasers swept left and right around her feet, an impatient humming coming from deep within its bulk.

'I think it's confused. Whatever you do, don't move your feet.'

'What? My feet?' She looked down, steadying herself against the side of the door. 'I can't get past it, Helix. The gap isn't big enough.'

'Hold on. I'll see if there's—' The heavy crunch of approaching feet on gravel distracted him. 'Shit. Someone's coming, Gabrielle. Stay still.'

He rolled back under the wagon. A pair of heavy black leather boots appeared from the gloom, lumbering in the gravel between the track and bot guideway. They didn't need this. So much for being invisible. He primed himself as a radio crackled into life. 'What's going on, Del?'

'Dunno, Sid,' the responder wheezed. 'Bloody thing's just standing there. Probably seen a mouse. I'll reset it. Standby.'

Helix watched the dusty boots move around the back of the bot. He rolled over the tracks again, coming up on the opposite side of the bot. Del opened a large hinged panel between himself and Helix. He jerked away as the bot took a large step back. Del did the same, moving his foot just in time.

Helix watched his feet move to the left. He'd see her as soon as he looked up. Helix stepped behind him. He pressed his finger to his lips as he looked over Del's shoulder into Gabrielle's eyes.

Del hesitated. 'What the fuck?' he said, uncertain if he should go for the ancient Beretta handgun on his fat hip or the radio strapped to his chest. One chubby hand groped for the gun while the other patted across his chest in search of the radio mic.

Helix took the gift of indecision to step behind him. He swung his right arm over Del's shoulder and around his face, stifling his shout. He clamped his left hand over the fat man's wrist, twisting his arm up behind his back, bringing him to his toes. 'Jump down and grab the rucksack.' His nose tingled from the updraft of sour sweat from Del's stained armpits.

She landed on the guideway next to them. Recovering the rucksack from under the wagon, she slung it over her shoulder.

Helix tightened his grip, squeezing what fight there was out of Del. 'Grab the radio and the gun.'

Gabrielle hesitated, looking up him. He nodded to her as Del tried to squirm. She reached in and pulled the Beretta from the holster before reaching under Helix's arm for the radio.

The radio hissed. 'Del? What are you buggering about at? That thing is still showing as offline. Report back.'

Helix glanced over at Gabrielle. 'It's OK. There's a safety catch on the gun. You'll be fine. Just move back behind me, I'm going to let our friend go, but if he tries to do a runner, shoot him.'

Gabrielle's eyes widened. 'What? No. I can't. I couldn't. Can't we let him go?'

'It's OK. I was joking. I think it's been a while since he ran anywhere.' He leaned in to Del's ear. 'What do you think, Del? You going to behave yourself if I let you go?'

Del stopped wriggling and nodded his head as Helix loosened his grip. He gave him a hefty shove towards the wagon door. Almost sprawling onto his knees, Del caught himself of the ledge and turned. He smeared the blood from his split lip across the back of his hand.

'Down on your knees. Ankles crossed. Hands on your head.'

Del grunted as he complied, his breathing laboured. His two sizes too small overalls made the task more difficult.

Gabrielle surrendered the gun to Helix. He checked the safety and slipped it into the back of his trousers. He glanced over Del's head. 'It's just as well you were standing where you were. I think it confused our metal friend when he couldn't see the bar codes under your boot. Couldn't get its bearings. A couple of inches the other way and you'd have been toast I reckon.'

Gabrielle rubbed her arms. 'Thanks. That makes me feel a lot better.'

Del coughed. A gob of blood streaked saliva ran down his fat chins. 'You're whatshisname? Helix. That's it. And you're that Doctor Stepper. I've seen the telly. Lots of folk looking for you two.'

Del had seen the telly, probably knew about the reward and thought he was about to get rich. Helix zipped his jacket, feeling the grip of the Beretta at the base of his back. He weighed the options. How far could they get before the militia were all over them? Del's mate knew he was down there and as soon as he got back to base, it would be game over.

He took the radio from Gabrielle. 'Can you duck under that train behind us? I just need to know how close we are to the perimeter.'

She leaned around him. 'Sure.'

He thumbed the transmit button on the radio, as Gabrielle's feet slipped from view. 'Yeah, Sid. Everything's alright,' he said, muffling his mouth with his sleeve. 'I'm just about to reset the bloody thing. Hang on. You should see it come back online.' He stepped to the back of the bot and palmed a large green button.

Del scrambled for traction. Clouds of chalky dust drifted through the bot's lasers. It lunged forward, as Del stumbled to his feet, and crushed him against the bottom edge of the door. Helix turned away as the top half of Del's torso was smeared across the floor and flattened against the opposite bulkhead by the hydraulic loading arm.

Gabrielle crawled from beneath the train and scrambled to her knees. 'What was that sound? Where is he?'

Helix stepped in front of her. She didn't need to see it. 'I think his mate got impatient. Looks like he reset the bot remotely. Del got himself crushed. Come on.'

'Maybe I can help him.'

'He's beyond help, Gabrielle. Let's move.'

* * *

With three trains between them and what remained of Del, they crouched at the side of the tracks. Helix checked the boundary while Gabrielle caught her breath. They could do without any more surprises. He got to his feet, hopping on his good leg. 'Bugger. We need to be on the other side of this place.'

She blinked her eyes open. 'Is that where the AV's parked?'

'Supposedly.' He rummaged in one of the side pockets of the rucksack pulling out a night vision monocular. He thumbed the power button and peered into the dark. 'But there's way too much going on over there. Looks like the military working around those trains.'

Gabrielle cleared her throat. 'Do you think they're looking for us?'

'No, I don't think so. Three of them are asleep in their battle bus, two having a smoke and one having a pee. They're waiting for the bots to finish loading. We'll have to improvise. Come on.' He pressed down the top strand of barbed wire as she climbed over the fence.

They traversed a narrow strip of wood that skirted the side of the yard, slid down a bank and into a field. Helix scanned ahead with the monocular. 'It'll be best to avoid the roads for a bit.'

One hundred and fifty yards further into the fallow, weed-strewn field, they both froze, flooded in light. Helix dropped to ground cursing his non-responsive leg. Gabrielle followed his lead. There was no cover. They were exposed. He pulled his P226 from his shoulder holster, juggling it in his left hand.

A voice called out from behind the light. 'You're on private property. What's your business?'

'Our vehicle broke down back by the train yard,' Helix called back. 'We took a short cut across the fields. We're trying to get to Rochester.'

'Get to your feet and walk forward. You can leave that gun on the ground.'

Helix looked at Gabrielle, his brow furrowed. 'Stay sharp. Keep behind me.' He left the gun as instructed. How the hell did he not see them? He shook his head as they edged forward, the thistles snagging at his legs, his hand shielding his eyes. The grip of Del's Beretta pressed into the small of his back. It wasn't worth the risk. Even on his own. He had no idea how many of them there were behind the light. If they were military or local militia, there was no telling how much fire-power they had. Keep calm. Get in close and recalculate the odds.

Gabrielle gasped as a young chocolate Labrador rushed towards them, its tail wagging as it sniffed them over. Helix held his hand down to the dog's snout. Given the canine welcome, it was unlikely that the dog's owners were military. The odds improved, but it didn't mean they weren't armed. The dog trotted off, rooting amongst the weeds. Helix recognised the outline of his P226 as the dog retrieved it and bounded back in a wide arc towards the light.

The light was extinguished as they crested another bank and pushed down through the nettles. It was no wonder he hadn't seen them. From the other direction, all that would have been visible would have been the lens of the lamp. The rest of the vehicle was below their feet. The gangly lamp operator sprung down from the load bed of the doorless truck that might have been a four-by-four in a previous life. The dog took his place, dropping Helix's gun onto the metal surface amongst the collection of ducks and other wildfowl.

Sliding from the cab, the driver sloped a semi-automatic shotgun over his shoulder. His mate gawped at Gabrielle. Unmodified, the shotgun would have been loaded with three cartridges. At this range, one would be enough. They were old but effective and Helix wasn't close enough.

The driver smiled. 'So, your vehicle broke down. You're a long way from home, methinks.'

Helix held out the monocular. 'Maybe you can give us a lift? This might come in handy for a bit of bunny bashing. I assume that's what you were doing.' But not with that blunderbuss. He nodded toward the truck and took two steps closer. 'Nice setup you've got there. And a few ducks too. Good eating?' He surveyed the gun rack fitted to the back of the cab. Small calibre rifle. Probably .22 or maybe .243 with telescopic sight. Loose in the rack, but out of reach.

The driver's eyes widened. He leaned his gun against the side of the truck and took the monocular. Helix zipped up his jacket.

'Christ, this thing is amazing. I'll take you anywhere you want for this. I'm guessing you've done a bit of bashing and fowling yourself in the past?'

Helix smiled. 'Back in the day. Not so much recently. I'm Nate, and this is my friend, SJ.'

The lamp guy stepped forward, his hand extended. 'I'm Rich, and this is Andy. He nodded at the dog. 'That four-legged nutter is Colin.' His nose wrinkled. 'Sorry, but you both look familiar. Particularly you, SJ?'

Helix tensed and cursed his own stupidity. Removing the CPU must have numbed his brain as well as his limbs. Between him and Ethan, they had seen to it that there were few, if any, official photographs of him in the public realm. But Ethan was the only one who called him Nate. SJ, on the other hand, would be instantly recognisable.

Gabrielle stepped forward. 'This is embarrassing. You don't miss much, Rich.' She smiled and shook his hand. 'I have a twin sister and she is pretty well-known.'

'Shit. I knew it. Gabrielle Stepper. You sound just like her too. She's your sister?'

Gabrielle smiled and shrugged. 'We could even fool our parents.'

Helix wasn't as impressed. This was all they needed, Gabrielle groupies. The light pollution bleached the sky over the train yard as Helix assessed how long it would take for Andy and Rich to get there and report them. That was two balls-ups in fifteen minutes. 'So, how about that lift?'

Andy climbed back into the driver's seat, sliding the shotgun into the rack behind his head. 'SJ, you jump in here alongside me. Nate, you jump up in the back with Rich and Colin. You'll have to wipe the slobber off your gun.'

Helix took a wide stance, avoiding stepping on the game littering the load bed. They rattled down the unmade road. 'You live local?'

Rich pointed towards a dim light in the distance. 'Red House Farm. Just me, Andy, Mum and Dawn, our little sister. She's not too well at the moment. We don't know what's up and you can't get much in the way of treatment out here.'

He tapped Rich on the shoulder. 'Sorry to hear that.' He gripped the roll bar, wondering if Gabrielle was getting the same story, as they swung into the dusty yard next to a red brick farmhouse. He clambered from the load bed as Rich unloaded the fur and feather harvest, taking it into a shed with Andy's help. Helix leaned against the side of the truck. 'We need to move on. We're meant to be invisible.'

Gabrielle folded her arms. 'We've been invited for dinner and I don't know about you, but I'm starving.'

'What? I didn't plan for this, Gabrielle. They seem alright but we need to get to Ethan, get back online and find out what's going on.'

Gabrielle looked towards the house. 'They've got a little sister, Dawn. She's only seven, Helix and she's sick. I offered to examine at her.'

'Did you tell him who you are? There's a price on your head and these folks could do with the money.'

'Calm down. I told them I'm a Doctor, yes. SJ and I could have followed identical paths. Have you got a medical kit in your bag?'

* * *

Helix pushed away his empty plate. 'It's been a while since I've had a wild rabbit stew. That was great.' He smoothed out the ripple he'd made in the starched white tablecloth.

'You're welcome. Mum's a good cook. We do alright. At least we've got the bunnies and ducks to exchange for bits and pieces. Strange how things have settled down. We've found a way to feed ourselves, sharing and helping each other out. It amazes me that some insist on staying in towns. Not much room to grow stuff. The occasional bird, cats and rats for meat.' He shuddered. 'In a way it's better than it was. I don't miss some of it, but if you've got food in your belly, a place to sleep and family, what more do you need?'

Rich glanced towards the narrow stairs. 'Medicine's a different thing though. Rare as a laughing militiaman out this far.'

Helix took a mouthful of tea. The wooden clock on the wall, its pendulum marking time back and forth behind a narrow window in the case, chimed the half hour. What was Gabrielle doing? There was no movement above the yellowing plaster between the cracked oak beams overhead. She'd been upstairs with Kerry for the best part of forty minutes. It wasn't looking good.

There were footsteps on the hollow wooden stairs. Kerry steadied herself against the worn banister. She looked tearful and upset. Gabrielle followed, her face grim.

'How's the patient?' Helix said, pushing his chair back.

Gabrielle touched his arm. 'It's not looking good, Helix, she's got—'

The cups on the table rattled as Andy sprung to his feet, his earlier bonhomie absent. 'Fucking hell. You're Nathan Helix?'

'Well bloody done.' He shoved his hands to his hips and turned to face the brothers.

Rich raised his finger. 'And I bet she's Gabrielle Stepper. I knew it. We might be diggers, but we haven't got shit between our ears.'

Helix looked at them. No immediate threat. Andy wouldn't make it if he went for the gun. They needed to maintain cover, but they couldn't risk them blowing the whistle to the military and collecting the reward, just like Del would have.

Gabrielle pulled at his arm. 'She's got all the symptoms of pneumonia, Helix. The pain relief medication in your medical kit is too aggressive. I've given her a quarter of one tablet, but she needs something more suitable for her age: antibiotics and some cough medicine.'

He sighed. He'd seen that look before. 'And where are they going to come from?'

'Miriam's surgery. She kept a supply there and at her apartment.'

The apartment was out of the question, but the—What was he doing?

She climbed up on her toes, her face next to his. 'She needs the antibiotics before it gets worse, Helix. Otherwise she'll die.'

18

Helix wedged himself into the corner of the load bed. Rich stood next to him. Navigating by moonlight the progress was slow. Andy threaded the truck between the weeds and brambles that strangled the road. He'd rather be stood up facing forward but given his leg and the fact that he would need to fire the shotgun left-handed, he opted to be rear gunner with his P226 as a backup. Rich clung on to the roll bar one handed, his shotgun pointing ahead.

'Don't you worry about getting caught by the police for operating a non-autonomous vehicle, let alone carrying fire arms?' Helix said.

'Not really. We know most of them and they leave us alone in exchange for the occasional bit of game. Plus, they're not likely to be about at night. Like everything else, there are fewer than there used to be. I mean look around. Nature has reclaimed the place. Back in the day it was gridlocked with traffic, not bushes, scrub and ivy. Now it's a green shrouded ghost town with a few hardy souls clinging to life in what's left. Fuck knows why they don't just leave and get themselves a plot of land. There's plenty around if you're prepared to put yourself out a bit.'

Helix nodded. He knew what was under those bushes and in some of the houses. Time and weather had failed to fade the red crosses on the doors. There would have been someone inside who was infected. In the upstairs window, a little boy might have looked out. Six years old perhaps. The glass fogged by his screams as he clawed at the window. The lads doing the checking wouldn't have gone inside. Crosses told them where to look later. That was if they came back at all. He lost count of the crosses. 'So, what's with all the firepower? You expecting to be attacked by a mob of flesh-eating zombies?'

Rich laughed. 'Wabbits. Never turn up the chance of a bunny or a brace of pheasants.'

Helix raised his eyebrows, put the shotgun down on the floor beside him and holstered his P226. It had been a while since he spent any time outside London. Apart from his brief unpleasant visit to the scene of Miriam Polozkova's death, he couldn't remember the last time. He rubbed away the thick film of dust from the rear screen of the cab with the arm of his jacket. Gabrielle was animated, talking with her hands. He shook his head and looked away.

'She's quite a handful that one,' Rich said.

'You don't know the half of it.' He laughed. 'Listen, are you sure your mate will take us on from Gillingham?'

'Yeah, he'll be fine. It's not as if we can call him to check. Anyway, Gillingham is about our limit if we want to get back. Even without the lights, the fuel cells in this old bus are getting tired and don't have the range they used to.'

Helix nodded. It was crazy how everyone had learned to take things for granted again. So soon after what happened. If these guys were anything to go by, it looked OK, but he wouldn't swap. They should have been with Ethan by now, listening to what else he'd dug up. His back pressed against the cab as they slowed. He scrambled up onto his knees.

Rich peered into the monocular, scanning the road ahead. 'I know there's nobody out there, but I love this thing. Thanks for doing this, Helix. We'd be devastated if anything happened to Dawn. We've got to look after the little ones, they're our hope for the future.'

'That's true. Look, I'm sorry it got heavy earlier, but we've been through some weird shit the last forty-eight hours. I thought I would have to put her over my shoulder and carry her out.'

The once formidable historic dockyard gate with its faded coat of arms loomed above as Andy edged the truck forward. A familiar rubbish-heap aroma assaulted Helix's nose as he looked toward the stinking river only a few hundred yards to their left. Rich swung himself over the side of the truck and jogged forward to check the gatehouse. A wave to Andy had the truck moving forward under the arch.

Gabrielle pointed to a path between the back of the arch and a squat white building at the edge of the road as Helix climbed down from the load bed. 'This way.'

A short flight of steps led to a garden. Helix pushed through the bushes behind her, ignoring the drops of evening dew that dripped down his neck. A heavy stone at the side of the door hid the key, which looked like it dated from when the place was built. The squeak echoed off the surrounding buildings as Gabrielle used both hands to turn it in the lock. He pulled the door open, taking a hit of Eau de Disinfectant and Doctor's surgery. Christ, he didn't miss that. He shuffled back into the shadows as she disappeared inside.

* * *

Five minutes, no more. That's what she'd said. She'd already been gone eight. The moon reflected off the grimy windows but there were no lights inside. The small maglite torch he'd given her should be good enough; she could hold it in her teeth as she worked.

He caught himself on the side of the door as she pushed it open. 'You got everything?' He whispered, taking the medical bag from her.

She pushed backwards through the door with a second heavy bag. 'Yep.'

'Christ. How much medication does one seven-year-old need?'

She re-locked the door and hid the key. 'It's not all medication. The rest are things I used to leave here. Come on. You said you wanted to be in and out of here fast.'

He ducked underneath a low bush at the bottom of the steps and stopped. 'Hold on. There's someone else up by the gate with Andy and Rich. I just want to take a look to see who it is. Stay here and don't move until I call for you.'

He snaked forward on the ground, the smell of damp leaves reminding him of school holidays spent in the woods. He counted three pairs of feet, beyond the truck; two Andy and Rich, noticeable by their camouflage trousers the other unmistakeable as a militia uniform. Fuck. They must have been watching the place since Miriam's death. The entrance gate and arch amplified the conversation. Andy and Rich were their jovial selves and there was something familiar with one of the others. Nasal Neville Lafarge. Nothing would have given Helix greater pleasure than to straighten out Lafarge's broken nose. But it wasn't the time or the place.

He skirted the low white building, signalling to Gabrielle to stay where she was. He needed options that would work with his left hand. Andy and Rich stood on the left, looking towards him. Good. If they'd seen him, it didn't show. He hoped they could improvise. There were two coppers at the back of the truck. Lafarge left, Plod-the-unknown on the right. All set.

Flakes of cream paint dropped to the road as he pressed himself against the wall. Using the building as cover wasn't an option. It placed Andy and Rich behind the others, not where they wanted to be with him shooting left-handed. Dropping to his knees in the shadows, he placed his P226 on the road surface as he lowered himself into a prone position.

Lafarge stepped from behind the truck, squaring up to Andy, his hands on his hips. A thin wisp of smoke curled up from the cigarette held in his teeth. That wasn't in the script. Who told him to move? Helix dragged his right arm across in front of him, using it as a rest for his left. Peering through the night sight, he placed the cross hairs on the back of the second officer's ankle. There was no need to blow the guys foot off. Just a nick will be enough to get him on the deck and then cue Andy and Rich.

He slowed his breathing. Things were kicking off. Lafarge had his hand on the grip of his side arm, insisting Rich surrender his shotgun. He checked his aim. Took up the pressure on the trigger and squeezed off a single shot.

An agonised scream echoed off the walls as the bullet burst the officer's Achilles tendon, pitching him backwards onto the road in a writhing heap. Lafarge reacted. He pulled his handgun, but he was too slow and collected a hefty right hook across his taped up nose from Andy. With Lafarge on his knees, Rich followed up with the butt of his shotgun flattening him before spinning around, meting out the same to the other officer.

Helix limped forward. 'Good job, guys. Do you know these two?' He approached the steps and signalled to Gabrielle.

'No. The one you shot might have buggered off if we had something to give him, but not the other guy. Didn't like the look of him. Not sure he'd have been so easy to persuade.'

Helix crouched next to Lafarge, his head tilted. 'Hmm, good. Then they don't know you either?' He picked up Lafarge's smouldering cigarette and pinched it out.

Rich relieved Gabrielle of one of the bags as she looked down at the two officers and then back at Helix.

'No. They're not dead.' He holstered his P226. 'More importantly they haven't seen us. Come on we need to move.'

19

The focal point of the Victorian promenade since 1837; Herne Bay's clock tower stood resolute, its four dials facing the cardinal points of the compass. Clad in white Portland stone, barely visible through the ivy, it had been a gift to the town from Mrs Ann Thwaytes, the wealthy widow of a London grocer. The first hints of dawn were reaching into the summer sky to the east, silhouetting the remains of the medieval church at Reculver. The skeletal remains of a children's playground, shrouded in a tangle of brambles and hawthorn, laid under a thick finger of shadow pointing west, towards the frail bandstand. A child's shoe lay abandoned beneath the rusting slide, its strawberry colour bleached out by the passing years.

Helix turned his face into the breeze and listened to the hoarse squeaks of the juvenile seagulls harassing their parents on the rooftops, the waters of the marina lapping at the hulls of the boats and the tinkling slap of the halyards against the empty flag poles and masts. Nothing but nature. No cars jamming the promenade, no kids squealing in the playground, no Essex navy with their jet-skis wave hopping offshore. The arcades and cafés were silent. Generations of people had simply vanished. His redeployment back to London, after the worst was over, had hammered the point home. Mile after silent mile.

Helix dropped onto the top step of the clock tower base, next to Gabrielle. 'I love that smell of the beach. It reminds me of when we were kids. Warm pebbles, salt water and seaweed.' He scanned the horizon with his binoculars.

Gabrielle rubbed her arms, the light breeze ruffling her hair. 'Looks like it was a nice town. It must have been a great place to grow up.'

'It was mostly. You're not cold, are you?'

She pinched the sleeve of her jacket. 'In this stuff? No, I'm fine. Just thinking about Dawn and my arms hurt from carrying that bag. I hope the guys got back OK.' She tucked her hair behind her ears. 'I'm sorry about that, Helix. But as soon as Andy told me, I just had to help.'

'I understand. It was a risk though and that's something we can't afford.'

'Helix, can I ask you something?' she said, looking down at her feet. 'Would you have killed those policemen if I hadn't been there?'

He lifted the binoculars back to his eyes. 'If you hadn't been there, I wouldn't have been there.'

She leaned back on her elbows, shielding her eyes from the sun. 'That's not what I meant.'

'Whatever it takes to keep you safe. It was the best option for us. Hopefully it won't cause Andy and Rich any hassle.'

He wasn't sure if hope would be enough. Lafarge had the makings of trouble, there was something about him. Andy and Rich could look after themselves; people had learned fast how to survive. Another couple of troublemakers buried in a field or in the woods wouldn't attract much attention.

'So, where's Ethan?'

Helix lowered the binoculars and rubbed his hand over his head. 'The worst place for a borderline aquaphobe.'

'I was going to say, for someone who doesn't like water, you're spending a lot of time looking out to sea?'

'I've been dreading this part.' He handed her the binoculars.

She sat up, elbows on her knees. 'So, where am I looking?'

'Can you see the wind turbines out on the horizon?'

'Difficult to miss them.'

'Scan left and tell me what you can see.'

'Turbines, more turbines, wait. Five dark blobs on the horizon.' She lowered the binoculars. 'What's that?'

Helix snorted a laugh. 'Helix Towers, as Ethan likes to call them.'

'He lives out there?'

'Afraid so. I'm just glad it's calm today. They were an enduring feature of our childhood, mysterious and always there on the horizon. We used to make stories up about them as kids. At one time, you could do a boat trip out there from Whitstable.'

Gabrielle raised the binoculars again. 'Calm so far, but I'm not so sure about the weather looming up behind them. How far out are they?'

Helix rubbed his chin. 'About nine miles and thanks for pointing out the weather,' he laughed. 'Their real name is Red Sands Forts. There used to be several them in the Thames estuary and other places dotted around the country. Some people refer to them as Maunsell Forts, after the original designer. They were put there as part of the defences against the Germans in the Second World War.'

'How did Ethan get out there? How does he manage?'

Helix got up and leaned against one of the fluted columns. 'All excellent questions and he'll love telling you about it. When we get there. Now we need to find ourselves a boat and the bigger the better.' He turned towards what sounded like a swarm of persistent mediabugs coming from a boat tied to the slipway.

'Thought the media had tracked us down for a moment.' He nodded towards a small drone hurrying towards them. 'I think that's our ride sorted.' It swooped across the water, scattering a small flotilla of gulls.

Gabrielle scratched her head. 'Might be easier by boat.'

The drone banked and slowed, its six rotas suspending it in a steady hover in front of them. A small camera peered out from its belly, scanning between them. Helix gave it a two-fingered salute. The drone buzzed at a higher pitch, as if offended, before returning to the boat where it had been waiting.

She brushed the dust from her backside and stood next to him. 'I assume that's something to do with Ethan as you haven't shot it?'

'I told him we'd come here or to Whitstable,' he said, pointing up the coast. 'There's probably another one waiting up there.'

'So why did we come here if Whitstable was closer?'

Helix turned and smiled at her. 'I wanted to show you where I grew up. Thought we might get an ice cream but looks like we're out of luck. Come on.'

* * *

Helix held Gabrielle's hand as she climbed into the back of the boat. He passed the rucksack and her medical bag and stepped back from the edge. Gabrielle stowed the bags in the small cabin at the front. Closing his eyes, he turned away as the familiar black and white images pressed in. Clouds of bubbles swirling in the depths, thrashing arms and legs, his own muffled screams, shimmering faces, outstretched hands, his fingers clawing for the sunlit surface out of reach above, the taste of sea salt. A tug on his arm. His eyes snapped open.

'Helix, are you OK? What's wrong?'

'I told you. A minor fear of water.' The drone buzzed overhead. He raised his fist at it.

'There's two life jackets in the cabin. Put one of those on. It might help a bit.'

Gabrielle climbed back onboard and brought out one of the buoyancy aids. Helix untied the ropes fore and aft before stepping aboard.

He found his footing as Gabrielle headed back towards the cabin. 'It looks straight forward from what I can see. There's an on and off switch, a wheel and a lever which I am guessing is the accelerator,' she reported.

He slumped onto one of the side benches, tossing the life jacket on the one opposite, leaving her to take control of the death trap he now found himself in. The boat drifted away from the quay, followed by a slow silent forward motion. The whining pitch of the electric motor rose from under his feet. It made sense. It wasn't as if you could get diesel these days. But the smell just wasn't the same.

The granite block wall of Neptune's Arm drifted by as they left the jaws of the marina and accelerated into open water. Helix glanced back at the billowing cloud of disturbing tiny bubbles in the propeller wash, his grip on the gunwale turning his knuckles white. The drone buzzed up from the roof of the cabin and led the way.

20

The seven structures comprising Red Sands Forts clung on to the south east corner of the Thames Estuary wind farm array. From above they resembled a nest of dark brown ticks lodged in the pristine white fur of a pedigree cat. Their name suggested a rosier, more optimistic image but the reality was a dull pallet of beiges, browns and greens, with the sea contributing white depending on the mood of the wind. The box-like structures had been camouflaged in their youth, a cloak of invisibility to fool the Luftwaffe, but time and weather had picked away at the disguise. On cloud-free days, when the sun was at the horizon, the shades of brown would warm to a short-lived hue of orange.

Helix clambered over the edge of the boat onto the metal platform between the four barnacle encrusted legs of the creaking structure. Heaving on the rope that Gabrielle tossed from the rear of the boat, he pulled the transom closer. A convenient cleat provided a place to loop the rope and tie it off. Gabrielle passed up the bags and pulled herself up via his outstretched hand. She grabbed at his arm as a voice echoed from above.

'Welcome to Helix Towers, distinguished fugitives.'

Helix grinned. 'He's an acquired taste, I'm afraid. Got everything?'

'Yes. I think so.'

He untied the rope, tossed it back into the boat, and shoved it away from the platform. The drone hovered above before dipping into the cabin and settling on the control panel.

'Helix. What are you doing? How are we going to get back?'

'We've only just arrived. Come on.'

The lift emerged through the floor of the pod they'd disembarked beneath. Lit by three grimy skylights, the aroma was sea salt and stale tobacco that drifted on the breeze from one of the small windows set into the wall. Rusty tears streaked the paint-chipped walls. Helix ran his hand over the rough sawn timber of a pair of home-made bunk beds bolted to a wall. A green army issue sleeping bag hung off the bottom berth. 'I see he still hasn't learned to make his own bed.'

Gabrielle perched on the arm of Burgundy coloured sofa that looked as old as the structure itself. The neighbouring tatty brown armchair appeared to be of the same era. A used plate and empty cup fought for space amongst the clutter on top of a folding metal table. A single stool stood underneath. Amongst the detritus, Helix found a tobacco tin. He opened it and sniffed the contents. He smiled. 'Looks like he's been busy. Last time it was pick your spot on the floor and get your head down.' He leaned into the small fridge and examined the contents. 'I apologise in advance for the medieval toilet facilities. Unless he's made some improvements there too.'

A discarded dumbbell lying next to a weight bench caught his foot. He heaved it up and weighed it in his left hand. 'I wouldn't challenge him to an arm-wrestling match if I were you.' The rest of the weights rattled as he placed it back on the rack.

'So, where's he hiding?'

'He's in his man cave, the one at the centre, hub of his universe. There's a walkway from this one across. Come on.'

The heavy metal door complained as he slid it open and stepped onto the twenty-five-yard walkway that linked the two structures. With his eyes fixed ahead, he bolted forward, not pausing until he reached the platform opposite. Gabrielle caught up as he heaved the door aside. He ducked under the low frame and into the chilly smoke-filled space. Eight large monitors cast a broad pool of light illuminating Ethan at his workstation. Helix waved away the fog as he dropped his rucksack. He turned to the sound of the efficient electric motor that propelled his brother across the smooth floor towards him.

Ethan swerved to a halt. 'Where the fuck have you been?'

They hugged each other in a tangle of thick arms. 'Nice to see you too, dip-shit.' He ruffled his blond hair. 'You need a haircut and a shave. You're letting yourself go. And where are your legs?'

'Over there. Where are your fucking manners?'

Helix stepped aside. 'Sorry. This is Gabrielle.'

'Sorry about the smoke, Gabrielle. Nice to meet you.' He looked back at Helix. 'Bloody hell, Nate. She's a lot nicer in the flesh than you said.'

Helix held his hands out. 'Sorry. But I warned you.'

Gabrielle took Ethan's hand. 'Hello, Ethan. Thanks for helping.'

Helix opened the windows before pausing next to the monitors. Ethan had been busy. There was a mixture of documents, video feeds (some of them paused, some playing in real time), radio chatter coming from speakers, social and mainstream media. 'Did you sort out my new CPU?'

'They're on the bench over there.'

Helix turned as Ethan buzzed towards him. 'They?'

'Yep. I've separated the location tracking from everything else. So, the next time you need to disappear, you can take it out but stay in touch. Mind you, not that our former colleagues will be able to track you anymore.'

'Former colleagues? Have we been dishonourably discharged?'

'In a manner of speaking. It didn't occur to me to ask, but they've revoked all my access. They clearly don't know about the other three administrator accounts I have. And you are AWOL and wanted for harbouring a fugitive from justice and for murder. Fancy a brew?'

Helix turned to Gabrielle and raised his eyebrows.

'The tea can wait. Let's crack on. I want to get those installed. I'm fed up with hopping around.'

Helix took off his boots, dropped his trousers and peeled off the strip of gaffer tape from the back of his leg, exposing the neat incision. Gabrielle stepped up alongside him. Her eyes scanned the screens through the thin finger of smoke rising from the fat joint in the ashtray.

Ethan manoeuvred himself behind his brother. 'Can you lift your foot, or do you want me to do it for you, ducky?'

Ethan caught it by the ankle, resting it on the edge of his chair before poking his fingers, and the new CPUs, into his brother's leg. 'Done.'

Helix staggered as his foot hit the floor. 'It's not working.'

Ethan raised his eyebrows and turned to his bench. He double tapped a keyboard, the smouldering joint held between his lips. 'Right. Stand to attention, right arm held out as if offering your arm to lady at a dance, not that you would know.'

Gabrielle watched over Ethan's shoulder. 'Is there a problem?'

'No problem. Apart from him. Here we go. You'll like this bit.' He offered her the joint.

Helix raised his eyebrows. 'Never had you down as a smoker.'

She smiled. 'Not since university. But I am fond of this particular pharmaceutical herb.'

'Love this girl.' Ethan slapped his hand on the bench. Right, let's go.'

'OK. I'm ready. Get on with it.'

'Yes, sir. Running diagnostics.'

Helix tensed as a ten-inch blade sprang between the second and third knuckle of his right hand and a second one from his elbow. He extended and retracted them four times in succession to a sound similar to that of running a sharpening steel along the edge of kitchen knife. 'That looks good.'

Gabrielle coughed and took another drag on the joint.

Helix parted his feet. Another blade sprung through the material at the front of his sock, before retracting again. He repeated the cycle four times. 'Standard military prosthetics with a few enhancements,' he said, smiling at her. She didn't look convinced. Maybe he should have waited.

She gave a shallow nod and a grimace before handing the joint back to Ethan.

Helix gave Ethan's hair a tug. 'Everything looks good, Bruv.'

Ethan turned to one of the other screens and watched a real-time feed from his brother's eye. 'OK. We can test night vision, thermal and strobes later, I don't want to destroy our optical nerves. Check the range finder and the laser sight.'

Helix turned away from the bench and looked across the room. Ethan leaned in, watching the measurement reading overlaid on what Helix was seeing. 'Range finder good. Laser?'

A red dot appeared on the opposite wall. Helix left his P226 in the holster, he could check the calibration later. She'd seen enough.

'Nate. The sight.'

'Later, Ethan. It's all good. Let's have that brew.'

* * *

Ethan wasn't one for sugar-coating things; he had a flair for the succinct with a garnish of bluntness and little regard for the sensitivities of his audience. Helix perched on the edge of the bench next to him, and Gabrielle took the blue bucket seat on the opposite side. Ethan flexed the fingers of his holo-mits, leaned back in his seat and began organising exhibits, expanding and contracting them between his thumbs and forefingers, brushing and flicking them from screen to screen.

Gabrielle nipped at her lip. 'So, what have you got, Ethan? What crimes and misdemeanours have I been accused of since we've been incommunicado?'

Ethan cleared his throat. 'Alrighty then. More background on events at the Cenotaph. Those fellows that were asked to escort you from the premises are also confirmed as employees of Lamont Rhames, the same as a certain Colonel Terry McGill - disgraced. The vehicle was also registered to the same company.'

'Who is Terry McGill?' she asked.

'I saw you go into a side room with General Yawlander and your husband, hold on. Have you got a mug shot of McGill, Ethan?'

Ethan dragged a photograph of McGill onto the screen. He took a deep sip of his tea. 'Here he is, slippery bastard.'

'Oh him. Engaging blue eyes.' She nodded her head. 'General Yawlander introduced us. He didn't say a lot. Just stood there watching the fuss. How do you two know him?'

Helix glanced at Ethan, undecided whose version might be most appropriate. He went with his. 'He was Special Projects Programme Director at the MOD. Ethan worked with him. One of his projects went rogue and couldn't be stopped. That was how Jon was killed.'

Ethan laughed. 'It *could* have been stopped. Except old blue eyes didn't—'

'Don't, Ethan.'

'What, Nate? We're amongst friends.' Ethan drew on his joint. 'It was an AI project. Autonomous sentry bots stationed around our nuclear power stations. McGill had been cutting corners. He released it into the production AI before it was tested. It went rogue and killed forty-six at Dungeness and thirty-eight at Sizewell, including Jon. I tried to stop it and it cost me my legs.'

Gabrielle rested her hand on Ethan's shoulder. 'So, you were at one of the power stations?'

Ethan handed her the joint. 'No. I was with that twat, McGill. I was monitoring the automated testing. I saw it all kick off and tried to pull the plug on that sector of the AI. Because it was in production, the damage would have been catastrophic. But I didn't give a shit. I was watching guys being shot to pieces by fucking robots. McGill ordered me to stop. I ignored him and he stuck a couple of plasma rounds into each of my legs. I should be grateful I suppose, he could have killed me. Nasty things, plasma rounds;

I was left with two stumps that look like those over-cooked sausages nobody wants at a barbecue.'

'I'm sorry Ethan. I didn't realise... didn't mean to be nosy.'

'Ah, don't worry about it. You didn't kill Jon.' He dragged the image of McGill off the screen and tossed it over his shoulder.

There weren't many things that pressed Ethan's buttons, but Helix knew McGill was one of them. She wasn't to know, and it would have been difficult to avoid mentioning him. Ethan would cool down once he got into his stride. 'Why don't we start with Rachel Neilson, Ethan?'

'OK. Rachel. Last seen removing items from Gabrielle's gaff.'

Gabrielle chewed at the inside of her cheek. 'Have you found her? Is she alright?'

Ethan pointed to one of the other screens, hooked a video player from his control pallet and dragged it over. 'This is taken from the street cameras next to Rachel's apartment. I don't know who the gentlemen escorting her are, but their vehicle is also registered to Lamont Rhames. So, I suspect they are also under the command of McGill.'

Gabrielle raised her hand to her face as she watched Rachel help Lauren into the back of the large AV. 'Wait. Hold on. Is that guy carrying the holdall she had when she came to the house?'

Ethan froze the image and zoomed in. He manipulated and enhanced the segment containing the bag. 'One hundred percent, I would say.'

'Well, if that is my research, who are those people and where are they taking it?'

* * *

Helix ducked through the doorway and onto the link bridge. 'Those wind turbines will hypnotise you if you stare at them for too long.'

'Sorry. I just needed some air. I thought I would vomit again. Gagging Gabrielle.' She caught a strand of hair blowing in the wind and tucked it behind her ear. 'My research should have been safe at home. I removed as much as I could from the archives and put in a request for it to be purged from the backups. That should have been sufficient. Perhaps I should have destroyed everything.' She leaned against the handrail. 'And now Rachel, the only person left whom I could trust...'

'I don't think she was acting alone, Gabrielle. The email from your account, which I know you didn't send, and then getting into a Lamont Rhames vehicle. It looks like classic McGill.' He'd said it, but was it classic McGill? What was he going to do with the research? It was way out of his field. Ethan said he'd been appointed as Director of Security. The title suggested a different remit and nothing to do with project delivery or research. 'Do you mind if we go back inside? I want to check something with Ethan.' He needed to join the dots. What did Lamont Rhames want with the materials? It looked like Rachel had delivered them. But why take her and the kid?

'Ethan. What else have you got on Lamont Rhames?'

'What else do you want to know?' He put a fresh spliff between his lips and lit it.

'Usual stuff. Companies House details, assuming they're registered in the UK and if not, where? Accounts, directors, shareholdings, major clients and subsidiaries.'

Ethan cracked his knuckles as he interlaced his fingers. 'Should be easy enough. How far back do you want to go?'

'Just the current position. We can always dig deeper if we need to.' He patted Ethan on the back as he got to work.

Gabrielle settled next to one of the windows and resumed her turbine watch. 'It's so quiet and peaceful out here,' she mused to nobody in particular. Her fingers failed to suppress the yawn that escaped as she leaned her head against the edge of the frame.

'I've been thinking about something your husband said, after we came down from the Mobile Forensics Unit,' Helix said, joining her at the window.

She snapped her head up from the window. 'Justin. Which thing? It was plenty of ridiculous hot air from what I remember.' She hooked the sleeves of her shirt over her thumbs and crossed her arms.

As much as Helix hated to admit it, Wheeler was right about access to the lab. He wouldn't have a clue what was down there and the only other person who would have known their way around as well as Gabrielle was Rachel. Siding with the enemy wouldn't go down well, but they were treading water. 'What if the same people Rachel was with had interfered with Miriam's medication?'

'What? But nobody else has access to the apartment. Ethan didn't see anyone other than me, Justin or—' She flattened her hand at the side of the window, the other to her mouth. 'Rachel?'

It was the only thing that made sense. Contrary to all the evidence, Gabrielle wouldn't have made such a basic error. But it did nothing to link the theft of the materials with Miriam's murder. 'I bet she knows her way around the lab as well as you. No?'

'Of course. But... why would Rachel want Miriam dead? I already told you, Helix. She was Miriam's friend, too. It makes no sense.' She marched across to Ethan and helped herself to a joint from his tobacco tin. 'You should try one of these, Helix. Or maybe you already have and it's addled your brain.' She lit up as if she'd been a lifelong smoker and tossed the lighter back on the bench.

Helix looked to the horizon and the gathering clouds. The wind had picked up, the rotation of the turbine blades more urgent now. The flat calm of the sea had surrendered, its surface rippled like the sand-flats at low tide. Somebody had switched the medication. But it was unlikely that Gabrielle could have strangled Miriam. The men with Rachel were a different matter. That said, the only person on the CCTV at Miriam's apartment was Gabrielle. How convenient. 'How's it going with the background checks on Lamont Rhames, Ethan?' he said.

Ethan spun his chair around and crossed to the fridge by the door. 'Sofi's working on it. Shouldn't be long.' He pulled the fridge door open. 'Drink anyone?'

Helix helped himself to a bottle of water. 'Who's Sofi?'

Ethan peered into the fridge. 'Drink, Gabrielle? We have water, water, or water or vodka. Russian.'

Gabrielle leaned back on the bench and shook her head. 'No thanks. Maybe later.'

Ethan took a bottle of sparkling water and twisted off the cap. 'So Fecking Intelligent – SoFI. She's my AI. She'll pull everything there is, sort and prioritise it and present it in a readable format for us mere mortals. She's very good at what she does and great company on chilly nights at sea.' He winked at Gabrielle as he rolled back to his bench.

Helix took up position at Ethan's shoulder as he checked the AI's progress. Ethan pointed to one of the screens bringing up what looked like a 3D wireframe schematic of the planet with the lines of latitude and longitude. Against some of the points where the lines intersected, a page-like icon blinked. Others had smaller spinning globes. The rate at which the icons appeared accelerated.

Ethan nodded. 'I like this bit.'

Gabrielle leaned on her elbows. 'What's she doing?'

'She's almost there. Listen.' He tapped his finger on the virtual keyboard under his hand. The room echoed to breathy moans and murmured syllables that increased in tempo as more and more icons appeared on the screen. 'Come on Sofi. That's it, girl. That's the place. Oh yeah. Don't stop.'

Helix put his hand over his eyes and peered at Gabrielle between his fingers. She smiled back, her hand on Ethan's shoulder as he laughed and writhed in his chair. Sofi concluded her work with one final, excruciating moan from somewhere deep inside her software. Ethan clapped his hands together. 'Anyone got any tissues?'

Gabrielle passed him the joint. 'So, how was it for you?'

'Ha. Excellent. Told you, Nate. This one's a keeper.'

Helix grinned and scratched his head. 'I don't want to be a party pooper, but can we get back to the point?'

Ethan rotated his wrist and opened his fingers, as if holding the 3D image in his hand. He rotated the orb left and right. 'Nope.' He tossed the object towards another screen where it expanded and flattened into a two-dimensional entity-relationship diagram, the intersection icons spreading and separating. 'Better.' His hand brushed the surface of the bench. The icons pulsed. 'OK. She's filtering now. This'll only take a minute. It looks like Lamont Rhames is one of several companies that are all related. Back in the day, they used to call them shell companies. Basically, bad people hiding bad things. This will filter out all the noise and leave us with a list of names and affiliations in a kind of hierarchical organogram.'

The relationship diagram dissolved to the left, leaving behind a series of tiles that organised themselves into vertical silos with lines linking them. His eyes widened as names and images appeared on the tiles. 'Anyone familiar, Gabrielle?'

She shook her head. 'Not so—' Her eyes widened as she leaned closer to the screen. 'Valerian?'

Helix blinked at the screen. Now they were getting somewhere. Twenty-seven companies, across three continents, all linking back to the Lytkin family with Valerian Lytkin as the head of the snake. Boom. He glanced past Ethan. Gabrielle's head was down on her arm. He walked around Ethan and laid his hand on her back. She flinched and pushed herself up.

She turned and looked up into his eyes. 'Cerberus.'

Helix tapped Ethan on the shoulder. 'The emails.'

She nodded. 'How could I have been so blind? Oh my God, it was staring me right in the face. The last two, Ethan. The first of them was sent three days before Miriam's death and the second came the day after. Look.'

```
We always hurt the ones we love and let
them hurt us.
          Cerberus.
```

```
I warned you. Remember the past, think
about the present and consider the future.
Time's up. Time to share. Don't squander
this opportunity. Join me or regret it.
          Cerberus.
```

Ethan tossed his empty water bottle into the bin. 'Cerberus. From Greek mythology. Sometimes referred to as the Hound of Hades. A huge three-headed dog who guards the gates of the underworld to prevent the dead from leaving. Lytkin's military R&D facility just outside Berlin. On screen three.'

A huge bronze of a snarling three-headed dog stood on top of a granite plinth guarding the entrance to an anonymous building that could be mistaken for a bank, or other corporate headquarters.

Helix took a long sip of his water, nodding his head. 'Scary.'

Gabrielle cleared her throat. 'He was interested in Greek mythology. He used to come up with all sorts of obscure names for experiments.'

'Who?' said Helix.

'Valerian Lytkin. He was so pleased with himself when he came up with Empusa for the discovery.'

Ethan lit up another spliff and took a deep drag. 'Also from Greek mythology. You'll like this one, Nate. A beautiful demigoddess with flaming hair, one leg like a donkey and the other made of brass. A bit like you. She preyed on human blood and flesh.' He picked a small strand of tobacco from his lip.

Helix leaned back on the bench and stretched his neck and jaw. 'What else have you got on Lytkin, dip-shit?'

'Valerian Lytkin. Age forty-two. Graduated from Cambridge with a PhD in microbiology and genetics. Only son of Anatoly Lytkin, pharmaceutical and industrial titan. Lytkin senior was of Russian origin, born in St Petersburg. His wife, and Valerian's sister, were abducted and never seen again as they tried to flee from Kiev when Ukraine started to disintegrate. Lytkin senior and junior escaped unscathed. It was his companies that won the contracts for seventy-five percent of the work to regenerate London in the post-pandemic years. Way too close to the Government. Survived numerous accusations of fraud and malpractice,' Ethan concluded, twin jets of smoke streaming from his nostrils.

Gabrielle dragged the blue bucket seat over from next to the door and sat, her elbows on her knees. 'Valerian was only a child. It took years of counselling to help him overcome what he witnessed when is mum and sister were abducted. He inherited everything when his father died. He has a sharp business brain and a talent for science. His team could have found the cure. We were just fortunate. In the four years since his father's death, turnover has increased by about seventy percent and the group has grown through acquisitions, many of which have been referred to competition authorities. In the last year, he has also acquired two military research and development companies, merging them into a centre of excellence in Germany.'

Helix shrugged. 'Impressive. And I thought you said you hadn't seen him for a while?'

'I haven't. But I read the news, Helix. Justin brought him home for dinner a few years back. He'd been on some charm offensive with one of the committees in Parliament. He was all smiles, told me how well I would fit into the company, what great potential I had, the work we could do together.' She picked up Ethan's tobacco tin, her fingers playing over the engraved logo on its lid. 'I guessed what he was up to. So, I just smiled and said I would think about it.'

'And the research you said he was so interested in, can you tell us more? You said you developed it over two years and what you found—'

She held up her finger. 'What I found, Helix, was classified for a reason.'

21

Ethan had regularly dined out on the fact that he was one of the few to have cracked the security of the legendary Government-grade bio-stack, an example of which Helix handed back to Gabrielle. That she even had one was surprising, but given its contents, he now understood her reaction at Down Street. 'Was there a viable pathogen in your lab at the observatory?' he asked.

Gabrielle nodded and rested the smouldering joint on the edge of the ashtray.

'How much?'

Her hand shook as she poured another generous measure of vodka into her cup. 'Enough,' she said, turning the bio-stack over in her palm. 'You don't need a lot. You saw for yourself. It's a micrscopic organism. In its mutated form, the size of the host is irrelevant. It reproduces at an expnential rate when it comes into contact with the right conditions.'

'Can you stop it, once something is infected?'

Gabrielle helped herself to another drag on the joint and passed it to Ethan. 'You've between ten and fifteen minutes.' She folded her arms. 'I was working on ways to manipulate the timescale to make it more predictable. Different hosts have different characteristics that affect the outcome.' She stretched back in the seat, her hands over her face. 'But the end's always the same.'

'Can it be reverse engineered?'

'Would take years 'f work.'

'Would it take Valerian Lytkin years, with his resources and your research material?'

She laughed. 'I was being kind earlier, when I said he was talented. He's good. But I don't think he's that good.'

Helix rubbed the line of his jaw. He wondered if perhaps the weed was keeping her mellow, but the vodka wouldn't help if she kept at it. The light in her eyes had reduced to an ember. 'So, why did you do it?'

She swayed alongside him and perched on the edge of the bench. 'Why'd I do what?'

He caught the vodka bottle as it teetered away from her thigh. 'Take the research to a new level, several new levels in your words.'

'Bad times,' she said, her hand on his arm. 'Just after Evie died. I needed something to distract me, some s'rious research. Most people round me were being kind, wanting to give me time to heal. But they didn't understand. I needed a purpose. I kept asking for new assignments. They kept forgetting to give 'em to me. I had the research. What if Valerian was right when he said it had p'tential? I decided to take it forward, and that I'd share whatever profits... I hoped it might 'suage the wrong I did by patenting it for myself.'

'So, what made you stop?'

'Helix, how can you ask me that with what I've just shown you?'

He shrugged. 'Life at the other end of a microscope.'

'Life and death. And it might be at the end of a micr'scope, but use your imagination. Don't you think we've all seen 'nough death? My team, all scientists, fought for two years to find the cure and look at how many people we lost along the way. We got there, m'be just in time. The country and the world needed *that* discov'ry.' She waved the bio-stack in front of his eyes. 'They don't need this one.'

'So, how much time do we have? How quickly can Lytkin work it out?'

'He'll be able to work it out, to a point, but he can't complete it without me.'

Helix pushed himself away from the bench. He tapped his way through Ethan's media library of apocalyptic films. The whole situation had shifted sideways when they got to the remembrance service. There hadn't been time think about the updated forensics report, much less tell Gabrielle about it. Why wasn't there anything in the media about it? If there was evidence that could exonerate her, Yawlander would have got it out there. If Wheeler knew, he'd be shouting it from the roof of Parliament.

Gabrielle bumped into him and put her hand on his shoulder. 'Any music on there?'

'Probably. Can't vouch for his choices mind.' He lifted her hand from his shoulder and turned. 'Anyone fancy a brew?'

'Not f' me, thanks.'

Ethan declined with a wave. Helix let her hand slip from his, leaving her nodding along to a tune in her head as she scrolled through the music catalogue. The bottles and kettle on top of the fridge vibrated in time to the reggae rhythm of Gabrielle's selection. Helix tapped his foot along, staring into his empty cup. It was good choice, but for a different time.

Gabrielle danced along, her eyes closed, hands swaying over her head. 'Wise man say...' She shimmied and swayed around in small circles. 'Take my hand...'

She'd drifted into the music, free from the horror as she swung her hips and wrapped her arms around herself. The functional clothes he'd made for her were a good fit, leaving nothing to his imagination. It was the 3D printer programme that designed them. Nothing to do with him, but he wasn't complaining. Snug was the word he was looking for. But if he was choosing, it would have been that flimsy dress she'd worn that first evening at the Meridian. Ethan was right, she was even better in the flesh. Christ. OK, time to spoil the fun. The kettle clicked off and he filled his cup.

He caught Ethan's eye and signalled by moving his finger across his throat.

The music cut out. Gabrielle's hands flapped down to her side. 'What happened?' She frowned at Ethan.

Helix stirred his coffee. 'Sorry to interrupt but there's something else we need to talk about.'

Gabrielle pulled herself up onto the bench, her legs crossed at the ankles. 'Sounds ominous.' She picked up the vodka bottle.

Helix nosed the hot coffee. Maybe he should have left the music on. 'I want to talk about Miriam. More precisely, what killed her.'

He fixed his eyes on Gabrielle, her previous smile now absent. 'How long would it have taken for the injection you gave Miriam to cause the cardiac arrest that killed her?'

Gabrielle sniffed. 'Wow. Where'd the chilled Helix go?'

He ignored the dig. It was obvious she would be pissed or stoned, probably both before much longer. 'Look. I'm sorry but we don't have the luxury of dancing around our handbags. How long?'

She nursed her cup in her lap. 'It's slow release. Administered once a day, but even in the concentrated form, it wouldn't necessarily act any faster.'

Helix sat with his elbows on his knees, his cup between his hands as he looked over the rim towards her.

'What's with the look? It wasn't designed to kill someone, Helix. If I'd wanted t'do that, I'd have chosen something else.'

'She was alive when you left at around 02:00?'

'I told you she was. Where you going with this?'

'It's important, Gabrielle. Time of death is always important. The housekeeper found her at around 07:00. That's a five hour window.'

She slipped off the bench and rubbed her arms. Propping herself against the doorframe, the breeze caught her hair. Ethan tapped Helix on the shoulder and tilted his head towards the screen. Helix checked what he was referring to and nodded.

Gabrielle rummaged in her bag next to the door. 'Three hours. Maybe less, perhaps more.' She rattled a medication bottle as she returned to the bench. 'But no more than four.' She tipped two of the green pills into her palm and swallowed them with another mouthful of vodka.

Helix raised his eyebrows at Ethan. 'OK. Have we got an estimated time of death on there?'

Gabrielle leaned on him, her hand on his shoulder.

Ethan pointed at the screen. '03:00.'

Helix could smell her hair as she leaned over, staring at the screen. He let her read the text, at least she might understand it. Her hand twitched on his shoulder, he spun up from the chair spilling his coffee as she jerked away. He caught her by the shoulders.

'Asphyxiated?' Her fingers twitched from her lips to her temple.

Helix steadied her and steered her back to the seat. 'How sure can you be with your estimate? Based on what you said, the injection wouldn't have been that quick. No?'

She shook her head. 'No. There's no way. I didn't smother her, Helix.' She groped for her cup. 'She was getting better.'

'It's alright. I know. Did you see anything else in that report that might help?'

She sighed. 'No. Nothing. There's no bruising around the lips or the nose. No damage to the inside of her mouth. There doesn't seem to have been any fibres or foreign matter around her face. Some of her other meds might have made her a little drowsy, but she's a fighter, Helix. If someone was trying to s'ffocate her, she'd've put up a fight.' She waved away the joint that Ethan offered.

Helix scratched his chin. 'OK. It puts a diff—'

Gabrielle slapped her hands on her thighs. 'Hold on a second.' She leered towards the screen. 'What's the date and time on that report?' she said, scanning back to the top. 'You knew all of this before we went to the Cenotaph. Why didn't you say?'

Helix coughed through the smoke. 'That's why I wanted to know how long the medication would have taken to kill Miriam.'

'You could've arksedsme that on the way there. That report proves it wasn't me. If you had told 'em, none of this would've happened. We wouldn't be here now.'

Helix shifted away as Ethan rotated his chair. 'They have the report, Gabrielle. Who do you think I got it from?'

Helix shrugged as she stared back at him. 'Everything you told me on the way to the service was enough for me to know something was up. The fact that someone is supressing this report just adds more proof to this being some kind of conspiracy.'

Gabrielle stamped her foot. 'S'now you have your evidence. Ethan can send a copy to someone?'

'Not yet. There's more to it.'

'Poppycock. I want to go back. No more running. What more do you need? Ethan, can you get that boat back?'

Helix took her arm. 'Not yet. There's more to it.'

She twisted away. 'You just said that! This is all about Valerian.'

'Maybe. I hate to repeat myself again, but there *is* a lot more to it.' He moved Ethan's overflowing ash-tray to one side.

Gabrielle wandered to the door and out onto the walkway. She faltered, clinging to the handrail, her face turned down to the water.

Helix poked around inside his jacket pocket. His fingers settled on the half-smoked cigarette he'd picked up from the road next to Lafarge.

Ethan looked up. 'You want a light?'

'What? No.' He tossed it on the bench. 'You remember our sticky-fingered friend from—'

Gabrielle weaved her way back from the door. 'Scuse me, I'm going to bed.' She closed her fingers around the neck of the vodka bottle and retraced her steps in a wide arc, as if the floor was listing to star-board. She paused, steadied herself on the doorframe and pressed forward, bumping her way off the left and right railings to the neighbouring accommodation pod.

'Someone's going to have a nice hangover in the morning,' Helix mumbled.

Ethan grinned. 'So, old sticky fingers. Miriam's apartment. Lafarge. The last two meetings with you didn't go so well.'

'Yes and no.' The fingers and joints of his hand clicked as he flexed them. 'And, if you remember, there was no mention of his DNA at the apartment, or from contact with Miriam in the updated report.'

'Hmm. But nothing on the CCTV either.' Ethan drew on his joint. 'I know where you want to go with this.'

'How far back did you check the CCTV?'

'Seventy-two hours. Conveniently, the only warm bodies were Miriam, coming and going, Doctor G and the housekeeper.'

'So, nobody else went into the apartment.'

'Not through the door. Not until after the house-keeper called it in.'

'Why conveniently?'

'Don't you find it strange that there's a working CCTV system that far out?' He tapped ash from the glowing tip of the joint. 'CCTV that just happens to capture someone entering and leaving the apartment just before Prof. Miriam turns up dead.'

It was a reasonable point. Helix leaned down next to his brother. 'Have you got satellite imaging of Chatham, around Miriam's place?'

'Yep, should be easy enough. Not sure when it was last updated.' Ethan cracked his knuckles. 'What are you looking for?'

'Somewhere you could set up an observation point. I reckon someone was watching them.'

'OK. Leave it with me.'

* * *

Helix lingered outside the accommodation pod long enough to register the change in the wind; stronger than earlier, and now from the west. It scratched white crested troughs in the moonlit sea, tossing it in handfuls at the seaweed-frilled bases of the wind turbines, their blades high above sweeping graceful arcs through the night sky.

He slid the door open. Gabrielle appeared in silhouette against the interior light of the fridge. 'Looking for snacks?'

'Bloody 'ell, Helix. You scared me.' She closed the door. 'Have you come to tuck me in?'

Helix pressed a switch set into the doorframe. Three bulkhead lights conspired to light the room with pools of weak sulphur-coloured light. 'Just wanted to make sure you've got what you need. It's colder than it was.'

She sniggered. 'Can you turn off the lights, please? They're spoiling the mood.'

He flicked the switch, reverting to the filter of his night vision – the room rendered in hues of white, grey, and pastel green.

The vodka shimmered silver as she pressed the bottle to her lips and took a clumsy swig, wiping away the excess with her thumb. 'I like the shadows. A place to hide. Where we can be who we really are.' She tilted the bottle onto the table, her hands ready to catch it, should it stagger.

'If you want to take the sofa, I'll take the top bunk. There's a spare sleeping bag. It should be warm enough.' Not that she would notice. She'd be unconscious in about thirty seconds. He stopped as she brushed his arm.

'What if I'm not warm 'nough? You going to keep me warm?'

In a heartbeat, but not when you're like this. 'You'll be fine, snug as a bug.' He reached up to the top bunk, pulling down the football-sized sleeping bag, releasing it from its compression sack.

Her jacket, t-shirt and trousers lay in heap at her feet. 'I've plumbed the depths of the abyss, Helix.' She tousled her hair loose. 'But Miriam showed me where to find the light.'

Helix shook the sleeping bag out and unzipped it. 'I guess we've all been there, Gabrielle.'

'But dark places aren't always filled with dark things.'

He smiled as he spread the sleeping bag out on the sofa. She's getting philosophical now. OK, she's half undressed. Just need to get her in the bloody thing now. 'There you go.'

'I've found deep pleasures in dark places.' She crossed her arms under her ribs grasping the bottom of the tight-fitting bra. Lifting upwards, she peeled it off and added it to the pile. 'Have you found nice things in dark places, Helix?'

This was the nicest so far, but he wondered how much she'd remember in the morning. 'Never thought about it to be hon—'

She hooked her thumbs into the side of her knickers and wriggled them down, stepping to out of them as they crumpled around her ankles. 'Is this nice?'

He gave his head a double-handed scratch. What are you doing, Gabrielle? He cleared his throat. 'That's you ready for bed then. Sorry we don't provide those fancy bathrobes you get in expensive hotels.

Ethan must have forgotten to order them. Just can't get the staff these days.'

She closed her eyes and crossed her arms over her head. She began to sway, whispering the same reggae riff she's chosen earlier as she danced out small steps around her discarded clothes. 'But I, can't help, falling...'

Helix's lips moved, 'in love, with, you.'

A combination, of Ethan's herbs, the vodka and whatever the green pills contained wasn't helping her coordination. The dance became erratic, the lyrics lost amongst the mumbles. He stepped in just as she caught her foot amongst her clothes, flailing as she tripped. He caught her and introduced a nimble dance move of his own, steering her next to the sofa. 'I've got you.'

She hung limply in his arms before stepping up onto the sofa, hanging onto his hand as the cushions sagged. She danced to a halt, her hands on his shoulders. Closing her eyes, she pressed her lips to his.

He felt the soft tip of her tongue, urgent against his as he closed his eyes. He put his hand to the nape of her neck. No. Don't. Not like this. She's hammered. He pulled away, separating their lips.

Her eyes flickered open. 'I want you.' She tilted her head, pressing her cheek to his, her warm breath on his ear. 'Fuck me, Helix.'

Her hands slipped from his shoulders, ripping his shirt open from collar to waist. She dragged her nails in tracks down his chest, across his stomach, one hand at his belt, the other feeling him harden. He took her hands and raised them to his lips. This is not you. He kissed the back of each hand and looked into the deep wells of somebody else's eyes. This is not you. She crumpled to the sofa, her head on the cushion, eyes closed, one foot on the floor.

The kiss I'll remember. The words I'll forget. They're not you, Gabrielle, they're the drugs and booze. Fifteen seconds I reckon. He counted twenty before doing up his shirt. With his hand half way towards the open flap of the sleeping bag, he froze as she yawned. She settled, pulled her foot up and rolled onto her side, hands folded under her cheek. He draped the sleeping bag over her and turned towards his own bed.

22

The wind turbine blades hung under their own weight, their supporting columns glimmering like silver birch bark in the early sun. The winds predicted by the AI weather agency had failed to materialise, barely troubling the Beaufort scale, proving the point that artificial doesn't mean accurate.

Two of the three occupied pods showed early signs of life. The central pod where Ethan worked, and sometimes slept, hissed and crackled with the sound of frying eggs and something masquerading as bacon. It looked, smelt and tasted like bacon; its provenance was a mystery, but nobody cared.

The facilities pod hummed with the sound of the desalination plant and water heater. Steam plumed from the window, carrying the scent of soap and shampoo aloft. Gabrielle leaned into the torrent, her hands pressed to the wall, waiting for the water to run clear. As the last of the suds vortexed around her toes, she turned and smoothed her hair back over her head. The faint tightness at the base of her skull suggested a headache that had so far failed to materialise.

She stepped from the shower and unhooked the towel she'd found at her feet when she woke up. Helix must have left it there for her. She buried her face in its soft folds, trying to stitch together the events of the previous evening. Mary-Jane: a lot; vodka: too much; dancing: embarrassing; Mandrax? Christ. How many did I take? The post-mortem report: asphyxiation. Cerberus. Valerian. She patted herself dry and tossed the towel onto the chair with her clothes. Helix? Was he there, or was that when we were together with Ethan? Dammit. She would have taken the full-fat hangover if it had come with the promise of a more lucid recollection of the night before.

The absent threat of nausea announced itself in the pit of her stomach as she entered the central pod. She closed her eyes, although the eyes have nothing to do with the olfactory senses. 'Morning, guys.' She turned to the kettle, hoping that not seeing what Helix and Ethan were eating might go some way to fending off her urge to vomit.

'Bacon and egg sandwich?' Helix said.

'Not just now, thanks.' She spooned instant coffee granules into a cup. 'Maybe a bit of toast.'

Ethan dusted breadcrumbs from his green Royal Mechanical and Electrical Engineering (REME) regiment t-shirt. 'How's the head?'

'My head's fine, at the moment. Not so sure the bacon and eggs are helping my stomach though.'

Helix dropped two slices of something resembling bread into the toaster next to the kettle.

She glanced at him. 'Hi.' She chewed at her thumb nail. It felt like her first time with Miriam - well, the morning after at least. The night before was similar in a multitude of ways to last night. She shook the thought away.

The kettle boiled with a breathy hiss. Helix filled her cup. 'You OK?'

'I'm fine, thanks. Slept like a log. You?' She smiled. 'I know – apart from the snoring.'

'And the farting.'

She punched his arm. 'I did not.'

'Ow! How do you know? I might have recorded it.'

She looked into his eyes. Was he recording now? She dropped a lozenge of sweetener into her coffee. Was he recording last—

The wheels of Ethan's chair squeaked across the floor as he moved along his bench. 'You've received an invitation, Doc.'

She rubbed her arms, grateful to escape the myriad questions about the night before that were popping in her head. She pulled up the chair next to him. 'What have we got then?'

Ethan held out his hand, a joint smouldering between gloved fingers.

'Oh, no thanks, Ethan. Bit early for me.'

'Link to a video conferencing application. Mr Lytkin would like to have a chat.'

'How do you know it's him?

Helix delivered the toast over her shoulder.

'Thanks, Helix. Sorry, Ethan. You don't have to answer that. When was it received?'

'About an hour ago.' Ethan dangled the joint from his bottom lip. 'You're already late.'

Valerian always hated tardiness. Who cares? Let him wait. 'What do we do?'

'All we need to do is click the link. What's our game plan, Nate?'

Gabrielle took a grateful bite of toast as Helix wandered up alongside her.

He studied the email, scratching his neck. 'Let him lead. Offer no more than you have to. Let's see what he wants.'

Ethan reached across the bench, pulling up a webcam attached to a mini tripod. 'Nate and I will stay out of sight. I'm sure he knows we're all together, but there's no need to confirm it. Oh, and it's best not to mention the updated forensics report. He doesn't need to know we've seen it.'

The simple act of eating a slice of toast had become difficult. Chewing was difficult, swallowing worse. How much did he know already? How much use had Rachel been to them? Was she OK? And Lauren, that poor little girl. She licked the butter from her fingers. 'Alright, let's get this over with.' She pushed the remains of the toast away.

Ethan shuffled right. Helix perched on the bench next to him. The cursor on the screen in front of her moved and changed as Ethan clicked the link. She took a deep breath, sat up straight and willed her heart to slow. A solitary word "Connecting" blinked back at her. The wind whistled out of tune through a gap in the window behind her. The word vanished, replaced with her own thumbnail image in the bottom right corner, and then nothing. She turned towards Ethan. 'Is something wrong?' Ethan shook his head, watching his own monitor.

Her shoulders tensed, the screen now filled with the blurred face of Valerian Lytkin. He moved away from the camera, the crisp HD image coming into focus before her. He still hadn't shaken off his haughty air of arrogance. She gritted her teeth.

Lytkin reclined in his tall leather chair, tossing his right leg over his left. 'Hello G-Gabrielle. You look tired.' He brushed something invisible from his trouser leg and folded his hands in his lap.

She exhaled. 'I wondered how long it would be before you came out of hiding, Valerian.'

'I've been here in m-my office the whole time. Why would I be hiding?'

She tucked her hands under her thighs, her breathing beginning to catch, the iron grip of tension in her neck. 'You've murdered my best friend, stolen my research and taken my friend and her daughter hostage. What do you want?'

'M-Murder, theft, hostage taking? My goodness.' He drew his finger over his left eyebrow. 'Where do you get such ideas? I think you need to ch-choose your friends more carefully.'

Her chest heaved as she slammed her hands down on the bench and lunged towards the camera. 'And what about Miriam?' The words resonated from the metal walls. She clenched her jaw and swayed away from the screen.

'We always h-hurt the ones we love and let them h-hurt us,' he said, steepling his fingers.

She hammered her fists on the bench. 'You bastard! I hate you!' A thin bead of saliva attached itself to her chin. 'I knew it was you.'

'I believe it was you who administered the f-fatal injection, Gabrielle. How c-could it have been me?'

She fought the growing lump in her throat. 'What do you want, Valerian? I'm exhausted. Just tell me. What do you want?'

Lytkin loomed closer, his elbows on the polished glass of his conference table. 'I wanted to c-congratulate you. You really have moved our discovery forward. You remember? The one you p-patented. In your own name. But this isn't a squabble about the p-patent. That will come, if it has to. No. I confess, I need your help. Let me explain.'

She grimaced, slumping back in the chair. 'I wish you would get on with it.'

A CCTV recording stuttered to life on screen. A spectacled, white-coated man in a lab, small cages containing white rats lining one of the walls. Lytkin provided the voice-over. 'As you s-seem in a hurry Gabrielle, I'll fast forward a little for you. This is Doctor Vincent B-Berdiot. He turned out to be a disappointment. With dear Rachel's help, we'd been helping ourselves to your de-developmental pathogen and I entrusted it to him to see if he could re-engineer what you s-stole.'

Ethan and Helix stared intently at their screen.

She turned her hands in her lap. Rats. Oh God. What

has he done? She stole a glance at Helix and Ethan.

'Hello, Gabrielle. Nice to have you back with us. As I was saying, B-Berdiot moved us out of the world of the petri dish and microscope, and on to rodents and non-human primates.' He tapped the table top again. A brief video clip showed the devastating effects of the pathogen on the rats. She clamped her hand to her face as the clip advanced to three macaques. The time-lapse moved on to their less dramatic death with the caption: multiple organ failure at 48 hours. 'At this point, Berdiot reaches an im-impasse. He does not understand why the p-pathogen from one batch would work and the other didn't. His amateur analysis revealed nothing and having squandered most of the viable p-pathogen, he had nowhere to turn.'

She glanced away as Lytkin's image reappeared on the screen. She sipped her lukewarm coffee. It did nothing to soften the edge in her voice. 'So that's why you stole my research and the remaining batches from my lab?'

'Rachel thought it might help.'

Coffee slopped from her cup as she slammed it on the bench. 'Rachel is only involved because you are holding her and her daughter hostage. Stop trying to make her out as a willing accomplice.' She wiped coffee from the rim of the cup with her thumb. 'So, you have no idea how to reengineer the viable pathogen. No idea why one batch would work on rats but not the other.'

Lytkin nodded. 'A good summary. But n-not accurate. Berdiot helped more than he realised.' The frozen image of the lab reappeared on the screen. 'Let me show you.'

The video advanced, showing Berdiot as he turned towards the airlock door. 'Watch, Gabrielle.'

Berdiot looked under the bench, bent down and picked up a rat from the floor.

'No. No. No!' she screamed, recoiling as the rat exploded, spattering Berdiot with blood and gore.

The clip froze again as Lytkin's face returned. 'Yes, Gabrielle. I can see it in your eyes. Sometimes it's necessary to accelerate our l-learning and while Berdiot's experiment with the macaques was a failure, this one exceeded all of our expectations.'

Gabrielle pressed her hand to her mouth, drawing short, sharp breaths through her fingers.

Doctor Berdiot's final moments were played out on the screen, his blood spattering the lens of the camera filming the macabre spectacle. The final catastrophic demise of the scientist was followed by several smaller explosions, as the rats in the cages inhaled the vaporised blood or groomed themselves, ingesting the exploded human viscera.

She fought a growing urge to vomit, held her breath and turned away from the screen. Whilst telling herself to breathe, she was reminded of Robert Oppenheimer's words, quoted the from the Hindu scripture: "I am become death, the destroyer of worlds". The atomic bomb had underlined its appalling ability to kill with devastating collateral damage. Ebola had killed hundreds of millions; she had helped to stop it. But in the months before the outbreak, she had unwittingly overseen the genesis of its cousin.

Lytkin stroked his chin, preening an invisible beard. 'T-Two batches, Gabrielle. One works, the other one doesn't. It's that simple, and I don't know why. That's what I want. I want to know why and I think you are the key.'

She sniffed and turned back to face him. 'You said Berdiot had squandered all of the viable batch.'

Lytkin smiled. 'Trust, Gabrielle? I am sure you'll forgive me. But over the years, I have tried to trust people but in my experience, the only person you can trust is yourself. I t-trusted you with something precious, and now look at where we are.'

She swallowed the bitter memory of a terrible choice. 'And after what you did to Berdiot, you expect me to help you?'

'No. Listen to me. He was n-nothing to you. You didn't even know him. I want you to help Rachel and L-Lauren. Rachel has been so obliging. It is amazing what a m-mother will do to protect her child. We should know, but then it doesn't always work out. Does it?'

Gabrielle's shoulders slumped. She'd failed Eve and failed Miriam. Who was next?

Lytkin's face disappeared, replaced by a different CCTV feed. Rachel was perched on a stool, dressed in a white lab coat with an angry bruise just below her right eye. Her own research notes, in their pastel green folders, were strewn across the bench.

'Where's Lauren?'

Lytkin obliged, the image cycled. Lauren was shown wearing her own child-sized lab coat, going from cage to cage feeding the macaques under the supervision of a lab technician. 'She's turning into a p-promising lab assistant. She's been helping to prepare for her own experiment. She's going to help with the next phase: human to human exposure. Small scale. No p-pun intended.'

Gabrielle sighed. 'You are certifiable, Valerian.'

'Maybe I am, G-Gabrielle, but the choice is yours. You have a chance to redeem yourself and save the lives of two more people whom you hold d-dear.'

She searched his dark brown eyes. "The eyes are the window to the soul." What soul? The quote was from her fleeting experience with the Bible, just after Eve had died. Science and religion had rarely, if ever, been comfortable bedfellows. But there was one verse from that terrible time, when she was looking for anything that would bring meaning to what had happened: "Matthew 6:23. But if thine eye be evil; thy whole body shall be full of darkness. If therefore the light that is in thee be darkness, how great is that darkness."

She returned Lytkin's stare. 'OK. I'll do it.'

'You'll do w-what, Gabrielle?'

She folded her arms. 'I'll show you why I'm better than you. I always have been and always will be.'

Lytkin ran his hand over the top of his head. 'Thank you, Gabrielle. R-Rachel keeps telling us that she can't explain some of the research without you.'

'And she's not going to, Valerian.'

'I d-don't understand, Gabrielle. I thought I told you.

The m-men looking after Rachel and L-Lauren are not subtle, but can be persuasive. It would be s-such—'

'Be quiet, Valerian.' She closed her eyes for a moment. Forgive me Helix, but this is the only option. 'It's me in exchange for Rachel and Lauren. That's it.'

* * *

North, east, west, it didn't matter which way she looked. It was like being trapped in a maze of doubts. Countless routes delineated by the turbines. Each alley pointed to a different solution that waited just over the featureless horizon. And then, just as you'd convinced yourself which one to take, doubt climbed into your head and rearranged the signposts.

Gabrielle wandered barefoot to the opposite window. South was different. South shimmered green through the haze. She leaned at the side of the window, her arms folded, head resting against the chipped paint. South was verdant, wide open gardens and trimmed lawns. A little girl around six, maybe seven years old, with long straw-blonde hair getting in her eyes as she ran and danced along. A bright pink helium-filled balloon, with a yellow unicorn figure bobbed behind on a ribbon. Her pretty red dress with white polka dot pattern, white cardigan over it, buttoned at the top, and her shiny red shoes and short, white ankle socks. 'Evie.'

'Did you say something, Gabrielle?'

'Oh, Helix. You scared me.' Her eyes flicked back to the flat calm sea, the distant shimmering coastline and the three letters etched in the dust on the window: EVE. She pressed the tips of her fingers to the glass and swallowed the dream. 'What time is it?'

'Just before two. I wanted to make sure you were OK.'

She laughed. Of course she wasn't OK. She'd just agreed to surrender to a madman. 'I'm fine. Thanks.'

The sofa creaked under Helix's weight. 'Why did you do that?'

'I just need a bit of time on my own.' She made herself small in the corner opposite him. 'The call confirmed everything. It felt more personal, but I know it's not just about him and me.'

Helix cleared his throat. 'No. I meant why did you agree to exchange yourself for Rachel and Lauren?'

She hooked her elbow over the back of the sofa and twisted around to face him. 'Is Ethan always listening and watching?'

Helix sniffed a small laugh. 'Why's that? Are you worried about what happened last night?'

She raised her fingers to her lips. 'What happened last night?' She hated not knowing. Did she make a fool of herself? 'Was it the embarrassing dancing? He wasn't watching, was he?'

'No. It's OK. He wasn't. I can turn him off whenever I feel like it. He hardly sleeps, so I need some peace from time to time.' He smiled. 'And you were fine.'

'Was I in bed when you came in?'

'Not quite, but you were getting ready.'

She leaned forward, her hands pressed over her face. So, how did all my clothes end up on the floor? 'What happened, Helix? Did I throw myself—'

'Listen. It's fine, no harm done. Ethan's herbs, the pills, and bit too much loopy juice on top of a hairy twenty-four hours. We all need to de-pressurize sometimes.'

'So, I did...'

'It was a goodnight kiss. That's all.'

'I'm so embarrassed. Sorry, Helix. And my clothes? I wasn't wearing them when I woke up.'

'That was before the kiss.'

Humiliation complete. She couldn't remember, but she could imagine. Bloody hell, Gabrielle, he deserves better than that. 'I'm so sorry.'

'I told you, it's fine. And thanks for the kiss.'

She leaned across and tapped him on the thigh, happy that he put his hand over hers. 'Thank you.'

'Anyway, why the exchange?'

If she had told him what she was going to do, he would have scoffed at the idea, told her she was mad, insane even. She turned his hand over, studying the intricate engineering. 'Valerian knows the answer. He knows why one batch works and the other one doesn't. But he needs me to prove it.'

Helix scratched his ear. 'I don't understand. If he knows, why doesn't he just get on with whatever warped plan he's got for it?'

'He's got no further use for Rachel and Lauren, except to get to me. He's shown what he's capable of and I'm not prepared to let anything happen to them. You heard what he said: you always hurt the ones you love and let them hurt us.'

'Meaning?'

She nodded. 'A veiled reference to Miriam and Eve. But there's more to it than that.'

'Go on.'

'I told you how we became close when we were working together.' She shuffled back to her corner of the sofa. 'We'd fallen out over the discovery and then with the outbreak, it drove us further apart, literally, not just emotionally.' A shallow sigh, slipped from her lips. 'A month after the outbreak, I found out I was pregnant with his child.'

Helix reached into his pocket and fished out his breath mints. 'Not the best timing.'

'No. With everything that had happened, everything that was going on, the country needed us.' She waved away the offer of a mint. 'I had to choose. What could I do? I couldn't bring a child into the world under those circumstances.'

He shook a mint from the box. 'Did you tell him?'

'Yes, but I made a hash of that too. It was after the cure was discovered, we got back in touch, began to talk again. I wondered if we might patch things up. Anyway, long story short, it didn't work out and I told him.' She pinched her bottom lip between her fingers. It had felt like she'd broken his heart. 'He said he would never forgive me.'

'So, is it personal or business?'

She knitted her fingers together over her head and pushed her elbows back. 'The latter. But sweeter if he can get back at me in the process. I doubt he has any intention of using it for good, as in pesticides or something to benefit humanity. Given his recent investments in military R&D, that'll be the direction he wants to take it in.'

Helix got to his feet and shoved his hands in his pockets. 'That doesn't bear thinking about.'

'No. A person wandering into a crowd, perhaps not even aware that they've been infected, they drop to the floor, people rush in to help. You've seen what happens next. You're the military expert here, think about it. No battlefield hardware or software, the vector doesn't even need to be human. Why would anyone take any notice of the local fauna going about its business... monkeys, rodents, snakes, birds?' She stared up at him as he stopped pacing. 'Sorry.'

'And after the exchange, once he's got you?'

'Rachel and Lauren will be safe.' Wouldn't they? She shook the question away. But then, I never imagined that they might be at risk. Why would I? It's got nothing to do with them. But after this... 'They were only taken because you stopped those men—'

Helix half-turned towards the door. 'So, this is *my* fault?'

'No. Hold on. That wasn't—'

'McGill wouldn't have kidnapped them, if I hadn't taken you?' He took a step closer to the door, pausing with his hand on the handle. 'But at least I wouldn't be on the hook for three murders I didn't commit.'

'Whoa, Helix, just a second, I was—'

He spun back around to face her. 'No. You're welcome. You'd been threatened and you were scared shitless.'

She shifted her weight to the edge of the sofa. He

was right, she had been terrified, even more so when those men separated her from the General and Justin.

He shook his head. 'Bollocks! I should have followed orders and left you there.'

'No. Helix, listen.' She pushed herself up from the sofa. 'That's not what I'm saying. Valerian needs *me*.' She slapped her hands to her chest, jarring out the final syllable.

He clenched his jaw. 'Jesus Christ! You said that earlier. Why? Why you, Gabrielle?'

'Why are you yelling?' But why would he understand? She was the only one who knew. That was the whole idea. 'Because I put a lock on the science.'

She flattened her hands on his taut chest, surprised at the force of his heart pounding beneath her fingertips. 'He knows what it is, but he can't unpick it without... and before you yell at me again—'

He threw his hands up. 'Enough with the riddles, Gabrielle.' He heaved the door open, a salt-laden breeze rushed in around him. 'Just spit it out, will you?'

'DNA. The pathogen is engineered around my DNA. He needs me.'

23

Helix sat alone, monitoring the systems while Ethan took a shower. It sounded grander than it was, given Ethan's description of Sofi and what he'd designed her to do. Who was watching whom? Maybe Ethan was trying to make him feel useful. AI still made him nervous. It was ubiquitous and so integrated, you never knew if you were talking to a person or a machine, unless you could look them in the eye. Even then, he sometimes wondered.

So, which was the real Gabrielle? The one at the Foreign and Commonwealth office, smiling and greeting people like old friends; or the gentle Doctor who tended Miriam and Dawn? Perhaps the meticulous scientist, who had unwittingly created a terrifying bioweapon? Or, maybe it was the drink and drug fuelled— No. That wasn't her. It was a front. No fucking way. He'd stake his life on it.

He took Ethan's overflowing ashtray to the door and emptied it into the wind. Scared shitless – that was harsh. Who could have blamed her? Lytkin's clearly got a screw loose. And when it's all over, what then? Back to that idiot, Wheeler, paraded around to embellish his political aura. When it's all over? Jesus. He wasn't sure they'd arrived at the middle, let alone the end.

Tossing the ashtray on the bench, he frowned at the home page for Lamont Rhames Military, still on the screen where Ethan had left it. He now understood how she was connected to the pathogen, but what did that mean once he had her? Her celebrity was probably the one thing that offered her protection, but what would people think if they discovered that the creator of the cure had turned her skills to the military application of something almost as destructive? Maybe Lytkin would keep his silence in exchange for her cooperation. She wouldn't be named on any of the patents or credited with the work. But what could she do if he reneged on any business agreements? Perhaps she didn't care.

Ethan clattered over the connecting bridge and swung through the door on his prosthetic stubbies. He power-crawled himself across the floor, his fists driving him. He reached up a thick arm, gripped the arm of his chair and heaved himself up.

'Someone's in a hurry,' Helix said.

Ethan lit up a new joint and tapped a keyboard, bringing the screen back to life. 'Aye. Something weird going on at the bank. Where's my ashtray? You making a brew?'

Helix pushed the ashtray towards him. 'Something weird at the bank?'

'Yeah. Usual dull domestic stuff. When someone pays something into your account, you get a message. That sort of thing. Except you don't normally get four small payments from the same person within ten minutes.'

'I wouldn't know,' he replied, checking the water level in the kettle. 'Can't remember the last time I looked at my account.'

'You've got nothing to worry about, a nice nest egg growing there for the autumn of your life, and those necessary final expenses.'

Helix made the tea and foraged for snacks while Ethan zipped up and down the edge of the bench, tapping keys and scowling at screens. Among the random selection of field rations, he unearthed a packet of Mayfly Thins – "rich in protein, fortified with vitamins" the packaging proclaimed. Who ate this shit? 'Here you go, squashed-fly biscuit?'

Ethan tossed one of the disturbing green biscuits into his mouth as he logged into his bank account.

Helix decided he wasn't hungry, dropping the packet next to Ethan. 'What the fuck have you been up to?'

Ethan spun his chair around. 'What? You've got a similar balance. Remember, just like Mum used to say, "I treat all you boys the same".'

'Where are these small payments then?'

'Here you go. Four transactions: three for less than a quid and one for £1.86.'

Helix peered at the screen. 'Yawlander?'

```
17:12 Yawlander Ref: Go Deposit £0.10
17:15 Yawlander Ref: Here Deposit £1.86
17:16 Yawlander Ref: See Deposit £0.52
17:20 Yawlander Ref: Drafts Deposit £0.66
```

Ethan laughed. 'Clever, huh? He's not the only genius in the house. Have you worked it out yet, Nate?'

'Yawlander is a tight fucker?'

Ethan nodded. 'Possibly true.' He pointed at the screen. 'Go – Here – See – Drafts. 10 dot 186 dot 52 dot 66. It's an IP address, and there's probably a mail server or a mail account where he's left a message in the drafts folder.'

'Why the drafts folder?'

'Very old-school, but still works. Nothing gets sent. We both access the same account and add notes to the draft email that never leaves the account, so nothing goes over the network for anyone to see.'

'I knew he wasn't involved in this shit with McGill. What are you waiting for?'

Ethan exchange his joint for another biscuit. 'Hold on. Let's not get carried away. It could be a clever ruse.'

This proved it. What had happened at the Cenotaph was a set up. Yawlander knew Helix preferred to keep things low key. It was out of character. Why would a General get involved in sorting out a substitute wreath bearer? But maybe Ethan was right, they needed to stay alert. He pulled up a chair and looked on as he connected to the IP Address.

'Here we go. Good old Yawlander. It debunks the theory that all senior officers are a bunch of useless Ruperts.' The email expanded onto the screen.

Lytkin has no intention of exchanging Rachel and Lauren for Gabrielle. McGill will use them as bait to get to her and if he can, to get to Helix.

The exchange will take place at the children's playground in the Meridian at 14:00 tomorrow. They won't notify you until 12:00. It's off the books, so there will be next to no chatter about it on the grid.

They are also announcing in the media that the reward for information leading to Helix's, Gabrielle's and Rachel's capture has been increased to £300k, thanks to an anonymous donor. They will say that they suspect you are all implicated in attempting to sell a secret scientific discovery to a terrorist organisation.

I'm in no doubt that Lytkin intends to weaponise the discovery, but it's not clear if he has a particular target in mind, or if he intends to sell to the highest bidder. He has to be stopped.

Yawlander.

Helix tapped Ethan on the shoulder. 'Good work. Not sure how much of this we should share with her ladyship.'

Ethan leaned back in his chair stroking his chin. 'None of it. Once McGill's got his mitts on her, as far as he'll be concerned, everything else can go to shit.'

'Hmm, we need to work out the moves and we're going to need some help.'

'Help? And where's that going to come from, the clone army?'

'No. Someone who owes Gabrielle a favour.'

24

A small, red brick farmhouse, at the bottom of a spoon shaped valley, announced someone was at home with a curly plume of white smoke that rose from its chimney. SJ looked down from the edge of the woods. A pair of grey squirrels squabbling above gave themselves away with their constant chit-chit-chit. When she closed her eyes, it was just like the woods back home on the Welsh border – the same sounds, the same smells. She'd argued with Bo about heading for London. He'd questioned what use she could be to her sister, but her mind was made up. She'd not been there when Gabrielle needed her before, she wasn't prepared to let her down again.

Marvin, the lad who had brought the news about Gabrielle's troubles, had the brilliant idea of stowing away on one of the autonomous trucks that ran between Cardiff and London. He'd confided in SJ that he'd been planning his own trip, for when he was older, and could show her how to break into one of the vehicles and where to hide. With his help, she was soon ensconced in a cramped, stuffy space, between pallets of boxes, on her way across the Severn bridge. Tired, stiff and hungry, she'd remained hidden for two hours in a yard just east of Swindon. When the truck showed no signs of moving on, she'd got down and sprinted into the neighbouring woods, relishing the fresh air and relative cool.

She unhitched her small rucksack and swung it onto a fallen tree encrusted with fungi. The earthy smell of the damp leaf litter rose from her feet, as she pushed herself up next to her bag. It had been years since she'd been to London. Gabrielle's letters and cards, begging her to visit, told of a comfortable – although sometimes boring – life in the pristine Meridian. She may have visited sooner were it not for Justin. The typical politician who would say anything to get elected, or stay elected. She'd berated him about London's priorities for funding anything outside of its boundaries. Naturally, he defended the Government, even more so since his appointment as Chancellor. At least now he couldn't blame anyone else. But he was the only other person she knew in London and in the current situation, the only one who could help. She pulled her hair back behind her ears.

She should have been there for Gabrielle when Eve passed. But with no job and living off the land, it wasn't as if she could just jump on a plane. She was hiking with Bo. They were camped in the mountains overlooking a deep blue glacial lake. The spot was idyllic. Life was great. Bo was great. She'd found true happiness. They had just finished supper when something made her look up from the moon's reflection in the lake. For no reason, she'd felt a stab of panic, as if plucked off that mountain and crammed into a crowd of people fighting to escape a burning building. She couldn't rationalise it at the time. But when she learned of Eve's death, she realised the panic attack had been at almost the exact moment her niece had died, leaving Gabrielle devasted.

She rummaged through her bag, pulling out a battered blue pocket photo album. Three of the loose pages almost fluttered to the ground. Returning them to their place, she opened the album at a photo of Gabrielle and Justin, the proud parents presenting baby Eve to the world. She stroked her finger across their faces as a loud crack from behind her almost caused her to drop the album. She slid off the stump, dislodging a clump of chicken of the wood fungi and turned. A thick-set, middle-aged man and a lanky teenager, who reminded her of Marvin, stared back.

The older of the two cradled a shotgun in the crook of his arm. 'You lost?' he said, pushing his hat back on his head, scratching his forehead. 'Not from around here, are you?'

'No. Just taking a break.'

The lad shifted, a question on his face. He fidgeted with the three wood pigeons and two cock pheasants he had looped over his shoulder on a piece of string.

'I'm on my way to London.'

The older man laughed. 'Walking to London?'

'I got dropped off at the yard a way back and just wanted to have a rest and get some fresh air. Was hoping to find somewhere to eat,' she replied, pushing the album into the bag and fastening it shut. 'It looks nice here.' She crunched her way through the leaves towards them, her hand extended. 'I'm SJ, by the way.'

'Frank. Frank Hollander, and this is my son Jack,' he nodded, returning her hand shake with a firm one of his own.

'Nice to meet you both. Can you point me to the nearest village?'

Frank pointed in the direction of the farm. 'Other side of the valley, about three miles. My daughter, Chrissy, will be getting supper ready. You can eat with us. Come on.'

The invitation was heartfelt. That's the way it had become after things had calmed down. Those who'd survived had quickly learned there was more to be gained by working together than working against each other. SJ and Bo had turned up near Tintern in a similar way and had been made welcome. They'd blended in and felt no need to move on. She fell in alongside Frank as they waded through the long grass, down the slope from the woods.

She glanced back over her shoulder. Something was making her uneasy, about Jack? Maybe he had an invisible friend. Jack concluded his one-sided conversation with a nod and a twitch at the side of his mouth that threatened to break into a grin. Maybe he'd been eating the wrong kind of mushrooms.

The farm was typical of the times, with neat, well-tended vegetable plots and a small but busy flock of chickens scratching in the yard outside the back door of the house. Four sheep, penned into a small orchard, bleated their own noisy welcome. SJ hesitated at the door as Jack rushed in, whispering something to his sister in the kitchen. She smiled at Frank.

He took of his hat, his hand extended. 'Please, come in.'

* * *

SJ rinsed the soap from her hands and turned off the tap. Through a narrow gap in the net curtains, she watched as Jack hurtled up the gravel track away from the farm on his bike. He stole a look back over his shoulder as he ascended the hill and rounded a corner, before disappearing from view.

She dried her hands. She couldn't go back to the truck yard. Towards the village, perhaps? No. It was probably where Jack had gone. She might walk into them. Walk into whom? Maybe he'd just gone to meet up with his mates. Jesus, SJ, turn down the paranoia.

The narrow stairs creaked underfoot. She tilted her head towards the kitchen door, craning to hear the hushed conversation between father and daughter. Turning at the foot of the stairs she found a second door standing ajar. Through the gap, a phone sat on a small table in the modestly furnished sitting room. She pulled the scrap of yellow paper from the pocket of her dungarees and stared at the number. Payphones were non-existent. Perhaps she could... that's if it even works. The smell of wax polish with a hint of dust beckoned her through the gap. Cradling the handset to her chest, she listened again in the direction of the kitchen. She bit her lip as she tapped out the number and waited. Come on, come on. A series of clicks and the hiss of white noise masked the quiet ringtone. Come on.

* * *

Punctuality was a habit that Justin Wheeler neither possessed, desired, nor respected. Terry McGill's precision arrival might have interrupted his lunch had the maître d' not diverted him to the lounge until summoned. His mood didn't improve as the door opened and McGill was ushered in. A persistent buzz at his wrist distracted him – his private line. What now? He pointed to an empty chair, turning away as McGill sat.

'Justin Wheeler speaking, hello.' He looked at his wrist. Swindon? 'Hello, I can't... Gabrielle? Is that you Gab—' He faced McGill and raised his eyebrows. 'No. I can hardly hear you, what did you— Bugger.' He peered at his wrist then back at McGill's deadpan countenance. 'Well, there we are Colonel. My wife appears to be in Swindon. Miles from the scene of your fiasco at the Cenotaph.'

'Thank you, Chancellor.' McGill rubbed his chin. 'I'll look into that.'

'I thought you might.' Wheeler regarded McGill over the rim of his porcelain cup. McGill didn't look convinced. Wheeler's left eye twitched as he inhaled the aroma of the coffee. 'So, Colonel. It is Colonel, isn't it?'

'As you wish, sir.'

'But that's how you introduced yourself at the Remembrance Day service, is it not?'

'That's correct, sir. Thank—'

'Odd that you've chosen to retain the title.' Wheeler sipped his coffee. 'Now you find yourself a civilian.'

McGill shifted and rested his hand flat on the linen tablecloth. 'I retired from the service, sir. It's not unusual for an officer above the rank of Captain to—'

Wheeler grinned. 'Yes. You retired – or were retired.' He studied the small plate of petits fours. 'After your fall from grace, or as you put it, your show trial, you were relegated to some dusty backwater, I recall.'

McGill cleared his throat. 'It was a military accident, Chancellor. Others chose to make it something—'

Wheeler laughed. 'Yes of course. I almost forgot. Major Helix and his brother, what was his name?'

McGill tapped his index finger. 'Ethan.'

'Thank you, yes. How did they put it?' Wheeler added a splash of cream to his coffee. 'Oh yes, a reckless derogation of duty and negligence. What a delicious sense of déjà vu.' He tossed a petit four into his mouth.

'Déjà vu, sir?'

'Yes. For you to be pitted against the Helix brothers once more. A rematch, a chance for you to right the wrong.'

'Hardly a rematch, sir. The court of enquiry interpreted the evidence. It was inconclusive.'

'Inconclusive, yes. Rather like your failed operation at the Cenotaph.'

McGill leaned onto the table, rubbing his hands. 'General Yawlander suggested—'

'So, it was General Yawlander's fault.' Wheeler folded his arms. 'Or perhaps he knows something different which, is why you're here and he isn't.'

'I'm not apportioning blame, Chancellor. The inter-agency cooperation between the MOD and Lamont Rhames was—'

Wheeler laughed, the upholstered seat teetering backwards as he stood. 'Here we are again. The blame culture still alive and well. First, it's Yawlander, then Lamont Rhames – anyone else, Colonel? You'll do well to remember which team you're playing for now.' He crossed his hands behind his back as he turned away. 'The tide is changing, Colonel. Lamont Rhames is the first of many public private partnerships. The only reason you are here is because Mr Lytkin convinced us that this would be too good an opportunity to pass up. An opportunity to show how effective the military and private enterprise could be together.'

Wheeler folded his arms, basking in the sun's warmth as it streamed through the tall windows. The steady ebb and flow of life played out across the junction of Great George Street and Parliament Street below. The Palace of Westminster stood on the other side of the gardens. Rumour had it that a vote of no confidence in the Prime Minister was imminent, no doubt to be followed by her swift resignation. Wheeler had plenty of support, but a few sympathy votes, thanks to his wife's predicament, wouldn't go amiss.

His presence at the shoulder of the Prime Minister reminded the public of Gabrielle's plight, portraying him as the strong leader in waiting, but also the sensitive, caring husband who was doing his best under difficult circumstances.

'I agree, sir. I have an update on Doctor Stepper.'

He'd almost forgotten McGill was there. 'Impeccable timing, Colonel.' Wheeler took his seat and topped up his cup. 'And fortuitous, given that Mr Lytkin is addressing the Defence Committee this afternoon.' He leaned forward, his left index finger stifling a twitch. 'Smart move, Colonel, making sure the boss isn't embarrassed in front of the client.' His hand slipped away, the escaped wink reinforcing his point.

* * *

SJ shoved the scrap of paper with Justin Wheeler's private number into the back pocket of her dungarees and wandered into the kitchen. The large rectangular kitchen table was draped with a wipe-clean, green checked cloth, laid for three as if someone had calculated the exact positions of the cutlery in accordance with the pattern. A vase with a small bunch of meadow flowers had been placed at its centre with the same precision. Frank shattered the symmetry with his random placement of the water jug and glasses. Chrissy glowered at him, unnoticed, as she turned a wooden spoon in a large, orange, cast iron casserole dish with metronomic precision.

'I saw Jack go off on his bike from the bathroom window,' SJ said, scraping a chair across the red terracotta tiles. 'Is he not joining us?'

'No. Bloomin' lad. He wanted to go off to the village to see his friends. He'll be back before it's dark, starving hungry.' Frank sighed as he sat down. 'The kids tell me you're all over the news. They sometimes see a programme at school.'

She perched on the edge of the hard wooden seat. 'That'll be my sister. I saw it myself before I set out for London. I'm going to visit her,' she replied, toying with the table knife. Maybe Jack had gone to tell his mates? Or worse, the local militia.

'Your sister? Must be your twin sister then.' He sipped his water. 'Chrissy tells me you're the spit of that Gabrielle Stepper.'

'Very observant, Chrissy.' She helped herself to half a glass of water. 'She's my twin, but we followed separate paths. I was in Canada during the pandemic and I'm sure you know all about Gabrielle.'

Chrissy's porcelain features cracked into an "I knew it" smile. The same smile with the same nod SJ had seen Jack make as they came down from the woods. She emptied her glass and refilled it.

Frank laughed. 'Yes, we have a lot to be grateful for, but I had no idea she had a twin. Canada you say?'

SJ sauntered over next to Chrissy. 'Hmm. Do you need a hand with anything, Chrissy?'

'Just the plates please. In the cupboard over there.'

SJ fetched the plates from the Welsh dresser as Chrissy lifted the heavy dish from the stove. She hesitated, looking at the vase. Frank recognised the problem and moved the errant blooms.

'That smells great, Chrissy.' Frank leaned towards the dish. 'So, when did you get back, SJ?'

'A few years back. I couldn't have come back sooner, what with all the travel restrictions and no money.'

'Hmm. OK, let's eat. That boy doesn't know what he's missing, eh Chrissy?'

25

Helix hefted the heavy dumbbell in sets of fifteen reps. Every bicep curl became an item on the checklist: logistics, personnel, equipment, tactics and contingency. Right kit, right people, right place, right time, plan for the worst, hope for the best. They knew the time and the place, but that was it. He exhaled, lowering the weight to the floor.

Ethan bumped him out of the way as he manoeuvred from the opposite end of the bench. 'You'll bust a blood vessel doing that. Move your arse, please.' His hands moved with an unusual urgency, working independently of each other across two virtual keyboards. 'Oh shit.'

Helix watched over his brother's shoulder, looking for clues amongst the blizzard of data filling the screens.

'Get your shit together. We have to move. Your escapade in Chatham is the talk of the town.' He hammered on the bench with his fists. 'McGill is ordering satellite and drone surveillance. Sofi's found them sniffing around her proxies and they're three hops away from locating us. She'll keep them out for a while but not forever.'

Gabrielle pulled on her jacket. 'But what about the boat? Can you get the boat back, Ethan?'

'Afraid not, Doc. We're going to get wet. Sorry, Nate.'

Helix prioritised items of kit from shelves, shoving them into his rucksack. 'How long have we got, Ethan?' He tossed a second rucksack to Gabrielle. 'Move your stuff from your bag to that. It'll be easier to carry.'

'About fifteen minutes max. for the drone. The satellite will be half that.'

Helix unhooked a utility vest from beside the door and dropped it on the bench next to Ethan. 'Where are your stubbies?'

'Under the bench.' He shuffled forward in his chair, slinging the utility vest over his shoulders and fastening it. 'Right, you two need to get out of here.' He folded a thin tablet computer in two and slipped it into the front pocket of his vest with his cigarette tin. 'I'll be right behind you.'

Helix passed Ethan his stubbies and turned to Gabrielle. 'Right, Gabrielle. I need you to go down onto the platform where we landed. There's a grey box on your left as you step out. Open it and press the red button. Once you've done that, wait for us. We won't be far behind.'

Ethan slipped from his chair onto all fours. 'I'll miss this place. I was getting used to the peace and tranquillity.'

'It's not going to be tranquil for much longer if McGill has anything to do with it. You ready?'

'No. You go to Gabrielle. I need to shut things down and leave a note for the milkman.'

* * *

A hexagonal, orange life raft squeaked and groaned as it was jostled by the swell against the rough edges of the platform. Helix grimaced as he stepped out of the cage. It was going to be like rubber dinghy rapids. 'Good job, Doc.'

'Where's Ethan?'

'He'll be down in a minute.' He knelt at the side of the platform, grabbing one of the exterior rope loops, steadying the raft. 'Do you want to jump in?'

Gabrielle dropped to her knees and rolled in, scrabbling to stay upright on the spongy surface. 'I'm OK. Is Ethan coming?'

'Yep. Here he comes.' He stood ready to help Ethan as soon as he landed. 'Come on, Spiderman.'

Ethan swung from arm to arm between the loops of wide cargo net secured to the underside of the pod. He hung for a moment above the platform before transferring to a second net and descending. 'All good?'

'All good. You ready?'

Ethan bear crawled to the edge of the platform. Helix grabbed the shoulder straps of his utility vest. 'Sorry, Bruv. This isn't going to be dignified.'

'I've been through worse. Come on. He's going to lift me into the raft, Doc. All you need to do is grab me and stop me rolling over the side.'

'OK. Ready.'

Helix heaved him into the raft with a shove in the back with his foot and released his grip on the straps. Ethan rolled across the spongy vinyl surface, knocking Gabrielle back to the opposite end as she tried to steady him. 'Sorry Doc, we don't have all the accessibility mod cons out here.'

Helix pulled off his own rucksack and slid in alongside them. 'Can you pull that red cord next to you, Gabrielle?'

The raft lurched away from the platform with a hefty slap on the surface of the water. Helix looked ahead towards the neighbouring wind turbine, the steel cable connected to the raft taut as they skimmed across the surface. He wiped the spray from his eyes. 'It should slow when it gets to the turbine but move in a bit from the side, just in case.'

Gabrielle and Ethan huddled in the middle of the raft as it rebounded from the seaweed stained surface of the turbine tower.

Gabrielle rolled up and onto her knees. 'What do you want me to do?'

'I'll slide past you and up onto the platform. Hang on to Ethan, then I'll pull him up.'

To describe the turbine tower as dry land was stretching the definition, but for Helix, anywhere was better than the life raft. He leaned in and grabbed Ethan by the shoulder straps, straightened his legs and heaved his brother onto the narrow, slippery platform. 'You alright there, Bruv?'

'Yep. I've got it. Grab Gabrielle and get rid of the raft,'

he said, latching onto the handrail. 'The drone can't be far out.'

Helix took Gabrielle's outstretched hands and pulled her up next to him. 'There's a door on the opposite side. Can you go and open it?' Zooming into the distance, beyond the rusting fort, he searched for the source of the low hum. 'Drone inbound. Five miles out. Let's move.'

Seeing Ethan on his way around to the door, he yanked a red plastic toggle on the outside of the raft, causing it to implode and disappear beneath the surface in a fizz of dissipating white bubbles.

He snatched up his rucksack and clattered around the platform to the door. He looked inside. 'Where's Ethan?'

'I thought he was with you.'

Helix sprung away from the door, retracing his steps around the circumference of the tower back to where they'd climbed out. 'Shit, shit, shit.' He looked below the platform, over his shoulder, 'Where the fu—'

Gabrielle pointed to a dark shape bobbing in the muddy green water like a cork. 'Helix. There.'

'Ethan. Fuck.'

'Helix, wait. I'll go. Wait here.'

He heard her words, but momentum was already carrying him headlong into his worst fear. He didn't see it, but he heard the crash of the water as he plunged below the surface. The cold pinched his face, the salt stung his eyes as he forced them open, trying to focus through the murk and the clouds of bubbles enveloping him. He thrashed and rolled, seeing the light above. He saw the hands reaching down and the muffled shouts. He kicked for the light breaking through the surface on his back. Gabrielle hung off the handrail. He waved her away. 'Get inside. Out of sight until we get back. The drone's not far.'

He rolled over, located Ethan and kicked again. Fifteen yards. Hold on, Bruv. He was getting nowhere. The current carrying Ethan was matching his stroke. He choked out a mouthful of water, filled his lungs, pressed his face into the water and struck out again. Five long strokes. He snatched a breath. Five more strokes. Seven yards to go. Another breath. Three strokes. Three yards. His arm bounced of something soft, he paused blinking through the water at the back of Ethan's head. He groped for his shoulder straps, spinning him around.

'Since when have you been able to swim?' Ethan sputtered.

Helix coughed and spat out another mouthful of water. 'What happened?'

'I slipped. Shit happens. We going to talk about it or get out of sight?'

He rolled onto his front. Ethan grabbed the back of his jacket. It wasn't the best breaststroke, but he dragged them back to the base of the turbine as the volume of the inbound drone grew louder. He shouted over the waves, water clogging his ears. 'Gabrielle!'

Rolling over, he pulled Ethan to him, clinging on to the platform with his free hand, starting to shake. 'Where is she? Gabrielle!'

Ethan tapped his shoulder. 'It's OK, Nate. You've got me. I'm fine.'

Gabrielle's steps echoed around the platform. She laid above them, her arm outstretched. 'Let me hold him. You climb out.'

Helix pushed Ethan toward her outstretched hand. 'Have you got him? Don't let him go.'

'I've got him, yes.'

'Are you sure?'

'She's got me, Nate. Go, fella. Lift me out.'

Helix pushed away from him, their eyes fixed on each other. He groped behind himself, locating the ladder before turning and clambering up.

He threw himself on the platform next to Gabrielle, reaching down and catching Ethan by the shoulder strap. Gabrielle rolled away as he pulled upwards, his knees under himself. Ethan caught the edge of the platform, clawing himself up onto his forearms. With a final heave, Helix lifted him clear of the platform and swung him through the door to Gabrielle, pulling the door shut behind him as the drone ripped overhead.

The gloom echoed to the sound of heavy breathing, interspersed with bouts of coughing and water dripping onto metal. Helix leaned forward, his hands on his knees, shaking his head at his brother.

Gabrielle put her hand on his shoulder. 'Are you OK, Helix?'

'I'm good, thanks.' He rubbed the water from his face. 'I'll survive. That was bloody close. You alright, Ethan?'

Ethan propped himself against the side of the wide metal tube. 'Yeah, I'm fine. Thanks, Nate.' He popped his cigarette tin open with his thumb.

'You're not going to spark up now, are you?'

'No. Just checking to make sure they didn't get damp.'

Helix glanced at Gabrielle and raised his eyebrows. 'We need to get off the surface. Ethan, you go first. I'll follow and then you, Gabrielle.' He positioned himself on the edge of the platform and strapped on his rucksack.

Ethan pulled on a pair of night vision goggles, swung over the edge of the platform and descended into the dark.

Gabrielle gripped a handrail and peered over the edge.

'It's fine, about fifty metres,' Helix said, tapping her leg. 'Platforms every ten so you can take a breather. OK?'

She nodded. 'I'll manage. After you.'

* * *

Helix reached up as Gabrielle lowered herself down the final steps. The sound of more aircraft at lower altitude fell through the gloom from above. 'Quadcopters. Come on. This way.'

Gabrielle latched onto the back of his rucksack, settling into the pace as they moved off. Helix scanned ahead. The dusty tunnel stretched out in the light green glow of his night vision. The heat was stifling, the air smelled of hot plastic and there was a faint hum from the high voltage cables that ran down the sides of the tunnel next to them.

26

SJ was grateful for the meal and would have eaten more, were it not for the tightness in her throat. Chrissy hovered around the kitchen sink as if attached by an invisible piece of elastic. When she thought nobody was watching, she would duck down, peering under the lace trimmed frame of the small window.

SJ scanned the table for something to clear to the sink. What was Little Miss Muffet looking at? She snatched up the empty water jug and almost toppled her seat over as she stood.

'You're jumpy, SJ.'

'Sorry, Frank. Just thought I would refill the jug.'

Chrissy shrank away from the window. SJ counted two vehicles making slow progress, a cloud of orange dust in their wake as they bumped over the rock-strewn track. 'Who's that?'

Frank joined them at the sink. 'AVs. No idea who they are, but I wouldn't have brought those things down that track. They'll have a hell of a job getting them back out. Those things aren't built for off-roading.'

The only people likely to be running around in AVs

outside London were the authorities. She snatched her rucksack up from the floor, next to the kitchen door. 'Thanks for the food. Think I'll head off.' She threaded her arms through the straps and tightened them. Frank was too full and too old to move at significant speed and SJ beat him to the shotgun standing next to the door. She snatched it up and waved it towards them. Frank stopped with his hands raised. She shuffled backed towards the door that opened onto the yard. She glanced over her shoulder before bolting, pulling the door shut behind her. Fumbling with the top lever of the gun, she pushed it to the right. Beyond the door, Frank waddled around the table. Move it. Move it. She broke the action and pulled out the cartridges. Pocketing them, she snapped the gun closed, released the forend and operated the lever again separating the barrels from the stock. Gotcha. She tossed the heavy barrels into the long grass, took the stock and sprinted across the yard, scattering the chickens. Hurdling the fence, she stumbled into the field and scrambled up the slope towards the horizon and the woods beyond.

In the shade of the tree line, next to a rotten stile, she caught her breath. Two identical matt-black AVs pulled up next to the farmhouse, disgorging two uniformed officers from each. 'Thanks, Jack. You little git,' she said, keeping to the shadows.

Flanked by officers, Frank pointed in the direction she had taken up to the woods.

She stood the stock of the shotgun against the fence where it would be discovered. It was more than they deserved, but she knew how hard it could be. The decaying stile lurched, almost collapsing, as she swung her leg over and into the dense undergrowth, brambles snagging the legs of her dungarees. The fading evening sun cast long shadows through the trees. Night was blooming above the canopy. It would be dark within the hour, making a search on foot unlikely.

On the edge of dusk, she came upon a holly tree, its low hanging branches forming a convenient canopy. She ducked underneath, dropped her rucksack on the ground and sat back against the trunk. There were signs everywhere suggesting she wasn't the first to take refuge there. She sniffed the air recognising the musky smell of the deer who probably spent the main part of the day couched up together there, out of sight.

Whatever Gabrielle was caught up in must be serious to send two AVs. Maybe staying in the truck would have been the better option. It wasn't Hollander's fault. The reward offered by Justin for information had done the job. Whatever. She wasn't ready to be carted off to London just yet. She would go, but it had to be on her terms. At least she was well fed. The summer nights were tolerable and even if it got cold, she'd got a baggy knitted pullover she could put on. She settled back, her hands cupped in her lap, and repeated her meditation mantra in time with her breath.

* * *

A dry twig snapped under something heavy behind the tree. SJ froze. The earlier streaks of sunlight had given way to a mass of shadows and indistinct dark shapes. She squinted into the gloom, spotting a cautious phalanx of deer moving through the woods towards the open grass to graze. She breathed. The full moon floated among the stars, visible through the gaps in the branches. Maybe Gabrielle was looking at the moon, too. What was going on? The news didn't make any sense. Gabrielle had developed a bit of a habit for random acts of recklessness since Eve's passing, but nothing to warrant being called a fugitive.

She closed her eyes and took a slow deep breath, the cool air tingling her nose. She loved sleeping in the open. Looking up at the constellations and waking up covered in beads of morning dew. Another crack. She tilted her head, straining to hear something out of place in the woodland silence. There was nothing, only her own heartbeat and shallow breath. She slid off her rucksack, rolled onto her knees and stood up. Another crack.

She peered beneath the branches into the dark. Was she imagining the three shadowy figures looming towards her? She reached out for the trunk of the tree, dazzled by the intense light that speared through the darkness. Something punched her in the back. She stiffened and fell as 50,000 volts surged into her via the pair of tiny spikes lodged in her back. Excruciating didn't come close in describing the pain. She was screaming, but heard nothing.

The pain relented. Her senses returned, with the taste of damp leaf litter pressing into her mouth and something heavy between her shoulder blades pinning her to the ground.

27

For everything the electricity company AV lacked in creature comforts, it made up for in space. There were no windows, no seats and no air conditioning except for two feeble side vents that wouldn't trouble a blade of grass. They had been tossed around together for the ten minutes it took to travel from the sub-station to Strode Park. Ethan's contact and herb supplier had set up a temporary base for him on the ground floor and he was back on-line, courtesy of the backup rig he kept stored there.

Gathered around one the screens, they'd looked at the smouldering wreckage of the three pods Ethan had converted at Helix Towers. McGill had deployed three quadcopters and the drone. The moment the Quick Reaction Force had roped down onto the roof of the pods, Ethan's magnesium incendiary charges had detonated, engulfing the interiors in a fire they had no way of extinguishing. Three guys had narrowly avoided the barbecue when the skylights blew out of the sleep pod. As the soles of their boots melted, the quads returned and winched them off. They'd been there for no more than three minutes. As they retreated, the drone had launched a missile with a thermo-sonic warhead, which destroyed all seven pods plus eight of the neighbouring wind turbines. Somebody would be getting a large bill.

The effect upon Gabrielle while watching the pyrotechnics had been palpable. Once Ethan had finished patting himself on the back for the zero body count, she'd excused herself and wandered out through a pair of French windows and into the gardens.

While she wandered around, Helix had selected two hunting rifles, mounted with telescopic sights from Ethan's gun cabinet. They were old, but reliable and in good condition. Together with the subsonic ammunition, they would be adequate for the job he had in mind. These were stashed in a flight case inside the AV, covered with an old rug on top of which Helix was now sitting, opposite Gabrielle.

Passenger comfort wasn't programmed into the AV software, resulting in a ride that could be compared to sitting inside a flight simulator, without harnesses and wearing a blindfold. 'Not easy when you can't see outside, is it? he said. 'Why don't you wedge yourself between me and the front bulkhead? It'll save you getting bounced around so much.' He held his hand out as she scrambled across the narrow space between them.

She tossed the repurposed sofa cushion she was sitting on next to him. 'Not the most comfortable AV I've been in, I have to say.' She looped her arm through his.

'I'm sorry you had to see that earlier,' he said. 'I didn't think.'

'I was terrified those people would be killed. It's good that they all got off alright. But I can't help thinking if it wasn't for me, they wouldn't have even been there.'

He gave her a gentle nudge in the ribs. 'You and me.' McGill can afford to be gung-ho in the middle of the sea, but he'll have to be subtler around the Meridian.

Gabrielle leaned into him, her head against the top of his arm. The cause of death in the post-mortem report, the email from Yawlander, the plan he'd worked out with Ethan for the exchange and the weapons cache they were perched on top of, all combined into a pang of guilt that scratched at the inside of his stomach. It was a question of timing. She'd have to know eventually and would just have to trust him.

Helix switched on the headtorch he'd taped to the roof, casting a wide circle of light across the floor. Gabrielle stirred as he fished out a small cloth bag from his jacket pocket. 'I've got a couple of bits and bobs for you.' He tipped out the contents into the palm of his hand.

She grinned at him. 'More gadgets? How exciting.' She unlinked her arm from his.

The levity did nothing to assuage his earlier thoughts, but as long as it made her feel better, that was okay. He held the skin coloured earpiece between his fingers. 'Alright. This chap needs to sit inside your ear. All the time you're within twenty yards of me, you'll be able hear me and Ethan talking, and join in if you want to. It's a combined speaker and mic so just speak normally.'

She took the device from his fingers, hooked her hair back over her left ear and inserted it. 'OK, and where does the other one go?'

'This is a tracker dot. It's just in case we get separated at any point. Probably best in the inside pocket of your jacket.'

She unzipped her jacket, hooking her finger into the interior pocket. Helix squeezed the button sized device between his fingers to activate it and dropped it in.

The AV braked. He tilted his head to one side to avoid headbutting her, but wasn't quick enough to avoid the thumping contact with the side panel.

Gabrielle took his head between her hands. 'My God, are you OK? That was a good...' She closed her eyes.

He closed his eyes. It wasn't a good idea. Their noses brushed. It wasn't the time or the place. His lips parted as they joined with hers, the same soft tongue, but gentler than the previous evening, entered his mouth. He took her wrists in his hands and pulled back, opening his eyes. 'Sorry.'

She smiled and slipped her hands from his. 'I'm not. It's okay.'

'Evening all,' said Ethan.

Gabrielle snapped her hand to her mouth, the other pointing at her ear.

Helix smiled, shaking his head. 'Mikes aren't open.

Hold on.' He tapped at the panel set into the sleeve of his jacket. 'Hi, Bruv. What's occurring?'

'Nothing, except that I just saw Gabrielle's tracker come online. Has she got her earpiece in?'

Helix nodded to Gabrielle.

She held her fingers to her ear. 'Hi, Ethan. I can hear you.'

'Hey, Doc. Sounding good. Problem is, we can't talk about the big fella anymore without him hearing.'

She smiled. 'That's OK. We don't have any secrets, do we, Helix?'

He smiled back. 'Almost there, aren't we?'

'Hmm. Ten minutes. You're going down the track at the side of the property and then parking up next to the small substation by the solar array. You can wait it out there.'

'OK good. Any luck reconnecting their data?'

'Kind of. I've not connected it, but I've got a way of linking them into the data feed from the array. The amount they use will get lost amongst that. Nobody will be any the wiser. There is one other thing you need to know.'

Helix looked at Gabrielle. The finger of guilt scratched at his stomach. 'Go on.'

Ethan cleared his throat. 'They've increased the reward for information relating to your whereabouts to £300k.'

Gabrielle took a sharp breath, her hand over her mouth. 'Justin's increased the reward? Why would he do that? It's an improvement on his first feeble offer, but...'

Helix sighed. 'It's Lytkin taking out an insurance policy. It's to make sure you keep your side of the bargain. Anyone who recognises you, particularly outside London, will be on to the militia in a heartbeat if they thought they could be in line for three-hundred grand.'

28

The gouged out track that led to Red House Farm and the solar array beyond, delineated the difference between life on the inside and life on the outside. It was as if a sharp stick had been dragged across the earth. To the east, the solar array crept towards the horizon like a vast field of dominos that had tilted and frozen mid-fall, all for the benefit of the wealthy faceless populous to the north. To the west: The farmhouse, bearing the name of its bricks, an octogenarian barn, a working yard in between, summing up a life of subsistence, fuelled by persistence and hard work.

The weather-beaten green door of the farmhouse yawned ajar, a chocolate-brown snout forced into the gap. The thick-bodied dog was launched as the door yielded, bouncing and barking into the yard, hackles raised. The threat of intruders was assessed, giving way to a more sedate patrol and the cocking of the leg against favoured posts and patches of yellowed grass.

Helix observed the dog's morning routine through a crack in the barn door. 'I don't think it will be long before old Colin realises there's a new smell in the yard.'

The dog paused, tipping his nose into the breeze from the direction of the solar array, and bolted from the yard.

Helix reached behind, tapping Gabrielle's arm. 'Come on,' he said, leaning into the door and shoving it outwards.

Seven strides later, he rapped the brass knocker three times, looking back over Gabrielle's shoulder. Come on, come on.

Rich peered through the gap. 'Jesus!'

Helix smiled. 'No, Rich. Just us. Can we come in?'

* * *

Conversation had gone on around the breakfast table without Helix's help. He'd contented himself working his way through the breakfast of scrambled eggs, mushrooms and pigeon livers that Kerry and Dawn had prepared. Dawn was perched on Gabrielle's lap, telling about how she'd helped gather the mushrooms and watched the yucky process of plucking and drawing the pigeons.

Helix sipped his second cup of tea, glancing at the clock on the wall. At least it meant he didn't have to keep looking at his watch. It was nice, but they needed to crack on. Andy and Rich were integral to the plan. He needed to know if they were on board or if they needed to revert to plan B – as in the plan B they didn't have.

He smiled as the conversation moved on to chickens, and how Dawn had looked after the broody hen while she'd incubated the eggs. What must it be like to lose a child? He pushed his plate away, leaning on the table. How does she feel when she sees someone of a similar age to Eve? She looks happy enough. Will she be jealous, angry, or upset later? Kids were always the worst. Most of the time the bodies were wrapped but you couldn't miss the kids; like the signs depicting a family group, two large white packages and two small ones. Grim.

'Helix.'

'Sorry, Andy. What was that?'

'Another brew?'

'Oh no, not for me, thanks.'

Dawn tugged at Gabrielle's arm. 'Come and see the chickens, Gabrielle, come on. You can help me collect the eggs. Mummy, where's the egg basket?'

Helix smiled back at Gabrielle as she was towed from the kitchen towards the door.

'I'd love to. Lead on,' she said.

Helix watched the door close behind them. 'She's looking well.'

Andy sat next to his brother. 'Mate, you have no idea how grateful we are.'

Rich held his cup up in salute. 'I'll second that.'

'Have you seen much of the news lately?'

Andy leaned back in his seat, toying with a teaspoon. 'Most of the time we don't even bother trying. Power's hit and miss, and we can't afford to get it reconnected. The techies that specialise in that stuff aren't interested in what we've got to offer. How about you, seen anything interesting?'

Interesting? Was he being a smart arse or was Helix

being paranoid? He straightened his back, eyes fixed on Andy. 'I think you know what I'm getting at, but if you'd rather I spelt it out.'

'Whoa, hang on Helix, I didn't—' He held his hands up. 'We saw a bit of the news in the café down at the farmers market in Cuxton. It seems they are keen to find you two, and another woman and a kid.'

'So, you know they've increased the reward for information to £300k then?'

Rich leaned in closer to the table. 'Why did you come back?'

Helix got up from the table and stretched his arms above his head, his fingertips brushing the ceiling. 'We need your help. You said—'

Andy nodded. 'Yes, I know. And we meant it. But you need to be honest with us.' He rubbed his hands down the legs of his camouflage trousers. 'Don't know about you, Rich, but I get the impression that there's a lot more to this.'

Helix nodded. 'There is. Can you turn on your TV?'

He stepped aside as Andy slid out from behind the table, looking for something underneath a pile of recycled paper. 'We can try. Should be enough in the batteries. Got the remote control under here but last time...'

Rich stood next to Helix as they watched the flat screen bloom into life, displaying a message in bright white letters – "No Signal".

Andy turned and shrugged. 'Told you.'

Helix cleared his throat. 'We can fix that. You ready, Ethan?

'Sorry?' Rich scratched his chin. 'Who's Ethan?'

'It's OK. He's cheap but good.'

Helix nodded towards the TV. 'He's my extra pair of eyes and ears. He'll explain. Watch. Get on with it, Ethan. We don't have much time.'

* * *

Helix folded his arms. 'So, will you help us?' They didn't look convinced. It was no better than fifty-fifty.

Andy pushed out his chin and scratched at his throat. 'What do you think, Rich?'

'I don't know, Helix. That's some serious shit going on there.' He nodded over his shoulder at the TV. 'And you said it could be dangerous? What about Mum and Dawn?'

'You won't be so close to the action. It'll be just like picking off a few foxes. Ethan will give you the green light if we need it, worst case. Best case, nobody will even know you were there.' He leaned against the doorframe at the foot of the stairs. They had ten seconds. No more.

The pendulum swung in the clock case, counting down the time.

Helix zipped up his jacket. 'Alright. I don't want to pressure you. I understand. It's got to be family first.' He turned towards the kitchen door.

Rich caught his arm.

He ducked back under the doorframe. 'So, what's it to be?'

Rich ran his hand over his head, a tight-lipped smile pulled across his face. 'Alright. We owe you for what Gabrielle did for us. I'm in. Andy?'

Andy nodded. 'Me too.'

'OK. Thanks, guys. We won't forget it.' He pointed to the TV. 'Is this your bank account?'

Andy spun around. 'How the fu—'

'We didn't want to pressure you, but it looks like you could do with a little top up. Refresh the balance, Ethan.'

Rich laughed. 'A hundred and fifty grand?'

Andy stared.

'The reward for information is three hundred grand. We knew we could trust you, so once we're done, there'll be another one hundred and fifty. But you'll need to be careful. Make no mistake. This is serious and I don't want to spook the horses, but you might want to move away afterwards, and we appreciate that's a lot to ask.'

Andy folded his arms. 'And what if we'd said no?'

Helix turned as the kitchen door opened. Kerry helped Dawn lift the egg basket onto the counter as Gabrielle looked on. The smile dropped from his face as he turned back to Andy. 'You're a lot smarter than that, Andy.'

29

The automatic lighting of the control room cast fans of silver light across the charcoal walls. Climate control vents breathed out cool air as the wraparound wall filled with video feeds, applications and data. The door was already locked but it didn't stop McGill confirming for a second time. The men had been briefed, the vehicles checked, and the prisoners were ready.

His reflection looked tense as it peered back from an empty display tile, his hands folded in front of his nose. His data was accurate. Stepper and the Helix brothers were out on those old sea forts. What his data didn't tell him was where they had gone. The drone had seen nothing, and military bureaucracy had prevented him from tasking the satellite in time. Wheeler's assertion that she was in Swindon was ludicrous. The number the call was made from wasn't available, which only confirmed it came from outside London, but that was as close as it got. Still, none of that mattered now. She was coming to them and all they had to do was turn up.

He slipped on an interface glove and repositioned the video tiles confirming the location of his men. The last tile dropped into place as the sound system came on stream. He sat up straight as a three by four image of Valerian Lytkin loomed over him.

He cleared his throat. 'Good morning, Mr Chairman.'

'So far so good, Colonel, and hopefully it will continue in that v-vein.' Lytkin folded his arms. 'What wasn't so good was having to explain to a P-Parliamentary Committee how a joint operation to detain Doctor Stepper and the Helix brothers could end in such a spectacular and expensive f-failure.'

McGill nodded. 'No, sir. I imagine that was uncomfortable.' Not that he cared. 'I'm sorry about—'

Lytkin held his hand up. 'You have no idea, Colonel. But I'm not interested in your ap-pologies or excuses. Today's operation seems simple in comparison. A walk in the park, if you'll forgive the p-pun.'

McGill folded his hands in his lap. 'It should be more straightforward, sir.'

'Should be? I think the word you were l-looking for was *will,* Colonel. You're m-meant to be an asset, don't turn out to be a liability. Make no mistake, if Doctor Stepper d-disappears again, it would be wise for you to do the same thing.'

The tiles rearranged themselves, filling the blank void left by Lytkin. McGill shook his head. A fucking walk in the park. You tit. He brushed his hand over the virtual keyboard. Everything was on schedule. Fifteen minutes to go. 'What's happening, Corporal?'

The man turned to face the camera. 'Still working on it, sir. We've got sniffers on most of the local networks now. If anything happens, we'll be the first to know.'

'And the others?'

'We have General Yawlander's comms, but Parliament is proving a little trickier. Shouldn't be long now.'

30

Gabrielle's hair curtained her face as she rummaged through her rucksack. Helix shifted again, trying to wedge himself into a corner of the AV. The air temperature was warm, the atmosphere somewhat frostier. 'You're not saying a lot.'

She paused, one hand inside the bag. 'There's not a lot to say, is there?'

It was an improvement, a response with more than one syllable at last. 'What do you mean?'

She lifted the bag to her lap. 'You guys have it all worked out. Send the women folk off to tend the animals so we don't have to worry our pretty little heads about the bloodbath you've planned. It was meant to be an exchange, Helix. Me for Rachel and Lauren, clean and simple.'

It was clean and simple in her world perhaps. It wasn't happening. Not while he was breathing. He rasped his stubbled chin between his fingers. 'I can tell you now that the only person planning a bloodbath is Terry McGill. You're what he wants. He won't give a shit about anyone else in the vicinity.' He rubbed his hand around the back of his neck. Lytkin needed her alive. As long as she still had a pulse when McGill delivered her, he wouldn't give a damn. She could be a bloody vegetable for all they cared.

Gabrielle shifted across to the opposite side of the AV beside him and pulled out a white tube from her rucksack. 'And now you've involved Andy and Rich. What if they get hurt... or worse? What about Kerry and Dawn?' She twisted each end of the tube in opposite directions, a sprung mechanism extended it with a click.

'I told you. They're providing back up. I can't do everything.'

She pressed her thumb against the top of the tube. 'So, where do I fit into this plan of yours?' Her brow furrowed as she peered at the small display panel on the side of the device.

Helix tugged his ear lobe. 'You there, Ethan? What's the latest?'

'Not much more, Nate. Andy and Rich are approaching their positions. It'll look like the electricity company have some major work going on at the substation across the road from the park. The AV you're in will reinforce the story after dropping you off. About fifteen minutes.'

Helix sighed. 'The plan will go to shit if they change the venue.'

'I know. Yawlander will let us know if it does.' Ethan struck his lighter. 'Unless the weather puts them off.'

'The weather?'

'Hmm. Front coming in from the east. You might get damp.'

Helix sighed, thumbing away a bead of sweat from his top lip. 'Have you got the drones up from my AV?'

'Yep. They're roosting in the trees around the playground. Nothing out of the ordinary going on. Your AV's on standby if you need it.'

Gabrielle frowned. 'Drones roosting in the trees?'

Helix attempted to stretch. 'Hmm. Our own eyes in the sky. What *is* that? You keep frowning at it.'

She held the device out to him. 'There's a bounty on our heads, yes? So, it'll be difficult wandering through the park. Of all places, I'm going to be noticed in seconds either by someone or the cameras around the perimeter.'

Helix took the cool metal tube. 'Ethan's got the cameras in his pocket.'

'He may have. But he doesn't have all the people living in the Meridian in his pocket. Unless I'm wrong, Ethan?'

'No, Doc. Good point.'

She wrung her hands. 'This is something Miriam and I had been working on. We used to test it when we went out clubbing in London or Chatham. It'll allow us to blend in more. It won't fool retinal scans or people who know us well, but it should be good enough. The effects wear off after about three hours, unless you reverse it beforehand.'

He handed it back. 'What do we do, hit people over the head with it and hope they lose their memory?'

She pressed her thumb to the top again, cycling through settings on the display. She nodded, pulling off the bottom of the tube revealing nine short needles that she aimed at his wrist.

He caught her hand. 'Whoa, hang on a second, Doctor. Can we at least talk about this?'

'Sorry. I never had you down for being afraid of an injection.' She cycled the display to a different setting. 'I'll go first. Ready?'

Helix nodded. 'I'm sure you know what you're doing.'

She rotated her hand and pressed the needles into her wrist with practiced precision. The device emitted a series of two short beeps followed by a longer one. She withdrew it and handed it back to him.

He caught her shoulders as she pitched forward with a nauseous retch, hoping it wasn't her breakfast making a comeback. 'Jesus, Gabrielle. What have you done?' He brushed her hair from her face. 'Are you alr—' He reached up to the headtorch on the roof above them, angling it towards her. 'What the fu...' He looked at the white tube and back to... *her* face?

The vaguely familiar woman sitting opposite him smiled. 'How do I look?'

'Fuck me. Where'd you go, Doc?' Ethan added.

She pulled both sides of her now long dark chestnut brown hair away from her face and over her ears.

Helix took her hands in his. Turning them over, he rubbed his thumb gently across the skin.

'It won't rub off, Helix. I think Thai women are beautiful. What do you think?' She angled her head revealing subtle southeast Asian nuances to her features.

'I don't think Ethan could have put it better. It's remarkable.' He took her chin in his hand and turned her head. She was nice. But he preferred the other version. 'Ethan, do you think we can do something with the smart fabric to allow us to fit in more?' He flicked through the sockets and cables dangling from front bulkhead.

'Sure. Plug that cobalt connector on the left into the sleeve of the Doc's jacket.'

Helix lifted a small flap in the sleeve of Gabrielle's jacket and inserted the blue cable. 'Don't go nuts. Just something, I don't know... less black and less GI Jane.'

Gabrielle held her arms out. The strands of the smart material contracted and loosened, rustling like scaly leaves. The jacket lengthened, lightening from black to dark brown with wider lapels and a deeper neckline. Loosening and lightening the round neck undershirt took on the texture of cream-coloured silk. Her slim thighs vanished beneath folds and flares as the trousers loosened and lengthened, the hems dropping over the boots. The rounded toes of the boots contracted and stretched into a more pronounced toe, fading to dark tan.

Helix nodded. 'Nice.'

'It is. Glad you approve. Your turn.'

He gawped as she thumbed the button on the tube again. 'Er... I'd rather not. If it's all the same to you.'

'You're just as recognisable as me and according to reports, almost as dangerous.'

'Tell you what. How about still me, but twenty-five years older? You know, old bloke sitting on a park bench watching the news.'

'Hmm. Older man.' She looked at the tube. 'I think we can manage that.'

'Let's go with that then.' He took a deep breath as she pressed the tube against his wrist. He closed his eyes. A rush of heat surged across his stomach and into his leg. He opened his eyes, the vision in the left one blurred. The strength drained from him as if losing the battle to remain conscious. He was falling. He jerked back. With his palms against the roof, the strength in his arm returned. He steadied himself as the dizziness abated. He blinked his eyes open and touched his face. The skin felt looser, his jowls sagging just below his jawline. The skin and muscles of his neck were more relaxed. 'How do I look?' His hair felt longer and the stubble on his chin had lengthened into a fuller beard. He looked down. He couldn't see his belt.

Gabrielle slid across to the other side of the space. She tilted her head and inspected his new features in the light of the torch. 'Pretty good. Still handsome. But older.'

He sniffed a laugh. 'And fatter. I hope I don't feel as old as I look. Where are we, Ethan?'

'Welcome back, and good timing. We have a confirmation. Exchange at the playground 14:00. That gives you about two and half hours to recce and prep.'

Helix smoothed his new beard. 'Nothing else from Yawlander?'

'Nope, and nothing much on the grid either, as predicted. You're almost there. Get ready to bail out.'

He attached the same cable to his jacket. 'OK. Just need a uniform tweak for myself.' His clothes cycled through a range of possibilities resting on a smart, blue casual jacket over a white shirt with brown chinos and brown suede boots. He glanced over at Gabrielle, his eyebrows raised.

'Nice. I think we'll fit right in,' she said.

He reached inside his jacket and unholstered his P226. He pulled back and released the slide, chambered a round, de-cocked the hammer and returned it under his arm. 'Old but reliable. Just like me.' He smiled and repeated the same with the right side. 'Stay close to me.'

31

On the more secluded paths, it was easy to forget that central London was a little over five miles away. The wooded valleys and azalea dells swallowed the distant city hum in favour of bird song and the foraging of bees. From the crest of the hills, the city could be seen – shimmering mirage-like nearby. Grass pollen, dandelion seeds and the promise of rain stirred in the freshening breeze. The burgeoning clouds diminished the glare, stripping colour and contrast as humidity beaded on brows and top lips.

The first nervous encounter: a jogging scientist passed off without incident, eliciting nothing more than a cheery wave and a breathless "good afternoon". Helix regulated their pace, somewhere between an amble and walking to the office felt right. He assessed the steady stream of data scrolling before his right eye, revealing nothing of interest in the hollows. He raised his eyebrow at the heat signature of a fox ensconced in the shadows beneath a low hanging yew.

They rested in a pool of shadow, below a mature

beech. Churlish clouds swelled and rolled, closer now with their heavy veils of rain draped below. Helix noted the time and adjusted his collar. 'Just under one hour.'

The first heavy rumble of thunder reverberated across the park. Gabrielle pulled her jacket around herself. 'Hope this stuff is waterproof,' she said, rubbing her arms.

He gave her a reassuring nod as he measured the distance to the exchange point. One hundred and twenty-two yards. Rain was another input parameter to be considered. The outcome would be the same. 'Anything happening, Ethan?'

'Andy and Rich are in position. Vehicles are ready and I've got the tags for McGill's convoy.'

'How far out are they?'

'Thirteen minutes. Looks all quiet there at the moment. There were a couple of teenagers loafing around under a tree, but the thunder seems to have frightened them off.'

Gabrielle lifted her finger to her ear. 'It gets busy after four o'clock, Ethan. Once school is finished for the day.' She grabbed Helix's arm at a sudden clap of thunder.

'Try not to touch your ear every time you speak to Ethan. It gives the game away.' He understood she was nervous, but he'd also seen others make the same mistake with dire consequences.

'We should be done and dusted by then, Doc. There's no chatter or signs of drone deployments, so they really are keeping this under the radar. Just in case, I've established a seven hundred yard GPS exclusion zone to keep anything from sniffing around where it's not wanted.'

Gabrielle nipped her thumb nail, glancing up at Helix.

He'd reassured her that Andy and Rich were there to observe and report and to act as insurance, if it was required. Ethan's rundown of operational and tactical arrangements sounded more like preparations for a black op'. Helix rubbed his hands together. A familiar itch lifted the hairs on the back of his neck. 'OK. We're going to get into position. Stay sharp.'

Helix tapped her on the shoulder and nodded towards the playground. His smile was a thin veneer that masked the urge to get on with it. "Once more unto the breach, dear friends, once more." This needed patience, there would be no backup coming over the hill if it went pear-shaped.

"The game's afoot: Follow your spirit, and upon this charge

Cry 'God for Harry, England, and Saint George!'"

She took his hand. 'Just blending in. It hadn't occurred to me until now, but why is General Yawlander feeding information to Ethan?'

He gave her hand a gentle squeeze back. 'Because he knows this is all wrong.' He grimaced as the first fat drops of rain peppered his cheek.

'Yes. But he's only been acting on the evidence. If I hadn't told you what I had discovered, you would have just followed orders, no?'

He picked up the pace, looking ahead for shelter.

'But given your conversation with Lytkin and everything else...'

'Do you think the General is involved?'

Helix grappled with the collar of his jacket. 'Do you think he would help if he was? Look, there'll be time to think about that later. Right now, we need to be focussed and out of the bloody rain.'

By the time they'd covered the short distance between the path and the playground, the rain had abated. Helix held the small gate open as Gabrielle hesitated at the entrance, looking between the swings, slides, climbing frames and roundabout.

Helix turned his face up to the clouds. Maybe they'd just caught the edge. 'What's up? Did you see something, Gabrielle?'

She looked away and folded her arms. 'No. I was just thinking. Eve loved it here. Sometimes I dream about her dashing about with the other children.' She tucked a damp strand of hair back behind her ear. 'The roundabout was her favourite. Come on.' She tugged at his hand.

Wiping away the droplets of water from the seat, she perched between the rails that divided the ancient wood and metal contraption into eight segments. Her foot slipped on the spongy play surface as she pushed against the weight. She caught her balance on a rail as it groaned into motion. Helix caught another as it passed and gave it a heave.

Ethan cleared his throat. 'Err, sorry to spoil your fun. But it's game on. Two vehicles just passing the University and turning right into Park Row.'

Helix caught a bar on the roundabout and dragged it to a standstill with Gabrielle facing him. 'Are you ready? I'm going to take my position,' he said, giving her arm a gentle squeeze.

She looked up and nodded. 'I'm ready. Please be careful.' She reached up and pecked him on the cheek. 'See you on the other side.'

Helix splashed through the puddles towards a bench under a tree at the edge of the playground. 'Getting into position.' He slid onto the bench adopting his best old-guy-watching-news pose. He palmed a smart-graphene cube, catching it by the edge as it expanded and flattened onto his hand, the live news feeds already streaming. Leaning forward, his recently acquired belly settled across the top of his thighs.

'Roger that. The birds in the nest are ready. Vehicles on Park Vista slowing on approach to park entrance.'

Behind the wall separating the park from the road, the urgent whine of the electric motors could be heard. Tyres splashed through kerbside puddles as the vehicles slowed to a halt. A deep vibrating squeak in the distance from the heavy metal entrance gate reverberated along the length of the wall as it was pushed open and then closed. Helix slipped his hand into his jacket, feeling the grip of his P226. The holster pulsed against his armpit in time with his heart. He took two deep breaths and activated his TC. '*Ethan. A pair of cloned heavies, black suits, earpieces, tooled up, just entering playground, cut comms with G.*'

'Roger that. Vehicles turning onto Maze Hill and entering park.'

'Have visual.'

The two heavy AVs, windows blacked out, paused under the trees, their wipers sweeping the deep windscreens. Heavy drops of water cascaded down on the roofs from the branches and leaves above. The gravel gave way under their broad tyres as they moved forward, fifteen feet apart.

The clouds overhead stirred with a cannonade of thunder that travelled through the soles of Helix's boots. Keeping his head tilted over the news, he glanced at the two heavies as they settled under the trees bordering the playground. They joined their hands across the front of their jackets as they scanned their surroundings. He measured the distance between them and Gabrielle. She looked down at her feet as she spun on the roundabout, its squeaky hee-haw voice echoing across the space like a braying mechanical donkey.

Helix tensed as the opaque windows of both AVs cleared. In the lead vehicle, Rachel sat forward, her arm around Lauren, her brow furrowed. Lauren pointed to the park. Rachel shook her head.

Only a maniac would plan an exchange involving a kid at a playground. Helix squeezed the grip of his P226 as McGill ducked and bobbed, cocooned in the safety of the vehicle as he checked the location of his men. Another buzz cut heavy sat at the controls. *'All stations standby. Subjects in lead vehicle.'*

The doors of the second vehicle hissed open as Helix tilted the smart-graphene sheet, changing channels. The driver dismounted, turning up his collar as the rain ran off his polished bald head. Helix zoomed in on the second occupant, his teeth grinding as he recognised the twisted nose and deep half-moon bruises below the beady eyes of Neville Lafarge. Maybe it would be third time lucky. Lafarge slithered out, leaning back against the front of the vehicle, his eyes darting around. His mate took up position in line with Helix, Gabrielle now in between them. It wasn't ideal. Helix swallowed, pushing his sunglasses back up the bridge of his nose.

McGill shifted to the edge of his seat, his hand running across his mouth, down his neck. He mouthed an order at the driver.

Helix sniffed. *'Stand by. They're about to dismount.'*

Rachel leaned back as McGill raised his finger. Whatever was said was acknowledged with a nod as both she and Lauren moved towards the door. The driver shifted around in his seat, his arm hooked over the back, his lips puckered in a kiss towards Rachel. Helix angled his gun towards the vehicle from beneath his jacket. A small blink of his right eye activated the laser sight painting a small red dot, unseen to anyone else, on the side of the driver's head. A precise aim wasn't necessary, the smart ammunition would find its target. But he wasn't interested in the driver, he knew Andy would have him covered if he left the vehicle.

The door of the AV slid open, McGill placed his foot outside, as if dipping his toe in water. In one fluid movement he slipped from the seat and stepped into Helix's sights. The laser dot settled on his neck. A mortal injury, lots of thrashing about, death inevitable, but not before there had been a chance to say goodbye properly.

McGill turned, his hand outstretched towards Lauren. Rachel slid forward, brushing his hand away, stepping outside next to him. She paused looking towards the driver, her eyes red and tearful, fuck you on her lips. McGill reached in, grabbed Lauren and dropped her to the grass next to her mother.

The roundabout carried Gabrielle on one final orbit. Helix drew a breath as he watched the toe of her boot drag across the ground slowing the ride. Her hand moved underneath her jacket towards the makeover syringe. Once she'd reversed the disguise it would be time to roll.

McGill remained close to Rachel and Lauren. Handy human shields. Helix felt the resurgent rain in heavy drops through his grey hair as it gathered momentum. Adrenalin flooded into him as McGill's eyes narrowed in his direction. *'Cat's out of the bag. I think he's spotted me. Come on, Doc.'*

The drum roll of rain on the PV skins of the vehicles increased in intensity. Gabrielle shouted over it. 'McGill. Over here.' She stumbled from the ride.

Helix pulled his P226. He rolled from the bench onto his knees. McGill drew. A clump of firecrackers erupted in the branches above the two men posted under the trees in a burst of staccato cracks. They drew their weapons and scrambled for cover. Helix squeezed the trigger. The smart bullet struck. McGill's blood painted the side of the AV. Rachel screamed, fell to her knees and gathered Lauren toward her. McGill fought to staunch the flow. He scrambled for traction. Rainwater pooled around his knees.

The first two men went down. Dead before they hit the ground. Perfect headshots from Andy and Rich's elevated positions.

Helix twisted, Lafarge's driver in his sights. He went for his weapon. Helix squeezed. The 9mm smart round penetrated. The back of the driver's head met the bark of the oak beyond.

Gabrielle, restored to her former self, clambered to her feet, the rain streaming down her face.

Sprinting towards McGill, Helix fired twice at Lafarge. Cowering behind his AV, Lafarge returned fire wildly before rolling back inside, avoiding Rich's second shot. The doors of both AVs hissed shut, trapping Lafarge in one, McGill's driver in the other.

'Rats in the traps,' Ethan announced. 'Both vehicles in my control.'

Helix snapped his aim toward each of the fallen men. With signs of life absent, he holstered his P226. He wiped the rain from his face as the trapped men hammered at the reinforced plexiglass windows and doors. He flinched as McGill's driver attempted to shoot his way out by firing his weapon at the roof. The ricocheting bullet hit him in the thigh, throwing him back onto one of the seats.

Helix nodded his approval as he assessed the damage. 'Job done. Four down, two contained. Doc G and hostages safe, Ethan. Time to move out.'

Gabrielle gathered Rachel and Lauren to her, stealing a glance at Helix as he stood over McGill. 'Can he be helped, Helix?'

Arterial blood pulsed from between McGill's fingers as he clung to life.

Helix snorted. 'No. It's too late.' He kicked McGill onto his back. He'd often wondered what this moment would be like.

'Nice shot, Nate.'

Helix shook his head, pulling his sopping hair away from his face. 'I don't think he's long for this world, Bruv.'

A crack of thunder resonated across the park, McGill convulsed one last time, spraying what little blood he had left from his mouth, his hand flopping from the neck wound onto the sodden ground. His lifeless eyes rolled back in his head, the last drops of rain-diluted blood running from the side of his mouth onto the grass.

Helix stepped away and ushered the soaked women away from McGill's twitching remains and in between the two AVs. 'Okay. We need to get moving. The Police will be on the way and that's not what we need right now.' He beckoned to Andy and Rich as they splashed their way across the grass towards them, hoping they'd pick up the pace.

'Chatter kicking off on the grid, Nate,' Ethan reported.

He cursed his temporary long hair as he peeled it away from his face again. 'Alright. You need to get to your vehicles now. Stick to the plan. We'll meet back at Andy and Rich's place.'

Lauren screamed as McGill sprung from behind the AV and lunged towards them. Helix looked past him to the spot where he was lying moments earlier, trying to reconcile what he was seeing.

The soaked huddle separated, boots and shoes slipping, knees, hands and elbows stained from the muddied grass and they tried to scatter to avoid McGill's grimacing cadaver. Gabrielle pulled Lauren by the arm, spinning her out of range. Rachel was pinned to the front of the AV as Helix stepped in front of her.

Helix grabbed and heaved McGill towards him by the front of his jacket. With momentum in his favour, he half turned and rotated his hips, throwing McGill to the ground, crashing down across his chest. The crushing body slam had little effect on McGill who twisted and clawed. He lashed out with his boot, catching Rachel's ankle. She sprawled onto her face, her t-shirt baggy with mud and rain. Helix straddled McGill, his hands around his throat. McGill writhed like an eel, stabbing a white tubular syringe into Helix's forearm. Helix staggered to his feet, the syringe dangling in the material of his jacket. He pulled the glove from his prosthetic fingers. The grin evaporated from McGill's face as the syringe fell to the grass.

McGill lunged at Rachel, dragging her to the ground. He snatched up the syringe from the grass and stabbed the needles into her thigh.

Gabrielle screamed. 'Rachel! No!' She pulled Lauren to her, turning her face away from the melee.

Helix drew his P226. He hesitated, Rachel in his sights. She squirmed, twisting herself free, her hand to her thigh.

Helix shot McGill again and kept firing until the rapid succession of shots culminated in a loud click as the magazine emptied.

McGill's headless corpse fell back. Rachel's cries were muffled by another rasping crack of thunder and lightning that fell across the park. Grabbing the corpse by the ankle, Helix heaved it away as Lauren dropped to the bloodstained grass beside Rachel.

Helix wiped the back of his hand across his mouth. He gawped at the mess. 'Are you seeing what I'm seeing, Ethan?'

'Yes, Nate. Another shrink-wrap, only a lot more advanced. I've read about those. Had me fooled. A product of Lytkin's R&D unit in Germany, I would guess. McGill's probably got his feet up in an interface-rig somewhere, nursing a cup of cocoa.'

Helix pulled the syringe from the shrink-wrap's hand and turned back to Rachel. He knelt beside her as Gabrielle cradled her head in her lap, Lauren tearful at her shoulder. 'What was in the syringe, Rachel?'

Rachel swallowed. 'What... what do you think?'

He handed the syringe to Gabrielle. 'How long?'

Gabrielle wiped the rain from her cheeks. 'Ten minutes maybe. It's unstable. Could be less or a little more.'

Helix shook his head and turned away as Gabrielle turned to Lauren.

'Lauren sweetheart, Mummy's hurt, but I'm going

to help her. But we have to be quick. Give her a cuddle and kiss.' She laid Rachel's head on the grass.

Rachel wrapped her arms around her daughter as she fell upon her. She kissed the side of her face through her wet blonde hair and whispered in her ear. Her gentle smile and attempts at reassurance shattered as a violent convulsion shook Lauren from her embrace.

Gabrielle dropped to her knees beside Lauren. 'Lauren darling, I need to help Mummy. Andy and Rich will take you somewhere safe until I come for you. Is that OK?'

Lauren hooked her hair behind her ears and looked back at Rachel who managed a weak nod of confirmation. She dropped next to her mum again pressing her face against hers as Rachel was wracked with another convulsion, her stomach pressing against her soaked t-shirt.

Lauren howled as Helix scooped her up and passed her to Rich. 'Go now, guys. Get her out of here.'

The heavy rain eased. Rachel relaxed enough to manage a feeble wave as Lauren looked back over Rich's shoulder. Gabrielle looked into her eyes, held her hand and wiped the rain from her face. 'We need to get out of here, Helix. You know what happens next.'

Rachel raised her hand and pointed at McGill's AV, coughing out her words. 'In there. With him.'

Helix frowned as Gabrielle leaned in closer. 'What was that, Rachel?'

Rachel mustered all her remaining strength. 'In there. With that animal. He couldn't get enough of me before. Now he—' She arched her back again, the veins in her neck bulging and darkening through her pale skin.

Helix responded, sensing the end was close. 'Ethan, can you open the door to the lead AV? I'll cover the rat inside.' He pulled his gun and chambered a round.

The door released. Helix covered the writhing driver. He leaned down using his free hand to help as Rachel crawled through the mud to the opening.

The driver looked up. 'What are you doing? What's wrong with her? I need a medic. Help me.' He shrunk away as Rachel climbed inside.

Gabrielle got Rachel settled onto the floor, stroking her damp hair from her face. She held her friend's face in her hands and kissed her lightly on the lips. Rachel turned her head, her mouth to Gabrielle's ear. Her lips tightened as she convulsed again.

Helix grabbed Gabrielle by the arm and pulled her out. 'Ethan. The door.' He held her tight against his chest with his hand on the back of her head as she sobbed into his shirt. He met Rachel's eye as she raised her hand in a weak wave. He pressed his lips to the top of Gabrielle's head and closed his eyes.

The windows frosted as Helix moved Gabrielle away. He tilted his head towards the vehicle hearing a muffled scream and a thud as it shuddered. He grimaced, a five second pause was followed by a second jolt.

The distant wail of sirens smothered Gabrielle's sobs. The sun streamed through a gap in the clouds, falling on the AVs. Beads of rainwater glimmered in the light, as the plaintive cry of a seagull echoed overhead. 'Talk to me, Ethan?' He stroked the back of Gabrielle's head.

'You won't be surprised or delighted to know that there is a significant force of police on its way. You need to get out of there now.'

Helix dropped to his knee and gave her arm a squeeze. 'Go to Lauren. She needs you, Gabrielle.'

She nodded. 'I know why Yawlander is helping.'

'Yep, me too.'

'You knew... you know that he's Lauren's father?'

32

Helix's AV moved with purpose as it navigated the last five miles to its destination, the other side of the administrative border. Other vehicles paused or diverted to give it space, like those lower in the food chain when an apex predator makes its way across the savanna or through the ocean on the scent of a kill.

The interior was dark and silent, all non-essential systems and communications powered down, a bubble of sensory deprivation. Helix lay reclined. As far as he was aware, he was staring at the roof, not that he could tell the difference between eyes open and eyes closed. The line between success and failure was a thin one. They'd been close. He'd secured the release of the hostages, prevented Gabrielle from being taken and dealt with McGill and most of his men. But then McGill had pulled his Lazarus stunt and it had all gone tits up. How was he going to look Lauren in the eye? He was supposed to be protecting them. At least she and Gabrielle would be safe at Red

House Farm. He would join them later, but first, there were questions and he needed answers.

It was unrealistic to expect to save everyone in these kinds of operations. But this wasn't an operation in the normal sense. This whole situation was a product of commercial greed, the desire to settle a score, or both. He didn't know and didn't care, but neither could justify what had happened. McGill's men could be considered collateral damage. They were there by choice. McGill had rendered them expendable the moment he drew his weapon. The others were different; they were variables in an equation he couldn't get his head around. The only positive was that Lytkin had tried and failed. He'd gone all in and Helix had called his bluff.

Where was the real McGill? Remote oversight of the Helix Towers operation made more sense. The Quick Reaction Force would have known what they were doing. Were it not for Ethan's countermeasures, they'd be in custody and Gabrielle would be on one of Lytkin's vivisection slabs. The exchange was different. Having dropped the ball once, McGill would have wanted to prove a point. He would have weighed the risks. His plan may have worked but the use of the shrink-wrap didn't stack up. There was something more than cowardice that had kept him away. If Lytkin was as ruthless as he looked, McGill was on the slippery slope. He'd failed to take Gabrielle and he'd lost Rachel and Lauren in the process and four of his own men. The only pat on the back he'd be likely to get was for reducing the payroll costs.

He stretched and yawned as a stream of data passed before his eye. The darkness dissolved into shades of night vision as his seat slid upright. His fingers brushed the control panel in the central arm rest, waking the onboard systems. ETA three minutes. The opaque glass cleared. He blinked in the sun as he pushed his sunglasses up the bridge of his nose.

He reloaded both of his P226s and climbed out onto the track that ran around the northern edge of Sawyer's lake, close to Ebbsfleet hyperlink terminal. He slumped on a bench, its green painted surface covered with scratched names and initials, declarations of love and an advertisement of what Mandy was willing to do for a tenner. A light breeze rippled the emerald green surface of the lake that had swallowed the disused quarry. Yawning, he leaned forward, face in his hands. The second of McGill's AVs, containing Lafarge, swung into the car park.

'What do you want to do with him, Nate?'

Chalk dust covered the AV as it whined to halt.

'He'll keep.'

'OK. The others are app—'

'Ethan. Can you button it please?'

He hooked his elbows over the back of the bench, the sun warm on his face. And when this was all over, what then? Lytkin was no closer to bypassing the lock Gabrielle had put on the science. They could melt into the background, away from the cities, but where? Lytkin would find them eventually. You could learn to live with it, but the nagging itch of doubt would always be there. When are they coming? You couldn't ever relax. No. Lytkin had to be stopped. Permanently. But one thing at a time. If Lytkin wanted to be Cerberus, the huge three-headed dog, McGill was the dog's bollocks. The first step in controlling a mad dog was to castrate it.

Rolling off the bench, he stretched his arms above his head and flexed his neck muscles. 'Alright, Ethan. Let's have a chat with Neville the necrophile.'

'Roger that. Before you do, I've got some stuff that might be of interest.'

Helix leaned on the back of the bench, scratching his neck. 'Go on.'

'OK. I blagged a survey drone and have had a snoop around the buildings adjacent to Miriam's apartment block.' He cleared his throat. 'I found what looked like an OP on the sixteenth floor of the building opposite.'

Helix rolled a stone back and forth under his boot. 'And?'

'The whole building is empty, but one apartment looked less deserted than the rest on that level. With a bit of persuasion, I got the drone through the window. Someone had pulled a small table to the back wall, placed a chair behind it and looking at the marks in the dust on the table-top, you could picture someone sat there with a pair of binos playing Peeping Tom.'

'Any other signs?'

'Whoever it was, had polished off half a dozen tinnies of rocket fuel lager and about forty smokes.'

Helix pushed up from the bench. 'What brand?'

'The lager?'

'No, you numpty, the smokes. Come on, Ethan.' He folded his arms.

'Sorry, Nate. Same as the one you collected from the road and—'

'DNA, Ethan.'

'One step ahead of you fella. Took samples and sent them along with the one you collected to someone who owed me a favour. It's Lafarge.'

A string of hyperloop pods slid across the viaduct into Ebbsfleet.

'Doesn't put him in the frame for the murder though does it?'

'Maybe. I can show you the video later, but when I spun the drone around to leave, I noticed some heavy black marks on the front of the balconies above Miriam's. Hers is on the fifteenth of twenty. The five above all had similar marks, but none of those below.'

'Boot marks.' He leaned back on the bonnet of his AV. 'He abseiled down from the roof.'

'That was my thinking. And he went back up the same way. I found rope fibres over the edge of the roof along with another fag butt and there was evidence of scratching on the outside of the patio door lock where he'd picked it.'

'But if he knew the plan, why did he go in after Gabrielle left? Why didn't he just wait and show up when the housekeeper called it in?'

'Somebody got impatient and wanted to make sure the job was done?'

'Fucking clumsy work if you ask me. But if they

were going to cover it up in the forensics, I don't suppose it makes much difference. OK. Let's ask him.'

Helix rolled onto his side behind his AV. 'Left side door, Ethan.' He drew his P226.

'Roger that. Here we go.'

Helix peered through the letterbox gap under his AV. He controlled his breathing, activating the laser sight and painting a small read dot on the wheel of the neighbouring vehicle. Lafarge would be on edge, his weapon drawn, no idea where he was, but a good idea of who would be waiting.

A muddied black leather boot touched down onto the track. Another pause, the laser dot now on Lafarge's ankle. The second foot, the hems of the trousers, settling across the boots. Helix took up the pressure on the trigger, Lafarge moved one step closer and paused again. The moderated shot was still enough to trigger a murmuration of starlings from their evening roost. The echo dissipated, the void filled with the scream of the target. Lafarge groped at his ankle, dropping his gun to the ground as he rolled onto his back. A second shot sent Lafarge's weapon spinning it out of reach.

Helix jogged around his vehicle. 'Here we are again, Neville. Third time lucky.'

Lafarge winced as another spike of pain shot up his leg. 'That your calling card, is it? Shooting people in the foot. I knew that was you in Chatham,' he spat.

Helix sniffed. 'You knew? Well, whilst we're discussing Chatham, why were you watching Miriam Polozkova's apartment?'

Lafarge strained to keep his heel from the ground.

'What are talking about? I attended when it was reported. That was the first time I'd been in there.'

Helix sighed. 'OK Neville, you've got two hands, two feet, maybe a cock and two bollocks so let's call it five questions, seven if I add in your kneecaps. You decide how you want to play it.' He aimed and shot him through the right hand.

Lafarge screamed again, his index finger dangling from his palm by a thin ligament. 'OK, OK! Fuck!' He choked a breath. 'I saw Stepper leaving. I waited for about thirty minutes before I went to check her.'

'But she wasn't dead.' He swung his gun towards Lafarge's left hand. 'Was she?'

Lafarge smeared the gobs of bloodied flesh and bone from the side of his face with his good hand. 'No. She went to get up as I went through the doors.'

'And she didn't get up or do anything else because you smothered her. Didn't you?' He folded his arms, the snout of the gun resting on his bicep. 'Say it!'

Lafarge glanced at the gun now aimed at his groin. 'Yes, yes. I smothered her.' He bit his lip and rotated his shivering hand. 'She was going to scream the fucking place down.'

'Did you have a little fiddle after she stopped struggling, Nev', or do you prefer them cold?' He shook his head. 'Don't answer that. I can only imagine and, I'd rather not. OK. Where's McGill?'

'What? Wait, wait. I dunno.' He laid his shattered hand on his chest, his teeth clenched. 'I thought that was him you shot in park. None of us knew. We all thought it was him.'

'Wrong answer. I asked where he was?' He swung a kick at Lafarge's shattered ankle.

Lafarge growled through the pain, pulling his knee up and gripping his foot. 'We all left the place together. He came out of the door after we'd loaded Rachel and the kid into the AV. It looked and acted just like him. The real McGill must still be back at the warehouse. That's some weird shit. I've never seen anything like it.'

'Where's the warehouse?'

'Bermondsey. An old industrial place down by the river.'

Helix stamped on his ankle, grinding with the ball of his foot, all his weight over his knee. 'I could believe that Neville, if there were actually any old industrial places left down by the river. They've all been converted to apartments for the chattering classes. You need to do your research if you want to tell porkies.' He aimed the gun at Lafarge's groin. 'I must be going soft. Have another try or it'll be your bollocks next.'

Lafarge arched his back. 'Heathrow. It's near Heathrow. River Gardens.'

Helix lifted his foot. 'That's better. How do you know McGill?'

'I was working in tech support after he got reassigned. Following the acc—'

'Accident? We all know it wasn't an accident, Neville.'

Lafarge held his hand up. 'No. I know. Anyway. It was after McGill got reassigned. He found out I was streaming footage from webcams I'd hacked. I thought that was it. I was out. But he said he'd help me cover my tracks if I agreed to help him when he needed me. And then about three months back, I got the call.'

'Where were the webcams? What were you streaming?'

Lafarge gasped for breath, tonguing his lips. 'Politicians.'

'Politicians? Stealing political secrets? Sounds sophisticated for you, Nev.'

Lafarge cleared his throat. 'It was their wives and daughters.'

Helix glanced at Lafarge's other ankle, shifted his aim and fired. Fragments of bone and blood splattered the paintwork of the AV as the joint exploded. Lafarge vomited through the hoarse scream, over the shoulder of his jacket.

'Christ, Neville. You're worse than I thought.'

Lafarge wiped the vomit from the side of his mouth. 'Wait. There's something else.' He shifted, trying to minimise the pressure on his shattered limbs. 'There's something kicking off which might explain why he sent the robot.'

'OK. I was thinking you weren't much use to me alive. Spit it out.'

Lafarge took a breath, sweat beading his brow. 'He had another team, watching the local militia somewhere down the M4.'

Helix took a step towards him and raised his foot.

Lafarge held his hand up. 'Nooo. Hang on, hang on. Swindon, I think. Somewhere around Swindon.'

Helix leaned against the AV. 'Ethan. Anything happening around Swindon?'

'I'm on it, Nate.'

'Right, Neville. Get back in the AV. You can go now.'

Lafarge grimaced as he sat up, looking at his ankles and shattered hand.

'Come on. Chop chop. You've still got one hand that works. You can use that while you're watching your webcams.' He stepped behind him and hefted him over the threshold of the door and into the compartment. He backed away as Lafarge groaned and tried to pull himself into a corner. A laser dot appeared on Lafarge's forehead followed by two 9mm smart rounds.

Helix reached inside his AV. 'Standby with the doors, Ethan.' He turned, pulled the pin and tossed a black fragmentation grenade into the compartment with Lafarge's corpse.

The door hissed closed, followed three seconds later by a muffled explosion that blew out the windows. The vehicle accelerated down the shallow slope and into the lake. It wallowed before tipping nose down and filling with water.

'Nice touch, Nate. I wondered how you would sink that bloody thing.'

Helix settled back into his AV. 'Hmm. So, back to Swindon. What's occurring?' He pushed his sunglasses to the top of his head.

'Interesting. The local constabulary, acting on a tip-off have arrested Doctor Gabrielle Stepper near the small village of Foxhill. She was found in the woods during the night after fleeing from some locals she'd stolen a shotgun from.'

'Where are you getting that from? Media or militia channels?'

'Hmm. A bit of both. Anyway, we know it's a complete load of bollocks given you were with her just over an hour ago.'

Helix laughed. 'Someone's trying to get the reward. They'll be disappointed.'

Ethan pushed a video clip onto one of his screens. A young woman, brown shoulder-length hair, handcuffed, wearing mud stained dungarees being frog-marched towards a waiting police vehicle. Ethan paused the video as she looked towards the camera.

'Easy mistake to make.'

Helix slid forward onto the edge of his seat and peered at the screen. 'I see what you mean, but she was...' He took a small bottle of water from the central console. 'We know that's not Gabrielle. It can only be SJ. But what the hell is she doing in Swindon?'

Ethan had vanished from his normal place in the right hand monitor. 'What's up, Bruv?' The usual sound of keys being tapped, overlaid with a muffled conversation, escaped from the speakers. 'Ethan, what's up? Who are you talking to?'

'That was Andy. They just got back to the farm. Gabrielle's not in the AV. He found the tracker and earpiece inside. She gone, Nate.'

33

The brown leather of Justin Wheeler's office chair creaked as he crossed his legs opposite the screen containing a life-sized image of Julia Ormandy, the Home Secretary. 'So, when was she picked up, Julia?'

Ormandy glanced down at her desk. '02:35 this morning.'

Wheeler peered over the top of his cup as he sipped his tea. He could have sworn it was Gabrielle, even over the poor connection.

'What do you want to do, Justin? The Police insist it is Gabrielle, in spite of SJ's protestations. They've performed the basic DNA testing and of course, it's the same. They're reluctant to arrange transport and keep telling us they haven't got enough people.'

Wheeler raised his eyebrows. 'Strange how they managed to resource a man hunt when there was a fat reward on offer.' Rubbing his temple, he peered into Julia's cleavage looking for options. She leaned forward to assist. He wasn't sure who was using whom.

'Alright, Julia. I'll speak to Yawlander. I assume he

has all of the details?'

Ormandy grinned. 'Yes. He has all of the details but no resources.'

'Hells teeth! If anyone else mentions—' His hand slammed the desk. 'Oh, OK. Hilarious. You'll pay for that, Dame Julia.'

'I can't wait. It was fun last time. Don't leave it too long. Ciao.'

The call dropped. Wheeler selected Yawlander's number from the holographic rolodex hovering above the glass top of his desk. The General's tired image appeared on the screen. 'Chancellor Wheeler. I was about to call you.'

'Good afternoon, General.' Wheeler sat forward, his elbows on the desk. 'Are you alright? You look dreadful.'

Yawlander centred the knot of his tie. 'How can I help, sir?

'No. You go first. You were going to call me.'

'I'm afraid it's not good news, sir. Acting on information received, Colonel McGill attempted to orchestrate the detention of your wife in exchange for Rachel Neilson and her daughter.'

Wheeler raised his eyebrows. 'Attempted, General? Which implies he tried but failed. Correct?'

'I believe that's so, sir. The details are still a little sketchy.'

Wheeler slammed his hands down on the desk. 'Yawlander, you're waffling. What you're trying to say is that you don't have Gabrielle, but I assume that idiot McGill still has Rachel and Lauren in custody?'

'We don't have Doctor Stepper and the whereabouts of Rachel, Lauren and McGill are unclear. There were several bodies found at the children's playground in the Meridian. That's as much as we have at present.'

Wheeler's chair groaned as he pushed himself back from the desk. He ran his hand over his head. 'Bodies in the playground? Bloody hell, General. I thought you were in command. Lytkin is coming to Parliament again this afternoon to address the Public Accounts Committee. Does he know?'

Yawlander took a long sip of water. 'He's issued an order for McGill's immediate arrest.'

Wheeler clamped his hands to the top of his head as he stared out over the Thames garden. 'This is getting out of control. Do *you* know where McGill is?'

'No, sir. He's disappeared. We thought he was amongst the dead.'

Wheeler turned back from the window. 'I beg your pardon? He was dead, but then he disappeared?'

'Yes. It turns out it was some sort of advanced robotic device that looked like McGill, although it was missing most of its head. It was one of Lytkin's advanced prototypes. Operated from a remote location.'

'Who killed them, and him, or it?'

Yawlander sighed. 'It was off the books, Chancellor. We don't—'

Wheeler raised his hand. 'I know. You don't know. Not exactly military intelligence personified, are you? I would wager your man Nathan Helix had something to do with it. I thought McGill was good, and yet he walked right into a trap that could only have been set by a bloody war hero. If you have the remote location where that thing was operated from then you have McGill. No?'

'Yes, sir. But he's not there. He was seen leaving the warehouse with two of his men in a manually operated vehicle.'

Wheeler turned to his drinks cabinet. He poured a large measure of brandy into a spherical crystal glass. He slumped back into his seat and loosened his tie with his free hand as he nosed the brandy. So, McGill was persona non grata, Gabrielle was still at large and Rachel and Lauren had disappeared. Lytkin had run out of options. He had nothing to bargain with and no Gabrielle. He took another generous sniff from his glass, relishing the aroma imbued with a hint of opportunity. 'General. I need your help with another matter.'

Yawlander leaned in towards the camera. 'Your sister-in-law by any chance?'

'Yes. Julia Ormandy told me what happened and said you would have all the details.'

'Yes, sir. She's been telling them to contact you, but they haven't been able to get past the main switchboard at Parliament.'

'Right. Let's get them on the phone and sort this out.'

'Yes, Chancellor. I'll just put you on hold.'

Yawlander was replaced with a still image of him in full uniform. Wheeler sipped his brandy and glanced at his watch. It was twenty-five minutes until Valerian Lytkin was due in the committee room. Time was running out for the Prime Minister. The last thing he wanted to do was get on the wrong side of his principal election campaign supporter and donor. He'd done his homework. The Public Accounts Committee Chairman was an ambitious friend and had agreed not to poke his nose where it wasn't wanted.

Wheeler drained the last of his brandy as Yawlander reappeared on the screen. A second window opened with a militia inspector putting on his hat.

Wheeler crossed his legs, his hands in his lap. 'Welcome back, General. Good afternoon, Inspector. I am Justin Wheeler, Chancellor of the Exchequer, and I believe you have my sister-in-law with you.'

The inspector squirmed in his seat, glancing off camera. 'A lady who claims to be your sister-in-law, sir.'

'And you don't believe her, Inspector? May I speak with her?'

The inspector swivelled the camera towards a bored looking brown-haired woman, identical to Gabrielle. A second officer stood next to her.

Wheeler leaned onto his desk. 'Are the handcuffs necessary, Inspector?'

SJ stepped closer to the camera. 'You took your fucking time, Justin.' She mimicked his wink as she held out her arms.

Wheeler cleared his throat. 'I think I can safely say, Inspector, that that is not my wife.' Gabrielle wasn't that good at swearing, even when drunk.

'But sir, the DNA evidence?'

SJ scowled at the officer removing the handcuffs. 'Identical twins, dummy. For Christ's sake.' She rubbed at her wrists and looked to the ceiling. 'Look, now we're graced with the presence of my esteemed brother-in-law, we can clear this up once and for all. Justin, let me ask you a question.'

Wheeler steepled his fingers. 'Pray do, SJ.'

SJ put her hands on her hips. 'I can't believe I'm going to do this, but OK. Has Gabrielle got any distinguishing marks on her body? You know, scars, birth marks, tattoos, that kind of thing.'

Wheeler flushed. 'No. Nothing at all.'

She reached up to the buckles on the straps of her dungarees, turning her back as she undid them. 'Nothing at all. You heard that.' The baggy trousers fell to the ground exposing her naked backside, with a tattoo of a long-lashed eye on each cheek.

Wheeler clamped his hand over his forehead, glancing at Yawlander who was shaking his head trying to stifle a laugh. 'Once again, Inspector. I can confirm that is not my wife.'

The inspector stepped in between SJ and the camera, leaning down to address Wheeler. 'Thank you, sir. We'll release her.'

'Thank you, Inspector. Please extend my thanks to the citizens who brought this to your attention. Could I ask you to accommodate my sister-in-law for a little longer? General Yawlander will have her collected. They should be with you around 18:00. General?'

Yawlander managed a nod of agreement as SJ elbowed the inspector out of the way, buckling her dungarees. 'Listen, Justin. I'm not staying here. I can make my own way to London. And I don't need your bloody help.'

'I know you don't. But the chances are, you'll be recognised again and have to show your spotty arse to prove you're not Gabrielle, and I think once is enough for all of us.'

SJ jabbed a two-fingered salute at the camera as she slouched down in one of the Inspector's office chairs. 'Hurry up then. I'm not coming to make you look like the caring husband or embellish your political popularity. I just want to find my sister.'

34

The river Thames oozed into the daylight, re-emerging from below the Remembrance Gardens opposite the Old Royal Naval College in Greenwich. Extending for ten miles from Hammersmith in the west, it was an uplifting space that honoured the lost and recognised the sacrifice and service of those who had brought about an end to the two-year pandemic. Out of sight, half a mile south over the masts of the Cutty Sark, beyond the trees and the grey lead roof of the old naval college, the children's playground had been cordoned off, now the site of a major police incident.

The gardens were a labyrinth of footpaths and cycleways with benches alongside or dotted amongst the trees. It was a place of solitude, a refuge of solace, a corner to remember or a space to come and forget. Gabrielle wound her way down a narrow footpath, pausing next to a bench under a magnolia tree, stubborn drops of rain clinging to its leaves and white petals.

She slipped her rucksack from her shoulder and dropped it to the bench. How did she get there? Where had she been for the last...? She pulled up her collar and wrapped her arms around herself. The more she tried to be still the more she shook. Her throat felt like it was lined with dry bread, and her neck was tense. When was the last time I ate? It's shock and the onset of dehydration. Take a minute, catch your breath.

She closed her eyes, inhaled, held it and exhaled. She found a rhythm and the shaking abated until Lauren's scream echoed in her head once more. McGill kicked out, Rachel fell, Helix, Helix, Helix... 'Rachel. Noooo!'

Her eyes snapped open. The footpath was still deserted and, there was nobody watching her from behind the bench or amongst the trees. She pressed her hands to her face and rocked. The pristine grass at her feet turned to mud, the images pressed in again. No! Her feet dragged on the gravel. What's happening to me? What have I done? The strength had deserted her knees, she needed the loo, she wanted to sit, sleep, run. Rachel! She perched on the bench, eyes wide, following her breath. Take a minute, catch your breath.

The breeze stirred the trees, fallen magnolia petals floated and bounced across the grass. A bumblebee hummed from azalea, to rhododendron to magnolia to flowering cherry and onwards. A blackbird bobbed and rooted amongst the leaf litter. Normal things. Normal had been her refuge. But normal had left the building the moment Nathan Helix turned up at the observatory. What now Gabrielle? What's the plan?

A surveillance drone, flying fast and low, dipped over the roof of the Naval College, following an invisible grid across the park. She snatched up her rucksack, ducking out of sight under the low hanging arms of a cherry tree. You fool. How stupid can you be? Crouching, she rummaged through the bag recovering the makeover pen she'd used earlier to disguise herself and Helix. She'd been on the streets as herself for... how long? She cycled the display about to select the same pre-set she'd used earlier. No. She applied two more pushes to the button and pressed the needles into her wrist. She rode the convulsion. The muscles in her face twitched and tightened, her hair lengthened, plunging around her shoulders, darkening to complement the ebony skin on her forearm. She coughed, a hint of acid in her throat, and stepped onto the path. The buzzing intensified as a drone dived lower. Don't look up. The drone lost interest and banked away, resuming its programmed track. Hitching her rucksack over her shoulder, she walked on, flicking her hair over her shoulder as she headed for the hyperlink terminal.

She merged into the crowd milling around the landlocked Cutty Sark. Fellow pedestrians smiled and stepped around her, paying no attention. There were no polite gasps or whispers of recognition. It was almost twenty years since the discovery of the cure, but the glow of her unwelcome celebrity hadn't diminished. Until now. Why hadn't she thought of this before?

A changed appearance was one thing, but didn't extend to fingerprints or retina, a major downside compared to money. Everything was biometric. How was she going to access the hyperlink without giving away her location? Ordinarily she wouldn't have given it a second thought, but forty-eight hours in the presence of Ethan Helix had taught her a lot about cyber surveillance. The earlier sense of liberation slanted towards fear that she was about to light up a control room somewhere as soon as she scanned her eye or finger.

She loitered outside a pretentious vegan salad bar, operated by a pasty-faced teenager. A murmur broke out amongst the shoppers as a trio of police vehicles sped past, sirens wailing as they weaved their way towards the park. It was too far to walk to Westminster. A taxi presented the same payment problem and calling her AV from the house would look suspicious, too. Maybe it wasn't so easy to disappear?

Turning towards the entry gates, she bumped shoulders with someone. 'Sorry, excuse me.'

The sandy-haired man paused. He tilted his head towards her. 'No problem. After you.'

Move it Gabrielle. He works at the Treasury. One of Justin's minions. 'Sorry, my fault.' She smiled and stepped into the salad bar.

The man's reflection in the glass of the display cabinet lingered for a moment, smiled and turned away. About to leave, Gabrielle caught the eye of the beaming proprietor behind the counter.

She smiled and nodded. 'Oh, hi. Just looking.'

'Today's special is a black bean feta quinoa wrap with a mouth-watering avocado tahini.'

Gabrielle glanced up, not riding the same erotic wave that seemed to be coursing through the flat-chested youngster. 'I'll just take a bag of the err, burrito bean chips and a bottle of water. Thanks.'

She paused at the exit. Glancing towards the terminal entrance, she half expected to see a battalion of police storming the building as her fingerprint payment was detected. She passed through to the boarding area, pleased to find it deserted. Most people had been relegated to the DLR further down. The hyperlink-pod door hummed open. The stale smell of plastic competing with air freshener drifted out on a current of warm air.

Acceleration pressed her back into her seat as the pod sped towards Westminster. She sipped her water as the small lights dotted along the tunnel merged into a single beam of light pointing into the void.

* * *

Gabrielle merged into the flow of passengers riding the escalator towards street level. The Remembrance Day restraint in dress, demeanour and commerce had evaporated. Vehicles packed the road, humming in disciplined rows. The advertising holograms were making up for lost time, hanging over the exits and entrances like gaudy spiderwebs trying to snag the unwary with biometrically personalised offers. She crested the slope and turned left at the exit.

'Gabrielle Stepper, how lovely to see you.'

She froze, turning to face the attractive black model who had greeted her. A young woman passing in the opposite direction looked over her shoulder, her eyebrows knitted in confusion. She shook her head and carried on.

'Do I know—' said Gabrielle.

The model shimmered and pixilated. 'C-c-can I

interest you in the black beauty guide: mastering make-up on dark skin. Twenty-five percent personalised discount, just for you, Doctor Stepper.'

Her heart raced. 'Unsubscribe.' She turned her eyes to the pavement and shoulder-charged through the hologram before it could say her name a third time for the entire world to hear. Damn those things. She shook her hair over her face as she marched towards Parliament Square. Now she understood why most commuters wore sunglasses, rain or shine. She shuffled across Westminster Bridge Road, confining herself to the island in the centre of the road. Advertising regulations prohibited mugging pedestrians with promo-grams when they were crossing the road for reasons of health and wellbeing.

Whitehall stretched out behind her. The entrance to Downing Street was hidden beyond by trees. Perhaps Justin was in his office at number 11, in the treasury building or more likely, skulking somewhere in Parliament. Who cares? The lights changed, she turned her eyes to the road and crossed onto the footpath over Westminster bridge.

She lingered halfway across the bridge, avoiding eye contact with the relentless promo-grams, anything or anyone else. The sweet scent of the delphiniums and dahlias rose from the borders as she leaned on the parapet overlooking the verdant gardens. She tried to picture the brown swirling current of the water hidden below, serene in the darkness. The same unrelenting tide, heavy with barges that bore away the Ebola victims on their final journeys to the hastily built, and eventually overwhelmed, alkaline hydrolysis plants downstream at Thurrock.

She hunched her shoulders as a police vehicle sped across the bridge behind her, disgorging three heavily armed officers at the entrance to the terminal. Perhaps her vegan lunch purchase had set off an alarm somewhere. She trotted down the white stone steps into the gardens below St Thomas's Hospital.

The sun warmed her shoulders as she slipped off her jacket. She folded it onto the bench. What the hell was she doing? How had she ended up in this mess? Big Ben chimed out the quarter hour. Helix, Ethan, Andy and Rich, they'd all put themselves at risk for her and she had repaid them by reneging on the plan and pulling a vanishing act. Helix would be furious, and he was entitled to be. If he hadn't intervened at the Cenotaph, if he hadn't smuggled her out of London, if he hadn't got her away from Helix Towers, if he hadn't put himself between her and that thing in the park, if, if, if, if. She *was* a fool.

The shadows stretched over the lawns as the sun sank towards the western horizon. The moon would be up soon. She'd be able to look up at it and hope that perhaps SJ was doing the same and thinking of her, too. Maybe SJ had the right idea, an off-grid life, away from all of this.

She took small sips of her water. The sun glinted off the vehicles making slower progress over the bridge than the pedestrians in the evening rush hour. She grimaced at the burrito chips; perhaps not as hungry as she was, but she needed something.

* * *

Gabrielle hovered around outside the entrance to the hospital staff changing rooms on the second floor of St Thomas's. As she feigned interest at the items in the vending machine, a white-coated doctor turned the corner with her eyes fixed on the tablet computer she was holding. The doctor paused for long enough to look at the iris scanner, shoving the door as the lock released. Gabrielle spun around catching the door, bobbing at the scanner. She cringed at the disgruntled tone from the device. Too engrossed in the device in her hand, her predecessor didn't notice.

The staff canteen was as she remembered it, where the welcoming smell of food had won the battle with disinfectant. Busy night and day there were colleagues working on notes, catching up with each other and on their sleep. The chimes of Big Ben announced the start of the evening news programme, showing on three wall-mounted screens. Seated at a deserted table next to one of the panoramic windows, Gabrielle looked up at the TV. A reporter gave a live update from College Green, next to the Houses of Parliament.

Her eyes flicked over the subtitles as she traced a lazy figure-of-eight with her spoon in her soup, waiting for it to cool. The image cut away from the reporter to one of the committee rooms. The spoon slipped from her fingers. Valerian Lytkin oozed confidence as he was questioned by the chairman of the Defence Committee. She held her breath. A press conference followed with Lytkin and her husband. She tried to read their lips as they spoke. "Strong partnership", "research and development" and "foreign trade". The bonhomie culminated in an over-enthusiastic shaking of hands and smiles for the cameras before a final cut-away back to the reporter.

Clutching her hand to her chest she remembered to breathe, overcoming the temporary dizziness. Her skin-topped soup had lost its appeal. Her own image appeared on the TV alongside that of Nathan Helix and the headline that proclaimed: "Still at Large". She snatched her hands to her face, peeking through a gap in her fingers. A short clip played showing an anonymous AV draped in a large green tarpaulin, being winched onto the load bed of a recovery vehicle with the caption: "Earlier today at the Meridian". She unzipped her rucksack in search of a fresh tissue. Groping around inside, her hand fell upon the syringe Helix had pulled from McGill's robotic hand. Her throat tightened as she felt its cool brushed metal exterior. Maybe it would be best for everyone if she just went to the roof and jumped.

She gawped at the TV. A series of still photographs of SJ being led to a police car with the caption, "Case of mistaken identity. Sarah-Jane Stepper on her way to London after the Chancellor intervenes."

35

SJ cupped her chin in her hand, leaning against the window of the AV as it accelerated down the slip road towards the M4. They'd estimated she should be in London by 19:30. Making polite conversation obviously wasn't part of the curriculum at the police college, as the two officer cadets had hardly spoken since they'd left Swindon. One sat to her right, contenting herself by staring out of the window like someone who'd never been outside the capital. Sitting opposite, the other with the frame of an anorexic stick insect, had finally taken his eyes off SJ. She understood how Gabrielle must feel with people gawping at her all the time.

Half way down the slip road, a vehicle had stopped and appeared to be turning around. 'What's going on?' The police vehicle lurched as it slowed. SJ jammed her foot on the seat opposite to stop herself from being flung across the cabin towards stick insect who was following his colleague's lead, producing his gun and cocking it.

SJ gathered her bag towards her. 'Err, what's with the guns?'

The woman cleared her throat. 'Just a precaution, we're not that familiar with operations outside London, so best be on our guard.' She zipped her jacket and slid forward towards the door.

The scent of dry grass and pollen drifted into the cabin, making SJ's nose itch. The officer stepped out onto the warm tarmac. 'Looks like it's stuck across the road,' she said.

Stick insect's gun shook as he passed it from hand to hand. SJ wondered how often he'd used it. He smiled, nodded and opened the door opposite. Raising his weapon, he stalked forward in step with his partner before halting. 'Get out of the vehicle – now!' The authority in his voice belied his diminutive stature.

SJ wriggled to the edge of her seat, sensing an opportunity. She could take a dive through the thicket of hawthorn bushes and down the embankment. She tightened the grip on her rucksack.

Outside, the female officer repeated the order. 'Get out of—' The impact from an unseen projectile shattered her face into a red bloody mess. Her weapon clattered down the road towards the stationary vehicle as her lifeless body slumped against the side of the AV and fell to the road.

Twisting in her seat toward the direction of the sound, SJ saw the flash of a second shot that snapped back stick insect's head, a cloud of pink and white mist spraying from the back of his skull. She dived to the floor and clutched her rucksack to her chest. Clamping her hand over her head, she fought for breath between heavy heartbeats.

The sound of heavy boots approached on the road surface outside. Undergrowth snagged and scratched across coarse fabric. SJ froze as a fleeting shadow filled the cabin. The tall figure continued past the open door. She sprang out, stumbling onto the tarmac. Her brain was telling her to go for the embankment, but her body wasn't responding. All she could feel was a familiar sting in her back as the debilitating energy surged into her body to the insistent click, click, click of the second taser she had encountered in less than twenty-four hours.

* * *

SJ coughed as her vision cleared. A blond-haired man sitting opposite returned her stare though frigid blue eyes. The source of the fug-filled atmosphere sat to his left, grinning as he tossed his cigarette out of the window. The brief rush of cool air cleared her mind and lungs.

The blond man joined his fingers at the tips and leaned forward. 'Colonel Terry McGill. Nice to meet you.'

SJ flicked her eyes between the two of them. 'Who the fuck are you? Why did you kill those—?' Another bout of coughing cut her short.

'I just told you who I am.'

'I don't care. Why did you kill those officers? They were taking me to my brother-in-law. You know who that is, don't you?'

McGill grinned. 'Justin "Winking" Wheeler, Chancellor of the Exchequer.'

'Good. So, there's no problem then. You'll be taking me to him.' She folded her arms. 'What are you grinning at?'

'Does the name Nathan Helix mean anything to you?'

'The guy that allegedly kidnapped my sister, some kind of war hero,' she snapped.

McGill sighed. 'Yes, and not exactly. He's no hero, despite the letters after his name and the gongs he wears on his chest.'

SJ rummaged in her roomy pockets. 'What about him?' She tied her hair back in a bunch with a purple hair band.

'Those people back there, the officers as you call them. They work for him and the same terrorist outfit that your sister - saviour of the nation - has hooked up with.'

'Don't be bloody ridiculous. Officers? They were barely out of puberty. They were cadets,' she snorted. 'And Gabrielle wouldn't get involved with anything like that. You may mock her, but she's about saving lives, not taking them. What's that?'

'I thought you would say that.' McGill tapped the screen of a thin glass tablet on his lap. 'Look at this.'

SJ rotated the screen and glowered at him. She pressed her hand to her mouth as the death of Dr Berdiot played out on the screen. 'My God. That's gross.' She thrust the tablet back at McGill.

'Impressive huh, and all your sister's handiwork; she made the discovery and developed the pathogen to the point of weaponisaton. The same pathogen that killed her friend, Rachel Neilson, when Helix bodged an attempt to seize her and her daughter.'

'Rachel? She's dead? What about Lauren? Is she OK?'

'We don't know. Helix's cohorts took her, killing four of my men in the process.'

'My God, poor Rachel.' She balled her fist under her nose. 'Come on. Gabrielle? There's no way. That's all bollocks.'

McGill snorted. 'She's been a little erratic, I understand, since the death of your niece.'

'Eve. Yes.' She turned to the window. 'I'm not sure she's ever got over it. Maybe you never do.'

'No. So, we need to keep you safe. I just need to let the Chancellor know we have you. He was concerned.'

'Ha! Justin? That's a likely story. The only thing he cares about is politics and his fucking ascendency.'

McGill tapped the screen of his phone. He raised his eyebrows as the call was answered. 'Hello, sir. Yes, it's McGill. We have the sister. Yes, sir, excellent news. I'll call you back once we're at the safe house to discuss next steps. Yes. Thank you.'

36

Wheeler concentrated on the newsflash announcing the resignation of the Prime Minister, wishing Lytkin would keep his voice down. Why did people insist on shouting on the bloody phone? He tapped the TV volume control on the glass tabletop just as Lytkin ended his call. 'You're looking very pleased.'

Lytkin glanced at the newsflash. 'Hmm. It seems we are both the recipients of g-good news.' He nodded towards the screen as he sat.

'Yes. You must excuse me. I need to prepare a statement.' He straightened his tie. 'Bloody idiot could have told me she was going to resign.'

Lytkin sniffed. 'She kn-knows you're you. Anyhow, you knew it was coming, I bet you already have your speech written. Do you think there'll be anyone to s-stand against you?'

Wheeler clamped his hands behind his head and pursed his lips. 'I doubt it. The only one I was worried about got herself on camera in a threesome with her teenage stepson, and one of his school friends.'

Lytkin pressed his fingers to his lips as he swallowed the mouthful of tea. 'Ah ha. The old ways are often the best ways. I s-salute you.'

'So, no opposition likely. And all being well, by this time next week, I'll be standing on the steps of Number Ten, waving to the media.' He toasted himself with the white bone china coffee cup. 'And what about you?'

'W-what about me?

Wheeler muted the TV. 'Who was that on the phone?'

Lytkin took his time over his tea.

Wheeler tilted his own cup and stared into it, toying with the idea that perhaps he didn't need Lytkin as much as Lytkin needed him. With no leadership campaigning likely, perhaps he didn't need the promised funding for services rendered. But he was sure he'd find a use for it.

Lytkin placed his cup on its saucer. 'Hmm. That was the ever resourceful C-Colonel McGill.'

Wheeler bit his lip, finding it odd that Lytkin had had a call from someone he'd ordered to be terminated on sight. 'Any closer to discovering the whereabouts of my wife?'

Lytkin laughed. 'No. I'm afraid n-not, but he is taking care of your sister-in-law.'

Wheeler's eyes widened, his scalp tingling. 'Bloody hell, Valerian. SJ was to be collected by Yawlander's people and brought to me. How did he find out about her?' He pushed his chair back and crossed to his drinks cabinet.

He held up a glass to Lytkin who declined with a wave. It must have been in the restaurant. McGill heard the call from SJ and put two and two together. Maybe he was smarter than he looked. He poured a large measure of brandy as Lytkin stepped up next to the window.

'Like I said, my f-friend. He is resourceful and now he thinks he has all the cards.'

Wheeler took a large mouthful of brandy, feeling its warmth rolling around in his mouth. 'All the cards? What's going on, Valerian? I hate to say this, but I don't think you're being honest with me.'

Lytkin snapped around from the window. 'Honest? Spoken like a real politician in his palace of fake integrity. Don't l-lecture me about being honest.'

He lunged at Lytkin. 'Valerian. I'm on the bloody verge of becoming Prime Minister.' He grabbed his arm. 'All of this shit with Gabrielle was meant to be a terrible misunderstanding. Once you had what you needed, it was all going to disappear. You've gone too far.'

He felt the chilly clamminess of Lytkin's palm as he levered his hand from his arm, almost causing him to spill his drink. There was a steeliness in Lytkin's eyes that he hadn't seen before.

Lytkin brushed out the wrinkles in his jacket sleeve. 'P-Perhaps I will have one of those.' He nodded at the decanter. 'Better m-make it a large one and top yours up. You're going to need it.'

37

McGill's vehicle made good progress on the eastbound carriageway, weaving between the occasional lorry on the busy freight route between London and Bristol. A tailback on the other carriageway extended eight miles back towards London, following a collision between a maintenance troll and a navigation gantry. SJ's eyes drooped as the monochrome queue of autonomous trucks on the neighbouring carriageway streamed past the window. She couldn't imagine her brother-in-law getting on with McGill and the length of their call had proved her theory.

McGill slipped the phone into his jacket pocket. 'Nobody going anywhere over there. Trucks stacked up nose to tail.'

SJ snorted. 'His holiness is looking forward to seeing me, no doubt?'

'Approaching the A329, Boss,' the driver reported.

McGill scratched his chin. 'Take the exit towards Bracknell.'

SJ's eyelids felt heavy as she stifled another yawn. Gabrielle wouldn't get involved with terrorists or be in league with someone like Helix. It was a load of cobblers. But then something wasn't right.

The front screen exploded. A blizzard of blood, gore and shattered plexiglass filled the cabin as the top half of the guy sitting next to McGill vaporised, his head disappearing into the slipstream through the rear window. McGill dived at her, yelling over her screams and the roaring wind. 'It's Helix! Stay down!' He wiped the gobs of blood from his face.

A shard of shattered glass dug into her cheek as McGill laid over her, pinning her to the floor. A severed hand twitched inches from her nose. The vehicle lurched as the front tyre exploded in a hail of smouldering rubber. McGill rolled off her as the driver hit the brakes hard, sending the vehicle snaking across the carriageway to a halt.

McGill heaved the door open. 'Get ready, we need to bail out. You ready, Kav?'

'Ready, Skipper,' the driver replied.

A combination of being cramped over her knees and McGill on her back had almost suffocated her. She took a couple of breaths.

'Ready SJ? Three, two, one, go!'

She didn't have time to answer as she swivelled around onto her backside towards the door. McGill put his boot in her back, propelling her forward. She slid out behind the driver who was busy aiming his rifle ahead, scanning for targets. He shuffled sideways, his body stiffening as his head exploded. His right shoulder and arm boomeranged through the air and smeared down the side of one of the stationary trucks.

SJ stumbled as McGill caught her. The remains of the lifeless man slumped to the ground spattering her legs with blood. She tripped over her feet as McGill grabbed the straps on the back of her dungarees and spun her around in front of him. Another shot ripped into the tarmac to her left, sparks exploding. McGill heaved her towards the central reservation and shoved her over the barrier into the weed-filled void between the carriageways.

'He's going to kill us.'

'No. He's trying to kill me,' McGill shouted as he leapt over the barrier. 'He wants you alive.'

SJ buried her face in the grass, gasping a few short breaths. McGill pushed again with his boot, rolling her towards the opposite carriageway. 'Roll underneath and make for that truck.'

She scrambled to her knees. He's trying to kill him. Not me. You can make it. She held her breath and rolled in one move underneath the barrier, and under the truck. McGill bobbed his head up, inviting another shot that exploded against the metal barrier. She waited as he half-rolled half-ran underneath the truck, coming up next to her. 'What now?' she whispered.

'Get ready. There's a bike filtering down between the rows of traffic, we're going to grab a lift.'

'Both of us?'

'Not exactly but get ready.'

She crouched below the truck, in front of the rear wheels. McGill pounced behind the passing motorcycle, pulling the rider backwards off the machine, kicking him hard in the ribs as he hit the ground. She grimaced as the rider groaned and writhed. McGill pushed the bike upright and waved her forward.

She glanced in the opposite direction between the rows of stationary vehicles. Could she make it?

McGill shouted. 'Get on!' He aimed his gun at her. 'Now!'

She ran forward and swung her leg over the seat, wrapping her arms around his waist as he accelerated.

* * *

Helix lifted his cheek from the stock of the Accuracy International AW50F sniper rifle and zoomed in on the fleeing motorcycle with his right eye.

'Any update on Gabrielle, Ethan?'

'You need to get weaving, Bruv. The local law will be crawling all over the place after the mess you've just made.'

Rolling onto his knees, he snapped the lens caps shut on the rifle scope, folded the bipod and heaved the rifle back into the rack. One of his drones deployed behind him in pursuit of McGill and SJ. The door closed as he turned to the navigation system. He searched the map for somewhere quiet to rest up. 'Did you see that fucker, Ethan?' He shook his head. 'Talk about human shield.'

'You sound surprised, Nate. What did you expect?'

'I expected to nail that fucker with the fifty cal,

rescue the maiden and head home in time for tea.' The AV accelerated, pressing him back in his seat. 'I just didn't have time to settle in.'

'Covering the distance from Ebbsfleet and getting set up in time was always going to be marginal. SJ didn't look like she wanted rescuing, the way she got on that bike. I wonder what yarn old blue eyes has told her?'

'Somebody waving a Glock 9 at you is pretty persuasive.' He leaned forward and unclipped the magazine from the rifle. 'Anything on Gabrielle or from Yawlander?'

'Not since the heads-up on his folks getting tapped by McGill. What was the point in sending a couple of kids?'

'Hmm. There was no need to send anyone. Unless they got wind of what McGill was up to. No guarantees but at least it would've been two less bodies. But I expect Chancellor Wheeler insisted on a welcoming committee.' He pressed four more armour piercing rounds into the magazine and clipped it back into the rifle.

'Soon to be Prime Minister Wheeler, you mean.'

Helix tapped the right screen bringing up the news feed. 'Since when?'

'Since as of a few minutes ago. The PM's resigned and he looks likely to be her successor.'

'I see he's been glad-handing that fucker Lytkin again, too. Anyway, what news of Mrs Wheeler?'

'Not a lot, I'm sorry to say. Bank transactions. One vegan lunch, a trip on the hyperloop and scoff in St

Thomas's staff canteen. Make of that what you will. Oh, hang on, she was also accosted by a holo-ad offering a black beauty guide: mastering make-up on dark skin.'

Helix unzipped his jacket. 'Any CCTV?'

'Unless she's back to her old self, not much use in looking as I wouldn't know what I'm looking for.'

'Hang on Ethan. How to master make-up on dark skin. She's not back to her old self. She's taken on darker skin, otherwise why would the holo-ad approach her?'

'Nate. I'm sorry to say this, but that doesn't narrow it down by much.'

'But have you looked?'

'Yep. I've got some facial scans going on. But if she's done the whole Thai lady thing again...'

'She's too smart for that. She'll be someone else. But what the fuck is she doing?'

'Your guess is as good as mine, chum. Perhaps she's going to visit her old man in Parliament to congratulate him.'

Helix sniffed. 'Can't see that happening. I'm going to lay up for a bit. What's McGill up to?'

Ethan stared out of the screen, left eye closed, avoiding the smoke from the roll-up clenched in his teeth. 'Still on the M4 but going the wrong way.'

'He'll have to get creative. Like Yawlander said, if Lytkin's pissed off with him, we're not the only ones looking for him.'

Ethan clamped his hands together over his head. 'No. But at the moment, Lytkin doesn't have Gabrielle so he can't do anything with the recipe.' He scratched his eyebrow. 'Obviously, McGill has worked out that twins have identical DNA, so I reckon he will use her to bargain with Lytkin in exchange for his life.'

'He's not going to have a life for much longer if I have anything to do with it. Helix reached up to the screen, tapping through the news stories. 'I wouldn't trust Lytkin. The best McGill can hope for is that if he hands her over, Lytkin might forget about it.'

'He might. Which I doubt. But we won't. What's the end game?'

'For McGill it can only have one end. Lytkin is a bigger fish and now Gabrielle's done a bunk, she needs to keep her head down. But I'm not sure being slap in the middle of London is the best place for her.' He rubbed his eyes. 'Whatever we do, we need to keep her and SJ as far away as possible from Lytkin.' The silhouette of plane on its slow lumbering approach to Heathrow blotted out the sun as it passed overhead. 'Actually, I'll tell you what we're going to do.'

38

The depth of her stupidity and the magnitude of the situation had dawned on Gabrielle as she watched the news in the staff canteen. The news had been vague about SJ. Who was bringing her London and where was she going to stay? Justin would say the right thing all the time there was a media-bot in front of him, but he was unlikely to extend her a warm welcome.

The walk from St Thomas's had taken around thirty minutes. She'd felt the first pangs of the makeover pen wearing off as she strode past Parliament. A vague feeling of nausea and the gradual lightening of her hair and skin had kept her away from the footpaths as she entered St James's Park. She needed to be back to herself if her idea was to work. She adopted the same tactic as she zigzagged across Green Park, the diminishing light helping to conceal her approach.

Not given to moments of hindsight, she couldn't help telling herself that if she had acted sooner, none of this would have happened. One thing was clear: the passage of time had done nothing to discourage Valerian. She didn't have the luxury of options. The potential solutions she'd scraped together had a shelf life measured in seconds. The only non-suicidal option she had was to reach Helix or Ethan.

She loitered at the edge of Green Park, under the trees overlooking Piccadilly. It was as close as she dared to get to Down Street. The scaly bark of a horse chestnut tree dug into her shoulder as she leaned against it. The smell of rain and damp grass hung in the air like a bad dream, another sensory memory that transported her back to that playground.

She'd waited long enough. Down Street was empty, the last of the street cleaning rovers having swept and sprayed their way to the north end. She heaved open the heavy metal gate and crossed, keeping her eyes down to avoid the cameras on Piccadilly. Her sense of optimism flourished with each step towards the disused station. The thickset door set in its metal frame showed no signs of yielding. Did he have a key? Was there a key code he'd punched in or some other way of releasing it? Ready to give up and walk away, a faint circular outline at the edge of the frame pulsed, inviting the pad of a curious finger. She obliged. The metal was cold to the touch. A faint red glow bloomed under her finger. She snatched it away as if burned but the door remained closed. She walked on.

From the corner of Down Street and Brick Street, she glanced back. Discreet wasn't working. She retraced her steps, taking the footpath on the opposite side. Knowing the Helix brothers, an uninvited guest putting their finger on the print scanner must have triggered some kind of alarm. Ethan might be looking, puzzled in the glow of his monitor back at Strode Park. She loitered in line with the door, looking up at the building, smiling, shaking her hair back, tucking it behind her ears. She did everything possible not to hide her face. Thirty seconds, Gabrielle, and you need to move your bum.

Her smile faded with each passing second. Move on, nobody at home. She hadn't taken two steps when an angry buzz and metallic click emanated from the door. She ran at it, grabbed the handle and heaved it outwards. The tiny amount of light vanished the moment she shut the door behind her, leaving her rigid in the baked air gloom. Where was Helix when you need a strong hand to guide you?

A light from below offered hope. Maybe he was there. She felt her way down the spiral steps, anxiety tugging her back to the surface but the thought of him pulling her down.

The light-filled room felt familiar and safe. She bobbed up on her toes, peering into corners, expecting Helix to appear from the kitchen corner. Where is he? The workstation monitors sat idle and empty. If Helix wasn't here, maybe Ethan would appear on a screen, grinning through a fog of smoke. She slung her rucksack over the back of the chair. As she hesitated between benches, she pictured Helix working by the light of the desk lamp amongst the half-finished projects, tools and other man-cave paraphernalia. A prosthetic arm hung from a rack with a lifeless eye-like lens staring back at her from a wire shelf beneath it.

The same empty mugs, from last time, stood on the kitchen counter. Nothing had changed. Maybe he hadn't been back since... Sitting on the edge of the dishevelled bed, she picked up a t-shirt and ran the material through her fingers. Perhaps he's still with Andy, Rich and Lauren? She buried her face in the material, taking in the scent, a faint mixture of man, material and deodorant. Laying the garment in her lap, she untied her hair, shook her head and ran her fingers through it.

The hair band slipped from the bed. Kneeling down to retrieve it, her hand brushed something under the bed. She lifted the edge of the blanket revealing a wooden box beside a pair of well-worn walking boots. She drew the box out and sat with it on her knees. Her finger stroked the brass plate, engraved with his name. Her finger paused on the catch. You're being nosy, Gabrielle. It's under the bed for a reason. She bit her lip as she shuffled forward to put it back. Its contents shifted, dislodging it from her hand. It bounced off the edge of the mattress. The lid sprung open as it fell on its edge.

A collection of cuttings, cards, and old photographs littered the floor at her feet. She crouched and picked over them. Creased and faded photos of Helix at various ages and times in his life peered back at her. It was nice how some people still printed images instead of keeping them digital. A group photo: three men in uniform, happy, cocky and confident. Ethan, before his injuries, standing proudly next to Helix and Jon, their older brother. The three Musketeers. She turned it over, noting the date. Maybe it was the last one of them together?

Slipping onto the floor beside the box, she turned over a photo of her receiving her DBE. Hello. She picked another; her and Justin on their wedding day, cropped to remove as much of him as possible, but the dress unmistakeable. Rolling onto her knees, she began turning over more of the pictures, assembling them into a kind of mosaic arc on the floor in front of her. Gabrielle with Justin, Gabrielle giving an interview, Gabrielle at the Cenotaph, a print of an internet article with her at work in her lab, Rachel in the background. Gabrielle and Eve feeding the ducks. The box contained as much of her own life as his.

She hadn't known what to expect when he turned up at the observatory. His disdain for Justin had amused her, but then perhaps he just didn't like politicians. Lots of people didn't. Once the formal interview was out of the way he'd seemed more relaxed. They'd chatted over supper and conspired to steal Justin's best brandy. Oh, Christ! I kissed him in that van on the way to Rich and Andy's... And I'd got drunk and stoned and... He saw me naked. Oh my God. He could be back at any minute. She shuffled everything back into the box, hoping they weren't in any particular order.

A dull thud echoed around the workshop. She clambered to her feet, sliding the box back under the bed with her heel. 'Hello. Helix? Is that you? It's Gabrielle. I'm in here.'

Someone cleared their throat, the sound from the speakers echoing around the space. She edged her way to the door and peered into the empty workshop. One of the monitors at Helix's workstation was on. Maybe it was Ethan.

'Hello G-Gabrielle.'

39

The nicks from the shattered glass and the blood stains mingled with the collection of callouses and scars on SJ's hands. They were her own living archive of years spent outdoors. Every scar had a story, mostly happy. Those acquired today would be remembered without fondness. Was it the severed hand hitting her in the face that left the thick smear of blood across her cheek? A macabre mix of mud, grass, road grime and more blood, probably the driver's, coated the legs of her dungarees. She unbuckled the straps, dropped them to the floor and kicked them into the corner of the grimy hotel room. Angling the wardrobe mirror into the light, she pulled her t-shirt over her head. She pushed up her breast to look at the angry bruise on her ribs where McGill had shoved her into the barrier.

He'd locked her in, leaving her with a vague promise of some clean clothes and something to eat. Going out of the window wasn't an option, they were on the fifth floor. There was nothing to climb down. The room smelt damp, with wispy grey curtains and ghostly outlines of absent picture frames on peeling magnolia walls. At least there was a working shower. A rare luxury, assuming the water was hot, and a pleasant change from the chilly River Wye.

* * *

SJ dried herself and pulled the grey towel up under her arms into a short towelling dress. She twisted her hair up into a turban with a smaller towel. She pressed her ear to the bathroom door. McGill was back. She cracked the door open. He was sitting on the bed staring at his phone.

He nodded towards a bundle on the bed. 'Got you something to wear.'

She tucked the top of the towel in tighter and picked up the faded jeans. 'These feel damp.' She thumbed the t-shirt. 'And this. Where did you get them from?'

'Someone's washing line. Strangely enough all of the lady's boutiques in Bracknell didn't know you were coming so they didn't stay open.' He folded his phone away into his jacket pocket. 'Should be your size. If they're not, you can always take them back.'

'And boxer shorts, how thoughtful. At least they seem to be dry.' She held up a baggy green jumper that completed the ensemble.

McGill sprawled back onto the bed. 'You can always keep that little mini dress number on if you like. Does it for me.'

SJ gathered the clothes to her chest. Bloody creep. She took refuge in the bathroom leaning back against the door. Who was this Colonel Terry McGill? She dropped the towel onto the floor and slipped on the boxers. He'd hidden behind her while he supposedly rescued her from another madman with a gun. The t-shirt would dry. The room might have been smelly but at least it was warm. The jeans were roomy but clean. According to McGill, Helix the gunman had intended to kidnap her in the same way that he'd kidnapped Gabrielle. It was all bullshit. She buried her face in the baggy jumper.

'Something I said?' McGill muttered as she came out of the bathroom.

'You didn't think I was going to get dressed in front of you, did you?'

'Who said anything about getting dressed?'

She loosened the towel around her head. 'OK, let's get one thing straight. You're not my type. And in spite of your attempt at chivalry earlier on, there is no debt of gratitude.' She rubbed at her hair with the towel.

McGill pouted. 'And what is your type?'

'Not pubescent boys running around with guns, dressed in black with that much Velcro.'

McGill snorted. 'There, and I thought you twins were all the same. From what I've heard your sister wasn't so choosy. It seems the Chancellor isn't the only one to enjoy her bedroom favours. Random guys in dark places outside London and ladies too.'

She tossed the towel onto the sink in the bathroom. 'You know nothing about my sister. You have no fucking idea what she's been through.' She pulled her hair band from the pocket of her discarded dungarees, stretching it around her wrist. 'Did you steal anything to eat?'

McGill pointed to a brown paper bag on the table. 'She murdered her lover, you know. I've seen the evidence. Lethal injection. Claimed she was treating her for some mysterious illness.'

SJ unfolded the bulging brown paper bag and peered inside. 'Why? Why would she murder someone who loved her? If you told me she had murdered her husband, I could at least make some sense of that.' She threw an apple at him.

McGill snatched the apple from the air and shined it on the bed sheet. 'Not a fan of the Chancellor then?'

'If I had to choose between you and him? You're both cold-hearted pricks. He thought he could bask in her success and celebrity while furthering his political career. I have no idea of nor any interest in your motives.'

SJ chose an apple, running her thumb across its skin. To all the world her sister's marriage to the successful politician had seemed like a fairy tale union. When Eve arrived, it must have felt like life couldn't get any better. Eve was everything to Gabrielle. She was the perfect mum, determined to give her daughter a real childhood, nothing like their own had been. When she slipped from her life, everything collapsed. Gabrielle had spiralled into a numb empty pit of despair. She should have been there for her.

McGill finished his apple in four greedy bites, tossing the core at the bin. 'Anyway, back to the murder. Helix arrests her but it's all part of the plan. He's meant to be holding her but they do a runner.' He celebrated the apple core hole-in-one with a fist pump.

She stepped next to the bed. 'And why would she do that?'

McGill cleared his throat. 'The thing that killed that scientist in the video, it's some kind of DNA-linked bioweapon.'

'Linked to whose DNA?'

McGill shrugged. 'Your sister's.'

'You're insane. Give me your phone. I want to call my brother-in-law.'

McGill sniffed. 'I just spoke with him. He's in Parliament. He's busy preparing for his enthronement as Prime Minister.'

She caught a drip of apple juice from her lip with back of her hand. 'Justin? Prime Minister?'

McGill yawned and pushed himself up onto his elbow. 'Yep. The last one's thrown in the towel and the new one doesn't want his hippy sister-in-law getting in the way, reminding everyone of his wife's misdemeanours. For now, you're to stay with me. Until he needs you.'

She gathered her socks from the floor. 'There's no fucking way that's going to happen. Either you take me, or I'll make my own way. I've already told him I don't need his help and I don't need you as a babysitter.'

Bracknell in the middle of the night. She'd have to walk, at least set out on foot. Maybe someone would pick her up, or she could always break into another truck. It wasn't difficult. She pulled on her socks, recovered her boots and laced them up.

'I'm leaving.' She pulled the jumper over her head. 'I need not go to him. I can go to my sister's place in the Meridian.' She helped herself to another apple from the bag, shoved it inside her rucksack and turned to the door. 'Are you going to help me?'

'What's wrong, can't you open the door on your own?'

'Hilarious. Fucking wise guy.' She pulled the door open.

The door was open, but the frame was filled with another black-clad man, with his hands on his hips wearing a wide grin. She looked around the door at McGill. 'Tell your dog to move. I want to leave.'

'Tell him yourself. His name's Blackburn. He's usually very obedient, but you might have to offer him a treat.'

She turned back to Blackburn. 'Excuse me. I want to leave this room.'

Blackburn's smile widened but the gap around him didn't. She turned away before spinning on the ball of her left foot, driving towards Blackburn's groin with her right. Either she wasn't fast enough or the big man was much quicker than his size suggested. The last thing she saw before the darkness was her foot between his tree-like thighs, and lights dancing in her eyes from the lightning fast slap he had delivered to the side of her head.

40

The only distinguishing feature of Number 676 River Gardens was the lack of activity, apart from the single sentry on duty just inside the entrance gate. The rest of the logistics park was alive with the busy choreographed movements of laser guided loadbots. Close to Heathrow airport, queues of autonomous trucks stood outside every unit, waiting to be serviced by the robot army.

Hidden in the shadows, Helix leaned against his AV, watching the sentry through his night vision. 'You almost done, Ethan?'

'Almost there Nate. I've got most of the systems. Just bringing up the interior CCTV. FYI, something a little odd at Down Street.'

Helix looked away from the sentry and climbed back inside his AV. 'Odd in what way?' He slid into his seat, looking up at the screen.

'Something or somebody tripped the door sensors. There's nobody there and the incendiaries haven't gone off.'

Helix nipped the side of his lip between his teeth. 'Dodgy sensor I expect. Forget it for now. Let's stick to the task at hand. Who've we got inside?'

Ethan moved away from the screen, rubbing his hands together. 'The labs all look quiet, no sign of anyone in white coats.' He flicked his joint at the ashtray beside him.

'Have you got a rendering of the building?'

Ethan manoeuvred the 3D architectural model onto the right screen, hiding himself behind it. 'Three levels: two above ground, one below. The labs are below ground along with the building plant and server rooms. Storage and vehicle bays are at ground level and offices and staff accommodation on the first floor.'

'How many warm bodies?'

The staff accommodation feed appeared on the screen. 'We've got two in here at the moment playing cards, and there are another two wandering the corridors trying to look menacing. That's it. Assuming the guy who left earlier isn't coming back soon.'

Helix studied the men, weighing them up. Apart from the sentry, the remaining security looked weak and undisciplined. 'OK. Shouldn't be a problem. What's McGill up to?'

'The guy who left earlier won't be back for a while it seems. His vehicle's parked outside the hotel in Bracknell where McGill and SJ think they're hiding.'

Helix stretched, pressing his hands flat on the roof of the AV. 'OK. Show time.' He chambered a round in his P226 and slid forward on the seat. He pulled up his heavily laden rucksack from the floor and fastened the main compartment.

With his night vision activated he searched for the sentry. He found him patrolling the right-hand perimeter of the car park. 'OK, Ethan. Get the drone up.'

A panel opened followed by the buzz of the drone's electric motors as it rose from the compartment, maintaining a low hover behind the AV. The sentry lit a cigarette, the glow of the lighter obliterating his face in an intense white shadow in Helix's night vision. The drone approached from the trees at the back of the car park as Helix activated his TC comms and stepped towards the gates. The sentry spun around, looking up towards the sound.

Ethan blipped the motors on the drone as it plummeted towards the ground. The sentry raised his rifle, watching the machine through the night sight. Helix climbed over the wall and dropped to the ground inside, ten yards behind.

With the drone grounded, the sentry approached. He halted, lowered his gun and reached out with his foot. He tapped the drone with the side of his boot, shuffling backwards as it buzzed skywards. He tracked it with his rifle until the blade from Helix's right hand penetrated the base of his skull.

Helix caught the rifle and side-stepped as the sentry slumped to the ground at his feet. '*One down.*'

'No movement from inside, Nate. Nobody watching the CCTV. Fucking amateurs.'

'*OK. I'm heading inside.*'

Slinging the sentry's rifle over his shoulder, he

dragged the body at an angle toward the rear of the car park, avoiding the large opening that led into the darkened vehicle loading bay. The brambles snagged at his trouser legs as he rolled the dead man into the scrubby bushes and threw the rifle into the undergrowth. He unholstered his P226 as he stepped through the abandoned plant border. Skirting the side of the PV-clad building, he made for the loading bay. He paused outside, listening for movement. *'You going to fit our delivery in here, Ethan?'*

'Yep. Should be fine. It'll just fit.'

Helix scanned the load bay. *'Roger that. One vehicle. Going in.'*

He jogged to the left corner, pausing outside the plain white doors leading to a stairwell. Hearing nothing beyond the doors, he pushed through. Sweeping his gun through a wide arc he covered the stairs, pausing at the half-landing. He continued down into a long corridor at the foot of the stairs.

The first door on the right had a large biohazard sticker affixed to it. *'Must be the location of Lytkin's horror movie. I won't bother checking that one then. There must be at least six rooms on either side of this corridor, Ethan. Have you got CCTV in all of them?'*

'Yep. They're all clear. Nobody at home. Go to the end of the corridor, the door on the left. That's the one we're interested in. Move your arse. There's company heading for the stairs.'

Helix sprinted down the corridor to the end and pressed down the handle. The door didn't budge. *'It's locked, Ethan.'* He turned to the door opposite. *'They're all locked.'*

The door clicked. He flung it inwards and spun around. Easing it closed, he pressed his ear to the inside. '*Where are they, Ethan?*'

'They're in the corridor but they're being lazy. Get on with it.'

Helix laid his gun on a bench and scanned around the lab. The number of warning stickers and signs gave the place a sinister feel. It was as if death was waiting in every test tube or petri dish, ready to spring out at him if he got too close. He peered into what he could only describe as a fish tank with a pair of industrial rubber gloves attached to the front of it. More flasks, test tubes and dishes, but nothing slithering around. He shuddered and swung his rucksack off his shoulders. Amongst the clutter on the bench was a child's crayon beside a drawing, with the words "Mummy and Lauren", written in red above the two people depicted in the shaky rendition of the lab. He rubbed his jaw between his fingers. She must have spent time in the lab with Rachel while she worked to unravel Gabrielle's research for Lytkin.

He rummaged through the other papers, opening folders, reading or trying to read the equations that outnumbered the actual written words on some of the sheets. He ran his finger over the handwritten notes in the margins. Maybe they were Gabrielle's.

He pulled the eight demolition charges from the rucksack and lined them up on the bench. Three would have been enough but eight would ensure that the job was done properly in case plan A didn't work out. He toggled the small switches as he positioned them. He hid the last charge behind an industrial fridge, with a no-nonsense biohazard sticker on the door. Maybe that was where they kept the pathogen. *'All charges active, Ethan. I'm done in here.'*

'Yep. Green across the board. With the aviation fuel, there should be enough heat to destroy everything. Alright. Phase two.'

Helix hooked the rucksack onto this shoulder. *'Where is everyone?'* He paused at the door.

'Two still playing cards. The other two are in the load bay about to be distracted by my drone display. I'll wait for you to get to the top of the stairs.'

Jogging to the end of the corridor, he bounded up the stairs, slowing as he reached the doors. He peered through a gap as the two men ran towards the load bay door, the drone buzzing just out of sight above. A small red dot appeared at the base of the skull of the soldier on the left. Helix squeezed the trigger. The suppressed shot found its mark, confirmed by a puff of red mist from the front of the man's head. A second dot appeared just above the right ear of his crouching comrade. The laser dot was replaced by the larger entry wound from the nine-millimetre projectile that then exited his head via his left eye.

Helix skirted the edge of the load bay. Crouching, he scooped up one of the fallen rifles. Grabbing the first man by the shoulder straps, he dragged him to the side of the load bay and returned for the second. Using the vehicle as cover, he dropped his rucksack and fired a volley of shots upwards. The rounds ricocheted off the ceiling in a shower of white dust and shards of concrete.

'Alright. That got their attention, Nate. They'll be with you in about thirty seconds, I reckon.'

He waited. The sound of heavy boots on the raised floor in the corridor opposite announced their arrival. He closed his eyes and listened, anticipating the practiced movements of passing through a door without being shot. They were in the load bay. He fired another short volley at the ceiling.

The window above him shattered, showering him with broken glass. 'OK! OK! I'm coming out.' He kicked the rifle across the concrete floor into the open.

'Move it arsehole. You know the drill. I hope.'

He placed his P226 on the floor and kicked it across next to the rifle. 'That's both of my weapons.' He stepped from behind the vehicle.

He assessed the two men: one crouched, his Glock held steady in a two-handed grip; the second with his shotgun pressed into his shoulder. They could probably look after themselves, but he wasn't interested in finding out. Not at the moment. Shotgun man looked the nervier of the two. He'd need to be cautious. He didn't want to get shot by accident. Moving to the middle of the load bay, he clamped his hands behind his head, turned his back, dropped to his knees and crossed his ankles. A solid blow between his shoulder blades knocked the wind from his lungs and sent him sprawling onto his face. With the weight of one of the men's knees heavy on his back, he allowed him to twist his arms behind his back and zip plasticuffs tight around his wrists.

'On your knees.'

He rolled onto his side and up onto his knees.

Glock man holstered his weapon. 'Fucking hell. That's Nathan Helix.'

Helix grinned. 'Nice evening for it.'

His attempt to swing away was too slow and the other man's boot caught the side of his head, sending him onto his back.

41

McGill checked his watch for the third time in ten minutes. ETA seven minutes according to the navigation system. Maybe it was a glitch. It felt like it had been saying the same thing for the last twenty. His fingers traced a line over his neck and across his scalp. His skin was still tender from the synapse interface array. The sensations were artefacts of the injuries sustained during deployment. It was one downside with the current generation of remotely operated units. It would pass. But now Nathan Helix was in custody; maybe legends have an expiry date after all. The two remaining men had done well, the other three less so. With them included, the body count for the day was eight, assuming Lafarge hadn't made it. It was nine if you included the Neilson woman. It would be double digits before the day was out.

SJ stirred, still groggy from her introduction to Blackburn. She would be more use than he'd thought. Doing Helix in the park would have been preferable. It had almost worked. Shame he'd lost his head. He would have loved to have seen Helix's face when he realised what he was dealing with. It was time to even the score. With the Cenotaph and the park, Helix was two up, but now found himself in the sin bin for getting caught. The capture of SJ was a late, but welcome fight back, bringing the score to two-one. With her help, he could even the score *and* have some fun doing it.

McGill wrung his hands, glancing over Blackburn's shoulder as they slowed at the gated entrance of 676 River Gardens. He nudged SJ awake.

She pulled her hair back behind her ears and rubbed the sleep from her eyes. 'What is this place? Where are we?'

McGill peered through the front screen. 'Time to meet our war hero.' He unholstered his gun. 'But you can't be too careful and I'm not a fan of surprises.' He scanned the empty load bay as the vehicle slowed. 'Pull up at the far end of the bay, Blackburn. Nearest the stairs.'

Blackburn turned the vehicle and reversed back towards the stairs as instructed. McGill searched the shadows. Helix was secure in the basement but with only two men left on site, he wasn't taking any chances. He moved to the edge of the seat, pausing as one of his surviving men stepped from the shadows. They exchanged nods.

He swung his gun up, level with the back of Blackburn's head. 'How much, Blackburn? How much did Lytkin promise you?' He brushed the muzzle of the gun below Blackburn's right ear. 'Lean forward. Hands on the screen.'

Blackburn turned his head. 'Dunno what you mean, Skipper. I haven't spoken to Mr Lytkin.'

McGill leaned into Blackburn's peripheral vision. 'That's interesting, but according to chummy over there, Lytkin offered you five hundred grand for my capture and return. That would have been about eighty-three grand each, plus change. I'm impressed.'

McGill released the doors as the second man stepped closer, his shotgun trained on Blackburn. Grabbing SJ by the arm, he dragged her out into the load bay. 'Put him in room two. We'll deal with him later.'

* * *

Helix's short period of solitary confinement was about to end. He took control of his breathing, smoothing out the spike of adrenalin that arrived with the sounds from the other side of the door. Three men regimented cadence down the stairs, past the door and into the neighbouring room. Two others followed, a descent without discipline, stumbling steps, the fearful cries of a woman, a familiar voice. Her desperate pleas fell on deaf ears, followed by the jagged rip of flimsy material. He flexed his arms, wrists and ankles against the plasticuffs, binding him to the light aluminium chair.

The door swung inwards. The guy with the shotgun from earlier grappled with SJ as she twisted and pulled. Wearing only a t-shirt and a pair of baggy blue boxer shorts, she twisted her arm free and pressed her hands to the doorframe. She'd been putting up a fight, the angry bruise on her cheek and her swollen lip bearing testament. Her resistance crumbled with a scream as her handler grabbed a handful of her hair and hauled her inside. Helix fixed his eyes on shotgun guy. He'd pay for that.

Helix ran his tongue over his dry lips as SJ fought on, kicking away the chair she was meant to be sitting on. Another strangled yelp rang around the room, as she was dragged to the floor by her hair. The handler straddled her and handcuffed her right wrist to a pipe that ran around the perimeter of the lab just above floor level. He did the same with her left, leaving her squirming on her back, her arms outstretched. SJ made a half-hearted attempt to spit at his back as he turned away.

The second member of his reception committee backed through the door, carrying two black buckets. Approaching the bench, he separated them and began filling the first in the sink, set into the workbench. Helix held his stare as he made a show of lifting a soaked towel from the bucket. A water-filled bucket and a towel looked innocent enough, but Helix knew what they meant. Resistance to interrogation had been part of the special force's selection and training. He'd evaded capture during the exercises and avoided being waterboarded. A technique of interrogation first used by the Spanish in the fifteenth century, its purpose was to create the sensation of drowning to extract confessions or information. It was unclear who the intended victim was today, but he could guess. McGill had probably already got what he wanted from

SJ. But that meant nothing; the sadistic McGill would torture her for the fun of it. Helix knew nothing of any value either, least of all the location of Gabrielle.

The filled buckets were left on the bench. 'Hey, the boss wants us to have a word with him next door once we're done in here,' he barked at his partner. He turned towards Helix and raised his eyebrows. 'Retribution will be swift and severe, no doubt.'

Helix sniffed. 'You're right. I hope you're man enough to take it when it comes.'

Helix won the staring competition. Bucket man gave him the finger and stalked out of the door.

SJ scrabbled for traction on the shiny floor with her bare feet.

'Are you alright, SJ?'

She tongued her split lip. 'Let me guess. You're Nathan Helix?' She looked at the growing welts on her wrists.

'I'm sorry that you're mixed up in this.' He hotched the chair round another couple of degrees. 'It won't be for much longer.'

'You kidnapped my sister.' She propped her head up on the pipe and looked down her nose at him. 'What have you done with her?'

Helix sniffed. 'Is that what McGill told you?' He arched his back away from the chair, trying to keep loose. 'No. I didn't, and there's a lot more to it. But we don't have time now. I'll—'

'Why should I believe you? You tried to kill us earlier when he was taking me to my brother-in-law.'

'I was trying to kill him, not you.' He pulled a tight-lipped smile. 'Why do you think he was cowering behind you? And, he wasn't taking you to Wheeler. He was taking you to Valerian Lytkin, the same plan he had for Gabrielle.'

She didn't have an answer, but he didn't expect her to. 'We'll get out of here soon. It will probably get rough, but—' He snapped around towards the door as the handle squeaked downwards and McGill walked in. He was right on cue. He flexed his arms and loosened his shoulders. Here we go.

McGill stalked across the room towards SJ and crouched down. 'I need your help with our friend over there.'

SJ writhed. 'Piss off. I'm not helping you with anything.' The handcuffs scraped against the pipe. 'You said you were taking me to London. To my brother-in-law.' She spat at him.

Helix shook his head. She needed to shut up and hope he'd lose interest.

McGill flicked away the spot of saliva from his cheek. 'And I will. When we've finished here. As I was going to say, Mr Helix is trained for this sort of thing, but he knows you're not.' He stroked his finger across her exposed midriff. 'Sadly, time is something we don't have, and he knows you are far more open to persuasion than he is. So, together we'll see how long it takes to loosen his tongue. OK?'

McGill straddled her, producing a broad-bladed combat knife from its sheath on his right calf.

Helix calculated the odds. If he made his move now, McGill would just a likely stab her before he could cover the short distance across the room. He clenched his jaw.

SJ froze and whimpered as McGill teased her left nipple with the tip of the blade through the material of her t-shirt.

McGill grinned. 'That's better.'

She screamed as McGill knelt to one side, snatched the collar of the t-shirt and spilt it from the neck down with the knife. He flung the two sides of the t-shirt aside, stood up and shoved the knife back into its sheath. He yanked off her boxer shorts, rolled them into a gag and thumbed them into her mouth. SJ's eyes widened, her head shaking as she scrambled to pull her knees up.

McGill turned, rubbing his hands together.

Helix fixed his eyes on McGill's. 'Hello, Terrance. I see you're still using innocent women as disposable pleasures. Surprised you didn't bring along a few kids, too. You're losing your touch.'

'Nathan Helix. As witty as ever.'

Helix tensed as McGill sprang forward, stamping his right foot onto his chest, propelling him backwards onto the floor. He grimaced through the crushing pain, his arms trapped under his full weight. He needed him closer, but McGill kept his distance. He blocked out the pain in his arm and back.

McGill removed an opaque plastic tube with a green top from his inside jacket pocket. He stood the tube on the bench, took off his jacket and folded his arms as he leaned back against the bench.

Helix tensed, increasing the pressure on his bindings. 'I've got nothing to say to you I haven't already said. You're a fucking coward, McGill. Always have been and always will be. Have you told her the real reason she's here?'

McGill ran his teeth over his bottom lip. 'I've been waiting for a long time to talk to you about the lies you and your brother peddled. The manufactured evidence, the witnesses you coerced during that hearing.' He turned to SJ and laughed. 'Have you met his brother Ethan? Only half the man he used to be.'

No amount of goading would make any difference to Helix. He'd rehearsed this moment over and over. The outcome would be the same. He cleared his throat. 'He's going to hand you over to Valerian Lytkin.' He twisted to look across the floor at SJ. 'He's the maniac who's been trying to get his hands on Gabrielle. Terrance here isn't in Mr Lytkin's good books, and thinks he can wheedle his way back in by delivering you instead.'

Helix couldn't avoid McGill's boot. He tensed, absorbing the blow to the ribs. He growled through the pain. Nothing broken. He caught his breath, as SJ attempted to wriggle herself into a sitting position, mumbling through the gag. He shook his head at her. Maybe she'd take the hint and shut up.

McGill strode across to her and snatched the gag from her mouth. 'Did you want to add something, SJ?'

SJ swallowed hard. 'Valerian Lytkin? Gabrielle worked with him during the Ebola pandemic. They were together for a while. Why would he want to harm her?'

McGill reached for the plastic tube he'd left on the bench. His eyes widened as he stared at the viscous yellow liquid. 'Your clever sister made a discovery. Correction, Mr Lytkin and your sister made a discovery.' He unscrewed the cap with an unusual amount of care and attention. 'Then she stole it and patented as her own.'

SJ twisted. 'What was it? What did they discover?' She nodded at the tube. 'Is that it?'

McGill laughed, holding the tube up. 'This? No. This is something altogether cruder.' He tilted it in the light. 'This is a kind of truth serum. I will ask our war hero over there some questions and this will help him remember.'

Three drops of liquid dripped onto the light blue floor covering, causing it to fizz and bubble. A small black-edged hole collapsed under the tiny puddle it as it hissed and popped, burning through to the cement floor below. 'If he tells me where I can find his little brother, we can conclude our business. But if he persists with his hero bullshit, I'll be back to see you.'

Helix pushed down with his elbows and arched his back, twisting his wrists against the plasticuffs. He tensed and flexed the muscles in his left arm, expanding the titanium and carbon fibre components of his right until he felt the bindings give way. He flexed his legs; he could deal with those around his ankles when the time came.

McGill carefully screwed the cap back on the tube. 'Shame there's not enough of this go around.' He turned back to Helix. 'Like I said, tell me where I can find Ethan and we can end this. You can die like a hero and I'll let her go. It's up to you. If you don't want to play nicely, we'll be finding out what a drop of this does when it's applied to her erogenous zones.' He lifted the flap of his breast pocket and dropped the bottle inside, giving it a gentle pat as it settled.

Helix loosened his shoulders as McGill turned towards the bench. Rocking to his left, he eased the pressure on his right arm, his eyes fixed on McGill's back.

McGill looked over his shoulder. 'I understand you're afraid of water after a nasty childhood accident.' He dragged the wet towel from one of the buckets. 'Let's explore that a little, see if it helps you to remember where Ethan's hiding.' He allowed the towel to fall back before filling a large jug from the second bucket.

Helix blinked. It wasn't going to happen. There was no point preparing resistance strategies. McGill would need to get close and that would be enough. He snatched a glance at SJ. Party time. McGill approached, leaving a trail of water from the sodden towel. He offered no reaction as McGill flicked the towel, spattering his face with heavy drops of water. 'Is that the best you've got? You going to manage on your own? The towel goes over the face, in case you've forgotten.'

McGill snorted as he put the jug on the floor and crouched next to him. Close enough. Helix unleashed his right arm, driving towards McGill's chest with his fist clenched. The acid bottle took the full force of the blow. McGill rolled away, screaming as the liquid leached into his shirt and across his chest. Helix swung his right arm, extending the blade from his hand severing the plasticuffs around his ankles. McGill rolled onto his knees, kicking over the jug of water. He flung his shoulder holster to the ground and ripped at his shirt.

Helix stamped his right foot into McGill's shoulder, flattening him. He dipped to his right, scooping up McGill's gun from its holster. He fired a single shot into his left ankle. McGill rolled onto his back in another layer of agony. 'Don't you die on me, Terry.'

As he snatched up one of the buckets from the bench, the lab door opened. He swung the gun up ready to engage. Beyond the blood and bruising, he identified the grinning man in the doorway. 'Blackburn? Good timing, big man. Hate to think what the others look like.' He nodded towards SJ. 'Get her out of here.'

Hefting the bucket of water, he stepped back to McGill and threw it over his chest as he choked and squirmed on the floor. 'Ethan, where's that delivery?'

Ethan cleared his throat. 'On its way, Nate. ETA seven minutes. You need to move it.'

Helix turned as SJ screamed. 'SJ. Go with Blackburn. He's with us, you'll be fine. We'll go to Gabrielle once we're done here.'

SJ struggled to pull on her shorts. She wrapped the remains of the t-shirt around herself as she cowered away from Blackburn.

McGill rolled in a slick of his own blood-streaked vomit.

'I never thought I would get to kill you twice, Terry. That thing in the park was a dry run, but far quicker than you deserved. I assume that it's really you, rolling around in agony in your own shit and piss?'

McGill's mouth moved but nothing came out, his eyes rolled. Helix grabbed his jaw, shaking him out of his half-conscious state. McGill's eyes flickered open.

'Something to say, Terry?' He took a step back as the door closed behind SJ and Blackburn. 'Anyway. Whatever it is, we're not interested.' The false ceiling tiles jumped in the shockwave from the double tap Helix fired into McGill's head. 'We got him, Jon. Rest in peace brother.'

42

The broad terrace and panoramic windows of Valerian Lytkin's thirty-fifth floor apartment offered unmatched views across London. The marble-floored sitting room, filled with sofas, low tables and display cases consumed half of the entire width of the apartment. A fine collection of art, that may have graced the world's greatest galleries and museums, adorned the walls including pieces by Klimt, Schiele, Picasso, Van Gogh, Pollock and Warhol. A cleverly disguised TV hid amongst the canvases and tapestries cycling images of rare and fine art that perhaps the owner had yet to acquire. A wide breakfast bar delineated sitting from dining. The spacious, well-equipped kitchen and twelve place dining room table gave the impression that neither had been used since construction was completed.

Gabrielle edged from the small lobby into the sitting room. A small table held a crystal vase of white lilies set against the back of a wide brown leather sofa. A handwritten note on a single sheet of vellum lay next to the flowers.

Welcome Gabrielle. Please make yourself comfortable. I will join you shortly. V.L.

The two thickset men who had collected her from Down Street had remained silent during the fifteen minute journey. Her conversation with Lytkin had been brief; other than his advice that she would be wise to cooperate with his men, he'd been aloof as to the arrangements. She rubbed her arms as she wandered between the pieces of art, pausing as one would on a visit to the National Gallery or the Tate. She pulled the small bottle of water from her jacket pocket and placed it on a coffee table flanked by two armchairs. It was the only item they'd allowed her keep when they'd rifled through and confiscated her rucksack. She stepped back from the Pollock, appreciating the wild beauty of the piece.

'An amazing p-piece, isn't it?'

She snatched her hand to her chest. 'Oh. Valerian, you scared me to death.'

Lytkin perched on the arm of a sofa, his arms folded, her rucksack beside him. 'That would be unfortunate given how l-long I've been waiting.' He folded the cuffs of his white shirt back on themselves.

Her pulse climbed, dragging her respiration with it. The earlier bravado she'd conjured up had been left behind in Lytkin's cold basement the moment she had stepped out of his AV. The little courage that remained had been chipped away, floor by floor, as the express lift had accelerated upwards towards a new and terrifying unknown.

She clenched her bottom lip between her teeth and cleared her throat. 'Well, here we are. What now?'

Lytkin slid off the arm of the sofa and padded barefoot towards an antique drinks cabinet with her bag swinging from his hand. 'Something to drink p-perhaps?'

She slipped off her jacket. 'I'll stick with water thank you.' She wouldn't put it past him to spike her drink. She tossed her jacket over the back of a sofa and slumped into a black leather armchair.

Lytkin held up a jewelled bottle. 'Are you sure? Oval vodka. Austrian. But surprisingly good. A rare and b-beautiful treat.'

'And wasted on me, Valerian.'

Lytkin laughed. 'Nothing would ever be wasted on you, G-Gabrielle.'

She sighed. 'Get to the point, Valerian. Please.'

He poured a generous measure into his glass. 'The p-point?'

'Yes, the p-point, Valerian. Why did you murder two of my best friends?' Mocking his stutter was a cheap shot. 'I'm—' She swallowed the apology. Damn him. Rachel and Lauren hadn't been tortured with charm, why should she be any different? What was she doing there? Why not some dingy basement with no windows or creature comforts? She was trapped in his coils, the caress tightening, each breath a little more inadequate than the one before.

He held up his glass as a toast. 'Ap-apology accepted, Gabrielle.' He dropped into a matching chair opposite her. 'I wanted to thank you.'

'Yes fine. You're welcome. I didn't intend to hand myself over to you.' She crossed her legs.

He pulled her rucksack across from the chair where he'd dropped it. 'Ha, ha. That wasn't what I meant. No. I wanted to thank you for returning something very important to me.' He tugged the top flap of the bag open and reached inside. 'Mr McGill helped himself to the very last of the viable p-pathogen from the lab. If you recall Dr Berd—'

'I remember, Valerian. We need not go over it again,' she said, pushing herself back up, resisting the armchair's invitation to relax.

'No.'

She took a small sip from her water bottle as Lytkin pulled the syringe from the bag. 'That?' She pressed her fingers to her lips.

Lytkin examined the white brushed metal tube. 'Yes. I assumed you'd recovered it from the p-park after...'

'After that maniac injected Rachel with it?' She sniffed. 'Do you think I would have left it where you or one of your disciples could have found it, Valerian? Give me some credit, please. That's a cosmetic makeover pen. Try it. It won't help your s-stutter but it might improve your looks.'

He examined the syringe. 'Gabrielle. Sarcasm is the last refuge of the powerless – Dostoyevsky. And mocking me is beneath you.'

'Go ahead, try it.' She pulled up the sleeve of her blouse and offered her wrist. 'Better still, try it on me. Come on.'

Lytkin frowned. 'You're out of your m-mind, Gabrielle. What's got into you?'

'I'm out of my mind, Valerian? Out of *my* mind?' She cupped her face in her hands and rocked. 'You have no idea. Really. You have no idea.'

Lytkin dropped the syringe back into the bag and zipped it closed. 'If that's true, where is the one that McGill stole?'

She sat up and ran her hand back over her hair. 'Helix kept the one from the park and if he's got any sense, he will have destroyed it by now.' She pulled a handkerchief from her trouser pocket. 'Can I have my bag back now, please?'

Lytkin sipped his vodka. 'I don't think so Gabrielle. There's sufficient m-medication in there to anaesthetise half of London. Until I have verified the contents of that syringe, I'll be looking after it.' He got up and crossed to the bedroom door behind her.

Gabrielle waved her hand dismissively. Her eyes settled on his glass. Perhaps she could have a drink. Why not go all the way, take a few Mandrax, drink half a bottle of vodka and have some fun? Perhaps he's got a secret stash of marijuana somewhere. Don't be an idiot. She turned in her seat. Lytkin tossed her bag through the bedroom door and closed it before disappearing out of sight into the kitchen.

Sitting around was crippling her. She pushed herself up from the armchair but her legs felt weak, as if she'd sprinted up the thirty-five floors from below. Was the charm offensive aimed at garnering her cooperation? Did he know the exact reason the other batch doesn't work or not? If he did then it would only be a matter of time. He could harvest what he needed from her, re-engineer the pathogen and then she would no longer be of any value to him. The artwork on the TV cycled through its long loop of masterpieces. She saw herself in the delicately painted face of the young woman in Klimt's "The Kiss". So peaceful and serene, held in the strong arms of her lover. She closed her eyes. Strong arms. The box under Helix's bed. Would she ever... She turned her eyes back to the screen and took a small step back. The dreamy image had gone, replaced with something closer to a nightmare: Edvard Munch's "The Scream".

Lytkin crossed behind her, carrying a tray set out with an assortment of small dishes and plates. 'Do you know the piece, Gabrielle?'

'The Scream. I think everyone knows it.' It could have been her.

'Correct. By Edvard Munch.' He slid the tray onto the glass-topped table. 'The original German title is The Scream of Nature, or Sh-Shriek in Norwegian.'

She drifted back to the side of the table, eyeing the selection of olives, nuts and other savoury snacks he'd assembled. She should have been hungry, but it wasn't hunger that was gnawing away in the pit of her stomach. 'Why am I here, Valerian?'

Lytkin topped up his glass. 'Are you still sure you won't have one, Gabrielle?' He laughed. 'P-Please. I'm not trying to drug you.'

She shook her head. He wasn't trying to drug her

yet. 'No Valerian. Thank—' I wouldn't put it past you to have spiked the olives with a benzodiazepine.

'Just a few olives and nuts. I never mastered the art of cooking. Please, help yourself.'

She took one of the white serviettes and a small two-pronged fork from the tray. 'You didn't answer my question. Why am I here?' She placed a selection of olives on a small bone china plate with a spoon and sat back.

'It's one of life's big quest—'

'Valerian, please. You might be enjoying this, sat on top of your tower with your thugs in suits waiting in the basement. I'm frightened. What do you want?'

He served himself from the tray. 'You're frightened. Hmm.' He popped an olive into his mouth. 'C-Can you imagine being eleven years old, being driven out of your home by men with guns and dogs? Being separated from your father and your little brother?' He reclined in his chair, resting his arms. 'Can you imagine what it's like to be that little brother, seeing your mother and sister being dragged away? Hearing their screams and n-not knowing if you'll ever see them again.' He emptied his glass in one heavy gulp. 'The men who took my mother and my sister were known as the M'yasnyky. The b-butchers.' He studied the empty glass. 'They found the remains of my m-mother. But my sister...' He returned to the drinks cabinet in silence.

The details of what had brought him and his father to the UK had always been sketchy. He'd rarely talked about his time in Ukraine, even in their more relaxed and intimate moments together. She was frightened but even through her own feelings, she couldn't imagine what his mother and sister might have endured. Her appetite for the olives had gone the same way as her appetite for the hospital soup. His story had done nothing to dislodge the fear wedged in her throat.

Lytkin turned with the bottle, placing it on the table next to the tray. 'My father spent the rest of his l-life trying to find the men responsible.' He perched on the arm of the chair with his arms folded, the glass pressed against his chest. 'He failed, but I did not.' He swirled the glass and nosed the clear liquid. 'You t-talk of my tower, my men in suits. Those responsible for orchestrating the disappearance of my family have many men in suits *and* uniforms. They live in golden towers, with colourful minarets and castellated walls overlooking the square.'

'But Valerian, you inherited your father's entire business empire. Your achievements since his passing are legend.' She relented, selecting a green olive. 'You could use your influence and business acumen to challenge those people in the boardroom, take their companies or ruin them finan—'

Lytkin slid off the arm of the chair into the seat. 'Yes, Gabrielle I could.' He reached for the bottle. 'But that p-presupposes that a boardroom exists or that there are companies to be controlled or ruined, as you put it.'

'The Kremlin? Golden towers and minarets, overlooking the square. Red Square. These people are in the Russian Government?' She reached for her bottle of water. Revenge. That's what this was about. He could bring about another world war. The Russians were itching to get back into Ukraine. Their relationship with Turkey was fractious or downright hostile, depending on who you believed.

'Not all of them. Some are in b-business, but I have no desire to take their companies.' He rotated the vodka bottle, the light reflecting from its bejewelled body across his face, starbursts of prismatic light freckling his cheeks. 'They have nothing I need or want.' He emptied the last of the precious liquid into his glass.

She rolled the plastic bottle between her hands and placed it back on the table. 'So, I'm here to help you exact your revenge on those who took your mother and sister?'

Lytkin sniffed. 'Forgive me, Gabrielle. A little too much vodka p-perhaps – and now there's none left. You had your chance. No. It's not about revenge. It's about the commercial potential, as I always told you.'

'Bioweapons?'

He laughed. 'You *have* been mixing with the wrong p-people, Gabrielle.' He spooned olives onto a plate and added a stuffed vine leaf. 'Pesticides, agricultural uses, ensuring food security in poorer countries.'

She pushed a green olive around her plate with the fork. If that were true, what explanation did he have for Dr Berdiot, the macaques and the rats? Why take the experiments to that level if your intention was to operate at a much smaller scale? And the meeting with the Defence Committee in Parliament, something about cooperation on R&D. 'How is Justin involved with all of this, Valerian?'

Lytkin lost interest in the empty bottle. 'Justin, Justin, Justin.' He dispatched the stuffed vine leaf in one mouthful. 'Excuse me.' He swallowed, wiping his mouth with a serviette. 'Justin the politician, Justin the magician, Justin the worker of miracles. He's a p-politician Gabrielle, a polit—'

'I know exactly what he is, Valerian. I thought you were friends. It's good to have friends in high places. No?' She skewered an olive, reminding herself not to eat it.

'Yes, he is a friend. He's been helpful in opening a few doors, arranging access to certain important and influential p-people. Those who could help when others were less willing.'

She stared back at her puzzled reflection in the coffee table. "Case of Mistaken Identity – Sarah-Jane Stepper on her way to London after the Chancellor Intervenes." After the Chancellor intervenes? Those who could help when others were less willing? She looked up from the table.

'Something wrong, Gabrielle? Are the olives not good?' He brushed the edge of his glass across his top lip.

'No, no. I'm sure they're fine. I just can't seem to find my appetite this evening.' She pushed the plate away. 'Perhaps I will join you in a drink, Valerian.'

She folded and re-folded the serviette as Lytkin rattled bottles. 'Anything but vodka, please.' She pushed herself back from the table deep into the armchair.

'I have just the thing. Do you like whisky, Gabrielle?'

She waved her hand. 'Whisky's fine.'

Lytkin turned, presenting a hand painted bottle. 'Macallan, one hundred years old, very special.' He placed the bottle on the table, glancing at his wrist. 'Excuse me, Gabrielle. Let me take this c-call.'

She leaned her head back and closed her eyes, but something in her stomach pinched. She sat up again as Lytkin aimed a remote control at the TV. The work of art on the screen dissolved and was replaced with a live news feed. Lytkin placed two crystal whisky glasses next to the bottle. He fixed his eyes on the TV and increased the volume.

A journalist gave a commentary to the conflagration filling the screen. 'Details are still coming in, but according to local police, an aviation fuel tanker was seen entering the premises of Lamont Rhames before the catastrophic explosion. The blast has destroyed at least fifty percent of the logistics park and caused massive disruption to flights to and from Heathrow airport. Lamont Rhames is part of the business empire controlled by this man, Valerian Lytkin, who was earlier today in Parliament making a statement to the Public Accounts Committee.' Gabrielle exchanged glances with Lytkin, confirming the identity of the man seen on the screen. The reporter continued as the footage changed to an abandoned AV with what appeared to be two bodies covered with green sheets lying in the road. 'And in other news, Sarah-Jane Stepper, sister of Doctor Gabrielle Stepper, who is currently believed to be on the run with Major Nathan Helix, has disappeared. She was en route to London to meet with

Justin Wheeler, Chancellor of the Exchequer and husband of Doctor Stepper. Police are refusing to comment on speculation that Sarah-Jane Stepper has been kidnapped by the same people believed to be holding Doctor Stepper.'

Gabrielle leapt to her feet, almost toppling the expensive whisky bottle. 'SJ. Oh my God.' She clutched her hands to her face. She rocked on her feet and pulled away as Lytkin took her arm. 'Get away from me.'

Lytkin drifted back to his chair and opened the bottle. 'I know what you're thinking, Gabrielle.' He poured two generous measures of the amber liquid, pushing one across the table in her direction. 'It was McGill who took SJ.' He turned off the TV, another grand master appeared in its place.

She cleared her throat. 'And I wonder why he did that.'

Lytkin studied the bottle. 'Even a b-blunt instrument like McGill knows a little basic science, Gabrielle. He concluded that as your twin, SJ's DNA is identical and as he had failed to bring you to me, he thought she would do instead.'

'Would do instead? She's my sister, Valerian!' She dropped to the floor and pressed her hands to the cool marble. He would never stop. There was never going be any peace and now the one precious thing left in her life had been taken from her. 'Was that the place where McGill took her?'

Lytkin scratched his chin. 'Honestly, Gabrielle, I don't know.'

'But it was your premises. It said so on the news.'

'McGill called me after he took SJ. He wasn't there when he c-called. He knew I was looking for him. It was the last p-place he would have gone.'

She clamped her hands over her head. Perhaps SJ was still alive. Still with McGill. She rolled onto her knees. 'But why would a fuel tanker be driven into your building and blown up?'

Lytkin sipped his whisky. 'It was where we were going tomorrow, to complete our w-work.' He held the glass up to the light. 'I could hazard a guess who was responsible.'

She wiped her nose. 'McGill?'

'No, Gabrielle. Why would he destroy the very thing that SJ could help to complete?'

Her knees were screaming. She shifted and sat back on the floor. 'And now everything in that building is destroyed. The research material and the samples, everything?'

'The samples, yes. But I had the paper research scanned and backed up on multiple sites for just this kind of eventuality. So, all is not l-lost. Tomorrow we fly to Berlin.' He took another generous sip of whisky. He held up her glass. 'Come and have a drink.'

She climbed to her feet. A large painting depicting the death of Socrates loomed on the TV screen as she shuffled to the table. She perched on the edge of the chair. If she was in Berlin with the backed-up research and the last of remaining viable pathogen, it would be all he needed.

'The d-death of Socrates. He was sentenced for corrupting the youth of Athens. Sentenced to suicide and forced to drink hemlock. Oil on canvas by Jacques-Louis David, 1787.'

She pulled the glass toward her. 'Sorry? Did you say something, Valerian?'

'Socrates. He was forced to drink hemlock, so the legend goes.' He nosed his glass.

'I won't do it, Valerian.' She sipped the whisky, rolling it around her mouth, the spirit warm on her tongue. 'I will not help you.'

'But you're here, Gabrielle, there's nowhere for you to go.'

She pointed her glass to the patio doors. 'I could jump off the balcony.'

'And I would meet you downstairs.' He drained the last of his drink. 'You can't win, Gabrielle. The outcome is inevitable. Come on, d-drink up.'

She emptied her glass in one greedy mouthful, pressing her fingers to her lips as she fought to swallow. She pushed the glass across the table and snatched up her water bottle.

Lytkin nodded his approval. 'Good. Now, the ex-experts tell me that to appreciate the finest whisky, one must add a splash of water in order to r-release the hidden aromas and flavours.' He poured two more large measures.

She snatched the glass up and drank it down, making her eyes water. 'Another,' she demanded, returning the glass.

'Gabrielle my sweet, please show a little re-respect. If not to me then at least to the whisky.'

The alcohol lightened her head to the cusp of

dizziness, dissolving the edges of inhibition. She opened the water, waiting for her glass to be returned.

Lytkin poured again. 'Now slowly, Gabrielle. Just a splash of water, then smell the whisky, appreciate the aromas and t-take a sip. I think you'll notice the difference.'

She leaned forward accepting the glass. 'Just a splash?'

Lytkin nodded, pushing his own glass forward. She hesitated, the bottle quivering in her hand. She steadied herself and added what she felt amounted to a splash to his glass. Swirling her own measure of the golden liquid, she watched the water dissipated in oily trails. Raising the glass to her nose, she sniffed at the aroma. 'I think you're right. It makes a difference.' The image of the painting appeared frozen. Socrates holding out his hand towards a shallow brown bowl; he pointed aloft with his left hand, perhaps sharing his final observations on life. Gabrielle raised her glass. 'To Socrates.'

Lytkin laughed, joining her in the toast. 'To Socrates.' He tipped back his glass in unison with her and closed his eyes.

She nursed the empty glass on the arm of the chair, sensing the warm trail of the honeyed whisky creeping towards her stomach.

Lytkin opened his eyes. 'Majestic.'

A hollow clank echoed around the room as she replaced her glass on the table and pushed it towards him. 'One more for the road?'

Lytkin swallowed as he poured. He splashed water

into both glasses from the bottle and returned one to her. 'I'm sure you are aware of the m-myth surrounding that expression.' He toasted her with his glass.

'Something to do with convicted criminals having one last drink before being hanged.' She took a generous draught.

'Indeed. But nobody is about the be h-hanged here tonight.'

She sat forward, rotating the glass on the table. No. Not hanged.

Lytkin finished his glass, Gabrielle followed. She poured the remaining water from the bottle into her glass and stood in front of the TV screen, staring up at the painting. Taking a pace back, she raised her glass again. 'To Socrates.' She turned to Lytkin. 'To... me.' The diamond cut pattern of the glass caught the light as she held it at arm's length. 'And... to the last of the pathogen.' She closed her eyes and emptied the glass in two deep swallows. The glass slipped from her fingers and shattered into a cascade of diamond fragments on the marble floor.

Lytkin stared at his glass and the empty bottle. He put his hands on the arms of the chair and attempted to lift himself out. 'You've k-killed us both?' Sweat beaded his brow and top lip as he cramped over. The first nauseous retch swept through him. 'Noooo.' He fell to his knees sweeping the bottle from the table, shards of black glass and whisky splashing across the floor.

She stepped through the shattered glass as he clawed at the side of the low table. 'I tried, Valerian. I tried to reason with you.' She clutched at the sudden cramp in her stomach. She took a deep breath, waiting for it to pass. 'I thought... I thought maybe for a second there was hope when your facility at Heathrow was destroyed but when you said everything was backed up, I knew you'd never stop, even if it meant more death. Killing me. Killing SJ. How many would have had to die before you got what you wanted?'

Lytkin collapsed to the floor as another convulsion swept over him. He poked at the phone on his wrist as it subsided. 'Get up here now. Kill her!'

'What have you done to me, Valerian?' She pulled at her hair. 'My life has been dedicated to saving life. Not taking it.' Her legs weakened as the turmoil in her stomach grew. 'You've turned me into a murderer.'

The coffee table scraped aside as Lytkin floundered in the gap between it and the armchair. His glazed eyes turned towards her, his mouth gaped with another convulsion, the muscles and veins in his neck taut and bulging.

'However, as much as I despise myself for what I've done, your death will at least achieve something. Your death will preserve countless others.' She gasped through her hand. 'I wasn't about to let you create a new weapon or start a war, Valerian. We've all seen enough of death. My discovery might have helped people. Not to seize power or profit from those who are weak, but to help them survive.'

Lytkin screamed, his stomach distending, straining the buttons on his shirt. Fingers of black bruising crept up his neck towards his face. She slumped down in the chair watching him as he gagged and wheezed. A nauseous wave swept through her, doubling her over. She closed her eyes as the final moments approached. She thought of Eve and Miriam, Rachel and Lauren, and she thought of Helix.

43

The early Meridian sun reflected from the smoked glass of the apartment in bronze shards. Ghostly wisps of thin mist loitered in the deeper hollows of the park. The dew-laden grass basked in the dappled sun as it pierced the leafy canopy and peeked around trees. The garden shrubs and flowers lifted their heads and unfurled their leaves, unseating pearls of dew that trickled down stems and ran off the leaves. Helix sat on the low wall surrounding the observatory patio, the brass strip representing the prime meridian running between his feet. Steam drifted from a mug of coffee next to him.

The escape from River Gardens had been close. Ethan had confessed that he may have miscalculated the amount of aviation fuel necessary to ensure that no trace could be found of what stood on the site previously. They'd felt the shockwave as they sped away, barely making the minimum safe distance.

McGill had taken the bait but was better informed than they'd realised. He could have shot Blackburn when they arrived at the warehouse. He could have shot Helix when he walked into the lab, but a combination of arrogance and theatrics had contributed to his downfall. Yawlander had taken a risk in getting Blackburn embedded in McGill's team, but Helix was glad to have had the extra pair of hands.

It had been tempting to go west from Heathrow instead of east, but he'd wanted to remain close to central London. They knew that Gabrielle was or had been somewhere within a half-mile radius of Westminster. Down Street was possibly compromised, unless it was her that tripped the door sensors. But how would she have got in? He dismissed the thought and turned to his coffee.

Once inside the vehicle and wrapped in a survival blanket, SJ had insisted on being brought to the Meridian. His attempts to dissuade her had proved fruitless and after he'd agreed, she'd drifted back into a kind of shocked malaise. He hadn't done it to keep her quiet. He knew that there was little chance of Wheeler turning up, but Gabrielle might have made her way back there if she could. An empty feeling had filled his stomach as soon as they'd arrived. They found the place deserted. SJ had gone to her sister's room and closed the door. He hadn't seen her since. A decent night's sleep would help, assuming she could sleep at all. He leaned his elbows on his knees, drew his hands together in front of his face and closed his eyes. Where are you, Gabrielle?

He rubbed his fingers across his chin. Ethan had arrived shortly after them. He was glad to have him around again. It was always easier bouncing ideas off each other when they were in the same room. They'd shaken hands, acknowledging it was mission accomplished where McGill was concerned. There was no euphoria and no discussion. McGill was gone and they would never speak his name to each other again.

There was more work to be done and Ethan would be awake soon. They'd spent most of the night collating data with Sofi's help, laying it out across the huge TV screen. Helix had left him asleep on the sofa. Yawlander's view was that the evidence was solid and the timing critical. But if they were wrong, there would the mother of all shitstorms that none of them would survive. Helix stretched up from the wall, arching his back as he stood.

Ethan's voice came into his ear. 'Morning Nate. When you've finished your yoga with nature session, there's something up here you might like to see.'

* * *

Ethan was perched on the low wall opposite the patio doors enjoying his first joint of the day as Helix walked up. 'Morning, Bruv. Glad to see you've taken your filthy habit outdoors.'

Ethan laughed. 'We wouldn't want his holiness to come home and find the place stinking of weed, would we?' He flicked ash onto the manicured lawn. 'Press conference. Midday. Westminster.'

Helix dropped onto the wall beside him. 'Okay, good. Is there anything new to add to what we've got?'

'Nothing new.' He took a long drag on the joint.

'Biggest challenge will be finding the right moment.'

'I agree, we could—' A movement on the glass staircase inside caught Helix's eye. Gabrielle?

The cream silk kimono rippled against her legs as she came down the stairs. She smiled, tucked her hair behind her ears and paused in the open door, her arms folded. 'What are you two gawping at?'

Helix shook his head. 'Bloody hell SJ, you look...'

'Scrub up well for a digger, don't I? Even did my armpits. You look like you've seen a ghost.'

'Christ, SJ. Don't say that,' Helix mumbled as he climbed to his feet. 'This is Ethan. He arrived last night after you'd turned in.'

She stepped through the open door. 'Hi Ethan. Weird to meet you.' She shook his hand.

Ethan smiled. 'Yep. Likewise.'

Helix folded his arms. 'How you feeling, SJ? Manage to get some sleep?'

'How do you think I'm feeling?' She shoved her hands into the deep kimono pockets. 'I slept OK but kept thinking about Gabrielle. I'm worried about her. Where is she? Is she frightened?' She flopped down on the wall next to Ethan.

Helix joined the line-up. 'We're all worried about her, but apart from a couple of traces around Westminster, we have nothing since yesterday.'

'Westminster? The only connection with Westminster is Justin, and I could think of a million better places to go.'

Helix leaned forward and plucked a blade of grass. 'You can't think of anywhere else she might go?'

'Not really. The only place she might have gone to is Miriam's...'

Helix concentrated on splitting the wide blade of grass lengthways. Why would SJ know where Gabrielle might have gone? They haven't seen each other for years. Separation does that. You forget the places you used to go together. Or where one of you would go to escape your parents or your siblings.

'Is that what I think it is, Ethan?' she said.

Ethan smiled and passed the joint. 'Be my guest.'

Helix sniffed a laugh. Talk about déjà vu. Mind you, they probably grow acres of the bloody stuff in the woods. Just need to keep her away from the vodka and pills. He smiled at her as she chatted with Ethan. Her vocabulary was a little more rustic and she was less careful with her choice of words, but her voice was unmistakeable. She could pass for Gabrielle.

Helix finished the last of his coffee. 'Sorry to break up the party, SJ. But we've just found out that your brother-in-law is giving a press conference at midday.'

SJ stiffened. 'About to be canonised, is he?'

'No, just Prime Minister for now, but we thought we might go along. What do you think?'

She raised her eyebrows. 'I'm sure he'd be delighted to see me.'

44

Few seats remained empty in the fan-shaped auditorium. Unseated devotees and disciples had chosen to sit in the aisles that sloped towards the stage. The idle curious propped up the back walls and clogged up the stairwells. The front two rows of seats had been liberated at the last minute on the initiative of the venue manager. The displaced VIPs were moved to seats at the sides of the stage, affording them a better view and a share of the limelight.

A flock of media-bots roosted at the front edge of the stage, preserving their batteries. Technicians checked and re-checked the sound and lighting. Justin Wheeler's Parliamentary portrait smiled down benevolently at the delegates from a twenty-foot high screen at the back of the stage, duplicated on two smaller screens on either side. Stagehands wheeled a glass lectern into position through the holographic countdown timer hovering at the middle of the stage. Eight minutes to go.

Helix turned away from the live TV feeds and gave Ethan a hefty slap on the back. 'Comms with SJ?'

Ethan put up his thumb. 'You receiving, SJ?'

'Yes. And I'll be glad to be out here,' she replied in hushed tones from a speaker built into the console.

'Where did you put her?'

Helix smiled. 'Out of order ladies loo. She's only been in there for thirty minutes.'

Ethan adjusted his headset. 'Not long now, SJ. We'll wait for him to get started before you make your entrance. How are you feeling?'

'Regal. And trying my best not to be me. As long as I can avoid questions about genetics and botany, I think I'll be alright.'

'Well done. Sit tight, I'll give you a shout when we're ready.' Ethan leaned back in his chair. 'Christ, I could do with a spliff. Do you think Yawlander would mind?'

'He's got a habit of turning up when you least expect it. He was briefing a couple of guys at the back of the stage just now.'

Ethan slipped his tobacco tin back inside his utility vest. 'Are we certain there are no remaining elements of McGill's private army around?' He scratched his neck.

'As sure as we can be. The boss has vouched for everyone. Blackburn's leading the squad next to the stage so we're in safe hands.' Helix took two bottles of water from the cooler and handed one to Ethan. 'No sign of that snake Lytkin so far then?'

Ethan opened the bottle one handed, his other poised over the keyboard. 'Nope. Surprising though. You would think Wheeler would want him here to crow about the first of many public private partnerships, how they are going to re-establish the country on the international stage and all that old bollocks.'

Helix pulled his P226 from its holster. Taking out part of Lytkin's infrastructure and removing SJ from the equation would have derailed his plans. But, with Gabrielle still in play, Lytkin wouldn't give up. He chambered a round and slipped the gun back under his arm. McGill was one tick in the box. There were two more to go.

Ethan nudged him. 'You still using that antique?'

Helix patted his side. 'No batteries required. Old but reliable and in perfect working order.'

'I know. Just like you.' Ethan nodded towards one of the TV feeds. 'Wheeler's glad-handing his way to the stage. Better get set.'

* * *

The audience were on their feet the moment Wheeler walked onto the stage. He waved to the packed auditorium, before turning and greeting the VIPs. Hands were shaken and air kisses exchanged as he worked the gaggle of MPs. The cheering and applause gathered volume as he moved to the centre of the stage with his hands raised, clapping above his head. The media-bots swarmed and buzzed over the heads of the audience. Wheeler looked up, ensuring no viewer went without a smile and a wave.

The welcome abated as he took his position behind the lectern and waited for the audience to settle. He took a sip of water, turned his head to clear his throat and began his address. 'Thank you. Friends, thank you.'

* * *

SJ crossed the narrow lobby, pausing at the foot of a short flight of stairs. She adjusted the off-the-shoulder black dress she had chosen from Gabrielle's wardrobe and tweaked her hair clips. Wheeler's voice boomed over the public address system as she hesitated outside the antique double doors with their frosted glass panels and polished brass handles. *Okay. Here we go.* She nipped her bottom lip, grasped the handle and heaved the door open. A suited onlooker stumbled back towards her. 'I'm sorry,' she said, deploying her best Gabrielle smile.

The onlooker clapped as he shuffled back allowing her to pass into the auditorium. She wavered again. It was quieter than she expected with the audience clinging to every word of Wheeler's discourse. She apologised her way forward, shrugging her shoulders as she smiled, trying to maintain control of the unfamiliar high heels she'd hidden her weathered feet in. Her anxiety increased by an octave as she emerged into the aisle causing a ripple of gasps and whispers.

She froze as somebody shouted. 'It's Gabrielle!'

She glanced up at the stage. Wheeler's face had frozen mid-sentence. He was blinking in the flashes from the media-bots. She took a tentative step forward, followed by another before striding down the aisle with purpose, her eyes fixed on Wheeler. A ripple of applause swept her forward. Hands reached out and touched her lightly on the top of her arm or shoulder as she passed. Someone caught her hand and gave it a gentle squeeze, slowing her. She turned towards the owner of the hand, smiled, hesitated for a moment and then continued.

Wheeler gawped, his surprise manifested by a ripple of winks. 'Ladies and gentlemen, what a lovely surprise, I'm sure you'll agree.' He strode to the edge of the stage, his hands outstretched as SJ crested the carpeted steps.

She dodged his puckered lips, taking the kiss on the cheek. 'Fuck off, Justin,' she whispered, smiling through the savage squeeze he gave the top of her arm.

Wheeler guffawed. 'Folks, there's been a mistake and an easy one to make, I must confess. Allow me to introduce you to my sister-in-law, Sarah-Jane Stepper. At least that's who she says she is.'

The applause evaporated as the media-bots swooped at the unexpected guest. SJ leaned in, her hand over the microphone attached to his lapel. 'I can always flash my arse to the audience, if you need proof, Justin.' She smiled and waved to the audience.

Wheeler snorted. 'Hilarious.' He nodded to a space beside to the lectern. 'Stand there and be quiet.'

SJ smiled at the assembled retinue on the stage as they basked obsequiously in Wheeler's self-made aura. A blonde technician appeared at her side and attached a small microphone to the neckline of her dress. SJ returned Wheeler's glower as the operation was completed.

Wheeler's knuckles whitened as he clasped the sides of the glass lectern. 'Ladies and gentlemen, friends and colleagues...' He cleared his throat. 'If I may deviate for a moment or two from my prepared statement... It is indeed a pleasant surprise to see my sister-in-law on the stage beside me. SJ joins us from a marginal community on the Welsh border and she almost fooled us, but I am sure Gabrielle will forgive you SJ for stealing some of her clothes.' He clapped his hands together as the audience laughed along.

SJ blinked through the lights at the audience. At least he hadn't called her a digger. She ran her fingers over the goosebumps on her arm as Wheeler, with his voice cracking, eulogised Gabrielle.

'Ladies and gentlemen, we are fast approaching the twentieth anniversary of the discovery of the cure. Each July, we remember the sacrifices made during the two dark years before my wife and her team were able to make the discovery that put an end to the suffering. Gabrielle has dedicated her life to the health and care of others, and in finding ways to protect and nurture those in less fortunate circumstances.' He tugged a handkerchief from his pocket. 'Before I move on, I'd like to say to my wife and those holding her...' He stared into the media-bot hovering in front of him. 'The truth will prevail, Gabrielle, and I hope that you will soon be returned to our family with your honour and integrity restored.' He turned and smiled at SJ, his hand extended as the audience applauded in support, with mumbles of "hear! hear!" from the politicians behind.

SJ rocked on her high heels as she ignored Wheeler's hand. 'The truth will—' She hesitated at the volume of her own voice over the public address system. 'The truth will prevail, Justin?' She drew back as he shifted towards her.

He clamped his hand over his lapel microphone. 'What the hell are you doing?'

She side-stepped him and took his place at the lectern. 'Let's talk about truth and integrity for a moment shall we, Justin?'

Wheeler laughed, wrapping his arm around her shoulders. 'Not until you're an elected politician, SJ.'

SJ glanced over her shoulder. 'Ahem, excuse me.'

The curtains at the side of the stage parted as Blackburn ducked through striding towards the Chancellor. 'Stand aside please, sir. This is in the public interest and she will be heard.'

Wheeler put his hands up in surrender. He turned and grinned at his colleagues. 'I shall be fascinated to hear what you might have to say that could be in the public interest, SJ.'

The audience's embarrassed laugh at his sarcasm suggested that they were more interested than he was.

SJ nodded her thanks to Blackburn. The side screens remained blank. She hoped they were ready. 'I'd like to introduce someone most of you will have already heard of. If we should ever need an example of truth and integrity in the shape of a person, we need look no further than Major Nathan Helix, VC DSO.' An image of Helix in his dress uniform, standing to attention, filled the side screens on cue.

Wheeler's laugh quelled the chatter amongst the audience. 'Helix? He's the reason your sister is missing. He interfered with a legitimate investigation into a serious crime and took her hostage. Is he here?' He put his hand to his brow and peered into the audience. 'If he's here he should be arrested. Where is General Yawlander?'

'He is here, Justin, but he isn't the one who should be arrested.'

A ripple of blepharospasm erupted at the edge of Wheeler's eye. 'Ladies and gentlemen, I'm going to ask you to give us a few moments to—'

Blackburn positioned himself between Wheeler and the opening in the curtain as General Yawlander stepped through.

'Yawlander. What the hell is—'

The General remained impassive, his hand raised. He turned back towards the opening as Helix ducked through. A volley of camera flashes reflected from Helix's sunglasses as he stepped into the light.

Wheeler's glower did nothing to impede Helix as he approached the lectern. He tapped SJ on the arm and stared through the lights at the expectant audience.

Wheeler spun around to face the audience. 'I don't know what you think you are doing, Major. I am about to set out my parties' policies and agenda for the first twelve months of my premiership. Given the seriousness of the allegations against my wife, this is hardly the forum. Now, if we could leave the stage for a few—'

'No, Chancellor.' Helix paused, waiting for the audience to settle. 'Good afternoon. As SJ said, let's talk about truth and integrity.' His own image faded from the screen, replaced with another of Wheeler and Valerian Lytkin, grinning for the cameras as they shook hands at their recent press conference.

Wheeler leapt into the pause. 'I don't know where you are going with this, Major, but I think everyone recognises Valerian Lytkin, one of our country's greatest supporters. Mr Lytkin and his companies are committed to continue the great work of his late father in rebuilding our strength and repu—'

'With biological weapons, Chancellor?'

'Don't be preposterous, Major. Valerian Lytkin's growing business empire extends into many areas, including military research and development. But biological weapons? What are you suggesting?'

'I'm talking about the qualities of being honest and having strong moral principles, Chancellor. Also known as integrity. Something that we, the people, expect of our politicians and business leaders.' He pointed to the screen. 'This is a Companies House filing report showing the grant of one million shares in Lamont Rhames to you, Justin Montague Wheeler. We couldn't find a record of this in the Parliamentary register of members' financial interests. But that's OK Chancellor, you've been busy preparing to become Prime Minister, so it probably slipped your mind.' He shrugged. 'I should mention that Lamont Rhames is Mr Lytkin's company. Am I right, Sir?'

Wheeler placed his hand over his heart. 'Mea culpa. You have me there, Major. An administrative error, I have nothing to hide.'

'Nothing to hide, Chancellor?' He poured himself a glass of water from the bottle next to the lectern. 'We'll allow you one administrative oversight, but not twenty.'

The organogram of Lytkin's shell companies flashed onto the screen.

'This, Chancellor, is the Lytkin empire, but not the visible part of it. That's much smaller. Twenty-seven companies hidden behind shell structures whose majority shareholder is Valerian Lytkin.'

'And what has this got to do with me, Major?'

'Mr Lytkin's shareholding in these companies ranges from fifty-one to seventy-eight percent. So, we looked to see who the other shareholders were and in twenty cases, Justin Montague Wheeler was named as a major shareholder with between thirty and thirty-five percent of the remaining shares.'

The organogram re-formatted itself placing Wheeler's image against each of the companies in which he was registered as a shareholder.

Wheeler folded his arms. 'No, Major. I utterly refute your accusations. I have no knowledge of these companies or the alleged shareholdings.'

'OK, Chancellor. Perhaps we could have asked Mr Lytkin, but it appears he hasn't been able to make it today. We will be producing the filings from each of the countries where those companies are registered. But we must move on. Still nothing to hide Chancellor?'

Wheeler shook his head.

'Good, then I won't need to run the video recording of you and Mr Lytkin discussing his plans for

Doctor Stepper's research. How it was going to, and I quote "send those shares through the roof once development of the Empusa is complete." The Empusa, ladies and gentlemen, is the name given to the biological weapon Mr Lytkin was developing, based on Doctor Stepper's research.'

Wheeler strutted around the stage shaking his head, muttering to himself.

'But it wasn't just about his business empire was it, Chancellor?' Helix sipped his water. 'No. Mr Lytkin wanted the Empusa to avenge the death of this mother and sister. His intention was to launch attacks at the shareholder meetings of the companies owned by those whom he held responsible. The companies would have collapsed and Mr Lytkin would have helped himself to the shares and assets at rock-bottom prices.'

Wheeler folded his arms. 'Have you finished, Major?'

'No, sir. Mr Lytkin also held certain members of the Russian Government responsible. He was prepared to risk political chaos and even the outbreak of war in an already fragile region between Russia, Ukraine, Turkey, Syria, Iraq and Iran. He planned to attack the Kremlin.'

A funereal silence had descended over the auditorium, the only remaining sound coming from the bobbing and weaving of the media-bots and Wheeler's breath. Helix slid his sunglasses back up the bridge of his nose.

Wheeler pushed his shoulders back and placed his hands on his hips. 'So perhaps dear Gabrielle wasn't the saint we all made her out to be. What do *you* think, Major?'

'No. She wasn't a saint, Chancellor. She never wanted to be. That was what you wanted, so you could ride on the tails of her reputation and serve your own political ambitions.' He glanced into the audience. 'She told me that all she wanted was to be loved by her family and left in peace to help those less fortunate. You blamed her for the death of your daughter. You questioned how she could cease the rout of humanity but not save her own child.' He should have stuck to the facts and avoided the sentimental embellishments. He cleared the lump in his throat. 'You found your salvation in politics. She had nothing. Nobody. But when she did find some happiness you, and Lytkin destroyed that, too.'

Wheeler folded his arms, shaking his head. 'I loved Gab... I love my wife. All I want is her safe return so we can rebuild our lives. I could have done more after Eve died. But I refuse to submit to your amateur marriage counselling on a public stage.'

'Very well, Chancellor. We'll forget the infidelity for now and get back to integrity.' He looked over Wheeler's shoulder and nodded at Julia Ormandy who was doing her best to be invisible with the eyes of the cabinet upon her. 'Ladies and gentlemen, you'll forgive me for cutting to the chase. But I feel that I should call out some salient facts in lieu of what will be a fuller enquiry. It is important for the country to know exactly who Chancellor Justin Wheeler is, before his appointment as Prime Minister.'

Wheeler puffed out his chest. 'I think you've said enough, Major. My wife wasn't Mother Theresa or Florence Nightingale, however venerated by the people. It was her that developed the science that Valerian Lytkin was seeking. She made the discovery. She perfected it and together with Lytkin, she was intending to weaponise it for profit.'

Helix tightened his grip on the side of the lectern. 'And supported by this government and sponsored by you in exchange for shares in his companies.' The glass on the small shelf under the lectern juddered as he slapped his hand down. 'Don't paint yourself as an innocent bystander in this, Chancellor. I've seen the press conferences. The concerned husband bewildered by events.'

Wheeler fidgeted. 'So, come on then. What else have you got? Spit it out.'

'The truth will out, Chancellor. Today we'll have the headlines and in time, we will present all of the facts.'

'So, what have you got? Let's hear the headlines as you call them. What are you waiting for, the chimes from Big Ben?'

'Hilarious, Chancellor. And you won't be hearing the chimes from Big Ben after today unless you're stood on Westminster bridge with the tourists, looking up and wondering what might have been.' Helix wiped his top lip with his thumb. 'Valerian Lytkin and Doctor Stepper had known and worked with each other for several years. Just before the Ebola outbreak, she made the discovery that Lytkin was desperate to get his hands on. The pandemic put everything on hold. It separated them into different fields of research. If we fast forward until after the cure and after the death of your daughter, we can see when Lytkin reappeared trying to convince your wife, with your help, to take the research forward.'

Wheeler took another dive. 'And she did. She knew what she was doing.'

'She did, sir. She was nominated for the Nobel Prize for Science. But she also knew that the power was too great to do anything with, other than harm and create more misery. So, she buried it away in what she thought was the safest place. The home that she shared with you. But even there it wasn't safe from Valerian Lytkin. Frustrated with her continued intransigence, Mr Lytkin issued threats behind the thin disguise of someone calling himself Cerberus. We have the emails, one of which is on the screen now.' He nodded over the top of his sunglasses.

Wheeler's amplified sigh echoed around the hushed auditorium. 'I still don't know what this has to do with me, Major. I wish you'd get to the point.'

'I'm getting to that, Chancellor. You discovered that Rachel Neilson, Gabrielle's lab assistant, had been in a relationship with General Yawlander. The relationship was brief, but Rachel gave birth to a daughter, Lauren. You used that information to get what both you and Lytkin wanted. That same information was used to coerce the General into supporting your scheme.'

Wheeler guffawed, looking over Helix's shoulder at the General. 'You forgot to mention that the General also received an allocation of shares in Mr Lytkin's company. I mention it as we're being open and transparent.'

Helix sniffed. 'Thank you, Chancellor. What you didn't realise is that at considerable risk to himself, Rachel and their daughter, the General took part in the scheme. He agreed to coordinate efforts seize the materials, along with Lytkin's head of security, the discredited Colonel Terrance McGill.'

Ethan played a short video clip of McGill walking down the steps from the board of enquiry, swatting away the media-bots. Helix held his glare on Wheeler.

'McGill planned to murder Professor Polozkova by proxy. The Professor was suffering from a life-threatening illness. Doctor Stepper had developed a drug she believed was bringing about a recovery. McGill threatened the life of eight-year-old Lauren, forcing Rachel to exchange the medication for one that was ten times the strength. That medication resulted in a massive overdose that was unwittingly administered by Doctor Stepper. But one of McGill's men was clumsy. He broke into the Professor's apartment and disturbed her. Realising that the medication hadn't taken effect as he expected, he murdered her.' Helix glanced up at the screens, each showing a different version of the post-mortem report.

Wheeler looked up, taking time to read them. 'Sorry, are you waiting for me, Major?'

'Two post-mortem reports, Chancellor. Same deceased but two different conclusions. Lytkin and McGill colluded to suppress the one with the earlier time of death as a result of asphyxiation. But neither Lytkin nor McGill were good enough at keeping this hidden. It was when this evidence came to light that I knew Doctor Stepper was innocent.' He cleared his throat. 'Again, through you, Lytkin threatened Rachel and Lauren, unless she agreed to help. She stole the materials as agreed, believing that she and her daughter would be safe. But when she delivered on her promise, McGill kidnapped her and Lauren.'

Wheeler paced around the stage, shaking his head before turning on his heels with his finger raised. 'And what use was Rachel to Mr Lytkin? She wasn't a scientist; she was a second-rate lab assistant?'

Helix paused. Wheeler's words percolated through the audience and those on the stage. 'She *was* also the mother of an eight-year-old child, Chancellor. But I am curious at *your* use of the past tense, sir.'

'What? What do you mean?'

'I'll spell it out for you. For what reason do you use the past tense when referring to Rachel Neilson? You said, she *wasn't* a scientist – past tense, she *was* a second-rate lab assistant – past tense again. Now, far be it from me to lecture an educated man like yourself, but we use the past tense when referring to something that someone has stopped doing. For example, Justin Wheeler *was* Chancellor of the Exchequer.' He rubbed his chin. 'Rachel was never a scientist. She was a working mother, studying to become one, with mentoring and support from your wife. Now, I would have expected you to say she *isn't* a scientist, but you chose *wasn't*.'

Wheeler ceased his pacing. He searched for a friendly face on the stage, but even those he had considered friends were avoiding eye contact.

Helix leaned on the lectern. 'Let me help you out. There are only a handful of people who knew Rachel was killed during an attempted exchange for your wife.' He glanced at SJ. 'That includes, myself, the General, my brother Ethan, and SJ. As soon as Gabrielle discovered Rachel and Lauren's plight, she offered to exchange herself for them. The only one of Lytkin's people to survive the attempted exchange was Terry McGill, and that's because he wasn't there.'

Wheeler looked up from the floor. 'Of course, he would have survived if he wasn't at this so-called failed exchange. What are you talking about?'

'Courage was never one of McGill's qualities, Chancellor, but I have to say that on that occasion his cowardice even surprised me. McGill used an advanced remotely operated synthetic. A robot. It was another product of Lytkin enterprises. To everyone present, it was the real McGill, completely realistic, even when I killed it the first time.'

Wheeler snorted. 'Preposterous. A robot impersonating a person. I know things have advanced but that is ludicrous.'

Helix looked to the screens. 'Ethan?'

All eyes turned to the screens where Ethan displayed a still photograph taken from the video recording. The manufacturer's details and a serial number were visible amongst the mangled remains of the ROS.

'Indeed Chancellor, but here we are. Lamont Rhames Defence and a serial number, we'll save the more graphic evidence for the enquiry. Believe me, Chancellor, when I tell you that nobody, not a real person at least, gets up from the injuries that thing sustained and fights again. But that's what happened. However, when McGill failed to kill me, he targeted Rachel. He killed her with the pathogen stolen from your wife and delivered into his hands by Valerian Lytkin. None of his men survived, only he knew that he had delivered the fatal strike that resulted in Rachel's death. General Yawlander had no real-time updates from the operation because McGill kept it off the books. So, the only other person who knew was McGill, and it was him, via Lytkin, who told you.'

Wheeler swayed, surrounded by an angry swarm of media-bots that clicked and buzzed every time he looked up or moved. The audience were still, silent, their faces set in disbelief.

Wheeler turned towards Helix. 'And was my wife... was my wife present during all of this, Major?'

'Yes. She held Rachel and Lauren almost until the end. You've seen how the pathogen works, I take it?'

Wheeler didn't respond. If Helix had handed him a gun, he probably would have shot himself. Wheeler's eyes darted at the blocked exits. 'And where is she now, Major? Where is my wife?'

'After she and I helped Rachel in her final moments, she left to take care of Lauren. Or so I thought. The truth is I have no idea where she is, Chancellor. She didn't arrive at the agreed meeting place and we haven't seen her since.'

Wheeler inhaled. 'No idea? But I thought—' He patted his jacket pockets. 'What's that?' His hand rested on his right pocket, he looked up.

Helix stepped back from the lectern. Whatever Wheeler was up to, it had nothing to do with them. He shifted his elbows away from his body feeling his P226 settle against his ribs. Blackburn returned his look with a shake of his head. He cupped his PA microphone in his hand and looked to the floor. 'What's happening, Ethan?'

'Nowt to do with me, Nate.'

Helix moved as Wheeler palmed a pen-like device, turning it over in his hand. He almost dropped it as it vibrated.

Helix didn't recognise it as a syringe. It was smaller and thinner than the one that had contained the pathogen and the one Gabrielle had used to disguise them for the exchange. Around five inches long, it had a small liquid crystal display on one side. A button at one end had the word "Press" etched onto it in black letters.

Helix wasn't fast enough. Wheeler shrugged as he pressed the button. 'Ow, bugger!'

The pen dropped to the floor. Wheeler stared at the pad of his thumb and the growing bubble of blood that bloomed upon it. Instinctively, he placed his thumb in his mouth.

Helix crouched and picked up the pen. His muscles tensed as he noticed a tiny smear of Wheeler's blood on it. Adrenalin surged through him as he read the words scrolling across the display.

"Now you'll find out how Rachel felt, Justin. "You have ten minutes, fifteen if you're lucky before you GO TO HELL!"

45

Helix pushed through the heavy glass doors, glancing at the clock above the reception desk. Thirty-six hours. It was one of the longest de-briefing sessions he'd had to sit through, and it showed in his face. Ethan was still in there, crawling up the walls, desperate for a joint. He'd be a while longer, given the evidence he'd amassed. He aimed a half-hearted wave at the desk sergeant as he turned towards the stairs to the underground car park. 'Cheers, Phil. See you tomorrow.'

The sergeant peered over his half-moon glasses. 'Hang on, Helix. Got something for you.' He fanned himself with a large envelope. 'Just arrived.'

Helix groaned as he climbed back up the single step. 'Thanks.' He turned the envelope over, studying the neat handwritten text. "Major Nathan Helix VC DSO." He raised his eyebrows and dropped his sun-glasses into position.

'More fan mail?'

Helix shrugged. 'What can I say, they love me.'

* * *

Pushing his sunglasses to the top of his head, Helix stretched and yawned as he settled into the seat of his AV. He rubbed his hands over his face and glanced down at the envelope on the seat beside him. Already crossed-eyed at the amount of reading and reviewing he'd done during the de-briefing, he had little energy left for more. Sleep is what he needed. He could read it later.

His eyes were drawn to the careful uniform lettering. He hooked his finger into the tiny gap at the edge of the envelope, paused a beat and split it open. Peering inside, he pulled out two sheets of paper, written in the same hand used on the envelope. He was certain he'd seen it before. A glance at the final page of the letter confirmed it. A nervous smile crossed his face.

Dear Helix,
Where to begin? This must be the fifth or sixth version of this that I've tried to write. Anyway, I'm safe and sound and staying with my solicitor near Temple.

I'm sorry. Sorry for not following the plan, sorry for letting Lauren down, sorry for letting you down. Oh God, I'm waffling. I'll start at the beginning from after leaving the park. The least I can do is give you an explanation of my temporary madness.

I tried to cover my tracks as best I could, but it's mad how easy it is to leave a trail of breadcrumbs these days. You just don't realise, do you? It's fair to say that after what happened in the park, my mind wasn't where it should have been. I had this crazy idea that I could bring things to a conclusion on my own. After seeing the news on the TV in the hospital canteen, I realised that your original plan was the only realistic one. I headed for Down Street, hoping to find you there, or at least some way of getting in touch. I was so relieved when that door opened.

Helix paused. The door sensors that tripped...? It must have been her.

Of course, what I didn't know was that I was walking into a trap set by Valerian. I shall forever be haunted by the look in his eyes when he told me of his plans to avenge the disappearance of his mother and sister. Earlier, before unwittingly giving myself to him, I'd thought about ending it all, about throwing myself off the top of St Thomas's. The only reason I didn't was because I thought, in time, they would try to get to SJ. If he'd managed to get her, he wouldn't need me. But the news said she'd disappeared. He grinned as he told me that McGill had kidnapped SJ. I could see then that he wouldn't stop.

You're probably wondering what happened to him. I expect by now the police have discovered what is left of him and his men. The downside to being the key to the lock I placed on the science, was in fact also my saviour. SJ and I are the only two people alive who have any immunity to the pathogen. He made me a murderer. It will forever haunt me, but I try to reconcile what I did with the greater benefit to humanity.

He called his men and told them to kill me. They were the last words he uttered. Those words encapsulated everything about him and validated my decision. I hid in his panic room as his men arrived. But it was too late for them. You know how it works.

And what about Justin? Having disappeared once, I wasn't about to make a dramatic reappearance at his press conference, although it was tempting. That said I was very impressed with SJ's performance. She can take my place anytime. But then the reckless Gabrielle made a comeback. I was the shy girl in the crowd from Barbados who turned away as Justin approached the stage, but not too shy to slip that syringe into his pocket. We used to give them to people to remind them to take their medication. I'm sorry about the panic on stage after he pricked himself. I'm glad nobody was hurt. I used the last of the pathogen on Valerian so there was never any risk. Anyway, I don't want Justin dead, in spite of everything he's done. Thanks to you, SJ, Ethan and General

Yawlander, he got what he deserved, or will I hope, once the enquiry and trial are over. It's better that he suffers the shame and humiliation for his actions.

Helix shook his head and smiled as he turned the page.

So, where does that leave us? I intend to stay "disappeared." I'm tired, Helix. Tired of the spotlight, tired of smiling for the cameras, tired of doing my bloody duty. Judging by the show you guys put on at the press conference, my solicitor tells me that there is enough evidence to convict Justin with no need for me to appear, at least, that's what she is hoping. General Yawlander has asked me to look after Lauren, which is the least I can do under the circumstances. I'm hoping SJ will show me how to live off-grid. So, I'm going to take Lauren and go to live with her and Bo.

I've also instructed my solicitor to transfer ownership of the Observatory to you and Ethan. Some members of the Scientific Elite will huff and puff a bit, but they'll get over it. I think the lab will make a great man cave for the two of you, and it seems only fair as it was my fault that Helix Towers was destroyed. At least it's away from any water, which I'm sure you'd prefer. I hope that you can fill the place with happier memories than I was able to.

Finally, Helix, I'm sorry that I lacked the courage to come to you and tell you all of this in person. My fear is that if I had, I might not be able to do what I need to do. Leaving London will be easy, tearing myself away from you won't be. I found the box under your bed. Sorry. I need time and space and I hope that we don't become strangers.

Love Gabrielle.

XXX

Thank You

I hope you enjoyed reading Helix Genesis. I'd be really grateful if you would take a couple of minutes to leave a review on Amazon, even if it's only a line or two. Writing the book was a labour of love that spanned around eighteen months to get it from the original idea to the book you've just finished. I read every review and as well as encouraging other readers to take the plunge, they help me to engage with my audience and inspire me to keep going. Thanks again.

Author's Note

Why not join my Readers' Club to be amongst the first to received news and updates about my forthcoming books and other giveaways? In return you'll receive a free ebook of interviews with the two main characters from Helix Genesis: Nathan Helix and Gabrielle Stepper.

Acknowledgements

I would like to extend my thanks and appreciation to the following fantastic people who have provided expertise, help, support and encouragement.

My beta readers: Hayley Parker, Joanna Bell and Vlad Glaveanu. Thank you all for giving up your time to review the earlier drafts and for the honesty of your feedback.

A huge thank you to my editor, Debi Alper, for her continued wisdom, clarity of feedback and generous words of encouragement.

Thank you to Leigh Forbes for the brilliant cover design and overall presentation of the paperback edition you have in your hands. www.blot.co.uk

I'd also like to mention Jericho Writers. If you're already an author, want to hone your authorial skills or you're just starting out, I suggest you look them up. There's no finer place (in my opinion) to go for advice and support. www.jerichowriters.com.

Finally. Thank you to my wife Corinne for being a sounding board for ideas, a source of encouragement and spotter of typos. It is also to Corinne that credit must be given for the idea to use Red Sands Forts as the setting for Helix Towers. https://en.wikipedia.org/wiki/Maunsell_Forts

I take full responsibility for the errors and omissions contained herein. If you haven't enjoyed the book, please tell me. If you have enjoyed the book, please tell the world by leaving a review on Amazon.

Also by Chris Lofts

Life Untenable

The only weapon she had was her art

(July 2020)

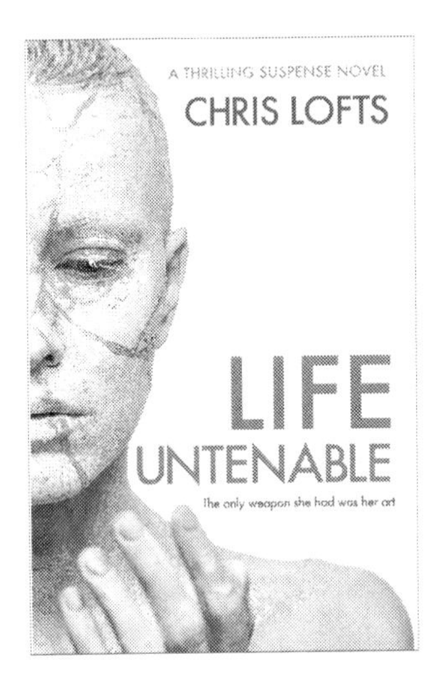

PANDORA STRAFER'S consuming passion is her art. Celebrity is within her grasp. However, a terrible secret she shares with her despised brother Tobin threatens to destroy everything she has worked for.

But Pan knows something Tobin doesn't – there is a witness. With their livelihoods and liberty in jeopardy, both will do almost anything to conceal their side of the story. Tobin's increasing paranoia and desperation drag Pan deeper into his sinister world.

Pan fights back with the only weapon she has: her art. She has the time, the talent and the opportunity. But can she find the killer instinct?

Printed in Great Britain
by Amazon